AN IMPOSSIBLE ATTRACTION

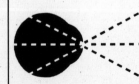

This Large Print Book carries the
Seal of Approval of N.A.V.H.

AN IMPOSSIBLE ATTRACTION

BRENDA JOYCE

THORNDIKE PRESS

A part of Gale, Cengage Learning

GALE
CENGAGE Learning·

Detroit • New York • San Francisco • New Haven, Conn • Waterville, Maine • London

GALE
CENGAGE Learning™

Copyright © 2010 by Brenda Joyce Dreams Unlimited, Inc.
Thorndike Press, a part of Gale, Cengage Learning.

Thorndike Press® Large Print Romance.
The text of this Large Print edition is unabridged.
Other aspects of the book may vary from the original edition.
Set in 16 pt. Plantin.

LIBRARY OF CONGRESS CATALOGING-IN-PUBLICATION DATA

Joyce, Brenda.
  An impossible attraction / by Brenda Joyce. — Large print
ed.
    p. cm. — (Thorndike Press large print romance)
  Originally published: New York : Harlequin, 2010.
  Summary: Once a lady, she has given up everything to take
care of her sisters and her wastrel father. Now, Alexandra
Bolton sews the clothing of those who were once her peers to
make ends meet. Yet her life is about to forever change. . . .
He is the most powerful peer in the realm—and the most
sought after bachelor. Yet the Duke of Clarewood has rejected
the creme de la creme of society for over a decade. But when
he first sees Alexandra, he is instantly intrigued—and he offers
her a scandalous proposition. And her stunning refusal only
whets his ambition. . . .
  ISBN-13: 978-1-4104-2545-4 (alk. paper)
  ISBN-10: 1-4104-2545-2
  1. Large type books. I. Title.
PS3560.O864I48 2010
813'.54—dc22   2009053952

Published in 2010 by arrangement with Harlequin Books S.A.

Printed in Mexico
2 3 4 5 6 7 14 13 12 11 10

Dear Reader,

I hope you enjoy reading *An Impossible Attraction* as much as I enjoyed writing it. I wanted Stephen and Alexandra's story to be a bit off the beaten path, and hopefully you'll be intrigued by their trials and tribulations. And now I am happy to announce that the story you have been waiting for — and asking me for — is on its way to you! I am halfway through Alexi and Elysse's epic love story, which will be released later in 2010.

This is truly a thrill ride! As you know from *A Dangerous Love,* Alexi married Elysse in 1833 — then left her at the altar and hasn't seen his bride in the six-year interim. In *An Impossible Attraction,* Elysse and Alexi are ecstatically together, with a child on the way. So what happened, exactly?

I always follow my muse. That is why I wrote these stories out of order; I simply wasn't ready to delve into Elysse and Alexi's incredibly intense and passionate love story. The novel opens in the spring of 1833, with Alexi returning home after a two-and-a-half-year absence. Elysse can't wait to see him, and to get his attention, she flirts shamelessly — with his friend. Her reckless

5

flirtation leads to murder and marriage — and to Alexi coldly and furiously leaving Elysse right after their wedding vows are exchanged.

Six years later, Elysse is one of London's reigning socialites. And Alexi has become a national icon — a China trader, he has set the record for the Canton to London run, and has been the first ship home two years in a row. Outwardly, Elysse is the woman every other woman wishes to be — beautiful, gracious, witty and wealthy, and not only are her invitations fought over, she is married to one of the country's most dashing men. But Elysse has spent six years maintaining a terrible pretense — that her life is exactly as she wishes it to be, and that her marriage is a successful one. But that lie is about to be exposed. . . .

That spring, when Alexi's ship is spotted off Plymouth, Elysse is convinced by her friends to greet him at the docks. Obviously he is not expecting her; obviously he has gone to great pains to avoid her. After six years, their reunion finally takes place. And nothing has changed. He is furious with her — and she is furious with him. But now he intends to stay in London, and she instantly realizes he must play the role of a proper husband, because her pride is at stake. . . .

And so begins the clash of love, pride and passion!

I can't wait to share their story with you!
Happy reading,
Always,
Brenda Joyce

For Sue Ball, one of the most generous
and caring spirits
I have ever known. My heartfelt thanks
for so many years of
kindness, friendship and support to me
and my family.

PROLOGUE

There was so much light, and Alexandra hesitated, confused.

"Alex . . . andra?" her mother whispered from the bed.

Gold-and-burgundy wallpaper adorned the walls, and dark draperies were closed over the bedroom's two windows. The bureau was a dark, rich mahogany, as was the bed, and the bedding was wine and gold. The room's single armchair was a dark, intense red. Yet the light within almost blinded her. "I am here, Mother," she whispered back.

And then, because Elizabeth Bolton was dying and would not last another night, because she had wasted away from the cancer eating at her, because she was so frail and weak now that she could barely see, much less hear, Alexandra hurried forward. She held back the tears. She hadn't cried, not even once, not even when her father had told her that her mother had a terrible and fatal disease. It hadn't been a shock. Elizabeth had been fading away before Alexandra and her younger sisters' eyes for months. Being the eldest — all of seventeen — meant she had to hold the family together now in this crisis.

Alexandra rushed to her mother's side, her heart clenching as she looked at her gaunt, unrecognizable face and frame. Elizabeth had been so beautiful, so lively, so alive. She was only thirty-eight years old now, but she looked ninety.

Alexandra sat, reaching for her thin, frail hands. "Father said you wished to see me, Mother. What can I get you? Do you want a sip of water?"

Elizabeth smiled wanly, lying prone on the large bed, dwarfed by the pillows behind her, the blankets over her. "Angels," she whispered. "Can you see them?"

Alexandra felt the tears rise. She batted her lashes furiously. Her mother needed her, as did her two sisters, who were only seven and nine. Father needed her, too — though he was locked in the library with his gin. But now she understood the odd light in the room, and the equally strange warmth. "I can't see them, but I can feel them. Are you afraid?"

Elizabeth shook her head ever so slightly, and just as slightly, her grasp on Alexandra's hands increased. "I don't . . . want to go, Alexandra. The girls . . . are so young."

It was hard to hear her, so Alexandra leaned even closer to her mother's face. "We don't want you to leave us, but you'll be with the angels now, Mother." Somehow she managed to smile. "I am going to take care of Olivia and Corey — you needn't worry. I will take care of Father, too."

"Promise me . . . darling . . . promise."

She laid her cheek against her mother's bony face. "I promise. You have done everything for this family, you have been its guiding light, its rock and its anchor, and I will do everything for Father and the girls now. We will be fine. *They* will be fine." But it didn't feel as if anything would ever be fine again.

"I am so proud . . . of you," Elizabeth whispered.

Alexandra had straightened so they could look into one another's eyes. She was the oldest, the firstborn, with years separating her and her two younger sisters, and she and her mother had always been close. Elizabeth had taught Alexandra how to manage the household, how to entertain and how to dress for tea or for a ball. She had taught her how to bake cinnamon cookies and how to make lemonade. She had shown her how to smile, even when upset, and how to behave with grace and dignity, no matter the occasion. She had shown her the true power of love, of family, of diligence and respect.

Alexandra knew her mother was proud of her. Just as she knew she could not bear this last moment with her. "Don't worry about the girls or Father. I will take good care of them."

"I know." Elizabeth smiled sadly and fell silent. And it took Alexandra a full moment to realize that her eyes had become sightless.

She gasped, hard, the intense pain blinding her. The tears finally overflowed, even as she fought them. She grasped her mother's hands more firmly and lay down beside her, already missing her acutely, the pain unbearable now, and that was how her fiancé, Owen, found her.

"Alexandra." He gently lifted her to her feet.

She met his concerned, searching gaze and let him guide her from the death room. It was dark and somber now — the warm light long gone. In the hall, he held her for a long time. Alexandra let him, even as her heart broke all over again.

Because she knew what she must do.

Owen was her best friend, her one and only true love, but that didn't matter now.

"Why are you looking at me that way?" he asked, eyes wide.

She clasped his beautiful cheek. "I love you, Owen."

He was alarmed. "You are in shock. This is the time to grieve."

She began shaking her head. "I can't marry you, Owen. I told her I would take care of this family, and I meant it. My life is no longer my own. I can't marry you, I can't be your wife, or the mother of your children. I can't. I have to take care of my sisters." And in that moment, she knew it was the truth and was overwhelmed by the turn her life had taken.

"Alexandra!" he cried. "Allow yourself a period of mourning. I will wait for you. I love you, and we will get through this together."

But she pulled away, the hardest thing she had ever done. "No, Owen. Everything has changed. Corey and Olivia need me, and so does Father."

"I am going to wait for you," he warned, and tears glistened on his lashes.

There were no choices now. She would

15

hold the family together, no matter what it meant or what it took. "Goodbye, Owen," she said.

CHAPTER ONE

"I can no longer afford you," the Baron of Edgemont said.

Alexandra Bolton stared in some surprise at her grim, rather disheveled father. He had just summoned her and her two younger sisters into the small, shabby library where he occasionally looked at the estate's books. Oddly, he seemed sober — and it was almost half past four in the afternoon. What did he mean, exactly? "I know how precarious our finances are," she said, but her smile was reassuring. "I am taking in additional sewing, Father, and I should be able to earn an extra pound every week."

Her father made a discouraging sound. "You are exactly like your mother. She was tireless, Alexandra, tireless in her efforts to reassure me — right up until the day of her death." He walked away, his posture slumped, and took his seat behind his equally worn and tired desk. It was crooked. One leg needed repair.

Alexandra was becoming vaguely alarmed. She had been doing her best to hold the family together ever since Elizabeth Bolton had died — no easy task, considering her father's terrible penchant for gaming and whiskey, which only their mother had been able to restrain. The last time her father had asked her and her two younger sisters into the library, it had been to tell them that their mother was fatally ill. Of course, Elizabeth had been fading before their very eyes. The news had been heart wrenching, but not a surprise.

Elizabeth had died nine years ago. Since then, her father had lost all self-restraint. He did not even try to refrain from his bad habits. Corey was tempestuous by nature, and did as she pleased when away from Alexandra's watchful eyes. Olivia had withdrawn into her world of watercolors and pastels, and although she seemed content, Alexandra despaired. She herself had given up true love to take care of them all. But there were no regrets.

"Someone must be cheerful," she said with a firm smile. "We may be short on funds, but we have a fine home, even if it could use some repairs, and we have clothes on our backs and food on the table. Our situation could be worse."

Corey, who was only sixteen, choked. After all, every rug in the house was threadbare, the walls needed paint and plaster, and the draperies were literally falling apart. The grounds were as bad, for their staff had been reduced to one manservant and the gardener let go last year. Their London townhome had been sold, but Edgemont Way was within an hour's drive of Greenwich, fortunately or not.

Alexandra decided to ignore her rather reckless, very outspoken and terribly beautiful little sister. "Father? Your demeanor is worrying me." And he was not yet foxed. He was always foxed well before noon. What did this turn mean? She couldn't be hopeful. She knew he had no reason to try to change his dissolute ways.

The baron sighed. "My last line of credit has been squashed."

Her unease escalated. Like most of their peers, they lived on rents and credit. But her father's obsession with gambling had forced him to sell off their tenant farms, one by one, and there were only two tenants left. Those rents might have been enough to support the family if he didn't game compulsively almost every single night. But he did game excessively and obsessively, so within a few years of their mother's death, Alexandra had turned her love for sewing into a source of income for them, though it was, at times, humiliating. The very women they had once enjoyed teas and dinner parties with were now her customers. Lady Lewis enjoyed personally handing over her torn and damaged garments, while making a huge fuss at how "sloppy" the repairs were upon their return. Alexandra always smiled and apologized. She was actually excellent with a thread and needle, and until the downturn, she had enjoyed sewing and embroidery. Now, given a choice, she doubted she would ever thread a needle again.

But they did have clothes on their backs, a roof over their heads and food on the table. Their clothes were out of fashion and well mended, the roof leaked when it stormed, and their diet was generally limited to bread, vegetables and potatoes, with red meat on Sundays. But that was better than nothing at all.

And her sisters did not recall a time of luncheons and balls. Alexandra was grateful for that.

But how would they get on without credit?

"I will take in more sewing," she said, determined.

"How can you take on more sewing? You are already up all night with the customers you have," Corey shot back. "You have calluses on your thumbs!"

Corey was right, and Alexandra knew it. She was only one person, and she simply couldn't manage more work, unless she forwent any sleep at all.

"Last summer Lord Henredon asked me if I would paint his portrait. I refused," Olivia said quietly. While Corey was a true golden blonde, Olivia was that indistinct shade that was neither blond nor brown, but she was also very pretty. "But I could offer my services to the shire as a portrait artist. I think I could make quite a few pounds within a very short time."

Alexandra stared at her middle sister, dismayed. Her sisters' happiness meant everything to her. "You are a naturalist," she said softly. "You despise doing portraits." But there was more. She knew that Henredon had made improper remarks to Olivia, and improper advances would no doubt have followed. Henredon was known for his gallivanting ways.

"It is a good idea," Olivia returned as quietly, steel in her green eyes.

"I am hoping it will not come to that," Alexandra said, meaning it. She was afraid her good-natured sister would be taken advantage of in many ways.

"I doubt that will be necessary, Olivia," Edgemont said. He turned to Alexandra. "How old are you?"

Alexandra was mildly confused by her father's odd question. "I am twenty-six."

The baron flushed. "I thought you were younger, maybe twenty-four. But you're still an attractive woman, Alexandra, and you keep a fine household, in spite of our means, so you will be the first — to show your sisters proper respect."

Tension began to knot in her stomach, but she kept a firm smile in place. "I will be the first to do what, Father?" she asked with care.

"To marry, of course. It's high time, don't you think?"

Alexandra was disbelieving. "There's no money for a dowry."

"I am aware of that," Edgemont snapped. "I am very aware of that, Alexandra. Despite that, an inquiry has been made about you."

Alexandra pulled a chair close and sat down. Was Edgemont mad? No one would ever consider marrying an impoverished spinster of her age. Everyone in town knew of her "profession," just as everyone knew that Edgemont gambled and drank every possible night away. The truth was that the good Bolton name was seriously tainted. "Are you serious, Father?"

He smiled eagerly now. "Squire Denney approached me last night to ask after you — and to enquire if he could call."

Alexandra was so surprised that she sat up straight, causing her chair to rock on its uneven legs. Was there a chance of marriage, after all this time? And for the first time in years, she thought of Owen St. James, the man she had given her heart to so long ago.

"You know him, of course," her father continued, smiling at her. "You sewed his late wife's garments for several years. He has come out of mourning now, and apparently you made a considerable impression upon him."

Alexandra knew she must not think of Owen now, or of the hopes and dreams they had once shared. She recalled the squire, a rather stately older man who had always been polite and respectful to her. She did not know him well, but his wife had been a valuable customer. She had been saddened for him when his wife had passed away. But now she did not know what to think.

She trembled. When she had given up the

idea of marriage nine years ago, they had still been a family with respectable means. But they had been reduced almost to abject poverty now. The squire was landed and wealthy. Marriage to him could improve their circumstances, their lives.

"He must be sixty years old," Corey gasped, paling.

"He is an older man, but he is very well-off, and he is only fifty, Corey. Alexandra will have a closet full of the latest gowns. You will like that, won't you?" He turned to her, brows raised. "He has a fine manor house. He has a carriage and a brougham."

Alexandra started, gathering up her wits. She had a suitor — one with means. Yes, he was an older man, but he had always been kind, and if he was inclined toward generosity, he could be a savior for their family. She thought again of Owen and his courtship, and she was saddened. She must put Owen out of her mind. Squire Denney's suit was flattering, and more than that, it was a boon. At her age, in her circumstances, she could not expect more.

"You know I don't care about fashion — I care about you and the girls," she said carefully. She stood up and dusted off her immaculate skirts, and stared carefully at her father now. He was sober, and he was no fool. "Tell me about the squire. Is he aware that there is no dowry?"

"Oh, dear," Olivia murmured. "Alexandra, you cannot be considering Denney."

"Don't you dare even think about marrying him!" Corey exclaimed.

Alexandra ignored their outbursts.

Edgemont leveled a firm gaze at them both. "You two will keep your opinions to yourselves. They are not wanted. Yes, he is very aware of our predicament, Alexandra." His stare was sharp.

"Is there any chance he will be able and willing to contribute to this household?" Alexandra asked, after a lengthy pause.

Corey ran over to her. "How can you consider marrying that fat old farmer?" She whirled. "You can't marry Alexandra to him against her will!"

Edgemont glared. "I have had enough of your harping, missy."

"Corey, please, I must discuss this opportunity with Father," Alexandra said, squeezing her sister's hand.

"You are elegant and beautiful. You are kind and good, and he *is* fat and old," Corey insisted. "This is not an opportunity. This is a fate worse than death!"

Alexandra laid her hand on her sister's arm. "Please calm yourself." She faced her father. "Well?"

"Our discussions have not taken that turn. But he is a very wealthy man, Alexandra. I have heard it said he has the largest lease of all the Harrington tenants. He will surely be generous with us."

Alexandra chewed on her lip, a terrible habit of hers. Lady Harrington was an old family friend; Elizabeth and Blanche had been fond of one another, once. Lady Blanche came out to Edgemont Way once or twice a year, when she was passing by, to check on Alexandra and her sisters. Alexandra no longer called on Lady Blanche, mostly because their clothes were so out of fashion and so shabby — it was too embarrassing. But it might be time to call now. Lady Blanche would certainly know all about Squire Denney.

"Father, I will be frank. If he is inclined to be generous, I do not see how I could refuse his offer — if he truly makes one."

Corey cried out.

"By God, Alexandra, you are such a fine and giving woman! You are exactly like your mother. She, too, was selfless. Morton Denney has implied he will be a benevolent son-in-law. And Olivia can certainly run this household once you are wed."

Alexandra looked at Olivia, who was

clearly distraught. She wanted to tell her not to worry, that it would be all right.

"He will call tomorrow afternoon, and I expect you to be turned out in your Sunday best." Edgemont smiled, pleased. "I am off, then."

But Corey rudely seized his sleeve as he turned to leave. "You can't sell Alexandra off to that farmer!" Corey said, flushed with outrage. "She is not a sack of potatoes!"

"Corey . . ." Olivia seized her sister's hand, jerking it away from their father's arm.

"But that is what he is doing." Corey was near tears. "He is selling Alexandra off to a fat old farmer so he can replenish his coffers — and then he will lose it all once again, gaming at the tables!"

Edgemont's hand lashed out, and his slap against Corey's face rang loudly in the room. Corey gasped, her palm flying to her red cheek, and tears filled her eyes.

"I have had enough of your insolence," Edgemont ground out, flushed. "And I do not like it when the three of you band against me. I am your father and the head of this house. You will do as I say — every one of you. So mark my words, after Alexandra, the two of you are next."

The sisters exchanged wide-eyed looks. Alexandra stepped forward, wishing Corey could forgive her father for their circumstances, yet knowing that she was too young and so she could not. But that was no excuse for their father's harsh behavior. She barred her sister from Edgemont, while Olivia put her arm around her. Corey kept her head high, but she was trembling and furious.

"Of course you are the head of this house. Of course we will do as you say," Alexandra soothed.

He did not soften. "I mean it, Alexandra. I have decided on this match, whether you agree to it or not. Even if he decides not to contribute to this household, it is high time you are wed."

Alexandra stiffened. She did not speak her thoughts, but she was amazed. She was too old to be forced against her will into marriage or anything else.

He spoke more kindly. "You are a good daughter, Alexandra, and the truth is, I have your best interests at heart. You all need husbands and homes of your own. I can't afford handsome young bucks — I only wish that I could. But I will do the best I can, and it is a stroke of great luck that you have attracted Denney, at your age. It has brought me to my senses at last. Your mother must be rolling about in her grave, the way I've neglected your future." He glared at Corey and Olivia. "And by damn, I expect some gratitude."

No one moved.

"I'm off, then. Plans for the evening, if you must know." Head down and avoiding their eyes, as they all knew what he would do that night, he hurried from the room.

When he was gone, the front door of the house slamming in his wake, Alexandra turned to Corey. "Are you all right?"

"I hate him." Corey trembled. "I have always hated him! Look at what he has done to us. And now he says he will marry you off."

Alexandra took her youngest sister into her arms. "You can't hate him — he is your father. He cannot help his gambling, and the drinking is an illness, too. Darling, I only want to help you and Olivia. I so want you both to have better lives."

"We are fine!" Corey wept now. "Everything is his fault! It is his fault we are living this way. His fault that the young gentlemen in town offer me flowers, and then, behind my back, send me rude looks and whisper about lifting my skirts. It is his fault my skirts are torn. I hate him! And I will run off before it is my turn to marry some horrid old man." She broke free from Alexandra and ran from the room.

Alexandra looked at Olivia, who returned her gaze. A potent silence fell.

Olivia touched her arm. "This is wrong. Mother would choose a prince for you. She would never approve of this. And we are happy, Alexandra. We are a family."

Alexandra shivered. Elizabeth Bolton had approved of Owen. In fact, she had been delighted that Alexandra had found such love. And suddenly Alexandra had the notion that Olivia was right. Mother would not approve of this eminently sensible and lucrative match with Denney. "Mother is dead, and Father has become entirely dissipated. This family is my responsibility, Olivia, and mine alone. This suit is a blessing."

Olivia's expression tightened. A long pause ensued. Then she said, "The moment father began to speak of this, I saw your face and knew that no one would be able to talk you out of this terrible match. You sacrificed yourself for us once, but I was too young to understand. Now you intend to do so again."

Alexandra started for the stairs. "It isn't a sacrifice. Will you help me choose a gown?"

"Alexandra, please don't do this!"

"Only a hurricane could stop me," she

said firmly. "Or some other, equally terrific, force of nature."

The huge black lacquered coach and its team of perfectly matched pitch-black horses careened down the road, the red-and-gold Clarewood coat of arms emblazoned upon its doors. Two liveried servants stood on the coach's back fender. Inside the coach's luxurious interior, as red and gold as the family crest, the duke of Clarewood held casually on to a safety strap, his gaze on the dark gray skies outside. His mouth curved as thunder boomed, as if he approved. Lightning forked a moment later, and his expression seemed to shift again. It was going to storm terrifically. He was amused — of course he was — a dull, dank day suited this dark occasion perfectly.

He tensed, thinking about the previous duke — the man who had raised him.

Stephen Mowbray, the eighth duke of Clarewood, universally recognized as the wealthiest and most powerful peer in the realm, turned his impassive blue gaze to the dark gray mausoleum ahead. Situated atop a treeless knoll, it housed seven generations of Mowbray noblemen. As the coach halted, it began to rain. He made no move to get out.

In fact, his grip on the safety strap tightened.

He had come to pay his respects to the previous duke, Tom Mowbray, on this, the fifteenth anniversary of his untimely death. He never thought about the past — he found the exercise useless — but today his head had ached since he had arisen at dawn. On this particular day, there was just no getting around the past. How else did one pay his respects and honor the dead?

"I wish a word, Stephen."

He'd been immersed in his studies. He was an excellent student, mastering every subject and discipline put before him, though achieving such excellence required diligence, dedication and discipline. However, the need to excel had been drilled into him from a very early age; after all, a duke was not allowed to fail. He couldn't recall a time in his life when he hadn't been struggling to master some thing or another. No amount of fluency in French was adequate enough; no fence was high enough; no mathematical equation complicated enough. Even as a small boy of six or seven, he would be up past midnight studying. And there was never any praise.

"This examination is marked ninety-two percent," the seventh duke said harshly.

He trembled, looking up at the tall, hand-some blond man standing over him. "Yes, Your Grace."

The examination was crumpled up and tossed into the fireplace. "You'll take it again!"

And he had. He had received a ninety-four percent. The duke had been so furious with him that he'd been sent to his rooms and not allowed out for the rest of the week. Eventually he'd achieved a hundred percent.

He realized one footman was holding the coach door open for him, while the other was extending an open umbrella. It was raining harder now.

His head ached uncomfortably. He nodded at the footmen and swung down from the coach, ignoring the umbrella. Although he wore the requisite felt hat, he was instantly soaked through. "You may wait here," he told the footmen, who were as wet as he was.

As he slogged across his property toward the mausoleum, he could see the Clarewood mansion just below the ridge where the marble vault loomed. Nestled in a magnificent park, it was pale and gray against the dark trees and even darker wet skies. Thunder rolled to the east. The rain was falling in earnest now.

Stephen pushed open the heavy vault door and stepped inside, reaching for matches. He lit the lanterns, one by one, as thunder kept rolling in the distance. The rain was coming down harder and faster now, like sledgehammers on the vault's roof. He was very aware of Tom Mowbray lying in effigy across the chamber, waiting for him.

He'd come into the duchy at the age of sixteen. He'd already known that Tom was not his biological father, not that he had been told or that it had mattered. After all, he was being groomed to be the next duke, to be Tom's heir. The realization hadn't been an epiphany or a revelation. It had been a slowly creeping awareness, a nagging and growing comprehension. The duke was renowned for his affairs, but Stephen had no other siblings, not even a bastard one, which was very odd. And even as isolated as his childhood was — his life was tutors and masters, the duke and duchess, and Clarewood — he was somehow aware of the rumors. They'd swirled about him his entire life, from the moment he'd first understood the spoken word. His young ears had caught the gossip many times, whether at a great Clarewood ball or below stairs between servants. And while he'd ignored the whispers of "changeling" and "bastard," eventually the truth had begun to sink in.

The lessons of childhood could serve a man well, he thought. Gossip followed him wherever he went, threaded with envy, jealousy and malice. He never paid attention to the barbs. Why would he? No one wielded as much power in the realm as he did — outside of the royal family, of course. If they wanted to accuse him of being cold, ruthless and uncaring of anything and anyone other than Clarewood, he hardly cared. The Clarewood legacy took up all his time, as did the Foundation he had established in its name. Since taking up the reins of the duchy, he had tripled its value, while the Foundation funded asylums, hospitals and other charities throughout the greater realm.

He stared across the chamber at the pale stone effigy of his father. His mother, the dowager duchess, had declined to join him that day. He did not blame her. The previous duke had been a cold, critical and demanding man — a harsh taskmaster for them both. He would never forget her endless defense of him — nor their unending rancor, their hostile debates. Yet Tom had done his duty, hadn't he? His duty to Clarewood had been to make certain Stephen had the character necessary to succor the estate, and he had succeeded. Most men could not have managed the vast responsibility that came along with the duchy. He looked forward to it.

It was shockingly still in the tomb, but not silent. The rain pounded on the roof over his head, almost deafening him. Stephen took a torch from the wall and slowly walked over to the white marble coffin, then stared down at the duke's stone image. He didn't bother to speak — there was nothing he wished to say.

But it hadn't always been that way.

"He is asking for you."

His insides lurched with frightening force. He carefully closed the textbook he was reading and looked up at his mother. She was so pale now that he knew the duke was finally at death's door. He'd been close to dying for three days now, and the wait had been almost interminable. It was not that he wanted his father to die. It was that it was inevitable, and the tension had become unbearable for everyone, even for him. Yet he had been taught that a duke could and would bear any burden in the name of the duchy.

He slowly stood, trying to hold his feelings at bay, uncertain of what they were, exactly. He was the next Duke of Clarewood, and he would always accept his duty and do what he must. He had been trained from birth for this day; if his father would die, then he would take over the reins of the dukedom — and he would excel as its eighth duke. Any uncertainty he felt he would simply quash. Uncertainty was not allowed — nor was fear or anger or pain.

The duchess stared closely at him, as if expecting tears.

He would never cry — and certainly not in public. He nodded grimly at her, and they left his suite of rooms. Even if she expected grief from him, he would never reveal such feelings. Besides, he was in control. He'd learned long ago, as a small boy, that self-control was personal salvation.

The man lying on the sickbed, one of the most powerful peers in the realm, was unrecognizable now. Diphtheria had wasted his body away, leaving a small and gaunt shadow in place of the man he'd once been. Stephen tensed, for one moment his control slipping. In that moment, he did not want his father to die.

This man had raised him, claimed him as his own, given him everything. . . .

The duke's eyes opened. His blue gaze was unfocused, but it instantly sharpened.

Stephen strode forward, aware now that he

wanted to take his father's hands and cling to them, to tell him how grateful he was for all that he had done for him. "Is there anything I can get you, Your Grace?"

They stared at one another. And suddenly he realized that in this last moment of the duke's life, he would like to know that the duke was pleased with him. Because there had never been a word of praise, only criticism, disapproval, rebukes. There had been long lectures on duty, diligence and the pursuit of excellence. There had been sermons on character and honor. There had been the occasional blow, the dreaded riding crop. But there had never been praise. He suddenly, desperately, wished for praise — and maybe even a sign of affection.

"Father?"

The duke had been staring, his lips twisted with scorn, as if he knew what Stephen wanted. "Clarewood is everything," he wheezed. "Your duty is to Clarewood."

Stephen wet his lips, oddly dismayed, a feeling he was unfamiliar with. The duke was going to die at any time, maybe within moments. Was he pleased? Proud? Did he love him at all? "Of course," he said, breathing in hard.

"You will do me proud," the duke said. "Are you crying?"

He stiffened. "Dukes do not cry."

"Damned right," the duke choked. "Swear on the Bible that you will never forsake Clarewood."

Stephen turned, saw the Bible and picked it up. He realized his hands were unsteady and his breathing uneven. He realized that no praise, no kindness and no words or sign of affection would be forthcoming. "Clarewood is my duty," he said.

At that the duke's eyes blazed with satisfaction. A moment later they were sightless.

Stephen heard a sharp inhalation in the tomb. He started and stared at the effigy, then realized *he* had made that sound. He certainly owed everything to Tom Mowbray, and he would not criticize him now.

"You're probably pleased, aren't you? That they call me cold, ruthless and heartless. That they see me in your image." His voice echoed in the chamber. If Mowbray heard, he did not respond or give a sign.

"Talking to the dead?"

Stephen jumped, whirling. But only one man would dare intrude upon him, and that was his cousin and best friend, Alexi de Warenne.

Alexi was lounging near the vault door, which was ajar, soaking wet and disheveled, dark hair falling over his vivid blue eyes.

"Guillermo said I would find you here. How morbid you have become, carousing with the dead." But he grinned widely.

Stephen was very pleased to see his cousin, not that anyone outside of the family knew of their biological relationship. They'd been close since childhood, and he supposed the old adage that opposites attracted was true. His mother had brought him to Harrington Hall when he was nine years old, on the pretext of introducing him to Sir Rex, who had saved Tom Mowbray's life in the war. That day he'd met so many children that he could not keep track of their names. Of course, they were all his de Warenne and O'Neill cousins. He hadn't known that then, as he hadn't realized until much later that Sir Rex de Warenne was his natural father, and he'd been stunned by the warmth and casual, open affection in the family — he hadn't known a family could be so loving, and that a house could contain so much laughter. And he hadn't known what to do, really, because he didn't know anyone and he didn't belong there. But his mother had gone off with the ladies, so he'd stood on the fringes of the crowded room, his hands in the pockets of his jacket, watching the boys and girls chattering and playing happily with one another. It was Alexi who'd come up to him, demanding that he go outside with him and several other boys and do what boys do: find trouble, and lots of it. They'd stolen horses and gone riding through the Greenwich streets at a gallop, overturning vendors' carts and chasing pedestrians away. Everyone had been punished that night. The duke had been livid with his behavior — he'd taken out his strap — but Stephen had had the time of his life. Their friendship had begun that day.

Although married and comfortably settled now, Alexi remained the freest spirit and most independent thinker Stephen knew. They could argue for hours on almost any subject; they usually agreed on broad conclusions, but disagreed on almost every detail. Before Alexi's marriage they had caroused together, and frequently — Alexi had been a notorious ladies' man. Stephen admired his cousin, and he almost envied him. Alexi had made his life exactly what he wished for it to be — he had not been the servant of duty or slave to a legacy. Stephen could not imagine having had such choices or such freedom. But Alexi had also followed in his father's footsteps and was one of the most successful China traders of the day. In fact, until he'd married Elysse, the sea had been his great love. Now, amazingly, his wife joined him on his longer voyages, and they had residences around the world.

"I am hardly conversing with the dead, much less carousing," Stephen said drily, walking over to Alexi and embracing him very briefly. "I was wondering when you would get back to town. How is Hong Kong and, more importantly, how is your wife?"

"My wife is doing very well, and if you must know, she is thrilled to be home — and she misses you, Stephen. God knows why. It must be your irrepressible charm." Alexi grinned and then glanced at the effigy. "It's pouring outside, and the road below is about to be flooded. We may have to wait out the storm here. Aren't you glad I have come?" He took a flask out of his pocket. "We can honor old Tom together. Cheers."

Stephen felt himself smile. "If I must be honest, I am pleased you are both back, and yes, I will have a drink." But he didn't add that they both knew Alexi had despised Tom Mowbray and wouldn't think of truly honoring him. Alexi had never understood Tom's methods as a father. He had been raised so differently. There had never been verbal lashings, much less whip lashings.

Alexi handed him the flask. "He does look better in stone, by the way. And the likeness is startling."

Stephen drank and handed the flask back. "We cannot disrespect the dead," he warned.

"Of course not. God forbid you fail in your duty to honor him and salvage the dukedom. I see you have not changed." Alexi drank. "All duty and no play . . . how respectable you are, Your Grace."

"My duty is my life, and I have not changed, for better or for worse," he said, mildly amused. Alexi loved to lecture him on his failure to seize upon life's lighter moments. Only rarely could he turn away from his responsibilites. "Some of us do have responsibilities."

Alexi made a sound. "Responsibilities are one thing, shackles, another." He drank again.

"Yes, I am so terribly enslaved," Stephen responded, "and it is a terrible fate, to have the power to buy, take or make anything I want, whenever I want."

"Tom taught you well, but one day, the de Warenne blood will emerge." Alexi was unperturbed. "Even if your power scares everyone else into abject obedience, obsequious fawning or outright submission, I will always attempt to steer you in the right direction."

"I would not be a very adept duke if I were not obeyed," Stephen said mildly. "Clarewood would be in shambles. And I believe the family has enough reckless adventurers." He smiled. The truth was, the de Warenne men were only reckless until they settled down, and Alexi was glaring proof of that.

"Clarewood in shambles? That is an impossibility, as long as you are at the helm." Alexi gave him a mock salute. "And I gather you have decided not to follow in my footsteps, after all. I am unbearably despondent."

Stephen smiled.

Alexi smiled back, then said, "So I take it nothing has changed and you are still Britain's most eligible bachelor?"

Now Stephen was truly amused. His de Warenne relations — those who knew that Sir Rex was his father — loved to nag him about his bachelor status. Of course, he did need an heir. He simply dreaded a cold, bitter and boring marriage. "You have been gone ten or eleven months. What did you expect? For me to find my betrothed at long last?"

"You have just turned thirty-one, and it has been fifteen years since you began searching for a bride."

"One can hardly rush the process." His tone was wry.

"Rush? You mean prevent. One can only delay the inevitable, Stephen, not prevent it, and I, for one, am glad you have rejected this Season's latest offerings."

"I will admit, inane banter with an eighteen-year-old, no matter how polished, has become a discipline I dread. Of course, you will never repeat this."

"You are growing up — and of course not!" Alexi exclaimed, crossing his heart.

Stephen laughed, something he rarely did, but Alexi could always make him see the humor in a situation. "I hope so — I *am* middle-aged."

They shared another drink, this time in silence. Then Alexi said, "So nothing has changed while I have been gone? You remain as industrious as ever, building hospitals for unwed mothers and managing mining leases for the duchy?"

He hesitated. "Nothing has changed."

"How boring." Alexi's smile faded, and he glanced at the effigy. "Old Tom there must be proud — finally."

Stephen tensed. He glanced at the effigy, too. And for one moment, it was as if Tom sat up and was staring mockingly at him, as alive as they were — and as accusatory as

45

ever. Stephen's tension increased but then the memory was gone. Tom had looked at him with such scorn a thousand times, and most of the time he preferred to forget, but today was the one day he always remembered. "I doubt it."

They shared a somber look. "Sir Rex is proud," Alexi finally said. "And by the way, you are nothing like Tom, even if you try to be exactly like him."

Stephen considered the comment, knowing that Alexi had overheard him talking to the effigy. "I have no delusions about my character, Alexi. But as far as Sir Rex goes, he has always been attentive and supportive. He was kind to me when I was a boy, before I even guessed at the true nature of our relationship. You are probably right. But frankly, it doesn't matter. I do not need anyone to admire me or be proud of my achievements. I know what I must do. I know my duty — mock it though you will."

"Damn it, your character is just fine!" Alexi was angry, his blue eyes sparking. "I came to rescue you from old Tom, but now I think I must rescue you from yourself. Everyone needs affection and admiration, Stephen, even you."

"You are wrong," he said instantly, meaning it.

"Why? Because you grew up without any affection, you assume you can and will live that way? Thank God you are a de Warenne by blood."

Stephen did not want to walk out on that particular plank and only said, "I do not need rescuing, Alexi. I am the one with the power, remember? I am the one who does the rescuing."

"Ah, yes, and the good work you do for those who cannot help themselves is admirable. Maybe it also keeps you sane — because it prevents you from realizing the cold truth about yourself."

Stephen felt a twinge of anger, which he quashed. "Why are you harping on me?"

"Because I am your cousin, and if I don't, who will?"

"Your wife, your sister and any number of other relations."

Alexi grinned. "Enough said, then. Let's make a dash for the coach, and if the road below is flooded, we will swim."

Stephen started to laugh. "If you drown, Elysse will drown *me!* I suggest we wait out the storm here."

"Yes, she probably would, and of course you would choose to be sensible and pragmatic." But Alexi opened the vault door anyway. The downpour remained torrential.

"I am bored with old Tom. I vote we adjourn to your library for the very finest and oldest Irish whiskey in your cabinet." He glanced back into the vault. "You know, I think he is here, eavesdropping on us, as disapproving as ever."

Stephen tensed and said sharply, "He is dead, for God's sake, and has been dead for fifteen years." But he wondered if his friend had felt the old man's presence, too.

"Then why aren't you free of him?"

Stephen started. What did that mean? He said carefully, "I am quite free of him, Alexi, just as I am free of the past. But duty rules me, and surely even you can understand that. I *am* Clarewood."

Alexi stared. "No, Stephen, you aren't free, not of him and not of the past, and I wish you could see that. But you are right, you are ruled by duty, and by now I should not expect anything else. Except, oddly, I do."

Alexi was wrong; Alexi didn't understand the Clarewood legacy. And Stephen didn't feel like arguing about it. He simply wanted to escape Tom. "The rain has let up. Let's go."

CHAPTER TWO

Alexandra paused, facing her sisters. "Wish me luck," she said grimly. Her smile felt far too firm, instead of being bright and reassuring. Squire Denney was waiting in the next room with Edgemont. Oddly, she was nervous. Or perhaps it wasn't so odd. After all, her family's future was at stake.

Alexandra knew that worrying about making a good impression was silly, given what she had to work with, but she glanced in the hall mirror anyway. Olivia had helped her with her hair, and the chignon seemed a bit severe. Worse, even though she'd chosen a dress that had fared better over the years than her other ones, it was clearly worn and out of fashion. She sighed. No amount of sewing could repair a frayed hem; only costly trim could do that.

"I appear ill kempt," she said flatly.

Corey and Olivia exchanged looks. "You look like a fictional heroine, one suffering

49

through tragic circumstances," Olivia said, "and awaiting a dark hero to rescue her." She reached up and teased several strands of hair from the tight chignon.

Alexandra smiled at her.

"I am not a tragic heroine, although the squire might very well be a hero. I suppose there is no putting this off."

"You don't have to be nervous," Olivia said softly. "He is predisposed toward you."

"I don't know why you didn't let me do your hair," Corey complained, the light in her eyes flickering.

"I would have gladly done so — if I could have trusted you." Knowing her sister, she might purposefully try to mess up her hair in the hopes of chasing off the squire. Alexandra could hear male voices in the parlor now. She started forward, resolved.

Both sisters followed. Olivia hugged her at the door. "I am with Corey, Alexandra. You can do better. He is not good enough for you. Please rethink this."

Alexandra did not bother to tell her what she herself had already accepted: she was, as always, doing what was best for everyone.

Olivia sighed, glancing at Corey, who appeared distraught now.

"This is not the end of the world," Alexandra said firmly, offering up a bright smile.

"In fact, this is a new beginning for us all." She shoved her anxiety aside and pushed open the door.

Behind her, she heard Corey cry softly, "Oh, Lord, I'd forgotten how short he was!"

Alexandra ignored that. She was exceptionally tall for a woman, and most men were shorter than she was. Her father and Denney were standing before the window, as if admiring their muddy and overgrown gardens. It had stopped raining that morning, but outside, the lawn had become a small lake. The squire was probably two inches shorter than she was — making his height quite average.

Both men turned.

Her heart suddenly lurched — as if with dismay. Denney was just as she recalled, a big, husky fellow with side whiskers and kind eyes. He wore a frock coat for this occasion, one she instantly saw was very well made — and very costly. Now she noticed a signet ring on his hand. It was gold and boasted a gemstone. And carefully inspecting him as she was doing made her feel like a fortune hunter.

But wasn't that exactly what she was?

You can't sell Alexandra off to that farmer!

But he could — it was done all of the time, Alexandra thought grimly. Very few in society married for love. Women in her position never did.

The parlor was small, the walls mustard-yellow, with fading green drapes and shabby furniture. Edgemont came forward, smiling, and looped his arm in hers. "Alexandra, there you are." He turned so that they faced the squire. And Alexandra was surprised — his eyes were shining.

"I am sorry if I have kept you waiting," she managed, her pulse pounding. Why did she suddenly feel saddened? Was it because if all went according to plan, she would be leaving Edgemont Way and her beloved family? Suddenly she thought of Owen and the deep bond — the passion — they'd shared. And she was resolute. Ever since her father had declared that she must marry, Owen had been on her mind. But that kind of love had passed her by, and she must forget about the past.

"This is my beautiful daughter, Alexandra," Edgemont said proudly, beaming.

"You could keep me waiting for days on end, Miss Bolton, and I would still be pleased to see you," Denney said, smiling at her.

Alexandra somehow smiled again. And she thought of how kind the squire had always been to his wife, before she'd passed away. He was a good man. Maybe, in time, she might come to love him a little. "That is far too kind of you," she replied, shaken.

"We had a chance to discuss the summer forecast, as predicted by the Almanac. Denney thinks it will be a good summer, not too hot, with plenty of rain," her father told her.

"That is wonderful," Alexandra said. She meant it, because every farmer in the shire depended on good weather for their crops and livelihood.

"I have had three good years in a row, enough to make a handsome profit, and then some other investments have paid off, as well," Denney said eagerly. His brown gaze had become searching. "I have invested in the railroads, mostly. I am now adding a fine wing to the house, for a grand parlor, if you will. There will be a small ballroom, too. I have decided that I will entertain in the future. I should love to show you my plans," he added.

"I am sure your plans are very pleasing."

Edgemont said eagerly, "His manor has fifteen rooms, Alexandra — fifteen rooms!"

She somehow smiled again. But her dismay had increased, against her will and intentions. The squire kept staring, his cheeks flushed, his dark eyes shining. Surely he wasn't in love with her? She did not want to hurt him by being incapable of returning such passion.

"You may come and visit Fox Hill anytime," Denney said. "In fact, it would be my pleasure to give you a tour of the house and gardens."

"Then I must call as soon as possible," she said lightly. She glanced at Edgemont. She needed to be alone with Denney so she could find out how he might be inclined toward helping her sisters.

Edgemont smiled at them. "The squire has been invited to the de Warenne fete tomorrow night. It is such an honor, as it is Lady Harrington's daughter's birthday celebration."

"I am impressed," Alexandra said. She hadn't heard about the party, but she knew both girls, even if she hadn't seen Sara or Marion in several years. They were close to Olivia and Corey in age.

"I am on very good terms with Lady Harrington and Sir Rex," Denney told her eagerly. "The party is for their youngest, Sara. I should love it if you joined me, Miss Bolton — with your sisters, of course."

Alexandra's first reaction was sheer surprise; then, instantly, she thought of her sisters, who had never been to a high-society fete. Her mind raced. Of course she must accept. This would be a wonderful opportunity for her sisters — and the kind of evening they deserved, and should have had and become accustomed to. But neither Alexandra nor her sisters had had a new gown since before their mother died. While the sad truth was that no one invited them out, due to their circumstances, even if someone had, they did not have the proper attire to attend most social functions.

Corey could fit into one of her old ball gowns, with some slight alterations. And surely they could find something for Olivia to wear from among their mother's clothes. They would be sadly out of fashion, but they would be able to attend.

"We would love to attend," she said quickly.

Edgemont looked carefully at her. Alexandra knew he was wondering how they would find the proper clothing. "Father, I was hoping to walk with the squire outside, as the sun has come out and all chance of further rain is gone."

His eyes widened, and he beamed. Then, "I'll be in the study. Enjoy your walk." He walked out, leaving the door wide-open.

Alexandra stared at the threshold until he was gone. Then she faced her suitor. "Squire

Denney, I am very flattered that you have called."

"A rainstorm could not have kept me away."

"Is it possible to have a very frank discussion?"

His eyes widened. "I so prefer candor. It is one of the things I like best about you, Miss Bolton, after your excessively kind nature. You are always direct."

She turned. "I fear you have put me high upon a pedestal, a stature I do not deserve."

His brows lifted. "If any woman deserves to be placed upon a pedestal, Miss Bolton, it is you." When she began to speak, he interrupted. "I have admired you for years. You have taken wonderful care of your sisters and father, and such selflessness and compassion is to be commended. And then, of course, there is your beauty. I am practically speechless, in fact, to be standing here with you now."

Alexandra almost blushed. She was hardly a raving beauty, but she would not dispute him. "I am glad you find my nature pleasing. And you are right about one thing — I try very hard to take good care of my younger sisters as well as my father. Olivia is only eighteen, Corey just sixteen."

A slight bewilderment crossed his bluff

face. "They are lovely young ladies."

She gestured at a chair, deciding to forgo their walk. He sat, and she took the adjacent seat, then clasped her hands in her lap. "I was on the verge of marriage nine years ago, before my mother passed on. When my mother died, I made the decision to devote myself to my family — and I broke things off with my suitor." She smiled firmly. There was some old sadness, thinking of Owen and their dreams now. "I promised her that I would take care of this family. I made a serious commitment to the care and welfare of my sisters and my father."

"The commitment you are speaking of only heightens my admiration for you, Miss Bolton." He hesitated. "I have the impression that you loved this gentleman."

She nodded. "Yes, I did."

"You are a paragon, Miss Bolton. But why are you telling me this?"

"How direct might I be?" She sat up straighter.

"As direct as is necessary." He flushed, suddenly seeming dismayed. "Are you about to tell me that you remain committed to the deathbed vows you made to your mother?"

"I will look after my sisters and my father until I die — although I hope my sisters will be wed well before that day." She smiled.

He slowly nodded. "I see. My intentions are honorable, Miss Bolton."

"That is what Edgemont indicated."

He held her gaze. "Do you know why I suggested your sisters accompany us tomorrow night?"

She shook her head. "Not really."

"Because it seemed to me that it would make the evening more pleasant for you — less awkward — but it also seemed to me that two such young ladies should be given the opportunity to get out and be seen."

Her heart sped. "That is so kind of you."

"I consider myself a kind man — and a generous one. If my suit progresses as I hope it does, you will not have to carry the burden of caring for your family by yourself."

Alexandra gasped. Tears came to her eyes. She was speechless.

But now she knew. He had means, his suit was a serious one, and he would be generous with her family.

"I have admired you for years, Miss Bolton — from afar, and very respectfully." He spoke thoughtfully now. "I never dreamed my wife would die so suddenly — she was in such good health until her final illness. I mourned her deeply." He paused, grim for a moment. "But she has died, and a year has gone by. You remain unattached — which bewilders me." He met her gaze. "I am of a very solid character, Miss Bolton. I am a dependable and honorable man. I am certain things will work out to both our satisfaction, if you give my suit a chance."

"I will give your suit all the respect and consideration it deserves," she somehow said. She could barely believe this was happening. Her sisters were going to have futures outside of Edgemont Way. It seemed like a miracle.

He stood, as she did. "Shall we walk outside?"

Alexandra took his proffered arm. "It will be my pleasure to stroll with you," she said.

But as they left the house, she glanced over her shoulder. Corey and Olivia were standing in the doorway, their expressions grim with dismay. Then Corey turned and stormed into the house.

Alexandra tensed as the squire's brougham queued up in the circular drive before Harrington Hall. It was a beautiful evening, and the sky was stained pink above the high gray stone roof of the mansion, with fingers of pink and peach drifting across the magnificent gardens and grounds. A fountain stood in the center of the drive, its waterworks a lavish display, bursting a dozen feet into the air. But she was exhausted, having stayed up the entire night to finish repairing and restoring dresses for herself and her sisters. In fact, she'd been sewing without interruption since Squire Denney had left her yesterday afternoon.

Of course she was tense, not excited, now. And her tension escalated. She, Olivia and Corey sat facing backward, toward her father and Denney, so she had to crane her neck to look outside. The coaches ahead were large, luxurious broughams, with perfectly matching horses and liveried coachmen, and the gentlemen and ladies alighting were in the finest tails and ball gowns. Even in the dusk, Alexandra saw jewels glinting from the ladies' throats and ears, and from the gentlemen's hands. She'd almost forgotten how wealthy the peerage was. She looked down at her bare fingers, her green satin gown. The fabric should have shone, but it had been hanging in the closet for too many years. No one wore dresses with full sleeves above the elbow anymore, but there had not been enough time to alter her own dress — she'd altered the sleeves on Olivia's and Corey's gowns, instead. Her skirts were too full for the current style, as well. At least, she thought grimly, her gown still fit.

"That is a beautiful dress," the squire said, clearing his throat.

Had he read her thoughts? Was she being transparent? She somehow managed to smile at him. His eyes had been shining yet again when he'd arrived to pick them up and escort them to Harrington Hall. Alexandra did not think she looked well — she was pale from her efforts to properly garb her sisters, and dark circles shadowed her eyes. He hadn't noticed, obviously. And maybe he didn't see how old — and old-fashioned — her dress truly was.

Olivia took her hand. Her eyes were sparkling with the kind of excitement she generally reserved for her paintings and sketches. She had never looked prettier. Her long tawny hair had been pinned up in curls, and she wore one of their mother's pale ivory ball gowns. Their gazes met. Alexandra was so proud of her.

"You do look beautiful," Olivia whispered.

Alexandra squeezed her hand. "So do you — and so does Corey. We are going to have a lovely evening — all because of the squire."

Denney beamed. "I hope so," he said.

Alexandra glanced at Corey. Her eyes were huge as she stared out of the carriage at the arriving guests, and her cheeks were flushed with excitement, too. She was almost as tall as Alexandra, and only a bit slimmer in build, and the pale blue watered silk was stunning on her. It was far too adult for someone of sixteen, but there hadn't been anything else in Alexandra's closet. Corey looked eighteen, at least, and terribly beautiful.

Alexandra felt a pang. Corey and Olivia had never been out in society, not like this — and though she did not want to blame anyone, there *was* one person to blame. She reminded herself that their father was no longer himself. Elizabeth Bolton's death had crushed him, leaving him with no passion but drink and gaming, and no spirit to challenge that passion. Did it matter? Her sisters deserved more, and maybe something good would come of this night for them. The gentlemen present would have to be blind not to notice them.

Suddenly hoofbeats sounded, as if an army was approaching. It was almost their turn to alight, but Alexandra turned, as did her sisters, the squire and Edgemont. A huge black coach, pulled by six magnificent blacks, red-and-gold crests emblazoned upon its doors, passed them, clearly cutting to the head of the line. As it did so, gravel sprayed their carriage.

Alexandra stared after the magnificently attired footmen, in red-and-gold livery, pale stockings, patent shoes and long, curled white wigs. She felt her tension increase. She reminded herself that when Elizabeth Bolton was alive, she had been to a few high-society fetes. Being nervous was absurd. Would anyone really care about their sudden appearance in society, or that they wore older clothes? But now she worried, and not for herself. She did not want her sisters ridiculed tonight.

The huge coach had halted, though she could not see who had gotten out. But she thought she glimpsed a tall, dark figure striding through the crowd, bypassing the queue and directly entering the house.

Oddly, her heart thundered, and she stared.

"Ah, it's our turn to alight," Denney exclaimed. A coachman had opened his door, and he got out.

Her father was about to follow Denney to the curb. He must not ruin this for them, she suddenly thought. And she did not trust him. She settled in her seat and faced her father, resolved. "I prefer that you do not overimbibe tonight."

His eyes widened in shock. Then, "You cannot talk to me that way, Alexandra."

She firmed. The one thing she could control, or at least try to control, was her father's drinking. "There is a flask in your pocket. May I have it?"

He gasped and turned red.

She held out her hand and somehow smiled. "If you want me to marry Squire Denney, it will not help if he sees you stumbling about. And, more importantly, what if Corey and Olivia attract suitors tonight? We are clearly in dire straits, and that means our behavior must be impeccable."

Grumbling, Edgemont took a tarnished silver flask from his pocket, and then, before handing it over, he took a swig. "Father!" Alexandra reproved.

"You remind me more of your mother every day," he groused, handing her the flask.

Alexandra uncapped it and poured the contents out the window. Then she exchanged looks with her sisters. "It is our turn."

Corey was somehow both pale and flushed at once. Alexandra murmured, "You will be fine." She gave her hand to Denney's coachman — he did not have liveried footmen, obviously — and stepped down to the ground. Her sisters followed.

Olivia came close and whispered, "What are you thinking? We are not here to attract suitors! How could we possibly do that? Everyone knows we are in dire straits."

Alexandra smiled at her. "Being here tonight makes me yearn for better circumstances, not for myself, but for you and Corey. Father and mother used to go to balls frequently. You should have had this life, Olivia. So should Corey."

"We are fine," Olivia insisted. "And right now, the only task we must concentrate on is getting you out of an unwanted betrothal."

Alexandra grimaced, glancing ahead of them, but the squire hadn't heard. "My mind hasn't changed. I am very pleased that the squire is courting me," she whispered back.

"Maybe you will find someone else here tonight," Olivia said. She was never combative, but her will was steel. It had always been that way. She was simply so good-natured that very few knew that fact about her.

"I am nervous," Corey suddenly said, interrupting them. "Enough so that I have a headache. And those men are staring at us."

Corey was never nervous, Alexandra thought, and looked past her sister to see three gentlemen standing by the open front doors, where the doormen were ushering other guests inside. The gentlemen were about Alexandra's age, and they were regarding her and her sisters. One smiled and touched his top hat, his look of admiration focused on her youngest sister.

Alexandra somehow smiled back. "He was smiling at you," she said to Corey. "And there was nothing bold or improper about it."

"He was smiling at Olivia," Corey said quickly. But she blushed.

Alexandra took her arm, reminded of just how young her sister was. Corey might be reckless and willful at home, but she was overcome now, and Alexandra did not blame her. She would not be so anxious if she'd had the kind of life she had been born into, she thought. And while Alexandra's marriage to the squire would not give her that kind of life, it would be a step upward.

The squire turned, gesturing for them to join him. They hurried to his side, following other guests up the walk. Alexandra had been to Harrington Hall many times, at first with her mother, and on two occasions, after Elizabeth's passing, with her sisters. Lady

Blanche had greeted them warmly, even after their fall from grace, as recently as last year.

The entrance hall was the size of their dining room twice over, and standing just outside the threshold of the ballroom, Alexandra saw their hosts, Lady Blanche and Sir Rex. He had lost his leg in the war and was leaning on a crutch. It didn't matter. They made a stunning couple as they greeted their guests, for she was pale and pretty, and he was dark and handsome. Sara was with them, a stunning, bejeweled and well-dressed brunette. Alexandra felt a twinge of envy as she studied her, but the envy wasn't for herself, it was for her sisters.

Then she realized that they were being remarked.

Alexandra started. Lady Lewis was staring hatefully at her — as if she wished her dead. But that was impossible, wasn't it? Lady Lewis was one of her best customers. The other woman turned away when she saw that Alexandra had noticed her, but then she began whispering to two other ladies, and Alexandra knew they were discussing her.

The squire was greeting several gentlemen, and he'd stepped ahead of them. Alexandra turned to her sisters, uneasy and dismayed. "Did you see that?"

Olivia met her stare. "Why would she look at us that way?"

Alexandra took a steadying breath. Now she noticed Lady Henredon across the room — and Lady Bothley, too. What had she been thinking? She sewed for all these women, and it was unacceptable for a servant — or a seamstress — to step out with her betters.

Her stomach churned. She turned — and bumped into Lady Lewis, who had approached.

"Alexandra, what a surprise. I did not recognize you in that dress."

Unable to manage a smile, she was aware of her sisters stepping close to her, one on either side.

Lady Lewis glanced contemptuously at the three of them. "I don't recognize any of you, dressed as you are."

Alexandra's heart thundered. "That is very unkind."

Lady Lewis lifted a brow. "It's not as if I said that I am accustomed to seeing you all in rags — and sewing my gowns."

Corey choked.

Olivia took Corey's hand.

Alexandra forced a smile. She wanted to explode, but she needed Lady Lewis's account, at least for now. "No, you didn't say any such thing, and I apologize. You would never speak so disgracefully. I am certain of that."

"My maid will drop off this gown to be cleaned and pressed tomorrow," Lady Lewis said, then huffed and walked away.

Alexandra trembled.

"What a witch!" Corey cried. "Don't you dare clean and press that gown for her."

"Of course I'll do exactly that." Alexandra spoke calmly, though she wasn't calm at all. Her temples were throbbing now. She was already exhausted, and the cruel confrontation had not been helpful. She glanced about, hoping to sit down.

"Miss Bolton, may I introduce you to my good friend, Squire Landon?" Denney said as he returned to her, smiling and in good spirits. "George, Miss Bolton and her two sisters, Olivia and Corey. And Edgemont, of course, you know."

Her father had caught up to them, as well, Alexandra noticed, then managed to smile at Squire Landon and wish him a pleasant evening. As Landon began to ask Denney about a bull he'd recently purchased, she heard a woman whispering behind her.

"A disgrace . . . drunk every single night . . . the gaming . . . his daughters . . ."

Alexandra felt her cheeks burning as she strained to hear exactly what the woman was saying, but the gist was clear. Edgemont was a disgrace, and everyone present knew it.

Corey was oblivious — peering wide-eyed at everyone and everything. Alexandra glanced at Olivia, who was staring at an oddly familiar blond man. She didn't think she knew him, yet the feeling remained that she did. She took a deep breath. Maybe the worst was over.

But then she saw that three older women were staring at her and her sisters now, and she knew that the worst was far from over.

They were whispering behind their gloved hands, and she felt certain they were discussing her or her sisters or her father. Alexandra trembled and turned her back to them. "Father, do you know those ladies?"

He glanced toward them and paused. "Actually, although it has been a while, those ladies were all friends of your mother's. Lady Collins was especially close. God, it seems so long ago! She is looking very well, actually."

"She isn't looking very friendly," Olivia remarked. "She is shooting daggers at us."

"That cannot be. She was very friendly with Elizabeth. Come, let's say hello."

70

Alexandra said quickly, "We haven't met our hosts yet."

"There are a dozen people ahead of us," Edgemont insisted. "And Squire Denney is preoccupied with his friend. Lady Collins!" He hurried over.

Reluctantly — exchanging grim looks with her sisters — Alexandra followed. Lady Collins's expression was as cold as ice.

"It is good to see you again," Edgemont said.

She inclined her head. "Hello, Edgemont. I didn't expect to see you here."

"I am most surprised to be here myself," he said cheerfully. "Do you recall my daughters?"

Alexandra held her head high as Lady Collins said she didn't believe they'd ever met. Polite handshakes were exchanged. "Enjoy your evening," Lady Collins said, then left them, making no attempt to hide her desire to get away as quickly as possible.

Edgemont flushed. "By God, she's changed."

"This is a mistake," Alexandra said softly. "I am a seamstress now. I sew for half a dozen of these women. They resent my being here."

"You have every right! You are Squire

Denney's guest, and Lady Harrington will be thrilled to see you."

Alexandra turned to look at her sisters, who seemed distraught and dismayed now. She wished she hadn't spoken so openly. Then, across their heads, she saw her escort. Denney smiled at her and indicated that he would return in another moment. He was surrounded by gentlemen now. Clearly he was well liked.

Three couples were ahead of them on the receiving line. The knot in her stomach had grown and was aching now. Her head hurt. What had she been thinking, to come out this way with Olivia and Corey? She overheard the matron at the front of the line going on and on about how lovely Sara was — how graceful, how genteel. It was true. Of course Sara de Warenne, a nice enough young lady, did not lack for anything.

"Jilted."

She turned and saw a woman staring cruelly at her. If looks could kill, she would have dropped over on the spot. She focused on making out what the woman was saying to her friend.

"At the altar?" The friend gasped, looking at Alexandra with malicious delight.

"Yes, she was jilted right at the altar. I recall it so well now." The first woman smiled with triumph at Alexandra. "She got what she deserved. St. James came to his senses — and married a proper title from a proper family."

Alexandra whirled, putting her back to the two matrons, aghast. Olivia whispered, "Did I just hear what I thought I did? Were those two ladies saying that Owen jilted you?"

Of all she had endured up to that point, that lie hurt the most, and to think Olivia had heard it, too. "It doesn't matter, Olivia," she said, feeling oddly faint now. She realized she was too exhausted to linger at Sara's birthday ball. She looked around for a chair. Seats lined the entry hall, many of them taken. But only two couples were ahead of them in the queue now; she would have to see this through.

She touched her throbbing temples. If she were at home, she would have lain down with an ice pack.

"Why would anyone say such a thing, when it is patently untrue?" Olivia demanded in a hushed tone.

Alexandra managed to sound calm. "I'm sure the lie wasn't deliberate. Undoubtedly they haven't recalled the past correctly, that is all. I'm sure those ladies made an innocent mistake." But she wasn't certain, not at all.

"Gossip is like wildfire," Olivia said. "Once it starts, it is impossible to control."

"I think those ladies are hateful," Corey said.

Alexandra's temples throbbed painfully now. She put her arm around Corey. "No one is hateful. And we should not be eavesdropping."

"They wanted us to hear," Corey said, twisting away.

"Why don't we change the topic? We came here to enjoy the evening," Alexandra suggested.

"How can we enjoy the evening now?" Olivia asked, clearly worried. "Although a small scandal might chase Squire Denney away."

Alexandra choked. Her despair seemed complete.

She had barely slept in days, mired in so much stress and anxiety since her father's shocking announcement. Last night she had worked herself to exhaustion — to the point of having numb fingertips. Suddenly she knew that no matter how close she was to the front of the queue, she must sit down — at once. She did not feel well, not at all.

The room spun.

The lights dulled and grayed.

I am not going to faint, Alexandra thought,

74

horrified. *If I faint, there will be even more gossip.*

But the floor tilted wildly anyway.

As she reached out blindly, she crashed into a hard male body — and a strong arm went around her. For one moment she was filled with disbelief; she hadn't felt such masculinity in almost a decade. Her heart slammed to a stop, then began hammering. Hard and muscular, her rescuer enveloped her in warmth. Breathless, Alexandra looked helplessly up. . . .

And found herself gazing into the most piercing — and most beautiful — blue eyes she had ever seen.

With utter calm, the man said, "Let me help you to a chair."

She meant to reply, she really did, but she couldn't form words. She could only stare at his stunningly handsome face — at those long-lashed eyes, which had turned languid and sensual now, at the straight, patrician line of his well-formed nose, at the curve of his cuttingly high cheekbones. She simply could not breathe. He was devastating, and it had been so long since she had been in a man's arms.

And her body knew it. It tightened, swelled. Her heart slammed again. Desire was a fist to her midsection, robbing her of all air.

And he was staring intensely back at her. His mouth was full, but chiseled into a hard line, and now, slightly, the corners shifted. But the expression was by no means a smile. "May I escort you to a chair?" he offered again.

His tone was so seductive that desire flooded her again. She wet her lips. As she no longer knew how to flirt, she decided she would not even try — assuming she could even find her voice. "You are very kind," she managed at last.

His mouth eased a bit more. "Many things are said about me, but I do believe that no one has ever called me kind."

His arm remained around her. Alexandra realized she was, for all intents and purposes, in his embrace. "Then you have detractors, sir."

He seemed amused — but it was as if he refused to smile. "I have many," he agreed. "But the truth of the matter is that kindness has nothing to do with rescuing a beautiful woman."

And as if she were a young woman, Alexandra blushed.

His brow lifted. "Shall we?" But before she could even nod, he was moving her through the crowd, which parted for them as if on command. Suddenly a red velvet chair was before them. Alexandra was vaguely aware of the whispers in the room behind them, but she couldn't make out a word and didn't even try — her racing heartbeat was simply too loud.

"I am reluctant to let you go," he said softly.

She knew she was blushing again. "I am afraid . . . there is no other choice."

"There are many choices," he said as softly, as he pressed her toward the chair.

He easily could have released her, but Alexandra was certain he held on to her as intimately as he did until the very last moment, when her bottom was securely on the plush seat of the chair. And even then, his large hand was on her waist, and his hard arm remained behind her back. She felt his fingers tighten.

"The pleasure has been mine."

She couldn't think of a thing to say. Worse, she couldn't look away from his warm, intent gaze. He was *flirting.* She was amazed.

He released her, straightened to his full height — he was over six feet tall, she thought almost inanely — bowed and walked away.

Alexandra just sat there, stunned.

And then, as her sisters rushed over and knelt beside her, she became aware of her hammering heart and throbbing body, and the fact that she was completely undone. *Who was that man?*

"Do you know who that was?" Corey asked excitedly, as if she'd heard Alexandra's silent question.

Alexandra looked up and saw that almost everyone in the entry hall was staring at her and whispering behind gloved hands. "No, I do not."

"That was the Duke of Clarewood," Corey breathed.

Alexandra stiffened in her seat. She knew all about the duke. Everyone did. He was a paragon of manhood — rich, titled, a great philanthropist. In fact, it was undisputed that he was the wealthiest peer in the realm — and possibly the most powerful one. And he was the most eligible bachelor in Great Britain.

She trembled. Because the most important thing of all was that everyone knew his reputation. He was, it was said, cold and heartless. He'd rejected the best Britain had to offer, time and again, for over a decade, refusing to choose a bride. But he kept many beautiful mistresses. And it was also said that he'd left a trail of broken hearts all across the realm.

CHAPTER THREE

He could not attend any kind of function without fawning ladies and obsequious gentlemen hoping to attract his interest and attention. The men wanted friendship, not because he was so likable, but for his connections; the ladies wanted his hand or at least an affair, or marriage for their daughters or sisters. However, even before he had come into his title, he had learned to put up a huge invisible wall between himself and everyone else. Because even when he'd been a boy, as the previous duke's son and heir, the sycophants had pursued him. Long ago, he'd become adept at walking through a huge crowd without making eye contact. When someone dared to approach, he either tolerated the intrusion, if so inclined, or sent the person such a quelling look that he or she instantly fled.

Now Stephen paused to glance back at the tall brunette who had almost fainted in his arms. His blood did not race at his first glimpse of a beautiful woman; he was too experienced and too jaded. But his blood was racing now.

He slowly smiled to himself.

She was surrounded by several women, two older gentlemen, and their hosts, and was obviously reassuring everyone that she was all right. The two youngest women seemed deeply concerned for her, so he deduced that they were relations or close friends. He thought he remarked a vague resemblance. Sisters?

He kept staring, unconcerned whether his interest was remarked. She was unusually tall and very attractive. Her face had strong planes and angles. He would not call her beautiful, and handsome was too masculine a word. But she was striking. He would leave his analysis at that, but he was intrigued.

And he was never intrigued so swiftly.

Because of her age, he instantly assumed she was a woman of some experience. And as she was obviously impoverished — no one with means would wear a gown so far out of fashion — there was no reason in the world why they might not reach some kind of mutually beneficial arrangement. His mistress Charlotte had already become tiresome. Besides, his lovers never stayed in his good graces for more than a few months.

"It is absolutely disgraceful of them to show up here. Imagine! Alexandra Bolton sews Lady Henredon's clothes! She makes a *living!*"

He glanced behind him at two flushed and furious socialites — one silver-haired and one a brassy redhead — and then saw his current mistress standing just behind them. Charlotte's blue eyes instantly met his, and she smiled.

He nodded politely at her, hardly dismayed. He was instead thinking about the fact that Alexandra Bolton sewed for the upper classes, which surprised him. He did not know of any noblewoman in strained circumstances who would do such a thing. It was actually quite admirable. He could not understand the upper class revulsion for "work." The truth was, he rolled up his sleeves every single day, whether he was at his desk, at one of his construction sites or at a Foundation office.

"And Edgemont has been banished from our circles for years. He is a *drunk,*" the redhead added. "I cannot believe Lady Harrington has allowed them through the front door."

The two women walked away, their faces

close together. He heard them murmuring about Miss Bolton being jilted at the altar and how she'd undoubtedly deserved it. He sighed. The bitches were gathering for a kill. He truly hated society at times, never mind that he stood at its peak. And he always despised gossip, especially when it was based on malice or ignorance. He suspected that, in this case, the gossips knew next to nothing about Miss Bolton — but they certainly wished her ill.

He felt a welling of compassion for her. Too well, he recalled and would never forget being a small boy and overhearing the servants or guests discussing him. Not that he cared any longer about being called a bastard, but as a child, those whispers had been confusing and hurtful.

He glanced back at Alexandra Bolton. She remained seated, but suddenly she looked up, as if on cue. His heart raced again. He did not mind, but he was now somewhat amused by his own reaction to an older, albeit attractive, and impoverished gentle-woman in a rather distasteful dress. It had been a long time since the mere sight of a woman could arouse him.

"Good evening, Your Grace," Charlotte Witte murmured.

He turned and bowed. He'd been enjoying Charlotte's favors for several months now. She was blond, petite, spectacularly beautiful — and very determined to keep his attention. Too determined, in fact, and her desire to become his wife had become more and more transparent. That was crossing the line. "Good evening, Lady Witte. You are in fine form tonight."

She smiled and curtsied, dutifully pleased, then glanced past him at Miss Bolton. "Such high drama, Your Grace. And I know how you like to avoid drama and theatrics."

He gazed impassively down at her. He did thoroughly dislike spectacles of any kind. "So you accuse Miss Bolton of deliberately attracting my attention? How unfair, when she is not here to defend herself."

"If she did not intend to make a spectacle of herself, then she is fortunate, is she not? For she *did* attract your attention." Charlotte was smiling, but her blue eyes were hard.

He managed not to sigh. She was jealous, as he supposed she should be. Except that she was only a lover, and he never made promises he did not intend to keep. He'd certainly made none to Charlotte. "I am hardly so cold-hearted that I would allow a damsel in distress to faint at my feet."

"I would never imply such a thing," she

said, as if taken aback. Then she smiled, glanced around, and stepped closer. "Did you receive my note?"

"I did," he said. She wished to know if he intended a rendezvous later that night. He'd meant to make the appointment, but now he glanced toward Miss Bolton, who was on her feet and sipping from a flute of champagne, while smiling at one of the older gentlemen. His gaze sharpened. The older man was besotted. "Do you know Miss Bolton?"

Charlotte managed to keep smiling. "I know of her, Your Grace, but no, I do not know her. How could I? She is a seamstress. Her father is a drunk. We do not run in the same circles."

He stared at her. "Pettiness is hardly becoming."

She flushed. "I do beg your pardon, Your Grace."

And in that moment, he knew he was done with Charlotte Witte.

She murmured, "Will I see you later tonight?"

He somehow smiled. "Not tonight." He had no intention of offering up any explanation for his decision.

She pouted so prettily that most men would have changed their minds. "I will console myself with my dreams."

He nodded at her, and she finally drifted away. But before he could find the new object of his interest, Alexi approached. "What is wrong with you?"

"Nothing is wrong with me. I am a paragon, remember?" Stephen said, and Alexi laughed.

"So why run off such a beautiful woman?" Alexi asked, but more seriously. "Oh, wait, I know the answer. You are bored."

Although they had shared quite a bit of his finest Irish whiskey the night before, the subject of his marital status had not arisen a second time. "Please do not lecture me on the impossible delights of matrimony."

Alexi's grin turned wicked. "The delights are only impossible if you are lucky in love."

"My God, she's turned you into a cow-eyed poet."

"Ah, an insult you will have to pay for. Drinks at the Stag?"

"Will she let you out of her sight?"

"I have my methods of persuasion." Alexi grinned.

An image of Alexandra Bolton passed through Stephen's mind. "At midnight, then."

"I'll round up Ned, if I can," Alexi said, referring to their cousin, the present earl's son and heir.

"And what about me," a woman said, "or is this evening meant to be strictly and exclusively one of male camaraderie?"

Stephen turned to greet Alexi's sister, Ariella, now Lady St. Xavier. He'd grown up with Ariella, as well. These days she was besotted with her husband and had somehow blossomed into a very beautiful woman, but she remained the highly educated and intellectually insatiable woman he had known since he was a child.

Brother and sister embraced. "This is indeed a moment of inherent male chauvinism. You are not invited to the Stag, but St. Xavier is."

"I'll *think* about allowing him out," she teased, "although I have much better plans for him tonight."

Stephen thought he blushed. "That is beyond polite conversation," he said mildly.

"I abhor polite conversation." She shrugged, smiling at him. "In fact, I have just come from a meeting of the People's Advocacy for Textile Workers." Then she pinched his cheek as if he were a small child. "I know you will donate to the cause of a labor union. By the way, I have been hearing odd rumors about you, Your Grace. Are you on the verge of a betrothal?"

He started, amused. "Don't you know better than to listen to idle gossip?"

"I thought the gossip unlikely, but one never knows." However, Ariella looked at him closely. "Is someone on your mind, Stephen?"

"If there was, he would tell *me,*" Alexi said. "His best and possibly only friend."

Stephen couldn't help thinking about Alexandra Bolton, who was very dignified, even while about to swoon. "The gossips have been claiming that I am on the verge for years," he said coolly. "It is wishful thinking."

Alexi laughed, rather wickedly. "You are staring at that brunette."

Stephen gave him a languid look. "I am simply concerned that she might not be feeling well."

"Really?" Alexi snickered. "And she isn't eighteen — how refreshing."

He gave Alexi a quelling look.

"Are you two arguing?" He turned at the sound of Elysse's voice, and she threw her arms around him, embracing him hard. "We have only just got home, Stephen. Why are you arguing with my husband?" she demanded.

"Because he is impossibly opinionated and his opinions are always wrong," he said. As a child, Elysse had been spoiled and snooty, as well as demanding, and she had been prone to putting on airs. They had often tired of her behavior and excluded her from their outings. She had certainly changed, but perhaps being abandoned at the altar and deserted by her new husband for six years had caused her to rethink her ways. In any case, he was truly fond of her now. And last night Alexi had shared his spectacular news — Elysse was expecting their first child. "I see that Hong Kong has agreed with you." He kissed her cheek. "Congratulations, my dear."

She beamed. "It is my husband who agrees with me, and my condition is one of the reasons why we came home now. Alexi has missed you, and so have I. But I see you two are already bickering like small boys."

"We are usually at odds," Stephen said. "Which you already know, as you have seen us sparring since we were small boys."

"And neither one of you ever wins," she reminded them both, her violet eyes stern. "So who was that woman who fainted in your arms?"

Before he could answer, Ariella cut in. "That is Alexandra Bolton. Her mother was a good friend of Aunt Blanche's," she said, referring to Lady Harrington, "but after she passed away, the family has fallen on hard times. I haven't seen her in years, and it is wonderful to see her and her sisters out and about."

"Is she widowed?" Stephen asked, well aware that she hadn't worn any rings.

Both women looked at him. "I don't think she was ever married," Ariella said, her brows lifted. "But I am not sure. Are you plotting your next seduction?"

He stared calmly at her. "A gentleman does not kiss and tell."

"Don't you dare!" she said, instantly outraged.

Before he could change the subject, a man behind them said, "Who is about to be seduced?"

Stephen turned in surprise as Elysse's brother spoke. He was friendly with Jack O'Neill, but he hadn't seen him in two years — O'Neill had been in America. "Ariella has a vivid imagination, or have you forgotten?"

Jack grinned and winked. Like Elysse, he was golden in coloring, though with gray eyes, and now he was bronzed from being outdoors. "I could never forget that."

Ariella huffed, "I am warning Mowbray off the woman he rescued from a swoon. I happen to know her, and she is not for him — not unless his intentions are honorable ones."

About to sip his champagne, Stephen choked.

"Really?" Jack laughed.

"I merely prevented the woman from collapsing," Stephen somehow said. "My God, I ask one innocent question and I am accused of the worst intentions." He gave Ariella a cool glance. What was wrong with her? Alexandra Bolton was in her late twenties, and a woman with such striking looks could not possibly be lacking in experience.

"Well, I have no problem confessing that my intentions might not be honorable, not at all, if I was in your shoes," Jack declared. "That brunette is quite pleasing to look at. Hello, Elysse. I am jealous. Are you happier to see Stephen, a mere friend, than me, your own brother?"

Elysse was wide-eyed — clearly, she hadn't known that her brother had returned to the country. "I haven't received a letter from you in a year, so we are not speaking," she said tersely, then gave him a cold look and turned her back on him.

"It is rather hard to write letters when you are warding off hostile Indians from the homestead," Jack said, amused. He kissed her cheek from behind. "I love you anyway, and I have a present for you." He then pumped Alexi's hand. "Congratulations."

Alexi grinned. "The Stag at midnight," he said.

"I wouldn't miss it," Jack returned.

Elysse faced Jack then. "Bribery will not get you forgiveness."

"But I have the stab wounds to prove my words," he said, eyes wide and innocent. "And an Apache warrior has a good hank of my hair."

"Why did you have to go to the wilds of America?" Elysse asked in dismay, all anger forgotten.

"That was so easy," Jack laughed, putting his arms around her.

For one moment, Stephen almost felt like the small boy he'd once been, standing on the edge of the crowded de Warenne salon, the only outsider in the room. St. Xavier had come up to join them, and he was aware of Sir Rex and Lady Blanche standing a few paces away, speaking to Tyrell de Warenne, the earl of Adare, who was standing with the duchess, his pretty, plump wife, Lizzie. Stephen was used to such feelings. It was impossible not to stand amid the great de Warenne family and not feel the sensation of not quite belonging, even though he shared their blood. But he would never share their name, and the blood connection was a family secret — society would never know. The fact of the matter was that he would always be on the fringes of the family and never truly a part of it.

Not that he minded, and not that it mattered. Every man of honor had a duty, and his was Clarewood.

Stephen turned away, certain Jack had meant every word as far as the Indians and his hair went, and just as certain that he had cleverly manipulated Elysse. The crowd in the hall had been reduced, most of the guests now in the great ballroom, for which Harrington Hall was famous. He scanned the room but did not see the most recent object of his interest. But across the room, he saw the Sinclairs arriving. Lord Sinclair had recently angled for Stephen's marriage to his very beautiful daughter. Young Anne was wedged between her parents, and she was so stunning that heads turned as they entered. His own blood did not race; instead, he had the urge to loosen his necktie. He hadn't dismissed Sinclair outright; Anne had all the proper prerequisites — on paper, anyway — and he had said he would consider such a union.

She was only eighteen. She would be meek

and eager to please; she would not have independent opinions; and she would make a stunning duchess.

"Why are you scowling?" Alexi asked.

"Am I frowning?" He smiled perfunctorily. He knew he would be bored with her before they ever got to the altar, and that was the end of that.

"Who is that? Oh, wait, don't bother — I know the answer."

"Anne Sinclair. Her father suggested a marriage."

"You will never get on."

"Do not tell me how splendid constant bickering is."

"I would die of boredom if Elysse obeyed my every command."

"She *disobeys* your every command," Stephen pointed out.

"And I am all the happier because of it."

"And while I am thrilled you are so besotted, I should be incredibly unhappy if my wife disobeyed me."

"Ah, yes, of course, Your Grace," Alexi said. He shook his head in disgust and lowered his voice. "You can pretend you are like the old man, but you are not. And we both know you will never get on in a dull, arranged marriage — which is why you have avoided matrimony for almost fifteen years."

Stephen was oddly annoyed, and they were once again at a stand-off. "I'll see you at the Stag later. I pray we can discuss your affairs, not mine."

"Coward."

Only Alexi de Warenne could get away with such an insolent statement. Stephen decided to ignore him and strode off into the crowd. He had better things to do — and an acquaintance to pursue.

Sara had been thronged with guests and admirers since she'd arrived. Stephen smiled, studying his half sister from a slight distance. She had never seemed so happy, and he was at once glad and proud. She was a very pretty girl, taking after her mother in both appearance and temperament; she was kind, shy and gentle. While he'd known her since she was an infant — she had been born shortly before he'd inherited the duchy — he hadn't spent as much time with her or Marion as he would have liked, due to the constraints of the situation. While most of the sprawling de Warenne family knew the truth about him, his half sisters had been told the exact nature of their relationship only two years ago. After all, children did not keep secrets well. Until that time, they had thought him a dear family friend.

He was aware that she was shy with him, as if he were an older relative who did not visit all that often. He also knew she was in some awe of him, and he wished somewhat wistfully that he could have been a brother to her openly, but that was simply impossible.

She was shining tonight, as she should be on her sixteenth birthday. As he watched several young men flirting with her, he felt a stirring of pride and protectiveness. He would always be her protector, even if from a distance.

He quietly awaited his turn to greet her, but the men and women in front of him realized who was standing behind them and allowed him to cut to the head of the queue. She was blushing profusely as Lord Montclair, who was far too old for her, congratulated her, and Stephen paused to smile at Lady Harrington.

"How are you, Your Grace?" Blanche Harrington asked, clasping both his hands warmly.

Blanche had been warm and kind to him from the moment of their first meeting, when he was nine years old. He liked her greatly in return, and understood that she had embraced him so genuinely because of her deep love for Sir Rex. "I am enjoying the evening, and apparently so is Sara."

"The truth is," Blanche said softly, "Sara was dreading this evening. You know how modest she is. She was afraid she would fail her guests. But she has been having a fabulous time."

He glanced at Sara, wondering how more confidence might be instilled in her. Sara saw him, and she instantly stepped forward, blushing. "Your Grace," she whispered.

Long ago, he had decided that having his half siblings address him formally was not awkward — just a necessity. He took her hands and said, "Congratulations, my dear. You are so lovely tonight, and I believe your ball is a great success."

"Thank you, Your Grace." She smiled shyly. "I'm so glad you could come tonight."

"I would never miss your birthday. In fact, your present is on the gift table in the front hall, and I hope you will enjoy it."

"I will treasure it," she said seriously. "Because it is from you."

He took her hand and kissed it. He had given her a diamond pendant necklace, and he hoped she would treasure it forever. But before he could straighten, he had a vision of Tom Mowbray standing behind her.

It was just for a moment, but the old man was mocking his sentiments, as if he thought him a fool.

Stephen tensed. Even though Tom was gone and what he'd seen had been a memory, not a ghost, he could hear him as clearly as if he still lived. *Your duty is Clarewood — not a half sibling! And you dare to yearn for more?*

But he wasn't yearning for anything. He was merely fond of his sister — and that was as much his duty as anything else.

Sir Rex detached himself from a group of guests and turned to face him. Stephen knew he was fortunate that his natural father was a man of such honor, and they had developed a friendship over the years. "Will Sara shriek and swoon when she sees your gift? I hope it was within reason," Sir Rex said, as they shook hands. "How are you, Stephen?"

Sir Rex refused to address him as Your Grace, and while it was odd, no one seemed to care, or perhaps society had simply become used to it. Stephen thought that he would hate being so formally addressed by the man who had not only sired him, but had had his best interests at heart for as long as he could remember. He had respected and even admired Sir Rex for years, before learning the truth about their relationship, while Sir Rex had always been more than usually kind and attentive to him. In retrospect, he understood why. "I am very well, and currently preoccupied with the Manchester housing project, amongst other things." He was building housing for textile workers, housing with proper lighting, ventilation and sewage disposal. The factory owners were not pleased, but he did not care; they would come around when they realized that healthy workers were far more productive than ill ones.

"Are the plans finalized?" Sir Rex asked with interest. He had been a huge supporter of all of Stephen's good works.

"No, they are not. But I was hoping to show them to you when they are done."

Sir Rex smiled, pleased. "I have not a doubt the plans will be a triumph, and I can hardly wait to see them."

Sir Rex was as different from Tom Mowbray as a man could be. He believed in praise and encouragement, not criticism and scorn. Stephen knew that he should be accustomed to such praise, but he was not. He was always vaguely surprised and a bit uncomfortable, and always warmed. "There might be several go-rounds," he said. "There are some issues still to resolve."

"You will resolve them — you always do. I am confident," Sir Rex said, smiling.

"Thank you. I am hopeful your confidence will not be misplaced." As he spoke, he saw Randolph, Sir Rex's son — his own half brother — enter the ballroom. Randolph instantly saw them, and he grinned, starting toward them.

"I am glad you are mentoring Randolph," Sir Rex said. "He has done nothing but speak of your good works since returning from Dublin."

"Randolph is determined, and he is very intelligent. He discovered some discrepancies in the Clarewood Home's Dublin accounts. I have had to replace the director there."

"He told me. He is astonishingly adept with numbers. He does not get that from me."

Randolph was not yet twenty, but he was tawny and handsome, resembling his father almost exactly, except for his golden coloring. He had tremendous confidence, present in his long, assured stride — and the many younger debutantes present were all ogling him as he passed by. He grinned as he paused beside them. "Hello, Father . . . Your Grace."

"You are late," Stephen said mildly. Randolph was flushed and very, very smug, and

Stephen damned well knew what he'd been up to.

"You are not the only one who has rescued a damsel in distress tonight," Randolph boasted.

"You will catch a dreadful disease," Stephen warned, meaning it. "And one must never discuss indiscretion openly."

Some of Randolph's exhilaration faded. "I did not mean to be late. The time somehow escaped me." But then he snickered again.

"Of course you did not mean to be late. You weren't thinking clearly — I doubt you were thinking at all. It is Sara's birthday, Randolph." He hoped he was not being too harsh, but Randolph was too often reckless, and that worried him.

The boy flushed now. "I will apologize to Sara." He glanced at his sister, and his eyes widened. "You have turned into a beauty!" he exclaimed.

Stephen was amused, and he saw that Sir Rex was, too. As Randolph hurried over to his sister, Sir Rex said, "I have spoken to him many times, but I am afraid my advice falls on deaf — though young — ears."

"He has assured me that he is careful and discreet," Stephen said.

"Thank you." Sir Rex sighed. "I cannot recall a male de Warenne who was not notorious for his philandering until the time he was wed." And Sir Rex gave him a look.

"Well, then Randolph is following in the family tradition," Stephen remarked. But he turned away, uncomfortable, wondering if he was included in the generalization. In a way, he hoped not. He considered his amorous liaisons rather routine, for a bachelor like himself.

Suddenly Stephen saw Edgemont hurrying through the crowd, and he quickly realized that the man was staggering drunk. He glanced around with some concern, but Miss Bolton was nowhere in sight. That was when he saw the dowager duchess entering the ballroom, and she was not alone.

The fact that his mother would be escorted to such an affair was hardly unusual, but he instantly saw that this was not a routine matter. The man on her arm was tall and golden, with a presence that was positively leonine. And his mother, he realized, was radiant — as if deliriously happy. In fact, she had never looked better.

Julia Mowbray, the Dowager Duchess of Clarewood, was one of the strongest and most courageous women he knew. She had devoted her entire life to the cause of advancing his interests, at great personal cost and sacrifice. She had suffered greatly at the previous duke's hands. A dowager for fifteen years, she had decided not to remarry, and he had applauded that decision. Now, he was concerned.

"Who is accompanying the dowager duchess tonight?" he asked sharply.

"I believe that his name is Tyne Jefferson, and that he is a rancher from California."

"Are you certain?" Was his mother romantically interested in Jefferson? "Is he wealthy? Does he come from a good family? He looks rather savage."

"You should calm down. Julia is a strong and sensible woman. Fortune hunters have been sniffing about her for years, and she has eluded every single one of them."

"So you think he is a fortune hunter!" Stephen exclaimed.

"No, I do not. I have heard that he has some business with your uncle, Cliff."

"I believe introductions are in order," Stephen said. The dowager duchess was a very wealthy woman — and she was his responsibility. He did not care for this liaison. He was worried. "Excuse me."

Julia was strolling across the ballroom with the American. The consummate diplomat now, as she had once been the consummate duchess, she paused before each party, making certain to politely introduce Jefferson, who looked to Stephen to be unperturbed by the entire affair. He barely spoke, but he watched Julia closely, with obvious interest. Stephen approached them from behind.

Jefferson sensed him immediately and turned. Stephen smiled coolly at him. As he discerned a challenge, Jefferson's gaze narrowed.

Julia whirled. "Stephen!" She took his hands and kissed his cheek. "I am so glad you are here. This is Mr. Tyne Jefferson, and this is my son, His Grace, the Duke of Clarewood."

"I am honored, Your Grace," Jefferson drawled. But Stephen knew from the American's tone that the man was not awed by him, or even impressed. "Mr. Jefferson. And are you enjoying my country?" Stephen returned, smiling. He gestured at the lavish room. "I imagine you do not attend many balls in California."

Julia stepped closer to Stephen and sent him a look that said very clearly that she was becoming angry with him.

It didn't matter. He had to protect her from disaster and heartache, at all costs.

"No, we don't have balls like this in California. The scenery here is quite a welcome change, as well." Suddenly Jefferson looked at Julia, the gaze direct, and she flushed.

Stephen was briefly shocked — and uncharacteristically speechless — by how obvious her feelings were for this man.

"I am enjoying my stay here," Jefferson added. "And I very much appreciate being invited to attend this ball."

Julia smiled at him. "It would have been remiss of me, sir, not to invite you to join me."

Stephen glanced sharply at her. What was she thinking? He turned back to Jefferson. "And what brings you to Britain?"

The American seemed amused. "A personal matter, actually."

He had just been told to mind his own affairs, and he was not pleased about it. "Sir Rex told me that you have some business with Cliff de Warenne." His uncle — Alexi's father — had built up a global shipping empire over the years.

"Stephen," Julia said swiftly. "I know you wish to become further acquainted with Mr. Jefferson, but we have only just arrived. There are still a number of introductions I wish to make." She was firm.

Stephen knew he must stand down — for now. But he would begin an investigation of the man, and tomorrow, first thing, he would summon Julia to Clarewood to find out what she was doing by promoting an acquaintance with such a man. "Perhaps I can be of some help in your business affairs, for not only am I on good terms with the de Warenne family, I am well connected throughout the realm."

"Nice of you to offer," Jefferson said, mockery in his tone but his expression as cool as a cube of ice. "And I'll definitely think about it."

Julia gave him another warning look, but Stephen barely saw it. He wasn't sure he had ever encountered such arrogance, and in spite of himself, he felt the dawning of a grudging respect for the American.

"Here, a sip of tea will undoubtedly help," Squire Denney said with concern.

Alexandra smiled gratefully at him, aware that she was still being stared at and, at times, whispered about. She had not dreamed of such a reception to her first social event in nine years. No one had spoken with her since they had arrived at Sara's birthday party other than her sisters, her father and the squire. She had done her best to pretend that all was well — she did not want to distress the squire or, worse, chase him off. But surely, once he realized what was happening and what society thought of her, he would flee.

They'd been at Harrington Hall for about two hours, and her headache was so bad now that she'd finally confessed to feeling a bit under the weather. Denney was being kind. She had the feeling that compassion was a large part of his nature. "Thank you," she said, accepting the tea and knowing he'd gone out of his way to find a hot cup at this hour.

She took a sip. She felt as if she had been standing in that corner of the ballroom forever, but it was only nine o'clock. She wasn't sure she had ever felt so humiliated. She couldn't believe she'd been so naive as to think she could appear in society when she made a living as a seamstress now. As for the vicious gossip that she'd been jilted by Owen, she couldn't bear to think about it. At least she could console herself with the truth. Even so, surely the squire would decide that he wanted a socially acceptable wife, ruling her out.

She glanced at her sisters, dismayed. They should have been out on the dance floor; instead, they refused to leave her side. They should have been having the best time of their young lives; instead, they were anxious and frightened, and determined to defend her from further slander and prevent another disaster.

Her glance wandered. And she knew she was looking for *him*.

Her heart thundered. Her cheeks felt hot.

"I will get you a small bite," Denney said, his concern as vast as ever.

Realizing he would leave her side for a moment, and that she might speak privately to her sisters, Alexandra nodded. "Thank you."

When he was gone, Corey whispered, "I think we should leave." She was pale with distress.

Alexandra faced her, a firm smile in place. "We will not cry over spilt milk, we will merely clean it up."

"These people are hateful," Corey continued in a whisper. "Who cares about being at this party?"

"Everyone is not hateful. A handful of these women are mean-spirited, that is all. Wasn't it nice to see Lady Harrington and her daughters again?" Blanche Harrington had been kind and concerned, and her daughters had actually seemed pleased to renew their acquaintances. Sir Rex had been equally magnanimous. "And, Corey, you remain the interest of several young gentlemen here."

"I don't care," Corey said, meaning it. "When can we leave?"

Alexandra exchanged a glance with Olivia and caught her staring at the same blond man she herself had noticed earlier. Her heart clenched. Whoever that gentleman was, he was not for her sister. "Who is that?"

Olivia flushed. "I don't know. I overheard someone saying he's been in the wilds of America for the past two years."

Alexandra sensed her sister's interest, and she took her hand and squeezed it sadly. Then she looked at Corey. "We can't leave this early. That would be grossly insulting to our hosts. And it would be rude to the squire, as well."

Corey was grim. "I know," she said. "But one can hope, can't one?"

"I think we should try to resurrect this evening — and enjoy the next few hours," Alexandra said.

Her sisters did not buy her optimism for a moment. Olivia said, "Where is Father?"

Alexandra froze. She hadn't seen him in an hour, and no good could come of that. If he was drinking, she would wring his neck when they got home, and this time she meant it. She could not bear any more disgrace. "Maybe we should look for him," she said, setting down her cup of tea.

109

Olivia pinched her — hard.

As she did, Alexandra felt *his* stare. She inhaled hard, tensing. The sensation of being watched by the Duke of Clarewood was unlike any other. And slowly she turned.

It remained unbelievable that she had almost fainted and that he'd caught her before she collapsed. It remained as impossible that he'd been gallant — and that he had even flirted with her. Just as impossible was the fact that a moment later she had caught him staring closely at her, as he was doing now. Their gazes locked.

Her heart leaped, lurched and then raced wildly.

She could not quite breathe.

He was speaking with several gentlemen, but his gaze was most definitely on her, at once confident and intense. Alexandra knew she would never forget the feeling of being in his strong arms. As for his interest, she was fairly certain she knew what it signified.

He was unwed, and so was she — but she was not in his league. She was too old for him, too impoverished, the family name too disreputable. His interest could mean only one thing.

She was stunned, but also dismayed.

"That is Clarewood," Corey breathed, clearly in awe and, just as clearly, having no comprehension of the situation.

"I am in his debt," Alexandra said tersely. She glanced at Olivia, who stared back. Surely Olivia understood that he would never be interested in her in any honorable way. And she still couldn't fathom his interest, not even in any *dis*honorable way. Why did he find her interesting? There were many beautiful women in the room. And then, from the corner of her eye, she saw their father heading toward them.

She froze. He was *lurching*. She had prayed things would not get worse, but clearly her prayers had gone unanswered.

Olivia saw him, too, and she gasped. Then, "Now we have to leave."

There was nothing Alexandra wished to do more. However, running now, with their tails between their legs, would leave a terrible impression. "The two of you stay here. I am sending him home, and I'll be back in a moment."

Olivia's regard was imploring. "Why?"

"I don't think Denney has noticed how foxed Father is. And we are staying until the squire is ready to leave — we are his guests."

Edgemont swayed toward her, grinning. "My beautiful daughter! Are you enjoying yourself?"

She took his arm, moving him into the

corner. "You promised not to imbibe."

"I haven't. Alexandra, I swear. Not one drop."

"You reek of whiskey, and you're staggering," she accused. She was livid, but even more, she was humiliated and dismayed.

"I did not take even one drop of whiskey," he slurred. " 'Twas gin."

"And that makes it better?" She looped her arm firmly through his, but even so, he almost fell on her. She hit the wall, flushing, his weight too heavy for her to bear. "You have to leave, Father. You cannot remain in such a state."

"Too shoon to go, my dear. There'sh cards in the game room." He tried to push her away and almost fell again.

Alexandra knew that they were being remarked. She seized his arm and tried to get him to stand upright. As he stood up, swaying, she did not know if she would ever forgive him for this.

"You're having a good time, aren't you?" he asked, grinning.

"Yes, I am having a splendid time," she snapped, wondering if she should try to drag him bodily from the room. She did not think she was strong enough to do so.

"Good." He suddenly pulled free of her and crashed into the wall himself.

"Whoops."

Furious, her cheeks on fire, Alexandra seized his arm and threw it over her shoulders. "We are leaving," she said, trying to speak as calmly as possible, no easy task when she was furious.

"Don't want to go," he said, balking. "Cardsh."

She looked at him, and when he smiled back at her, she wanted to cry. So this was how he was once he left the house every night? It was simply heartbreaking. And the most heartbreaking part was that she was certain that, had her mother lived, his propensity for alcohol would have never become so out of control.

"May I?" the Duke of Clarewood asked.

She went still. Then, her father's weight half on her, his arm over her shoulders, her hair now coming down in absolute disarray, she looked up.

His brilliantly blue gaze met hers. There was no scorn on his handsome face, no condescension. He seemed suitably grave, and in that moment he seemed like the Rock of Gibraltar.

Alexandra felt her heart explode. "I beg your pardon?"

"May I be of some assistance?" He sent her a dazzling smile.

113

It was the kind of smile no woman could resist. Alexandra felt like dumping her drunken father in his arms and bursting into tears. Instead, she jerked her father's arm more tightly over her shoulders, held her head high and blinked back any rising moisture. Even as she did so, she knew she couldn't possibly carry him out of the room, much less the house.

And Clarewood, the most devastating man she'd ever laid eyes on, was witnessing this humiliation.

"You can't possibly carry his weight," he said gently.

He was right. She wet her lips as it crossed her mind that this gesture — which was truly heroic — would only cause more attention and more gossip. "You are right." She dared to meet his gaze again.

It was the most speculative and intelligent, the most penetrating regard she'd ever encountered. Then he stooped down and removed her father's arm from her shoulders, firmly clasping him about the waist. Edgemont began to drunkenly protest.

"Father, you are going outside with the duke," Alexandra said as calmly as possible. "I will follow — and you are going home."

"Don't want to go home . . . the duke?" Edgemont gaped at Clarewood now.

114

"Easy, my man," Clarewood said, a quiet authority in his tone. "The night is over, and you are going home, as Miss Bolton has suggested."

He knew her name.

Edgemont's eyes widened comically. "Your Grace," he whispered, clearly awed and submissive now.

Alexandra fought more tears as Clarewood practically carried her father away.

She realized her sisters had come to stand silently beside her, filled with the same despair and distress she herself was feeling. As Clarewood started across the room, she became aware of the silent, gawking crowd. Every pair of eyes in the hall was trained upon Clarewood and his drunken, clownish burden.

Suddenly a pair of gentlemen came rushing over to the duke. She recognized the young man with tawny hair — he was Randolph de Warenne, Sir Rex's son, who was perhaps twenty or so. The other man was unmistakable, even if she hadn't seen him in years — he was the dark and dashing shipping merchant Alexi de Warenne. Both men quickly divested Clarewood of his drunken burden.

"Find a coach to take him home, and a proper escort," Clarewood calmly said, straightening his tailcoat.

"I'll see him home," Randolph said quickly, with a grim smile.

"Thank you." Clarewood gave the younger man a smile in return. "You can use my coach if you wish. I appreciate it, Rolph."

Alexandra thought that Randolph was eager to please the duke, not that it mattered to her, except as far as it meant that he would get her father safely home. But she also noticed how much the two men resembled one another — in spite of the fact that Randolph had tawny hair and Clarewood's was pitch-black. The similarity of their features struck her, as did the darkness of their complexions, and just before Randolph turned away with her father, she glimpsed the brilliant blue eyes the de Warenne men were renowned for. Clarewood had striking blue eyes, as well. None of this mattered, of course. She wasn't sure why she was noticing such things now.

Clarewood turned and approached her again.

Her heart slammed. Beside her, both her sisters stiffened, and Alexandra felt a flush begin. He had rescued her from a swoon. Had he heard the gossip? Did he think her reprehensible? A castoff? What did he think of her father's behavior? Of the fact that she had to earn her living by sewing? Why did she care?

Suddenly he took a flute of champagne from a passing waiter without even breaking stride. A moment later he was handing it to her. "Champagne hardly cures all ills. But you appear as if you might need a drink."

She gratefully accepted the glass. Clarewood glanced idly at her sisters as she did so. As if on command, they nodded at him, turned and hurried a few steps away. Alexandra couldn't look away from him, but she knew her sisters were staring, too — along with everyone else in the room.

"I am sorry for your distress, Miss Bolton."

What did that mean? Why would he care? "You have no reason to be sorry for anything. You saved me from a swoon. You escorted my inebriated father from the room and have made certain he will be taken safely home. Thank you."

"The first instance was my pleasure. The second, my choice." His mouth curved.

Still, she wondered why he had bothered. "It was certainly an unpleasant choice and one you did not have to make. Again, thank you, Your Grace. Your kindness is astounding."

He studied her for a moment. "Kindness

had nothing to do with it." He bowed. "You seem to have a suitor waiting in the wings. A gentleman knows when it is time to take his leave."

She tensed, glimpsing Squire Denney hovering behind them, his eyes wide, and she knew she hadn't mistaken the mockery in Clarewood's tone. Her dismay increased. So did a sense of embarrassment. Somehow, he'd ascertained that Denney was courting her.

The duke gave her an odd, almost promising look, as if telling her that he would return, and then he was gone.

Alexandra just stood there, feeling as if she'd somehow withstood a hurricane — or some other impossible force of nature.

CHAPTER FOUR

The Stag Room of the Hotel St. Lucien was as exclusive as a private club. While one did not have to be a member, the maitre d' had no trouble encouraging the wrong sort to turn away from its massive carved doors. Merchants, bankers, factory owners and lawyers were simply not allowed without a proper introduction or the right escort. Simply put, it was a refuge for the country's upper-class elite. Stephen rarely bothered with the Stag Room or any similar establishment, but once in a while such isolation was welcome.

Now he propelled Randolph forward, his hand on the younger man's shoulder. The maitre d' bowed. "Your Grace. Mr. de Warenne."

Stephen nodded as he and his half brother strolled into the dimly lit salon filled with fine furniture, gilded antiques and Aubusson rugs. At this late hour, nearing midnight, the gentlemen present were all his age, with only a few exceptions, and many were well into their cups. Murmurs of "Your Grace" followed him as he walked past the various groups. Alexi, Jack, Ned and his younger brother Charles, generally known as Chaz, were all slouched in their plush seats at the salon's far end. The windows there overlooked the park. The moon was bright tonight.

"We were wondering if you got waylaid," Jack O'Neill said, one leg crossed over the other, a cigar in hand.

"I had to pry my young friend away from a particularly voracious baroness," Stephen said drily. "He was making advances toward Lady Dupre."

Randolph flopped down onto the couch beside Alexi, who poured a fine cognac into a snifter for him and pushed it over. "She was the most beautiful woman at the birthday soirée, and may I say, in my own defense, she ogled me before I ever approached?"

"They are all beautiful, where you are concerned," Chaz said.

"Discretion would have been a better course," Stephen admonished, "as her current paramour was standing beside her and her husband within earshot."

"Lady Dupre," Alexi murmured. "Well done, Rolph."

Randolph saluted him with his snifter.

Stephen took the chair beside the couch, glancing at Alexi as he did so. His friend was lounging against the cushions in a manner that suggested he was hardly drunk and was very intently preparing for their next go-round. He looked like a black jaguar in a cage, one waiting for the gatekeeper to dare to come inside. He smiled indolently at Stephen.

"As long as we are speaking about impending conquests, has Miss Bolton indicated that she will be grateful to you for rescuing her not once, but twice, tonight?" Alexi asked.

Stephen poured himself a cognac, recalling Alexandra Bolton's humiliation at the hands of her father with a stirring of anger. "Edgemont is a disgrace."

"Miss Bolton handled herself well," Ned said firmly. "Grace under fire, all around."

Stephen silently agreed.

"She is a striking woman," Jack remarked. "She is almost as tall as I am."

Stephen gave Jack a deceptively mild look.

"I would never poach," Jack laughed. Then he sobered. "I did feel sorry for her. And for her sisters, too. Edgemont should be shot."

"That's a bit extreme," Ned said, amused. "You're back in civilization, Jack. Or have you forgotten?"

Jack flexed his hands. "I suppose I have become a bit extreme, actually." He glanced around. "Let's find a tavern and some good lusty tavern wenches. I am bored."

Chaz and Randolph exchanged looks. "I know a place," Chaz said, attempting to remain blasé.

His older brother looked at him. "You are the spare," Ned reproved. "You do have a reputation to maintain."

"Exactly. I'm the spare, not the heir," Chaz said, unperturbed, and he finished his drink, whispering to Randolph as they made their plans for the rest of the evening.

Alexi turned to look at Stephen. "I ask again. How goes the latest seduction? Is Miss Bolton disposed to be properly grateful?"

He felt his blood warm. He thought about how proud she was as he said slowly, "She seemed cautiously grateful . . . as if you care."

"But I do care." Alexi smiled. "She is no Charlotte Witte. In fact, you may find yourself with some resistance this time. By the way, Elysse has decided she wishes to know Miss Bolton. Ariella has decided to introduce them."

Stephen sighed. He expected his cousins to interfere in his personal life — they certainly harped on him for his bachelor status from time to time — but he couldn't imagine why they would care about his interest in Alexandra Bolton. Now he wondered if Alexi could be right. Not only had she been proud, she hadn't flirted with him, not one single time, when every other woman who crossed his path was coy and flirtatious. "Considering her dire straits, I am sure that, in the end, we will both come to very agreeable terms. And perhaps you might instruct your wife and sister not to meddle? As there is really nothing for them to meddle in."

Alexi smiled at him. "But I happen to think that perhaps, this one time, they *should* meddle — Miss Bolton is so original."

Stephen stared. "What are you up to?"

"She is not your type, not for an affair," Alexi said quickly.

"How wrong you are."

His look was almost smug, and that made Stephen uneasy.

"Isn't she unwed?" Ned asked, his gaze unwavering. "And isn't she a gentlewoman?"

Stephen felt a twinge of discomfort. "She is an older woman, Ned, a spinster, for God's sake. And there was some scandal already, so she is hardly an innocent debutante whom I wish to ruthlessly take advantage of."

"She is a woman of substance," Ned said. "And pride. Anyone can see that. You should look elsewhere for your entertainment."

Stephen stared coldly at him, but Ned wasn't daunted. One day his cousin would be the Earl of Adare, a powerful title and position. He didn't expect Ned to bow to him, but he did not appreciate being questioned, and he didn't like his cousins interfering in this instance. No one had ever bothered to say a word to him about Charlotte, or the mistress before her, or the one before *her*.

But Alexi was right on one account: Alexandra wasn't anything like Charlotte.

"I wonder how Anne Sinclair would handle the drama of such a night, if she were ever in Miss Bolton's position," Alexi said softly.

The other men chuckled. Stephen smiled wryly, sipping from his drink, wondering why Alexi had raised such a comparison.

"I'm sure she would be equally graceful and dignified," he said, though he hardly thought so. "Are you interested in Lady Anne, Alexi?"

"Me? Of course not. Let's see . . . how old is she? Eighteen? And what are her accomplishments? Oh, wait, she has been spoiled and pampered her entire life. But she is an excellent dancer. Her manners are impeccable, as well. The two of you make a pleasing couple, by the way — she would make a stunning duchess. Doesn't everyone agree?"

Everyone was silent now. Interest was acute.

And Stephen was now very annoyed. "I have considered Anne, and I have decided to reject her."

"Of course you have. And I do support your decision," Alexi said. "Tell me, have you heard that Miss Bolton sews to support her sisters and her father?"

Alexi was baiting him. He simply did not know why. "I admire her resourcefulness."

Alexi gaped. "Really?"

Someone laughed.

"I think it is a tragedy that she must work to support her family," Randolph said.

"It *is* a tragedy," Stephen said, staring

closely at Alexi. "Life is filled with trag-
edies."

"And life is filled with beautiful, young,
spoiled debutantes." Alexi saluted him with
his glass.

"What is your point?" Stephen asked
crossly. But he recalled the parade of young
ladies he'd been offered over the course of
the past decade — every single one of them
a mirror image of Anne. "Because I seem to
recall another terribly spoiled and pampered
young woman . . . before, of course, you
jilted her at the altar and took off for parts
unknown." Stephen saluted Alexi with his
glass, which he realized was almost empty.

Alexi's smile remained, but it no longer
reached his eyes. "I made a terrible mistake,
leaving her after our vows. I cannot imagine
Lady Anne becoming the spectacular
woman that my wife has become — a
woman of opinions, ideas, of will, of *substance*. Miss Bolton reminds me of Elysse
— not in appearance, but in courage." He
drained his drink and said, "I believe you
have just insulted my wife."

He knew he should apologize, but Alexi's
latest reference to Alexandra Bolton was
even more jarring than the previous ones —
though Alexandra had been courageous
tonight. No one could dispute that. "I

126

personally have no use for a woman with opinions," he muttered.

"My God, you've insulted me, then Elysse, and now you've just insulted every woman in the family," Alexi said, standing abruptly.

"That is not what I meant," Stephen said, standing, as well.

"I think you should marry Anne or someone just like her," Alexi said. "You can be such a jackass. Marrying a woman who will bore you to tears just so you can please that bastard who raised you — so you can be *just like* that bastard — is exactly what you deserve. Apologize."

Jack started laughing.

Stephen finally lost his temper. "I am a jackass? Because you meddle like a woman."

Alexi's eyes widened, then narrowed to slits. "Oh ho," he said.

Stephen tensed for the blow.

But just as Alexi clenched his fist, Ned stood and interposed himself between the two men. "You can't possibly strike *His Grace.*"

"His Grace, my arse. Why not? I've done so a hundred times." Alexi glared.

"Stephen deserves it," Jack said, grinning with relish. "He did insult Elysse — who happens to be my only sister. And if he called *me* a woman, I'd take a piece of his scalp." He winked at the two younger men, clearly relishing the prospect of a fistfight.

"Go ahead, hit me," Stephen said softly. "I won't hit you back."

But Alexi knew him too well. "You won't hit me back because you know that in a roundhouse, I will win."

Stephen rolled his eyes.

"I'll place a wager," Jack said. "Do you want in?" He looked at Chaz and Randolph.

"No one is coming to blows," Ned said. "Not at this table." Then, "Are you considering Anne Sinclair for a wife? Is that what this is about?"

"No, I am not," Stephen said firmly. "And I truly don't know what set Alexi off tonight. Obviously I will have to marry one day — and yes, I will choose a debutante. I am sorry I insulted Elysse. I am very fond of her. I consider her a sister, in some ways."

Alexi smiled, instantly in a good humor. "I know you do. But you are still an ass. You've considered a hundred different debutantes. However, it isn't your fault, it is Tom's. You will imitate him after all, living with a wife you despise, in splendid isolation."

Ned seized Alexi's shoulder. "He apologized. Let's end this subject."

Stephen folded his arms, staring. He truly

hoped that Alexi was wrong. But as a boy, he'd found Clarewood a cold and lonely place, something he recalled vividly now. "Splendid isolation? Now you are a poet," he said, holding back his rising temper.

"The truth can hurt." Alexi shrugged. "I have changed my mind. You should cease your pursuit of Alexandra, and you should most definitely marry Anne."

"Your point is made. It took you long enough."

"What point has he made?" Jack asked.

"That someone as young and inexperienced as Anne is the wrong choice, which is why he keeps comparing her to Miss Bolton. Next, he will espouse the delights of matrimony with a woman of independence, of ideas, a strong will and opinions."

"Unlike the rest of this family," Jack said, "I am against marriage in theory *and* in practice." He smiled.

"Those will be infamous last words," Alexi promised.

"Alexi is too besotted to know that smugness is not becoming," Stephen added.

"More infamous last words." Alexi patted his shoulder. "Don't worry, there is hope. You are a de Warenne, after all, and one day we will laugh about how stubborn and stupid you were."

"I am so pleased you care so much, but can we sit down and enjoy our drinks now? Or will you continue to egg me on?"

Alexi shook his head. "I've done enough for tonight — I am going home. To my independent, outspoken, opinionated wife." He grinned. "Enjoy your drinks."

When he left, they looked at each other, all of them bachelors, for even Ned was inclined to carouse. "He has lost his manhood," Jack said.

Stephen tended to agree — almost. "Don't let *him* hear you say that."

"I think we should toast our freedom — and count our blessings," Jack said. "I, for one, will never become like that."

Stephen accepted a glass, thinking about Alexandra. "At least he is genuinely happy," he said.

Alexandra went about her morning routine in a daze. She could not stop thinking about the previous night. And while it was impossible to forget the vile gossip that had targeted her, it was the Duke of Clarewood who loomed largest in her mind.

Having washed and dressed, she was on her way downstairs for a terribly late breakfast — at eleven, it was already nearly lunchtime — when she paused, her hand on

130

the worn wood banister. Her body tensed, and her heart seemed to clench before hammering hard. His devastating features were crystal clear in her mind. Their paths having crossed as they had, he was a man no woman could possibly forget.

She still couldn't fathom why he'd rescued her and her father. But most of all, she couldn't understand why she had been, and remained, so terribly attracted to him.

She could justify the passion she'd felt for Owen — she had loved him, and she had meant to marry him. But Clarewood was an absolute stranger.

And last night he'd indicated that he had an interest in her, as well — one that could only be scandalous. As if she needed more scandal! But it didn't matter, not at all. Today he would surely come to his senses. He would forget about her. And that was as it should be; she wasn't the kind of woman he seemed to think she was. Whatever he had intended, she was simply not interested.

Her heart continued to race, but she had awakened saddened, and she remained so. She'd made a mistake by accepting the squire's invitation, that was obvious, and her sisters had suffered because of it, as well. But going out last night, and winding up briefly in Clarewood's arms, had opened up all of her old wounds. She hadn't been able to sleep. She kept thinking about how she'd felt being in his embrace. Her body had become somewhat feverish just recalling it. And she was constantly thinking about Owen now, too, and what they'd almost had. The pain of the past had somehow returned, and it hurt worse than ever.

She almost wished she had chosen differently. And that was just as terrible. She'd never before doubted the choice she'd made. Her decision to take care of her sisters and father had been the morally correct one. She had sworn to Elizabeth as she lay dying that she would take care of the family. That vow meant more to her than her own happiness.

"Why are you standing on the stairs like a statue?" Olivia's soft voice cut into her thoughts.

Alexandra jerked back to reality, and she smiled, then moved swiftly down the stairs to join her sister. "I overslept," she said. She'd finally drifted off to sleep at dawn. No wonder she had slept long past her usual rising time.

"You never sleep in," Olivia said, her green eyes filled with concern.

There was no point in increasing her sister's anxiety by confessing how distracted and distressed she'd been all night, so she merely ignored the comment. "I am hungry," she lied. "Will you join me and at least have a cup of tea?"

Before Olivia could respond, the library doors opened and Edgemont lumbered through them, still in his tailcoat, which was thoroughly wrinkled now. Unshaven, he looked entirely disreputable. "Good morning," he boomed, then blinked at them.

Alexandra was so filled with outrage that she did not answer — she didn't trust herself to speak. Not yet, anyway. She marched past him to the kitchen, Olivia on her heels.

But Edgemont followed. "How rude!" he exclaimed. "What's wrong with you today?"

Alexandra went to the stove and used a match to light a burner, her hands shaking. She pumped water into the teakettle and set it on the burner.

"Are you angry?" He winced and rubbed his temples. "Was it a good evening? I can't seem to recall most of it."

Alexandra whirled. "No, it was not a good evening, as you were falling down drunk!"

He drew himself upright. "I won't have you speaking to me in such a manner."

She inhaled. She never lost her temper, never shouted, but she'd just shouted at him. She had just insulted her own father. She fought for calm. "Why not? You humiliated yourself in front of everyone at Harrington House." She spoke quietly now. "Do you even know how you got home last night?"

He was puzzled. "No, I do not."

"The Duke of Clarewood carried you across the ballroom, Father. Yes, you were that foxed. And then Randolph and Alexi de Warenne took you outside. I believe young Randolph de Warenne escorted you home."

Edgemont paled. Then he straightened. "A man has his rights, and I have every right to my gin. You're exaggerating — I recall it all now." He paused, breathing hard, and looked at Olivia. "Prepare my breakfast," he said.

Olivia walked past him to do just that, her mouth pursed.

The kettle began to sing. Alexandra turned slowly, though she felt like whirling in anger, and took the kettle from the fire and calmly set it on the counter, when she felt like smashing it down. She had Clarewood on her mind again. Bloody hell, she thought.

She also never cursed, not even in her thoughts.

"How is the squire today?" Edgemont

asked carefully, apparently having come to his full senses.

"I wouldn't know." She poured two cups of tea for herself and Olivia. "Would you like a cup, Father?"

"Yes."

She poured his tea and faced him. "He will surely call things off now, and it will be your fault. Your drinking has to stop. It is disgraceful, and we can't afford it."

Edgemont stared at her, and she stared back as she handed him the cup and saucer. Without a word, he went from the kitchen to the dining table and sat down.

Alexandra looked at Olivia. They both knew that he would not change.

"We have callers," Corey said. "Or rather, we have *a* caller."

Alexandra had just finished her toast and jam. Corey was standing at the kitchen window, and Alexandra got up to see who could possibly be calling before noon. As the dark carriage got closer, she realized it belonged to the squire.

She tensed. He'd brought them home last night, but it had been late, everyone had been tired, and the conversation had been perfunctory. Corey had even fallen asleep on the way, and the squire had encouraged

Alexandra to do so, as well. She hadn't, but she'd pretended to doze, to avoid speaking to him. Now she wondered if he was sending a note breaking things off. Or would he come in person to do so? A note would be kinder. On the other hand, he need only speak to Edgemont. And she was dismayed, because he was her sisters' last hope.

She refused to go down that path. *She* was her sisters' last hope. She would not give up on securing them a decent future.

Corey turned from the window. "He is here. Do you want us to chaperone you?"

"That won't be necessary." Alexandra removed her apron and tucked a stray hair behind her ears, the behavior instinctive.

"He is going to break things off, isn't he?" Corey asked. She was somber.

"Undoubtedly. You should be pleased, being as you are dead set against him."

"You were accused of horrible things last night, Alexandra! I would never want the suit broken off this way."

Alexandra patted her shoulder. "Forget about last night, Corey." She gave Olivia a glance and went to the front door. Rejection was always unpleasant, and her heart lurched with dread as she turned the knob.

The squire had come in person, looking flushed from the drive over, and he was not smiling — he seemed grave. "Good afternoon, Miss Bolton."

Tamping down her dread, she returned the greeting and let him in, walking with him to the parlor.

"Is it too early to call? I could not sleep last night, Miss Bolton, for all my thoughts of you."

Alexandra smiled grimly. "I must apologize for my father's behavior last night, and thank you yet again for inviting us out."

"You do not have to apologize," he said.

Alexandra inhaled sharply. "Of course I do."

"No." He shook his head. Then, "I am so distressed. I am so sorry you had to suffer through the evening. That was not my intention!"

"I am fine," she said lightly. "And it is forgotten." She managed a smile. She had to let him off the hook. "I know why you have called, Mr. Denney. And I understand."

"Good. Then you must know that I am furious with the mean-spiritedness of the gossips last night!" he exclaimed.

She went still. "You heard?"

He nodded gravely.

"But you never let on."

"I did not want to add to your distress."

Realizing that he'd heard all the ugly gossip, including the lies about her and Owen, she flushed. "You are let off, Mr. Denney." She finally said. "No gentleman wants a socially unacceptable wife."

He recoiled, eyes wide. "What? Is that what you think? I do not believe the ugliness I overheard, not for a minute! And you are the most socially acceptable woman I know. You shine, Miss Bolton, and those harpies cast shadows. I cannot understand why they would want to cast such aspersions on your character."

She was taken aback, disbelieving. Morton Denney hadn't believed the gossips. He hadn't judged her as everyone else had. He had faith in her character.

That was when she saw her sisters standing in the hallway, the parlor door ajar, faces pressed to the crack. "I am surprised, sir, that you would believe in me."

"You sewed my wife's clothing for five years, Miss Bolton. I believe I know your true nature."

She chewed on her lip, then breathed out. "So this is a social call?"

"What else would it be?"

She could not contain herself. "You did not come to end things?"

"No, I did not. I came to make certain

that you had survived the evening."

Alexandra could not believe his magnanimity. She turned, found a chair and sat down. He walked over to her. She looked up and said, "I am not socially acceptable. You can and should do better."

He hesitated. "How could I do better, Miss Bolton? How?"

She fought for composure, filled with both dismay and relief. He would not walk out of their lives after all, and even as she thought that, she was dismayed — he was so clearly in love with her. God, if only she could come to love him in return. And she had to stop thinking about Clarewood! Taking a few deep breaths, she stood. "I was not jilted by Owen St. James, Mr. Denney. When I told you about my vows to my dying mother, and my decision to send Owen away, it was the truth."

He nodded, and as he did, Edgemont came bursting into the room. He looked back and forth between them with alarm. "Father," Alexandra said, hoping to ward off disaster. "The squire has called."

Edgemont rushed forward. Denney seemed uncomfortable now. "Did you have a pleasant evening last night?" her father asked transparently. "Alexandra was lovely, was she not? Just like her blessed mother, a true lady."

"Miss Bolton is always lovely," Denney said.

"Will you have some tea with me? As it is too early for brandy." Her father laughed, slapping the squire's arm.

Denney glanced at Alexandra.

Even though he didn't seem interested in socializing with her father, the two men would have to get on if this marriage was to go forward, so she smiled a bit at him, and he nodded, then turned and walked off into the library with Edgemont. The moment he did, her sisters rushed into the parlor. They were both pale and wide-eyed.

"He isn't breaking things off," Alexandra said.

"We heard," Olivia whispered.

Corey glanced past her, out the window, at the front drive. "There's a rider approaching."

Alexandra turned to see a rider cantering a lathered mount up their rutted dirt drive. The animal was one of the finest specimens of horseflesh she'd ever seen, and she couldn't imagine who the rider might be. Then she faced her sisters. "The squire is a generous, kind and forgiving man."

Olivia suggested, "Maybe we should forgive him the crime of being twenty-four years your elder."

"That was your charge, not mine," Alexandra said softly.

Their caller was knocking on the front door. Alexandra decided that the rider had to be lost. Still stunned that the squire had not wrongly judged her, she started from the room, her sisters following, and opened the door.

Randolph de Warenne stood there, his boots muddy, his cheeks reddened from the wind. He was holding a very large paper-wrapped bouquet in his hand.

Was he calling on one of her sisters? Alexandra wondered in confusion.

"Miss Bolton." He smiled and bowed. "These are for you."

The delight that had begun vanished. Her confusion absolute, she glanced over her shoulder at the closed library doors. Denney would not have Randolph de Warenne deliver flowers to her.

Her heart slammed.

Behind her, one of her sisters inhaled.

He grinned. "There is a card."

"I have forgotten my manners," Alexandra said, beginning to tremble. No, it was impossible. Surely Clarewood hadn't sent her flowers. Absolutely not. She took the wrapped bouquet, gesturing Randolph inside. "Was it a long ride?"

"Very — but my mount is fast and fit, and we galloped most of the way." He smiled at Corey and Olivia. "I made the journey in barely an hour and a half."

She was shaking, she realized, and shocked. She did not know what this gesture could mean. Or did she? Alexandra walked into the parlor, saying, "They expect the new rail between Kensett and Clarewood to be completed in forty-seven."

"I'll ride anyway," Randolph laughed. He glanced at Corey.

"Open the flowers," Olivia whispered.

Alexandra clutched the bouquet and said, "Poor Randolph looks frozen. Can we get him some hot tea and scones? Oh, dear." She turned back to him. "I never thanked you for your kindness last night."

Neither sister moved.

"I am fine, really." Randolph grinned. "And it was my pleasure to see your father home. Open the flowers," he said. "I am not allowed to leave until you do."

He was not allowed to leave until she opened the bouquet? Clarewood's image consumed her now. He had so obviously sent her flowers; he hadn't forgotten her or even come to his senses.

Still stunned, and very reluctant now,

Alexandra tore the wrapper off. Two dozen huge burgundy-red roses, each one fully opened and perfect — and clearly hand-picked — were revealed. A small cream-colored envelope was pinned in their midst.

She could not move.

What did he want?

Why was he doing this?

The squire meant to *marry* her.

Corey gasped. "Those are the most perfect roses I have ever seen."

"I have never seen roses that color before," Olivia said as breathlessly.

"They cost a small fortune," Randolph boasted.

Alexandra stared at the stunning flowers. The gesture was excessively bold, excessively dramatic. And it was even seductive, though she wasn't sure it was romantic.

"Read the card," Corey said.

Her hand continuing to tremble, she handed Olivia the flowers, then took the envelope, opened it with her nail and pulled out the small card within. There was nothing written on it except for a large, bold *C*.

"What does it say?" Corey demanded.

Alexandra showed her the card, looking up at Randolph. He was expectant, grinning at her now. She turned to Olivia, somehow finding her voice. "Can you find a vase, please?" But even as she spoke, she realized she should return the flowers — that she should not accept them.

"Wait!"

Olivia froze. "What is it?"

Her heart thundering now, Alexandra looked at Randolph determinedly. "I cannot accept the flowers."

His eyes widened.

Corey cried out, "Why not?"

"Alexandra, we should discuss this," Olivia said tersely.

Alexandra trembled, but she took the roses from Olivia and handed them to Randolph, whose eyes widened still further. But he did not take them. "Please," she said. She tried to smile and failed. "If anything, I am the one who owes His Grace flowers or some other token of my gratitude for his rescue last night."

Randolph said, "He wishes for you to have them, Miss Bolton. In fact, he specified the exact roses he wished for me to find — the most perfect, the most costly. He even said one dozen would not do. You cannot return them — he would be offended."

"I cannot accept them." She heard the uncertain tremor in her tone. She did not want to offend Clarewood; no woman in her right mind would.

"Why on earth not?" Randolph asked sharply.

She wet her lips and glanced at the library doors. "I have a suitor, sir, who has made it very clear that he will soon offer marriage." She inhaled. "That is, I am being courted." She pressed the flowers into his arms. "Once he realizes I am practically engaged, His Grace will hardly be offended."

From behind, Olivia seized her. "I want a private word with you," she snapped.

As Alexandra turned to face her, she kept seeing Clarewood, and her heart was shrieking at her now. Oddly, a part of her wanted to accept those flowers, as inappropriate as that would be, and cherish them for a while.

Clarewood had sent her flowers.

"I am in no rush," Randolph said firmly, clearly determined not to leave with the roses, in spite of what she'd said.

"I'll make you tea," Corey said, rushing off into the kitchen.

"I'm going to step outside to cool my horse. May I water him?"

"Of course," Alexandra said. "The pump is by the stables." She waited until he was gone and she could see him leading the magnificent hunter past the house. Then, finally, she inhaled.

"Those flowers are too beautiful to re-

145

turn," Olivia said.

"How can I accept them?" Alexandra pleaded.

"What if his intentions are honorable?"

Alexandra simply looked at her. "It's impossible."

"Is it? What if there is the slightest chance that he is interested in you as a wife? If you return those flowers, you are closing the door in his face."

She stared. He wasn't interested in her that way, she was certain. She thought of Owen then and hugged herself, missing him and their dreams terribly.

"Just keep the flowers," Olivia said. "It can't hurt to keep them, but it *can* hurt to send them back."

Alexandra's resistance was rapidly crumbling. *She had never seen such beautiful roses.*

"Besides," Olivia smiled, "I want to paint them in oils."

Alexandra smiled and gave in.

CHAPTER FIVE

At half past one Stephen left his architects poring over the changes he'd scribbled on their carefully executed drawings, his mind filled with his visions of the housing the textile workers would soon enjoy. He was running late; he had been immersed in the Manchester project, and he was expecting the dowager duchess at any moment.

Clarewood had been renovated by his father, and it was now comprised of exactly a hundred rooms, with a mostly gothic facade, one of tall towers and pinnacles. Guillermo would most likely show her to the Gold Room when she arrived, if she wasn't there already. It was the most spectacular salon in the house, where his most significant guests were entertained. He shifted mental gears, now thinking about the American. Investigating him would be a time-consuming matter, because the man lived abroad. By the time he learned anything of interest, his mother's relationship with the man might have gone too far.

He was grim. Julia was fifty years old, but she remained a beautiful woman, at once trim and slender, graceful and elegant. She was a horsewoman who rode every day, and he felt certain that her activities kept her so youthful. He kept recalling the look he had witnessed. He had not a doubt that Jefferson was attracted to her.

Unfortunately, the man was no doubt just as attracted to her fortune, if not more so.

As he reached the front hall, which was the nucleus of the house, he glanced outside. He could see the huge fountain, and the pale shell drive circling it. Beyond, he saw a portion of the mile-long drive, lined by stately elm trees. He did not see a rider approaching, but Randolph was due to return at any time. He smiled to himself.

He hadn't slept well last night. He often tossed and turned, mulling over plans, unresolved issues and new ideas. But last night his interest in Alexandra Bolton had kept cropping up. If she'd thought to whet his appetite by rejecting his initial advances, she had certainly succeeded.

Guillermo suddenly intercepted him. He was holding out a calling card. "Your Grace, Lady Witte has just arrived."

Stephen was instantly grim; he could not delay the inevitable. It was time to inform her that their liaison was over. "Where is she?"

"She is in the Spring Salon with the dowager duchess."

He nodded, striding swiftly to the salon. His mother was standing in front of the doors that opened onto the terraces outside, chatting pleasantly with Lady Witte. Both women heard his approach, and, in unison, they turned.

His mother's smile vanished, and he instantly saw that she was distressed. He suddenly recalled how radiant she had been last night, when on Jefferson's arm. They had made a striking couple. Even he had to admit it.

Then he glanced at his mistress, who was smiling brightly at him. Charlotte was clever and shrewd, and undoubtedly she had come hoping to shore up their relationship. "Good afternoon, Lady Witte, Mother," he said. He smiled at Lady Witte, but lightly kissed his mother's cheek.

"I hope I have not called at an inopportune time," Charlotte said softly.

"I wish a private word with Stephen," Julia said firmly, her blue eyes dark.

"I am hardly in a rush." Charlotte smiled.

149

A seductive light was in her eyes.

"Will you give us a moment?" Stephen asked politely, knowing her answer. When she nodded, he led his mother into the adjacent room, dominated by a grand piano and a harp. Two rows of gold velvet chairs faced the musical instruments. "Thank you for coming on such short notice," he said.

"Even I, your mother, recognize a summons when I receive one."

He winced and spoke carefully now. "I hardly summoned you, Mother. But it has been a while since we last spoke, and there are some subjects I wish to discuss with you. However, I can see that you are somewhat distressed."

She smiled tightly. "You did your duty last night, as always, Stephen, by interviewing Jefferson as you did. We both know you instantly decided not to like him. So yes, I am distressed."

He was oddly tense now. "I know nothing about the man — he is a stranger and a foreigner, and to make matters worse, you seemed terribly happy with him."

"That makes matters *worse?*" she said. "I cannot decide, even now, if Tom taught you to be so cold and dispassionate or if it is your nature. Yes, I am quite distressed today — I am distressed with *you.*"

150

He was grim. "Well, as you seem to wish to be brutally frank, I will be frank, too. It is my duty to protect you from charlatans and fortune hunters."

"Of course it is," she ground out. "Tom taught you too well."

He stiffened. They never argued, but they were arguing now. "You believe in duty as much as I do," he finally said quietly.

She paced away from him, her silk skirts billowing. Then she turned, hands fisted on her slim hips. "Yes, I do. I spent my life fulfilling my duty to Clarewood — and to you. And you always came first — it is why I chose to stay with Tom and suffer his abuses. Everything I have done, I have done for you — so you would be Clarewood's next and greatest duke."

He was uncomfortable now. No one knew as well as he how she had suffered as Clarewood's wife. As far as Stephen was concerned, Tom had been cruelest toward her. He had despised his wife, and in the end, he hadn't even tried to hide it.

Julia, in turn, had never tried to defend herself from his attacks. She'd cloaked herself in dignity and endured the abuse. She had only become a lioness where her son was concerned. And then her fights with Tom had been vicious and vehement. He'd all too often fled those hateful scenes.

Even as a child, he'd despaired at seeing his mother forced to fight for him as she had. Once he was older, he had begged her to retreat, to ignore Tom when he decided to go on the attack against either of them. She had refused. His mother had been so courageous and determined when battling Tom. And she had also been the ultimate diplomat, because she had always known what was truly at stake: his future as the next duke.

"No one knows more than I do, the sacrifices that you made."

"Good. Then it is time, is it not, for me to take care of myself?" She stared.

Wariness settled over him. "What does that mean? Because you are, and will always be, the dowager duchess, my mother and my responsibility."

"It means that Tom died fifteen years ago, and while his death set me free, allowing me to live the life of my choosing, I was always afraid to allow any man too close. I never wanted to be shackled in marriage again, Stephen. And I know you are aware that is why I refused to ever remarry."

He did not like her bringing up the subject of marriage now. "Go on," he said tersely.

She suddenly paused, facing him, her

cheeks flushed. "There is something about Tyne Jefferson . . . he is kind, but also manly, solid, like the earth! I know he should be with a much younger woman — we are the same age, I think — but I believe he finds me interesting and . . . somewhat attractive. Stephen, I like him. I like him very much, but you will try to ruin it, I have realized that now."

Was his mother thinking of marriage to Jefferson? He was aghast. Or was this merely some kind of middle-aged love affair? "How long have you known him, and why am I only just learning about this affair now?" He controlled his anger. "Is it an affair?"

She stiffened. "I have only just met him — at a supper party — and then we bumped into one another on Pall Mall. And last night was our first chance to really converse. We had a lovely time, in spite of your overbearing behavior."

"Considering the way he looked at you, it was my privilege to be overbearing," he said.

"It is my privilege to have this second and maybe last chance!" Julia cried. "I was faithful to your father," she said tersely. "And God knows that any other woman would have sought comfort and kindness elsewhere."

Stephen was alarmed. "If you are lonely, I

will find a husband for you."

She started. "Do you know why Tom came to hate me, though he was madly in love with me when you were born? Enough so to accept you as his own child?" When he did not speak, she said, "He came to hate me for my not bearing him a natural son. It is so ironic! He was impotent, yet he directed his anger at me — and at you. Jefferson has made me feel like a young woman again." She smiled, and he blanched, dismayed. "It was lonely, being the Duchess of Clarewood. And I didn't realize that I was still lonely, not until I met Jefferson, not until he made me feel so alive again."

He was uncomfortable with the extent of their intimacy. "Again, it seems to me that you deserve what you seem to wish for now — a husband. I am going to begin a search. But you can do far better than an uncouth American who ranches for his living."

"When did you become such a snob?" she gasped, paling.

"Is there a difference between ranching and farming?" He knew his mother would never become involved with a farmer, not even a gentleman farmer.

"He is far more than a farmer — he has carved his ranch out of the wilderness with

154

his bare hands," she said. "And don't you dare start looking for a husband for me. I am interested in Jefferson, not marriage — there is a vast difference."

Was his mother telling him that she wished to pursue an affair? He would accept that — as it was the lesser of two evils. "I don't trust him. And you seem to know as little about him as I do."

"Which is why I am pursuing a friendship. I wish to learn more. And that is why you must mind your own affairs now, and leave Jefferson be," Julia said flatly.

He simply could not do that, so he was silent. Then, "Do you want to stay and have an early supper? I will cancel my evening plans."

She stood up. "I am going to go. I have plans for tea. I hope I was clear, Stephen. As much as I love you, if you ruin this for me, I may never forgive you."

"I will see you out," he said, taking her arm, knowing he would do what was best for the dowager duchess, even if it meant losing her trust and her love. As they left the salon, he added, "I am merely asking you to proceed with caution."

She suddenly smiled, her blue eyes sparkling. "It is hard to be cautious, Stephen, when someone makes your heart race so madly you can hardly think straight. But you wouldn't know the feeling, would you?"

Suddenly he thought of Miss Bolton. She certainly made his heart race, but he was having no problem being careful and pragmatic in his pursuit of her.

Guillermo already had his mother's coat and gloves in hand when they entered the gracious, high-ceilinged front hall. His doorman rushed to open the front door while Guillermo helped her on with her coat.

"Just promise me," she said, "that you will be polite the next time you meet. In fact, I am asking you to give him the benefit of the doubt."

"I will do my best," he said, aware that he was lying.

"By the way," Julia added, "it was gallant of you to help that young lady with her inebriated father. Miss Bolton seems like a rather interesting woman." She turned a questioning gaze on him.

He smiled indifferently. "I can be gallant, Mother. I am a gentleman, after all, never mind the gossips."

"You could have sent Alexi and Randolph de Warenne to her aid without your having to bother at all."

"They did come to her aid."

Julia stared closely. "You went out of your

way to attend her. She seems like a proud young woman, Stephen. She is very different from the kinds of young ladies you are normally introduced to."

He simply smiled. And when the dowager duchess was ensconced in her carriage a moment later, he returned to the Spring Room. Charlotte was seated on a settee, at once tiny and lovely, reading a weekly magazine. He knew her pose was contrived, as it revealed every lush curve she had. She smiled at him and stood up as he came inside.

He did not smile back.

"You should close the doors," she said softly, walking to him, her movements languid now.

She had proven to be a highly experienced lover. "We had an arrangement," he said. "And I do not recall sending you a note asking for your presence today." He had been very clear from the first — he did not like unexpected calls, and he preferred to manage their schedule of trysts.

She paused before him, reaching for the lapels of his waistcoat. "I never liked that stipulation, Stephen," she murmured. "You can summon me, yet I can never summon you. I have passions, too. It has been a week."

"I will not argue with you," He clasped her hands and removed them. "I am sorry, Charlotte. I have been very distracted with my projects, and I remain preoccupied." He intended to be as polite as possible.

Her face hardened. "Preoccupied with your projects, Stephen, or with that gawky seamstress you rescued twice last night?"

He was in disbelief.

She flushed. "I beg your pardon, but of course I noticed your gallantry. You never go out of your way for a woman — unless you are interested in her."

"I have no intention of discussing Miss Bolton with you. I am very sorry, Charlotte, but I am ending our affair."

Her expression tightened. "So you can pursue *her?* Or is there someone else, as well?"

"I have very much appreciated your favors. But there is no point in continuing if my passion has waned." He stepped aside, a gesture indicating that the interview was also over.

She did not move. "I do not mind your wandering. I have little doubt you will tire of her after a night or two."

He had no intention of debating this particular subject. "I am afraid I have many affairs to attend to. May I see you out? I will send your things on."

She trembled. "You may call at any time, Stephen. I know you will come to your senses."

He sighed. "You may think as you wish, obviously."

She widened her eyes innocently and said, "I'd like to get my things."

He knew she was scheming — he saw it in her eyes — and that was worse than insisting they were not over, or even a display of hysterics. "Fine. I will ask Guillermo to help you."

"I'd like a moment," she said softly, her eyes now shimmering with unshed tears.

He wasn't moved; he knew theatrics when he saw them. He nodded, leaving the salon, instantly relieved. His interest had been dying for some time, and he only realized that now. And perhaps that was why he was so keenly aware of Miss Bolton. He preferred that conclusion to the notion that she somehow stirred his desire as no previous woman had managed to do.

A few minutes later he had forgotten Charlotte Witte and was thinking about his drawings. He was about to enter the study when Randolph came running up the corridor, his boots muddy from the long ride to and from Edgemont Way.

Stephen halted, smiling. He glanced at his pocket watch. "You made good time. Did she like the roses?"

Randolph met his gaze and hesitated.

His smile vanished. "The roses were exquisite, I presume?" Heads would roll if they had been anything less.

"They were beyond exquisite, and yes, she did admire them . . . somewhat." Randolph hesitated again, as if searching carefully for words.

Stephen could not imagine what was wrong. "She admired them — *somewhat?* What, exactly, did she say? Surely she was very flattered."

"I am not sure she was flattered, Your Grace. But she did say thank-you," he added with haste.

Stephen was taken aback. "She was not flattered by my interest?"

Randolph sighed. "The truth of the matter is, Your Grace, she intended to refuse them, and I had to argue with her and convince her to keep them."

Stephen was disbelieving now, shocked. Alexandra Bolton had wanted to return the flowers? She thought to reject his advances? She thought to reject *him?* A dark mood overcame him. "Why would she wish to return the flowers?"

Randolph pursed his lips. "It seems as if she has a suitor who intends to ask for marriage."

Stephen was surprised. Surely she was not interested in the elderly squire? He'd already learned that the man who'd danced attendance on her the night before was Morton Denney, the largest of Sir Rex's leaseholders. He was twice her age, but that did not mean anything. And while he was a gentleman, he was also a farmer. On the other hand, he had some means. For someone as poorly off as Alexandra, his means might seem like a fortune.

But they were not. He, Stephen Mowbray, was the one with the fortune.

"She seemed to feel it inappropriate to accept the flowers, Your Grace. She even said she should be sending flowers to you, as a sign of her gratitude for your aid with Edgemont last night."

His interest seemed to have spiraled dangerously high. No woman had ever rejected his advances, and in fact, she hadn't done so, either. But she had thought about it. Apparently, however, in the back of her mind, she wasn't really ready to dismiss him. Of course she was not. In the end, she would bend to his will.

And now amusement began to rise. He

had a rival? *Really?* He loved a good battle. He was only sorry his rival wasn't someone more interesting, a peer who was closer to him in means and title. Stephen slowly smiled. "I want to know the moment the squire asks for marriage," he said softly.

Randolph started. "I'll contact our London lawyers, find out which firm Denney uses, and make certain we stay apprised."

"Good." Stephen turned, gesturing for Randolph to follow him into the study, and that was when he saw Charlotte backing away from the salon doors. Obviously she had been spying. He hoped it had brought her to her senses. And then his ex-mistress was entirely forgotten once again.

"I have some things I wish to discuss with you. I have started looking over the recent Ridgeway statements, and I'd like you to examine them," he said, pushing open the study door. As his mind turned back to the affairs of Clarewood and the Foundation, he had one last thought. Tomorrow night he would extend a supper invitation. And because he did not expect her to accept a conventional invitation, he would make it a persuasive one.

A very persuasive one — the kind no woman could refuse.

■ ■ ■ ■

Two days later, Alexandra smiled at the squire as his open carriage approached Edgemont Way. It was a gray cloudy day, the still-wet roads littered with red and gold leaves, and she'd just taken a tour of his home. She was impressed. He had a beautiful country house with immaculate grounds; clearly, he was doing very well.

Her home was ahead, a two-story rectangular country house built of beige stone with gray shingled roofs. The single stable, also of stone, was to the left. A caretaker's cottage stood alone off in the distance, but it had been vacant for years. A low wooden fence encircled the front of the property, and in springtime, blooming bougainvillea climbed the rails. In the spring, Elizabeth's red roses were a wild array against the front of the house. Now, only ivy graced its stone facade.

The squire turned into their short drive, and instantly, the coach hit a deep rut. Alexandra did not exclaim as she was jarred hard in her seat. She merely sent the squire an apologetic look. "I am sorry," she said.

"Do not apologize to me. It will be very easy to improve the drive," he said, smiling at her. He then added, "May I say you look lovely today, Miss Bolton?"

"Thank you." She did not flush, and her heart did not race. Instantly, her thoughts veered to Clarewood.

How could they not? His magnificent red roses were in her bedroom, and when she went upstairs, she remained in disbelief. Why choose her for his improper advances?

She was grim. She'd had two days to think about his advances. She still could not comprehend them. But that was the end of that. She'd told Randolph about the squire and his suit, so no doubt Clarewood would move on to other, greener pastures.

It should have been impossible, but she felt a twinge of dismay and another of regret.

She pinched herself — hard — through her navy blue skirts. A wonderful gentleman with means was courting her. He could have turned tail and fled after the fiasco at Harrington House, but he had not. He was staunch, he was generous, and he was kind. Most importantly, his intentions were honorable and he could change her sisters' lives.

Denney halted his two-horse carriage in front of the house. Alexandra silenced her wandering thoughts. She would have to entertain him for a bit, but she was impatient for him to leave. Lady Lewis had brought her gown by as she'd promised, the day after the birthday ball, and she was expecting to pick it up tomorrow. Several other ladies had also left their ball gowns with her yesterday. She had hours of labor ahead of her.

Denney got down from the coach, which he was driving, and helped her alight. Then, gravely, he said, "Would you be offended if I did not come inside? I'm afraid that I have some accounts to go over and a meeting with one of my most important tenants."

She realized he leased out some of the land that he himself leased. She was suitably impressed by his business acumen — and relieved that he would not linger, so she could get to her repairs and cleaning. "I would not be offended at all, Mr. Denney. It has been such a lovely afternoon."

He beamed and then, impulsively, took both of her hands in his. "I am trying to restrain myself, my dear, but would you be offended if I pressed my suit with your father sooner, rather than later?"

Her heart slammed. She told herself she was surprised, not alarmed. Then, somehow, she smiled. "I doubt you could ever offend me, sir."

His wide smile increased. A moment later

he was driving off, and Alexandra waved after him. He returned the gesture.

He intended to offer for her soon. She simply stood there, staring after his carriage, trying to control her dismay. She had expected a courtship of several months, if not longer.

But of course he was impatient. Her birthday was in the spring. She would be twenty-seven years old. And she wondered, her heart lurching, if he wanted more children. He had two grown sons and a daughter, all married, none of whom she'd ever met.

She decided that now was not the time to think about it.

Behind her, the front door opened, and Alexandra turned to see Olivia standing there, wide-eyed. Instantly she knew something was amiss. She hurried toward her. "What is it? Is something wrong?"

"Come inside."

Alarmed, Alexandra increased her stride and followed her sister into the house. "Father is out," Olivia said tersely, leading Alexandra into the parlor.

But Alexandra stumbled on the threshold, because six vases were on the table behind the sofa, each filed with a dozen perfect burgundy roses. Her heart slammed. Then it began racing madly.

He wasn't giving up.

"The florist delivered them himself. They came an hour after you left with the squire," Olivia said, her tone hushed, her eyes huge.

Alexandra sat down, in shock.

Corey rushed into the room. "Can you believe it?" she asked in excitement. "This time there's a letter!"

Why was he doing this?

Olivia handed her a letter. She said, "There's something inside, Alexandra."

She looked at the envelope, and saw the bulge in it. It was addressed simply to her at Edgemont Way; obviously, the florist had been given directions and a precise address. She could not imagine what the bulge meant. She turned the envelope over and saw that her hands were trembling. His crest was a magnificent one: the letter *C* was book-ended by two rearing lions, a crown atop it.

"Please open it," Corey begged.

She looked up at her sisters. "I was very clear. I told Randolph that the duke's previous gesture was inappropriate. I explained that the squire is courting me, and that he intends marriage." She did not recognize the tone of her own voice. It was high and strained. Tension had stiffened her so much that her back hurt.

"He is so romantic," Corey breathed.

Alexandra felt like screaming at her silly sister. This was not romantic. It was sordid.

But she wet her lips and took the letter opener that Olivia was holding out. She slit the envelope. And as she saw the gleaming contents inside, sprawled almost carelessly against a folded letter, her eyes widened and she went still with shock.

"What is it?" Olivia asked urgently.

Alexandra felt incapable of movement, of speech. She lifted the diamond bracelet from the envelope. It glittered wildly, even in the dull and gloomy daylight.

Corey gasped and sat down in an adjacent chair. Olivia cried out. Dumbfounded, Alexandra simply stared at the bracelet. It was two centimeters wide, consisting of hundreds of diamonds set in platinum squares. Her heart was pounding so fiercely now that she felt dizzy.

"That is worth a fortune," Olivia managed, also sitting down.

"Why is he doing this?" Alexandra asked helplessly. That bracelet could purchase new wardrobes for her sisters, she thought. It could provide small dowries. What was in his mind?

"Read the letter," Olivia whispered.

Alexandra gasped, realizing she'd forgotten about the note. She handed the bracelet to Olivia, who exclaimed over it, still stunned, and took out the letter and unfolded it.

My dear Miss Bolton,
I would be pleased to have the honor of your presence for supper tonight at 7:00 p.m. I look forward to furthering our acquaintance.

Yours,
Clarewood

"What does it say?" Corey demanded, but her tone was hushed with awe. She was holding the bracelet now.

Alexandra handed the letter to Olivia, who read it aloud. Her own mind raced, spun. She could not go. Of course she could not go. Because now there was no doubt as to his intentions. If he were inclined to court her, he would never send her this kind of invitation, or the kind of gift one bought one's mistress — if one were exceedingly rich.

"You have to go," Corey said, leaping to her feet.

Alexandra looked up at her. "Corey, he is intent on seduction. And I have a suitor, remember?"

"The squire?" Corey demanded scornfully. "Alexandra, what is wrong with you? The most handsome — and wealthiest — bachelor in Britain is pursuing you. How can you possibly refuse?"

"If I go over there tonight, I will return a fallen woman, a harlot with no shame!" Alexandra said, distressed.

Corey paled. Then, stubbornly, "I think he is a gentleman. He would never force you to do something against your will."

Alexandra stared desperately at her youngest sister. She longed to believe as Corey did — not that it mattered. What her sister did not know was that she dreamed of his strong arms, of his kisses. He'd awakened her dormant body, reminding her that she was an unfulfilled woman. But, dear God, he wasn't Owen. She did not love him. She did not even *know* him!

Olivia got up. "Corey, I believe that the duke is a gentleman, but I also agree with Alexandra that his intentions are scandalous." Olivia turned and looked carefully at her.

Alexandra stared back, aware that her sister sensed just how attracted she was to him.

"He has refused to take no for an answer,"

Olivia murmured.

"Are you going to reject the supper invitation?" Corey asked. "Even if you do, you still should keep the bracelet."

"Corey!" Olivia was aghast. "This is a stunning development, but Alexandra can't keep the bracelet." She turned to stare at Alexandra very closely again, her regard searching.

"But it would feed us for years. It would pay our debt," Corey said flatly. And she looked at Alexandra, too.

Alexandra's temples were throbbing. "I cannot keep the bracelet, because that would send the signal that I am open to his advances." She knew what she had to do. "Corey?" She held out her hand.

Corey seemed highly reluctant, but she handed Alexandra the glittering bracelet. "I would go," she said angrily. "And I would rather be the duke's mistress than the squire's wife."

Alexandra felt her heart lurch wildly, but she refused to identify her feelings. Nor did she want his image in her mind, as if engraved upon her memory. "He knows I am being courted. He obviously doesn't care. This has to stop."

Reluctantly, Olivia agreed with her. "It does have to stop — that is, if you mean to go through with marriage to the squire."

Alexandra ignored another jolt in her heart. "I do." She looked at the table with the six dozen roses. "If Father saw those, I do not know what I would say. He would be furious. The Lord only knows what he would do." She inhaled. "I am going to Clarewood."

Both of her sisters jumped in surprise.

Alexandra was grim as a tremendous wave of anxiety began to roll through her. "I will return the flowers and the bracelet, and I will make myself clear to the duke once and for all."

CHAPTER SIX

Shrugging on his frock coat, Stephen left the study, where Randolph was going over some Foundation accounts, to join Elysse and Ariella, who had come to visit at his request. "I am impressed," he said, entering a smaller blue-and-gold salon with long strides. "I'm impressed that you've ventured from town on such a terrible day." It had begun to drizzle an hour earlier, and now the skies were thunderously black, indicating a turn for the worse.

His cousins were seated on the pale cream-and-gold sofa, Elysse in a green pin-striped dress, Ariella in watered blue silk, making a striking picture, one any artist would have loved to paint. They leaped up to greet him, Elysse kissing his cheek warmly. Ariella followed suit, neither one caring that Guillermo was witness to their open display of affection. The butler was the epitome of discretion, and he was accustomed to such episodes. Society and staff knew he'd become closely acquainted with the de Warenne family years ago.

"Your note was intriguing," Ariella said, her blue eyes mirroring her curiosity. "You wrote that you were in dire straits and that only Elysse and I could be of help." Her tawny brows arched questioningly.

"I told Ariella it is a ruse of some kind. You are never in dire straits. If a hurricane dared to come this far inland, you would point at it and send it away," Elysse said, laughing. "Meanwhile, I am famished and must eat before you confess your troubles to us."

He smiled and turned to the butler. "Please bring refreshments, Guillermo."

"Immediately, Your Grace." Guillermo left, closing the pale blue-and-gold doors behind him.

Stephen gestured for them to retake their seats, and when they had done so, he sat, as well. Crossing one leg, he said, "I will get right to the point. I wish to find the dowager duchess a husband."

Both women gaped at him.

"I know. After fifteen years, it seems odd. But I think Julia would be more content with a husband than living alone as she does now."

Ariella and Elysse exchanged looks. Ariella spoke. "Stephen, what has brought this on? It is no secret that your mother suffered horribly when married to your father. I believe she is very content right now. She has no one to answer to, except for you, and you allow her to do as she pleases. Whenever I see the dowager duchess, she seems in good spirits. I would seriously reconsider a second spouse. I believe she is enjoying her freedom from matrimony."

Ariella always spoke her mind, and just then, he was glad. "I would never force her into a marriage. And you have missed my point. I want to make a good match — I want to find her someone attractive, witty and noble."

Both women were silent, staring, eyes wide. Finally Elysse said, "Are you saying you want to find your mother a *love* match?"

He winced. "I want to find her a gentleman whom she can become fond of, and who will be fond of her, as well. If you wish to call it a love match, so be it." He stood, thinking of Tyne Jefferson and feeling a twinge of guilt. He knew Julia well. She would not be pleased with his scheme, not now. But in the end, if all went as planned, she would be thrilled. "I prefer their relationship to be one of mutual admiration and respect. Obviously the prospective groom must have means, to foreclose any possibility of his interest being in her fortune."

Ariella and Elysse exchanged looks, and then they burst into smiles. "You are romantic after all!" Elysse exclaimed.

He sighed. "I am *not* romantic, Elysse. But Julia has been acting oddly recently. It has become evident that she is lonely."

"Really?" Elysse suddenly snickered, the sound unladylike. "She did not seem lonely at Harrington Hall the other night."

He bristled. "I am sure that in all of Britain, there must exist an older gentleman who might become genuinely fond of my mother."

Elysse turned to face Ariella with some excitement. "What was his name?"

"Jefferson — like the President. I can't recall his first name, though." Ariella turned to Stephen. "She seemed utterly taken with the American. What about him?"

His tension spiraled. "Tyne Jefferson is a rancher from the wilds of California," he said. "In Britain, those who raise cattle are *farmers!* He also trades — he sells his beef to Midwestern and Eastern markets. He is not suitable for the dowager duchess." He was firm, and he had even spoken briefly with Cliff de Warenne about the man.

The women exchanged glances. Elysse said flatly, "Alexi trades, and so does his father. Would you deny her someone like Alexi or Cliff?"

"May I remind you of precisely how blue their blood is?" His temper was rising, but he controlled it. He knew he was being a terrible snob.

Ariella stood, frowning with disapproval. "I despise it when you are at your snottiest. America is not Britain — it does not have our class system. It is a frontier society, and an open one. The standards that apply here do not apply there."

"He is very attractive," Elysse said, standing, as well. "And he seems to be a gentleman."

He was annoyed that they had closed ranks against him. "My standards apply everywhere — even in Hong Kong."

Ariella rolled her eyes. "Of course they do, Your Grace. Because you have inherited a fortune and a kingdom, and you are as controlling as a tyrant. Can you not admit to your prejudice?"

He roiled with anger. "Yet I am accused of being a Whig and a republican by everyone else."

"No, I am the true liberal, Stephen. In spite of your good works, your values are antiquated."

Only Ariella — or Elysse — could get away with such a statement. "And you remain impossibly overeducated," he said with characteristic calm, though inside he was not calm at all. "Must you always refute me? I am amazed St. Xavier allows you the liberties that he does. Do you dispute him, as you do me? For heaven's sake, the Foundation is at the forefront of social and political reform."

"I debate my husband when I believe that he is wrong." Then Ariella sighed. "I do not want to fight with you, Stephen. I am terribly fond of you, hypocrisy and all. And yes, you are at the forefront of reform. But your reforming tendencies have vanished where your mother is concerned. I think she is fond of Jefferson, and I think we should look into that."

"I agree," Elysse said flatly.

He was aghast and affronted. "I wish to enlist you to find my mother a suitable *peer* — one who is British and blue-blooded, not an American rancher who sells beef!"

"But what if Julia is falling in love? Would you deny her that?" Ariella asked.

"She is not falling in love. She is lonely, and he has simply turned her head."

Elysse hurried over. "I would love to

178

help," she said, seeming pleased by the prospect, and as if she hadn't heard his earlier words. "Wouldn't you, Ariella? I have always been fond of the dowager duchess. Let's find her a *love* match."

She glanced at Ariella, and he knew they were conspiring against him.

"Very well, Stephen," Ariella said. "We will do it."

He put his fists on his hips. "I meant my every word. I will not accept Jefferson, not now, not ever. I want you to find her a respectable, titled Englishman. After you have done your research, you will present me with a list of prospective husbands. You will not arrange an introduction to anyone, not until I have approved it."

They shared a look. "Of course, Your Grace," both women chorused innocently.

Alexandra was chilled to the bone, and Bonnie, the poor elderly mare drawing the carriage, was wet and exhausted, too. But Clarewood was finally in sight.

Holding the reins in her gloved hands, Bonnie walking tiredly now, Alexandra stared down the shell drive, past the monumental water fountain and the surrounding front gardens, at the stately four-storied gray stone house. It was palatial, she thought with sudden dismay. It seemed fit for a king, not a duke.

She shivered, and not just from the rain and the cold.

It had been impossible to remain in a state of moral indignation, if she had ever truly been in such a frame of mind. The mare was twelve years old and accustomed to two-mile jaunts to town — not traversing what felt like half of Surrey. Randolph de Warenne might have made the journey between Edgemont Way and Clarewood in an hour and a half, but three hours had surely elapsed since she'd left home. The rain hadn't helped matters.

The roads were slick, if not muddy, and her roof leaked. The carriage was not a closed one, so the wind had brought gusts of rain inside. Alexandra wasn't sure she had ever been so cold. She shouldn't care about her appearance, as she meant to drive Clarewood off, but she knew she must be utterly disheveled and shamelessly bedraggled. Most importantly, she was filled with trepidation now, all moral indignation gone.

What woman in her right mind would confront the Duke of Clarewood?

She almost dreaded the ensuing encounter. But she was proud of being a strong, determined and decisive woman. Now was not the time to weaken and lose her backbone — or her courage.

But he was so terribly daunting.

And she still couldn't fathom why he'd chosen *her.*

She was so lost in her anxiety that she realized Bonnie had come to a halt. She clucked to the chestnut mare, lifting the reins. "Come on, Bonnie. We'll be there shortly."

Her pulse had picked up its beat. Bonnie jogged forward, ears pinned back in annoyance. Ancient and stately elm trees lined the drive, the foliage overhead so thick, it at least provided some shelter from the rain. A few moments later she drove the carriage past the water fountain, and, in spite of the downpour, she gazed around, admiring the huge sculpted hedges that formed an identical mosaic on each side of the house. Alexandra halted the mare in front of the wide stone steps that led to the front door. A number of outbuildings stood off to the right, including stone stables. A very costly black brougham was parked beneath an archway between two buildings, four bays in the traces. The duke had other guests.

Her dread became acute. She hadn't thought about the possibility that he would surely be entertaining, if at home. But she had no choice now but to proceed, she thought grimly. Except that she had no wish for a conflict of any sort. She did not want to dismay, annoy or even anger the duke. If possible, she wished for some kind of peaceful acquaintanceship to emerge from the impending encounter.

Alexandra took off her gloves and tucked her wet hair back into place, resetting several hair pins more firmly. She then adjusted her once-jaunty blue felt hat. There was no way to dry her navy blue skirts, but at least her wool coat had protected her bodice from the rain. As she pulled her gloves back on, a doorman materialized by the driver's seat with an umbrella. Alexandra smiled gratefully at him as she got down.

A moment later she found herself in a huge front hall. The ceiling was high, and a massive crystal chandelier hung from its center. It was the size of a grand piano. Black-and-white marble floors were underfoot. Gilded chairs upholstered in dark red velvet and claw-footed tables stood against the walls, which were covered with works of art. Alexandra recognized masterpieces by Titian, Raphael, Constable and Poussin.

Her heart was thudding now.

Her dismay had somehow increased. She wasn't sure, especially as he had guests and she was so sodden, that her idea of speaking with him now was truly the best one. But she'd come this far, and she would go forward. She handed off her coat and gloves, then swept her hands down her soggy skirts. A tall, narrow mirror in a gilded frame hung on one wall. A glance at it told her that nothing would improve her appearance, outside of a change of clothes.

A dark-suited butler was hurrying across the hall. Alexandra managed to smile. "I am afraid I have forgotten my cards," she lied. She no longer had calling cards. She hadn't used a card in years.

His impassive expression did not change. "Whom might I declare, madam?"

"Miss Alexandra Bolton of Edgemont Way."

The butler left. Alexandra realized she was wringing her hands nervously, the duke's image now assailing her mind. She did not know him at all, except by reputation, but she was certain he would not be pleased with her response to his invitation. He did not seem like a man who was used to being countermanded.

She wet her lips nervously and wished the encounter over.

The butler returned. "His Grace will see you now."

Alexandra followed the man across the entry hall, glimpsing a magnificent white-and-gold salon with at least a dozen seating areas. She'd never seen such lavish furnishings, she thought. Her heart rate increased. They passed a large library, dark and masculine, a fire dancing in the emerald marble hearth. She somehow knew it was his favorite room, and she could see him on the sofa there, immersed in the day's journals. Her temples ached. She could not recall ever being this nervous. She wished she hadn't caught his attention at the ball.

And then she could see past the open doors of a small, intimate but airy salon, the walls eggshell-blue, trimmed in gold. Clarewood was standing by the handsomely sculpted white plaster fireplace, a lush nude painting over the mantel, as devastatingly handsome as she recalled. Her heart lurched so hard as she looked at him that she forgot to breathe.

He turned his head immediately, and his blue gaze slammed into hers, intense and direct.

For one endless moment his eyes remained locked with hers, his regard penetrating. Alexandra felt her cheeks warm impossibly; she was no longer cold. She had forgotten how intense his regard was, how unnerving. She'd forgotten how his presence could dominate a room.

She'd forgotten how he could ignite the heat in her body, too.

And then he looked her quickly up and down. It broke the impossible moment, and she became aware that he was not alone. Two elegantly turned out ladies were with him, and Alexandra recognized them instantly. All three pairs of eyes were riveted upon her. She should have waited for another day to confront him. Aware of how disreputable and untidy her appearance was, she felt her cheeks heat and her stomach churn. She held her head a notch higher, determined to hide her embarrassment.

"Miss Alexandra Bolton," the butler intoned.

Clarewood said calmly, "Please bring refreshments for Miss Bolton. And hot tea, Guillermo, immediately." He strode toward her.

Alexandra curtsied, aware that she was breathing harshly. "Good day, Your Grace," she managed.

"This is an exceedingly pleasant surprise, Miss Bolton." His gaze had become searching. "Good afternoon. I am sorry you have had to endure such unpleasant weather."

She gave up and trembled, having just noticed that her skirts were making a puddle upon his beautiful parquet floors. "It is a nasty day, and I must apologize for my rather unkempt appearance. My vehicle is not a closed one."

"Do not apologize. I cannot imagine what possessed you to come across Surrey in such weather." His stare intensified.

She knew she must respond, because his statement was in fact a question; instead, she fought to hide her nervousness as they stared at one another. Did he think her so eager for an illicit rendezvous that she had come earlier than invited? She prayed that was not the case. "I believe there is a matter we must discuss," she finally said.

His lashes lowered. They were thick and lush, and as black as coal. "Perhaps you should come to stand before the fire." It was not a question, and he touched her elbow, clasping it firmly and moving her that way.

His touch, though light, jolted her. It was hot and searing, as if his hand was directly upon her skin, not merely her wool sleeve. His hand was large and firm. It was even possessive. She instantly recalled his hands upon her at the ball, but then he'd clasped her waist, and later her shoulders. Now the chill in her bones vanished, replaced by a sudden warmth. She glanced at him, and their gazes collided. He stared. Helplessly, she stared back.

The tension that had begun the moment she'd seen him deepened, thickened, crackled between them. And it added to her dismay. The shocking attraction she felt for him had not changed, either, she thought dismally. And he knew. His mouth curved ever so slightly.

Alexandra looked away. As he guided her toward the hearth, her heart raced madly, but it was hard to think with his clasp growing firmer upon her elbow. She desperately looked forward to the conclusion of their encounter, and yet, oddly, there was something almost reassuring about his grasp.

She glanced at his striking profile. His strength was what was reassuring, she thought. She was so unused to strong men. He would never recklessly gamble or over-imbibe, or lay waste to his fortune. He would never behave foolishly. In fact, he would undoubtedly never so much as tolerate foolish behavior.

He said, "May I introduce Mrs. Alexi de Warenne and Lady St. Xavier?"

Alexandra somehow smiled at the two women, awaiting rude stares and falsely polite greetings. But as she paused before the warm fire, they instantly smiled at her, as if they were not taken aback by her disheveled appearance or her forward social call. She knew they must be thinking hatefully about her, however. The other night, she had learned how mean-spirited society was.

"I am somewhat acquainted with Lady St. Xavier," she said as calmly as possible. She hadn't seen Ariella St. Xavier, whom she'd known as Ariella de Warenne, in years. "But I do not believe I have had the opportunity to be formally introduced to Mrs. de Warenne." Suddenly she recalled that Elysse's husband had been the one to escort Edgemont from the ball, with the help of young Randolph.

"We have never met, but I am glad we are doing so now," Elysse de Warenne said warmly. "His Grace rescued you from a swoon the other night. Are you feeling better? Maybe you should not have come out on such a deadly day."

Alexandra stared at the beautiful blonde, trying to decide if there was an innuendo in her words, one hinting at the ugly gossip that had raged about the ball that night.

But Elysse de Warenne was smiling so pleasantly that Alexandra decided there was no rancor or malice in her words. Was it possible that these women would treat her fairly after the other night? She was so uncertain. She glanced at Clarewood.

His unwavering regard was filled with male speculation, and her tension increased. She thought again of how it had felt to be in his arms. Flushing, she addressed the women carefully. "I am afraid I have an urgent matter to discuss with His Grace." And then she wished she hadn't said anything at all. What could possibly be of an urgent nature between them? What would the two ladies think?

"Really?" Elysse smiled at Clarewood now. "Isn't Edgemont Way quite some distance from here?"

"Elysse," Clarewood reproved. "Not everyone is as candid as you."

This time there *had* been an innuendo — that she had gone out of her way to call on the duke, perhaps for personal reasons relating to their interaction the other night. If only Elysse knew. "Edgemont Way is quite a distance, yes," Alexandra said, then stopped, because there was no possible way to explain to them why she had called on Clarewood. She turned to him to change the subject.

189

"Is there any chance my poor mare could be cared for in the stables? I'm afraid she is a bit advanced in years, and Bonnie is as wet as I am."

"Of course." He wheeled and went to the door, leaving the women to their own devices.

Alexandra glanced around the room, inspecting it, hoping to avoid the topic of why she had come to Clarewood. "What a delightful salon," she said.

The bait was not, precisely, taken. "I am glad you have called, it gives us a chance to get reacquainted," Ariella said quite pleasantly. "How have you been, Miss Bolton?"

She must have heard the gossip, and she'd certainly seen Edgemont in his cups. Like Elysse, she did not seem hateful, but pleasant and polite. She even seemed sincere, though no one was sincere in society. Alexandra smiled carefully back. "I am very well, thank you. I understand you live some distance from town now?" She wanted to steer the conversation back to polite banalities.

"Yes, Woodland is in Derbyshire, and I do love it there. We will eventually build a home in London, but right now we enjoy staying at my father's London residence when we visit."

Alexandra suddenly made the connection between the two women — they were sisters-in-law. "I have not been to Derbyshire in years, but it is a beautiful part of the country," she said, keeping one eye on the door, wondering how she would manage a private word with Clarewood when he had guests.

"If you are ever in the country, you must stop by." Ariella smiled.

Alexandra felt her eyes widen. Did Ariella mean it?

"While Woodland is a country home, we have a Racket Hall, and there are some quaint shops in the local village. Have you ever played Rackets, Miss Bolton?"

She breathed, shocked by what sounded almost like an invitation. "No, I have not, but it looks amusing."

"It is very amusing, and more difficult than one would think. You must come and play sometime."

Alexandra remained stunned that Ariella had just invited her to her country home. "I have no plans to get out that way, but if I ever do, I will try to call." Flustered, she turned to gaze out the window at the rain.

"You should get out of those wet clothes," Elysse suddenly said. "You fainted the other night, or nearly so, and you could become terribly ill."

Alexandra had to face her. "I am afraid I do not have a change of clothing, and I will be returning home as soon as my business with the duke is concluded."

Elysse and Ariella glanced briefly at one another, the exchange a silent one. Alexandra had the feeling that they did not quite believe her — and she did not blame them.

Just then Clarewood returned to the room. He sent her an indolent look so seductive that her heart lurched wildly. That look was filled with confidence, as if he expected her to accept his outrageous supper invitation. Was he mad?

"She may stand in front of the fire until her clothes are dry," he said, and again, it was not a question but a command. "Your mare will be well cared for, Miss Bolton."

Alexandra was grateful. "Thank you."

Ariella came forward. "I have to go, Stephen," she said, surprising Alexandra by her use of his given name. "We have a supper affair, and with this weather, it will take longer to get back to town than usual."

"I am pleased you called, Ariella," Clarewood returned, an odd note of warning in his tone. "And I am grateful for your aid in the matter we have just discussed."

Ariella grinned and kissed his cheek,

surprising Alexandra even more. "I cannot wait to get started on our little endeavor," she said.

Elysse also kissed him. "You look worried. Have no fear, Your Grace." Her tone was teasing. "We shall humbly obey your every command."

"I am quaking," he said drily. "You gave me your word," he added.

"Of course we did," Elysse murmured. She turned to Alexandra. "It was a pleasure, Miss Bolton. I expect to see you again soon."

Alexandra tried to hide her surprise, because it had sounded as if the other woman meant the words.

Ariella then added, "Stephen's bark is worse than his bite. Whatever you intend, remain staunch, my dear."

Alexandra's eyes widened.

Ariella went on, "We have been friends since childhood." Then she wiggled her fingers at Alexandra and started for the door.

Clarewood turned to her, his gaze suddenly searing. "I will be right back," he said, then turned to walk them out.

The moment she was alone, Alexandra looked for a place to sit down, but she did not want to ruin the furniture. She finally took a window seat and exhaled hard, then began to shake.

The two women had been pleasant and even kind. They had been unusually candid, too. She did not know what to make of them or of that. As for Clarewood, they seemed very fond of him. They certainly weren't intimidated by him. That was good news, she supposed, because he certainly seemed too powerful and too sure of himself. Maybe he was, as Ariella St. Xavier had suggested, more bark than bite.

She doubted it.

But she wasn't intimidated by him — was she?

She trembled all over again. Images flashed, of his holding her as she'd started to faint, of his direct blue stare, and then of the squire's bluff countenance and kind smile. An image of Owen followed, and he was laughing, so dashing and in love with her. She rubbed her temples, which ached with more insistence now. His presence, his power and his masculinity were so overwhelming. This was going to be the most difficult interview of her life.

"Miss Bolton?"

She hadn't heard him return to the room. Alexandra leaped to her feet, and their gazes collided. He was smiling ever so slightly, ever so smugly. "It isn't seven," he murmured. "And I was planning to send my coach for you."

She inhaled, the sound ragged. "No, it isn't seven . . . I believe it's half past three or thereabouts."

His dark brows lifted.

"Should I be flattered?" he asked softly. "Or dismayed?"

"I shall be dining at Edgemont Way tonight."

"I see." His stare never wavered, but the slight curve of his mouth was gone. "Why?"

Why, she wondered, did she feel this slight twinge of regret? Why did he unnerve her? Why did she feel that if she said the wrong thing, or made the wrong gesture, he might pounce?

"The roses are in my carriage. They are stunning . . . but I am afraid they did not survive the rain very well." When he did not speak, simply continuing to stare, she opened her purse and took out the bracelet. "I have come to return this, as well. Obviously I cannot accept the flowers or such an inappropriate gift."

"I fail to see why not. Especially when I wish for you to have it," he purred.

She grew impossibly tense. His tone was seductive — but it was also dangerous. He was the lion inviting its keeper into the cage, hoping to make him its next meal, but only after toying with him. She knew then that her assessment of him had been correct: he was not accustomed to disobedience of any kind. "Your invitation wasn't a proper one."

"No, it was not."

She stared in surprise; he stared calmly back. And because he wasn't speaking, because his stare was unnerving, because her heart was slamming, she cried, "I explained to Randolph that I have a suitor, Your Grace. One with marriage on his mind."

His mouth curved. His eyes gleamed. "I hardly mind a rival, Miss Bolton."

She gasped. Wasn't he going to admit to the folly of his advances? Didn't he understand what she was saying? Wasn't he going to give up? "His intentions are honorable. Are yours?"

"No. They are not."

Alexandra was shocked speechless by his candid admission.

And he slowly smiled. "I believe in being direct, Miss Bolton," he said, "as I find it frivolous to waste time. I am taken with you. I believe that you are taken with me. Considering the circumstances in which we find ourselves, I do not see why you are reluctant to proceed — unless, of course, you are enamored with the squire."

He was seeking an illicit affair. She could not believe he had continued to be so direct. She breathed hard. And what did he mean by "circumstances"?

"How do you feel about the squire?" His stare was hard, but his tone was wry.

Was he amused by the other man's suit? "How I feel about Squire Denney is not your affair." But if he would not back down and give up, what was she going to do?

Mildly, he said, "I am making it my affair."

She inhaled, shaken again. His mind seemed made up — about her. He did not care that she was a gentlewoman, even if her name was in tatters. Images flashed through her mind again, of his face close to hers as he'd held her in his arms. Her dismay escalated. So did her tension. Her body was hot and throbbing. Of course she could not do as he wished. She was a proud, moral woman.

"Have I insulted you? Because, let me assure you, that was not my intention. Most women are flattered by my interest."

She shook her head. "I am flattered," she managed. "But, Your Grace, I am also affronted."

His brows lifted. "Why would my interest be insulting?"

She steadied herself and spoke. "Your Grace, I am in a difficult position. Of course I am flattered. What woman would not be? But you have misinterpreted my situation, not that I blame you, and that is why I am trying to reject your advances."

He seemed amused. "Will you coddle me now? I find your rejection almost refreshing, actually. Women generally are eager to kiss the ground at my feet."

She doubted he'd ever been rejected before. "I do not want to reject you entirely," she whispered, her heart slamming.

His brows rose. "Is there such a thing as a partial rejection?"

It was hard to speak. "Perhaps we can be friends."

He laughed. "Miss Bolton, that is a very quaint notion." He gave her a shockingly bold look. "Do not be insulted, but friendship has nothing to do with roses and diamonds — or my interest in you. I am very intrigued," he stated.

The insult should have been the final blow, but his last admission outweighed it. Her insides tightened. Desire fisted. As he stared into her eyes, she somehow said, aware that this was her last chance to escape him, "Your Grace, I have come to explain that, if the squire offers marriage, I will accept."

He was silent. He did not seem taken aback, or affronted or even dismayed. Just possibly, he seemed amused, except that his gaze was steel.

"Therefore I am returning the flowers and the bracelet. Therefore I must decline your supper invitation. And I must ask you to cease your pursuit." When he kept staring, she exclaimed, "I *am* sorry! I truly wish to remain on a friendly basis."

"Not half as sorry as I am," he said. "You should reconsider."

She laid the bracelet on a table and shook her head, feeling tearful and helpless. "I am so grateful for your aid the other night. . . . And I am flattered, but . . . I must go." She stumbled past him. The sooner she got in her carriage, the better. She did not know when she had last been this upset. True, she had achieved her goals. She had set him straight. She had stopped his advances.

Then he stepped in front of her, barring her way. Alexandra gasped, just before he seized her arms, firmly but not hurtfully. What was he doing now?

He said softly, "I rarely make errors of judgment."

His gaze was searching, and she could not look away. Her heart was thundering so loudly, she was certain he could hear it. "You have made such an error this time."

"I do not think so. I believe you are determined to accept the squire out of economic necessity."

"And if I am?"

He suddenly slid his thumb across her jaw. Pleasure exploded within her body, while she trembled in despair. He murmured, "I intend to be a very generous benefactor."

It was so hard to comprehend him when he was caressing her face with his thumb. Desire was a huge fist now, deep in her stomach, churning the confusion there.

"I look forward to being generous with you in all possible ways, Alexandra," he said throatily.

There was no mistaking the desire in his tone, no mistaking the lust smoldering in his eyes. She trembled, breathed, meant to pull away, meant to refute him. But she did not do any of those things.

He tilted up her chin. "You are sodden, even disheveled, but even so, you are capable of taking my breath away."

"Stop," she tried to say, but she wasn't sure she'd even spoken aloud.

His long, thick lashes lowered, and then

his face moved closer to hers.

He was going to kiss her.

She went still, her mind going blank. She forgot about everything, including why she'd come to Clarewood that afternoon. All she knew was that he was about to kiss her, and her body exploded in a frenzy of excitement

Clasping her shoulders, he brushed his firm mouth over hers, not once, but several times.

Alexandra did not move, stunned by the sensation of his lips on hers, her entire body a sudden conflagration of desire and urgent need. She caught his massive shoulders. She felt him smile. She softened in response.

Why was she denying him?

He made a sound and claimed her mouth, opening it, hard.

She cried out, throwing her arms around him, pressing close as he wrapped her tightly in his embrace, their tongues instantly entwining. He was hard and stiff against her hip. Excitement blinded her. She desperately need to be in this man's powerful arms, just as she desperately needed his mouth on hers and his hard, aroused male body pressing insistently against her.

Alexandra kissed him back.

Not softly, not gently, and not as a genteel

woman might. She kissed him wildly, urgently, demanding he open for her, trying to drink all of him in. He grunted, the sound one of triumph. His grasp on her tightened, every inch of his body straining against her now. She did not know how long they stood there that way, in a fierce, deep kiss, his tongue questing against the back of her throat, his manhood massively aroused against her pelvis. She wanted to shout his name and weep in pleasure — she wanted to demand more, beg for more. There was desire, and there was relief. There was joy.

How had she managed, these past nine years?

And then he broke the shocking kiss.

His handsome image swam before her as he held her so she would not fall, regarding her closely, his eyes ablaze. Alexandra clung, dazed. Sanity slowly returned.

And when her vision became focused and she saw how fiercely aroused he was — and how pleased — when she felt her own aroused body, and knew what it signaled, she released his shoulders. Shock washed through her.

Dismay rapidly followed.

What had she just done?

"You will stay for supper," he said flatly.

She shook her head and tried to back

away. For one moment he did not release her, his eyes widening with surprise. "No. I cannot. Let me go . . . please!"

She did not know if he released her or if she broke free. Their gazes remained locked, his now dark with what appeared to be anger. "If you are playing games, Alexandra, then you are a superb player, the best I have encountered."

Now he thought her the sort of woman who would toy with a man. She turned and ran for the door, horrified by his indictment and her own moral failure. She was too distressed to think clearly or hear if he was following her. She ran through the house, so intent on escape, she did not pause in the front hall to ask for her coat. She reached the door before the startled doorman, now fighting tears. *What was wrong with her?* As she wrenched the handle, the doorman opened it for her, and she ran outside and down the front steps, into the rain.

Her carriage was not in sight. She realized the mare had been taken to the stables at her own request. She choked down tears. What had she done?

"Miss Bolton." Clarewood's tone was like the lash of a whip. He held an umbrella over her.

She refused to turn and look at him; instead, she started resolutely for the stables.

He followed, holding the umbrella over her head.

His strides were longer than hers, and he seized her arm as he came abreast of her, his face hard with anger. "Stop."

"Let go."

"You remain soaking wet, and your nag will never make it back to Edgemont Way."

She finally looked into his piercing blue eyes, wrenching free. "So what would you have me do?" she asked hysterically. "Remain here with you, give in to your needs, satisfy your desire, your command?"

In spite of his anger, he spoke quietly now. "I am sorry you are in such a moral dilemma. And I will hardly hold you captive, Alexandra. Leave the mare. She can rest here. I will send you home after you have dried off. And I will leave you to your own devices while you do so."

She stared at him.

He stared coldly back. "But I suggest you reconsider the benefits of involvement with me, especially in light of what just happened."

CHAPTER SEVEN

"Alexandra," her father said jovially the next day. "Did I tell you? The squire will be coming to dine with us tonight."

It was half past ten the following morning, and Olivia was preparing Edgemont's breakfast, as she always did. Their father could not rouse himself any earlier, due to his late hours and his consumption of alcohol. Alexandra had set up her ironing board in one corner of the kitchen and was pressing the last ball gown from the Harrington Hall birthday party, having stayed up virtually all night. "No, Father, I do not think you told us that," she said calmly, when she was anything but.

Clarewood had been true to his word. He'd returned her to the front of the fire in the blue-and-gold salon, and then he had vanished. It had taken her a good hour to dry off, and in the interim she had been served a hot meal, which she had tried to decline, but then she had thought the better of it — the journey back to Edgemont would be a long, wet and cold one. But she had been wrong; his coach was well equipped, and as dry as a summer cupboard. Hot bricks had been placed on the carriage floors, furs on the backseat. The roof did not leak. The windows had glass. The return trip to Edgemont Way had been so pleasant that she had eventually managed to fall asleep — in spite of her distress and despair.

Now she carefully concentrated on the task at hand — she would have to replace a costly gown if she ever ruined one. But no matter how hard she stared at the gown and the iron, it was Clarewood's dark blue eyes that she saw. No matter how tightly she gripped the iron, it was his muscular shoulders she felt. Her despair was complete. All she wished to do was forget he even existed.

Last night Edgemont had been out when she had returned. It was the day's one saving grace. She had not been able to form a reasonable or believable explanation for why she was coming home in the duke's magnificent coach. Fortunately, she hadn't had to deliver one.

But Corey and Olivia had been speechless. Then they had pestered her with questions.

Refusing to answer a single one, she'd stumbled upstairs, where one of his burgundy roses sat on her dresser in a big vase, and her distress was renewed all over again.

It was impossible to be fully diverted by her father's declaration now. She had a meal to plan, and very few funds with which to do so. Carefully pressing a raspberry-red silk sleeve, she said, "Did you explain to the squire that we dine at seven?"

"He plans to come a bit earlier, for a sherry. He said he wishes to have a private discussion with me." Edgemont was obviously pleased.

Alexandra felt her heart lurch with dismay as she set the iron down on the wood cutting board by the sink. Clarewood's powerful image remained front and center in her mind; when she looked at her father, it was the duke that she saw. And his eyes were filled with anger.

He had hated being rejected.

But there had been no other possible recourse.

Her mind tried to veer to the passionate kiss they had shared. Moisture welled in her eyes, and it was suddenly hard to breathe. She did not know why she was so sad. She must never allow herself to remember, not even for an instant, that shockingly passionate encounter.

"I wonder what he wishes to say." Edgemont grinned.

She faced her father and tried to smile in return. Surely Denney would not offer for her now. It was too soon, no matter that he had said he intended to make haste with his suit. "I hope he won't mind a roasted chicken." It would be a respectable main course, and not a costly one.

Olivia set a plate down on the kitchen table, one containing a single poached egg and two slices of toast. Ham, sausage and bacon had vanished from their pantry long ago.

"He is so besotted with you, I'm sure you could serve him gizzards and he'd be pleased."

Absolutely dismayed and confounded, Alexandra turned away. She carefully turned over the dress, then retrieved the iron. But it had already cooled.

"Alexandra, you already did that side," Olivia said softly, her gaze worried.

Alexandra dared to meet her sister's eyes, incapable of summoning up even a false smile. "You're right. Silly me."

It was over now. And there was no reason

to be so distressed.

But it was as if she'd gone back in time to the days when she'd trysted with Owen — except that she wasn't certain she had ever felt such an explosion of desire.

She missed Owen so much. It had become painful all over again.

Edgemont was wolfing down his egg and toast. He'd already stated he would be gone for the day. Alexandra had no idea where he was going, nor did she particularly care. She carried the dress from the room, Olivia following on her heels.

Edgemont called after them, "Make certain you serve a fine meal tonight, Alexandra. Spare no expense!"

She did not answer, carefully hanging up the dress in the hall.

Olivia said, "Why won't you talk about whatever it was that happened yesterday? I am so worried."

Alexandra did not want her sisters worrying about her. She placed the hanger on the coatrack and turned. "There is nothing to worry about. I explained my situation to the duke. There will be no more inappropriate advances."

"You are near tears," Olivia pointed out. "You cannot even form a smile. What happened? Was he unkind? Cruel? All kinds of terrible imaginings are dancing about in my head!"

Alexandra put her arm around her. "Oh, Olivia. He was so very angry. He did not take my rejection lightly. But it is over, and there is no valid reason for me to remain upset."

"Yet you *are* upset!"

She would never tell Olivia about the kiss. And she could not tell her that she missed Owen and what they had shared, and thought about him now as she hadn't in years — while his image faded in and out, being constantly replaced by the duke's. Olivia would use that as ammunition against the squire and his suit. "I am just overtired," she said, and it was partly the truth. She forced a smile. "At least Bonnie is on a holiday. She is probably in the finest stall she has ever known, with more hay than she knows what to do with."

Olivia did not smile. Her gaze was searching. "Something happened at Clarewood, and you are not telling me. We have never had secrets before."

Alexandra bit her lip. Tears formed. "He kissed me."

Olivia gasped.

"I am sorry," Alexandra said, leaning against the wall. "I'd forgotten what it is like to be kissed by a young, handsome man."

"He isn't young. He is thirty or so," Olivia said. "What a despicable cad."

"Yes, he is despicable." But the moment she spoke, just as she heard her father approaching, she was aware that she didn't believe her own words. The two sisters shared a look and smiled at him as he ambled past, reaching for his coat. "Have a good day, Father."

"Spare no expense, Alexandra," he admonished, beaming. "And wear something pretty." He walked out of the house.

They waited until the door had closed and then looked at each other again. Olivia shook her head. "So I was wrong about his intentions. I am sorry, Alexandra."

"It's all right. It is over." She was firm. Nothing felt over, really, but she had to think about the evening to come. There was so much to do. "We need to start housecleaning. Where is Corey?"

"I'll get her," Olivia said.

For the next hour or so, the sisters swept, mopped and dusted the house in preparation for their dinner guest. Alexandra still could not shake Clarewood from her mind. Nor could she understand her sudden despondence. And she continued to miss

Owen terribly. It was as if Clarewood had taken a knife and sliced open all her old wounds.

Alexandra and Corey began to polish the wood furniture. Olivia was sweeping the front steps, the new day a bright, cold and sunny one, when she came rushing back into the house. "Alexandra, come quickly!"

Alexandra felt her heart lurch in alarm. She had the immediate and odd notion that Clarewood had sent her another gift; instantly, she told herself that she was wrong. She hurried outside, Corey on her heels. And she saw that Clarewood had sent her carriage home, but Bonnie was not in the traces. A beautiful, young, powerful black horse was pulling the carriage, instead.

"Where is Bonnie?" Olivia whispered.

"Look at that horse!" Corey exclaimed.

The gelding was part draught horse, clearly. He could undoubtedly go back and forth to Clarewood several times in a single day without even tiring, and probably pull a wagon filled with mortar and bricks the entire time. And now she saw Randolph's splendid hunter tied behind the carriage, and instantly realized he was driving it. He waved at them.

What was Clarewood up to now?

She was alarmed. She was dismayed. She

was also oddly breathless.

Randolph halted the carriage and braked it, leaping easily out as only a young man can do. He sauntered up the brick path to where they stood, just in front of the house. "Good day, ladies," he said gaily.

Alexandra hugged herself, while Corey asked, "Where is Bonnie?"

"Your mare remains at Clarewood. I am afraid she is lame, but do not be alarmed, His Grace has a singular veterinarian, and rest assured the mare will be ready to return home in five or six weeks. Apparently she has bowed a tendon."

"Five or six weeks!" Corey exclaimed in open dismay. "She's our only carriage horse! How will we get on?"

She turned to Alexandra, who inhaled. "Father will have to give up his mount, that is all. It is only temporary."

"He will never do such a thing," Olivia said softly.

"Ladies, have no fear," Randolph interjected, smiling. "His Grace wishes for you to have use of Ebony until the mare can come home."

Alexandra looked at him in astonishment. "I beg your pardon?" She looked at the powerful black gelding again.

"You may borrow Ebony until the mare

returns," he said firmly. "His Grace insists."

She jerked her gaze away from the striking horse. Randolph was staring at her — as if expecting a debate. Clarewood had sent them a horse. It was a thoughtful gesture, a generous one.

I will be a very generous benefactor.

I suggest you reconsider our involvement.

"He is lovely," Corey whispered. "He is the most beautiful horse I have ever laid my eyes on. Can he go under saddle?"

Randolph looked at her. "Yes, he hacks very well. Do you like to ride, Miss Bolton?"

"Of course I do, but it has been years since I have done so." She shrugged, the gesture feminine and helpless. "I have never had a mount of my own, sir, but as a child, I used to gallop Bonnie bareback all over the countryside."

"Corey," Olivia rebuked.

Alexandra barely heard them. She was shaken. Was this gesture an act of consideration and kindness? Or did it mean that he intended to continue his pursuit after all?

She looked at Randolph, breathing hard — as if she'd run back and forth to the house several times. "We appreciate the offer. It is very thoughtful and terribly magnanimous. But I am afraid we cannot accept even the temporary use of such a horse." But what she really wanted to say was that she could not accept the use of *his* horse, not now and not ever.

"Why not?" Corey screeched at her.

Randolph's eyes were wide, but he seemed to be restraining a smile. "Miss Bolton, His Grace insists. Why not humor him?"

She stared. It was so very hard to think clearly. "May we have a private word, sir?"

Before he could answer, Corey seized her arm, her green eyes blazing. "Alexandra, I love that horse. We need that horse. We cannot get on, even for six weeks, without a carriage horse. Look at him! If you send him back, I am never speaking to you again."

Olivia took Corey's arm. "Let's step inside." She looked at Alexandra meaningfully before she left. "I am siding with Corey, Alexandra. We do need a carriage horse. It is only a loan. Do not send him back."

Alexandra refused to speak. She waited until they were gone before turning her gaze back to Randolph. "I believe I have explained my situation to you, sir."

"It is only a horse."

"It is a very expensive horse, one that belongs to Clarewood."

Randolph folded his arms. "He said you'd refuse."

She started.

He smiled. "Come, Miss Bolton, why refuse? He will not give up, especially not in this instance — he truly wishes to help you in your time of need."

How could she answer that? "If only I believed you, sir."

"I am not allowed to return with Ebony," he added. Then, slyly, "So I am leaving him here, in your stable. So if you truly feel driven to return him, you will have to do so yourself."

Her defeat was complete. She would never go back to Clarewood, not even to return the horse. So she must accept his gift. The Duke of Clarewood had won.

"Has anyone ever told you just how clever you are?" Elysse asked, smiling, as the handsome St. Xavier coach turned down Pall Mall.

Ariella smiled at her friend. "Actually, this was Emilian's idea. He pointed out that Mr. Jefferson is courting my father and I could surely use that to our advantage." She warmed impossibly as she thought about her husband. It had been seven years now, and they had two beautiful children, a son and a daughter, but she loved him more than ever. Although he had been dark and distant and so intimidating when they had first met, he was now far more than a lover and a husband — he was her best friend and closest confidant. He'd been amused when she'd begun to tell him about their plans to ignore Clarewood's plans and encourage a match between the Dowager Duchess of Clarewood and the big, handsome American. But he'd also noticed the couple and agreed that there was obviously some connection between them.

"We will tell Mr. Jefferson that my father suggested I show him London. Being as he is eager to do business with my father, I doubt he will refuse our offer." Ariella smiled, pleased with their scheme.

"And we will just happen to drive by Constance Hall, and when we do, it is incumbent upon us that we call." Elysse grinned and squeezed her friend's hand.

"We can only put the two of them in the same room," Ariella said. "After that, it is up to them."

"Not necessarily," Elysse said, dropping her hand.

Ariella looked carefully at her beautiful friend, who was somber now, and she instantly knew that Elysse was thinking about the beginning of her own marriage and the six terrible years of separation that had immediately followed their vows.

She had suffered terribly. Alexi would probably never admit it, but Ariella knew her brother, and she was sure he had suffered, as well. His anger had been a disguise. But in the end, they had reconciled, and Ariella knew they were deliriously happy together. She had never dreamed her rakehell brother could turn into a devoted husband.

"Sometimes a couple needs a helping hand." Elysse smiled grimly at her. "Alexi and I might still be living apart if you hadn't encouraged me to pursue and seduce him."

"Those were terrible times," Ariella said softly. "And I am glad they are over and you are so enamored now."

Elysse smiled brightly, her brief lapse into the past over. "My point is, there is a gulf between Julia and Jefferson. She is a dowager duchess, he a rancher. She is English, he is American. She has a fortune, he does not. If there is a deep attraction, they might need some help overcoming their apparent differences."

"Has anyone ever told you how clever you are?" Ariella asked.

"Only my terribly dashing husband."

■ ■ ■ ■

Tyne Jefferson had refused to take the forward-facing seat, even though the two young ladies had tried to insist upon it. Instead, he sat across from them in the rear-facing seat, his long, strong legs crossed. He might be an American who had traversed the country three times before there had been a transcontinental railroad, meaning he had bested both mountains and deserts, suffered through heat waves and blizzards, while surviving Indians and wolves, not to mention just plain bad men, but when around the fair sex, he considered himself a gentleman of sorts. At least he would always try to be on his best behavior.

Cliff de Warenne's daughter was pointing out another landmark, this one the home of a renowned British artist. He was bemused. He'd been very surprised when the two ladies had appeared at his hotel, sweetly introducing themselves and asking if they could give him the grand tour of London. And even when Cliff's daughter had explained that her father had suggested they call on him and make him feel at home, he sensed a plot and a scheme. But he couldn't imagine what the conspiracy might be, and he was not about to refuse Cliff's daughter, not when he was trying to convince the man to start a shipping line in Sacramento. Besides, his time in town was limited. He was more than happy to take in every sight that he could.

But two hours had elapsed and they were no longer in town. He never went anywhere without studying maps first, and he knew they were in Greenwich. This was a suburb where the titled and the rich resided. It was a beautiful part of greater London, filled with palatial homes and smaller mansions, with carefully tended gardens and tree-lined drives. His bemusement had increased. "Should we go back to town? If you ladies care to join me, we can take tea, as you put it, at the hotel. And I can repay you for your hospitality."

Lady St. Xavier smiled oddly at him. "You hardly need to repay us, Mr. Jefferson."

"It's just Jefferson," he said.

Mrs. de Warenne blinked a bit innocently and said, "Oh, look. Constance Hall. I wonder if the dowager duchess is in."

His heart slammed.

"I believe you have met the dowager duchess, have you not?" Lady St. Xavier said, far too sweetly. "If she is in, we should call. Our families are very close, and I did not get to speak to her at any length at the Harrington ball."

He stared at the pale white pillars and the closed iron gates that barred trespassers from entering the grounds. His pulse had calmed now. But he wasn't very happy with his reaction to their *accidental* arrival at the duchess's home.

He looked at the two women, who smiled innocently at him. There was nothing accidental about this, he decided. But he could not imagine why they had brought him to call on the dowager duchess. He did not have business with her. If this was social, he could accept that. But in that case, why bring him there with so much subterfuge?

Surely they did not have matchmaking on their minds!

Her image came forcefully to his mind, pale, blond and beautiful. "I don't mind stopping by," he said slowly. And it was the truth. The dowager duchess was one of the most interesting women he had ever met. But then, where he came from, the female gender was rare, ladies even more so.

And as the coachman was instructed to turn into the drive, he had to admit to his tension. He rubbed his suddenly stiff neck, wondering at it. He almost felt nervous. He was never nervous, not even when facing a mountain lion on foot and in the dark.

If someone had ever asked him to imagine a duchess, he would have imagined a lady exactly like Julia Mowbray, but he hadn't realized a woman could truly be so elegant and so refined, so graceful and so gracious. He hadn't realized anyone could be so wealthy. He'd been very surprised to receive her invitation to the ball. He'd accepted mostly because he had never been to a ball before — not even in his younger days in Boston.

Since they'd met at a supper party last week, he had tried hard to think of her as a dowager duchess and not as a beautiful woman. But when they'd spoken that night, it had been clear how intelligent she was, and how gracious — causing his admiration to grow. It had been hard not to steal glances at her all night.

He'd bumped into her on the street a few days later. She'd been shopping with a friend, and he'd been alone, doing the same thing. He'd meant to merely say hello, the polite thing to do, but that simple greeting had turned into half an hour of conversation.

A man would have to be blind not to notice the dowager duchess's petite figure and pale beauty, her femininity and grace.

But it was all wrong. He had no right to think of her as a woman. He needed to remind himself that she was a duchess . . . and a lady. Not only was she out of his league, he would never lay a hand on a woman like that. It would be the height of disrespect.

He liked his women hot and lusty, anyway. Ladies did not enjoy sex, they suffered it. So that was another reason to keep things tidy and neat — not to mention polite and respectful — between them.

But he'd had a really good time at the ball — and not because of the hoity-toity crowd. And damn it, now he was nervous.

"I hope this isn't an intrusion," he said flatly, as her doormen opened their carriage doors for them.

"She will be thrilled to see us," Mrs. de Warenne said. "We are close friends with her son and have been so since childhood."

He made a mocking sound. Clarewood had been overbearing and arrogant, as if he thought the world of himself. "Ah yes, I've had the pleasure of meeting the Grand Duke."

Lady St. Xavier looked at him seriously. "There is more to Stephen than meets the eye," she said. "He may have airs, but he is at the forefront of reform. He is renowned for his philanthropy — he has built and maintains hospitals and asylums all over the country, and he is currently building proper housing for the working poor."

He hadn't realized that. Still, Clarewood had been an ass. "I'm sure he's a swell fellow." He realized he was about to get in really hot water, so he smiled at her and added, "I am very impressed."

A moment later they were in the dowager duchess's entry hall — which was the size of many northern California frontier homes. The women handed a butler their cards, which he promptly put on his small silver tray, asking them to wait. A few minutes later they were shown into a magnificent salon with turquoise-painted walls, gold wainscoting and plasterwork and gilded furniture.

He realized his heart was beating just a bit more swiftly than usual. He told himself to get a grip and grow up. She was a *duchess*, for God's sake.

And then, just as the two ladies were taking their seats, she came gliding into the room.

He was surprised, because she was in a riding habit, one with split skirts. And while it was an elegant outfit, it was somehow so feminine, an effect that was dissipated not a bit when he saw a bit of mud on her black boots — and noticed small, English spurs. He jerked his gaze to her face. She was flushed from the outdoors, while several pale tendrils had come loose from the chignon she seemed to favor and curled about her face.

He was incredulous. His heart was thundering.

She instantly went to the women and embraced them, kissing their cheeks warmly. "This is such a delightful surprise!" she exclaimed.

His heart was racing. He'd never seen her look as lovely, and he reminded himself to cool down. But he couldn't get over the fact that she had been on the back of a horse. He'd assumed she was always driven around. And she had long hair. . . .

She turned to face him, smiling politely. "I am so pleased you have called, Mr. Jefferson."

He'd learned his manners and took her hand, kissing the air above it, hating the foolish gesture. Her hand was small and petite in his own rather large one. "The ladies insisted we drop by. I hope it's all right." He meant his every word, and he looked into her eyes, wondering if she was really pleased to see him. And now he caught the scent of female perspiration, sweaty horse and something crisp, like the turning autumn leaves, mixed with lilies. His damned loins stirred.

And then he realized he was still holding her hand and quickly dropped it.

"I am very pleased that you have joined Elysse and Ariella," she said, and the color in her cheeks was a bit brighter now. "And I must apologize for my appearance. I didn't realize you would be calling, and I'm afraid the time simply slipped away. It usually does when I am riding."

Like an idiot, he stared. She rode often, and she enjoyed it enough to lose track of the time.

It was Lady St. Xavier who broke the silence. "The dowager duchess is one of our most renowned equestrians."

He looked at the young lady, wondering what that meant.

The dowager duchess said softly, "I enjoy my horses very much. Do you like horses, Mr. Jefferson? I imagine they are the life-blood of your ranch."

He came to his senses. And even though he wasn't sure he should tell her about life on a ranch, he explained, "I run five thou-sand head of cattle, Your Grace. In the spring, they're turned out, and by summer, they're in the high country. We round them up in the fall. It takes a few weeks. No cowboy could get the job done without having a couple of good horses." He was surprised at how rapt she was. Was she really interested? *She was a renowned equestrian?*

She said, "I've never tried to imagine a roundup before."

"It is hard work, and it can be dangerous. You don't want to be near a stampede." And then he wished he hadn't said that, because he knew the English aristocracy had a disdain for hard work. But she really seemed to be interested.

"I would love to see a roundup," she said softly.

He was speechless, because clearly she meant her every word. *What if he invited her to California?*

"Have you ever ridden in a foxhunt, Mr. Jefferson?" she asked, smiling. "It is the sport I prefer."

He went still, wondering if he'd misheard. "You hunt foxes — on horseback?" Did this woman chase a fox across the countryside, astride, with a pack of hounds?

She smiled. "Yes, I do, and I am rather passionate about it. You should join us in a foxhunt, if you can. The hounds are given a scent, and then they set chase. We follow on horseback, wherever we have to go." She met his gaze and stared.

He remained incredulous. "I've never been to — or seen — a foxhunt. But I've read about the sport. Aren't jumps involved?"

"Yes, there are fences — and other obstacles — of all kinds. In fact, the master of the hunt often works with a course designer to add interesting obstacles to the terrain. Our mounts are expected to take hedges, as well as stone walls and fallen trees. Balking is considered extremely bad form." And now, as she spoke, her eyes were shining — and still locked with his.

This woman rode in foxhunts. She jumped her horse over fallen trees and stone walls. It was amazing. He would never have guessed that the pretty little dowager duchess was such a horsewoman. "The fences are small, I hope," he somehow managed to say.

She laughed, and the happy sound made his heart leap. "That would not be very amusing, Mr. Jefferson. Nor would it be very challenging."

"Of course not," he managed.

"If you wish, I can show you my stable sometime. I have one of the best hunting strings in the country. And I will admit I've bred most of the barn myself."

She bred horses, too. He was going to have to reassess, he realized. Breeding was as earthy as anything could be. "I'd like to see your horses," he said gruffly, then added, "when it's convenient."

"You seem very surprised," she suddenly said, but her blue gaze was direct. "And if I am boring you, I apologize, but I am very passionate about my horses. And, of course, I am allowed my eccentricities. I even feel I deserve them. I'll show you my hounds, as well, if you wish. They are a formidable pack."

He was recovering somewhat. "I'll bet. Do you breed them, too?"

"Of course. The hounds need to have the drive to pursue prey, and we breed specifically for that drive."

"I'd like to join a foxhunt before I leave," he suddenly said. He wanted to watch the duchess ride.

"I'll try to arrange it. But it may take a while. Would you care to ride with me sometime?"

He looked at her now. She'd just extended another invitation to him. Why? And why was she even alone? Why hadn't she remarried? "If it's no trouble, I'd like that." Almost disbelievingly, he heard the seductive tone of his own voice.

She must have heard it, too, because she flushed. "It would be my pleasure," she returned slowly.

He had stopped smiling. So had she. And he was staring when he knew he should stop — but she was returning his gaze.

He was genuinely surprised when one of the younger ladies said, "Why don't you show Mr. Jefferson your house dogs?"

He'd forgotten about the other two women. He turned — suspicious now — because he thought there was laughter hidden in Lady St. Xavier's tone. But he met a pair of straight faces and wide, unblinking eyes. Then he glanced at the duchess, who quickly smiled, as gracious as ever. While his own heart kept thundering.

"When you next call, Mr. Jefferson, I will give you a tour of both the stables and my kennels." She looked at the two young women. "I'm sure Mr. Jefferson has no interest in my personal dogs."

"Thank you. I'd like that. And I'd like to see your lapdogs," he added, mostly to be polite.

She looked at him oddly and went to the door and said, "Send Henry and Matilda in, please."

He knew a pair of fluffy, noisy lapdogs

would be released into the room any moment, and he felt some relief, because that was how he wanted to think of her, as a regal, elegant untouchable duchess, seated in all her finery in her fancy gold salon in her palatial mansion, with a pair of silly lapdogs by her side.

A moment later, a pair of black Great Danes almost as tall as she was came trotting into the room. Instinctively, he backed up.

"Don't worry," the dowager duchess said. "They are well trained and only attack if I say so."

CHAPTER EIGHT

Alexandra sat with her sisters in the parlor, clasping her hands tightly in her lap. The chicken was roasting and red potatoes were baking, along with a vegetable dish. A purchased pie was in the icebox. A bottle of red wine had been opened. The dining-room table had been set with their best plates and crystal, two silver candlesticks in its center. Everything was ready for the squire.

And no one said a word.

The squire and her father had been closeted in his library for well over half an hour. By now they'd had at least one sherry. When they finally came back into the parlor, Alexandra was afraid of what would happen next.

To complicate matters further, Edgemont had seen Ebony. Corey had developed the lie. She had baldly told him that the horse was a temporary loan from Lady Harrington, of all people. According to Corey, they'd called earlier to thank her for the ball, and Bonnie had gone lame. Edgemont had believed her, had in fact been pleased. They knew he was thinking about using the horse, himself.

Olivia reached for her hand. "Maybe they are discussing the races. Please do not worry."

Newmarket would close in a few weeks. The last races of the season were on everyone's mind. "I'm fine," Alexandra lied.

"You're as white as a ghost. And you're trembling," Corey said. "If they return to us and declare a betrothal, you must stand up for your rights and refuse."

Alexandra was grim. "I will do no such thing," she began, and even as she spoke, the library door opened and the two men came ambling out, both smiling so widely that clearly they were in vast accord on something. Her heart clenched. She was certain they'd decided on the betrothal, and she reminded herself that this opportunity was a miracle, one that would benefit everyone, including herself. And she was not going to think about Clarewood now.

"We have news," Edgemont declared, beaming.

Alexandra stood up, refusing to look at

her sisters now, trying to smile. "I can see that you are both pleased."

The squire strode up to her, reaching for her hands. Oddly, today his palms felt clammy. "My dear, I have asked for your hand, and your father has agreed!"

She looked into his shining eyes and wished he did not love her so much. It was so hard to speak. "How wonderful," she managed.

"There hasn't even been a courtship!" Corey exclaimed, flushing with outrage. "He's courted her for all of five days!"

Denney faltered, Edgemont was furious and Alexandra quickly turned. "Corey, the squire indicated that he would move swiftly, and I agreed."

"No, you did not!" Corey exclaimed, eyes ablaze. "You wished for a proper suit, and you said so."

Alexandra bit her lip, aware that Corey was desperate to prevent her from making this marriage purely because she loved her.

"One more word and you will go to your room!" Edgemont roared, trembling with rage.

"Don't worry, there is no place I would rather be, for I have no wish to see Alexandra sell herself off. She deserves love!" Corey glared at the squire, then ran upstairs.

A moment later they heard her door slam.

A shocked and awkward silence fell. Alexandra turned to Denney, afraid that he would despise her sister and retreat from his previously stated intentions to be generous with her entire family. She was determined to soothe him now. "I am so sorry. My sister is quite young. Please, forgive her this outburst."

Denney had paled. Grimly he said, "May we have a private word, Miss Bolton?"

Dread began. "Of course." Alexandra waited for Edgemont to escort Olivia into his library, where he shut the door. "I am so sorry," she said again, meaning it.

"Is it true? Did you yearn for a proper courtship?" he asked.

She swallowed. "This is indeed hasty, sir, but I am very fortunate, and I do not intend to quibble." But even as she spoke, her mind treacherously demanded that she do just that.

He touched her arm. "I am so eager to wed, Miss Bolton. I simply cannot wait."

She tensed. "I am flattered," she managed, then wondered if he was in such a rush that they would be married by week's end.

He touched her cheek, and Alexandra was immediately incredulous, and then she was aghast, for his fingers lingered on her jaw.

He said softly, "You do deserve love, Miss Bolton. On that score, I happen to agree with you sister."

"Very few marry for love," she managed, wanting to pull her head back.

He dropped his hand. "Miss Bolton . . . *I* am in love with *you*."

She wanted to cry out in dismay. And damn it, it was Clarewood's fierce image she now saw, there in her mind's eye. Shaken, she breathed out.

"In time, I believe you will come to love me, too," he murmured.

What could she possibly say to such a statement? "I hope so." Now all she could recall was Clarewood's anger at her rejection and the black horse that was in their stables.

He clasped her shoulder, smiling gently, and her alarm escalated wildly. His regard was so tender, but his eyes were warm, and she knew he was about to kiss her. Panic began.

He leaned toward her. Alexandra told herself not to move and reminded herself that there would be many kisses. My God, they would share a bed, there would be intimate relations. And that was as it should be. They were going to be man and wife — it was best for everyone.

I will be a generous benefactor.
I suggest you reconsider our involvement.

His dark blue eyes had been dark with anger, his voice filled with authority. It hadn't been a suggestion. . . .

The squire's mouth brushed hers.

And because, for one moment, she had been transported back in time, as if standing with Clarewood in the rain, she cried out, surprised. His hands tightened on her shoulders and his mouth firmed, becoming more demanding.

She pushed at his shoulders, horrified. Her body screamed at her to run away. She hated the feel of his mouth, its taste, his touch. She did not want to do this!

He pulled away abruptly.

Alexandra backed up, trembling with shock. *She had hated his touching her.*

She would never love this man.

"Please forgive me," he rasped. "I was overcome by your beauty, Miss Bolton."

She somehow shook her head, wanting to wipe her mouth with her sleeve. "You are forgiven," she managed.

"Truly? I can see that I have shocked you. I am so very sorry."

"I was surprised," she somehow said. "It is forgotten, Mr. Denney. Oh! I have a chicken in the oven! Will you excuse me?"

With that, Alexandra fled.

After supper, when Denney was gone, Alexandra sat down on her bed, her bedroom door locked. She couldn't recall the last time she had locked her door; maybe she never had. Now she picked up a pillow and hugged it, staring at the burgundy roses on the bureau. In her mind's eye, Clarewood seemed mocking now, as if he'd told her so.

How do you feel about the squire?

Had he guessed that she could not care for or desire Morton Denney? Had he somehow known?

I hardly mind a rival.

Or was it simply that he was so arrogant that he knew there could not be a competition? How could anyone compare the handsome, powerful duke with the kind, elderly squire?

I am taken with you . . . I believe you are taken with me.

I will be a generous benefactor.

She started to cry. How was she going to marry the squire, never mind that he was so kind and generous, and that he was in love with her? His kiss had repulsed her. But in Clarewood's arms, she had been in a delirium of rapture. Worse, she had felt so oddly safe.

She was a shameless woman, that had become clear, to dream about and want a man who wanted only to make her his mistress. It had been different with Owen; they had intended marriage. She had loved him. She didn't love Clarewood. And there was *nothing* safe about him. He meant to ruin her — even though he would be financially generous.

What was she going to do?

Alexandra lay down and stared at the ceiling, cuddling her pillow, forcing her thoughts of Clarewood aside. Instead, she imagined herself the mistress of Fox Run, the wife of Squire Denney. She tried to imagine living in his handsome home, keeping the household, managing the staff. She saw herself arranging flowers in the grand salon, then sitting down to lunch with her sisters, a meal she had not been forced to prepare herself. And they were served by his two maids.

Then she imagined the squire appearing during their meal, beaming at her, kissing her warmly and sitting down to join them. Dismay rose up.

She would pretend to be pleased to see him and have him join them, when she wouldn't really care at all. She might even wish he'd allowed her a private luncheon with her sisters.

Tears leaked again.

She was not going to feel sorry for herself! There might be children. She'd wanted children once. She loved children and she knew she would be a good mother. So she changed the scene. Now two little girls raced about the dining room as she enjoyed a luncheon with her sisters and her husband. They were so pretty, one brown haired, one blond — they resembled Corey and Olivia as children. Her distress increased.

She imagined her sisters having handsome husbands and added them to the table. Everyone was smiling and content — the little girls, her sisters, their husbands, the squire. Everyone except herself . . .

The luncheon became supper. Everyone was in evening clothes — her sisters were so fashionable now. Olivia even wore pearls. And the supper was over. The squire was sending her warm looks. She was forcing a smile, going upstairs. He followed. And then he came up behind her and wrapped her in his arms, instantly amorous. She simply stood there and let him nuzzle her.

Alexandra sat bolt upright, clutching the pillow, Clarewood's roses front and center in her vision now. *She could not do this.*

She wanted to go through with it, she truly

did, and she wanted to be a loving wife. But she did not love the squire. She would never love him. He was too old, and the only man she'd ever loved and would ever love was Owen. He had been a prince. She deserved a prince!

Clarewood mocked her now. Even his roses mocked her!

And she wished her mother were there. "What am I going to do?" she asked the empty room.

The bedroom had a single window. Outside, the night was black and a few stars were shining. And suddenly Elizabeth was standing in front of the window. She could see her mother so clearly now, as if she were real, and not a warm and wonderful memory. As always, her mother was calm and reassuring. *You will do what you have to do.*

She hugged her knees to her chest. Elizabeth had been so happy that she'd found love with Owen. Her sisters were right, her mother would not approve of the squire.

"But he loves me."

You don't love him.

She would never love the squire. "I so wanted to save my sisters from destitution."

Elizabeth smiled. *He is not your prince.*

She looked again at the burgundy roses,

thinking of Clarewood, who was as close to a prince as a man could be, in every possible way. He would be generous. He had said so. His fortune made Denney look like a pauper.

Oh, God, what was she thinking?

What she was thinking was that if she turned the squire away, her sisters did not have to continue on as impoverished young women with no possible future. If she turned the squire away, she could turn to the duke, who would be generous with her.

Alexandra bit down hard on her lip. He had said he would be generous. And she would not mind being in his arms. To the contrary. She felt as if she *needed* his embrace, his passion. No, she did not need him; it was only that she missed Owen, who belonged to another now, and it had been so long. . . .

You deserve love.

She jumped, looking at her mother, recalling Corey's words. "He doesn't love me. It will be merely an arrangement."

And it would be short-term. It would not be for life.

Her mother smiled.

Alexandra hugged the pillow harder, knowing that if her illicit affair were ever discovered, her fall from grace would irrevocably ruin her sisters. So there were terrible pitfalls ahead — if she really meant to go forward.

"What should I do?" she asked.

Elizabeth came forward, touching her hair, the caress a maternal one. *I never meant for you to sacrifice yourself for your sisters, Alexandra. And I believe that deep within yourself, you know that.*

Her mother had never meant for her to sacrifice herself, but taking care of her sisters hadn't been a sacrifice, had it? She smiled tearfully, but suddenly Elizabeth was gone.

It didn't matter. One thing was clear. She could not marry the squire. And her relief was overwhelming.

"You locked your door last night," Corey said, wide-eyed.

"I needed some privacy," Alexandra told her, hurrying downstairs. Her mind was made up. She would not marry the squire and spend her life as his wife. She'd spent a very sleepless night, thinking about the duke and the arrangement he had in mind. There was trepidation, but there was also so much relief.

Alexandra smiled at Corey and Olivia now. "By the way, I have changed my mind.

I am not marrying the squire."

Their eyes widened.

Alexandra reached the ground floor; Edgemont had not answered his door, and she assumed he'd fallen asleep in the library. He hadn't gone out the night before. He'd gotten foxed at supper, instead, drinking several bottles of red wine.

He was indeed in the library, asleep on the small sofa. Alexandra strode over to him and shook his shoulder. "Father? I am sorry to awaken you, but we must have a talk."

He winced, waking immediately, sitting up. "What? What time is it? Did I fall asleep?" The bleary look left his eyes. "You got engaged, by God! This calls for a drink."

She clasped his shoulder, restraining him from getting up. "It's the next morning, Father." She turned. "Olivia, would you bring Father his coffee?"

"What time is it?" he groused, now glancing outside.

"It's only half past eight," she said, sitting down beside him. "Father, I have come to my senses. Olivia and Corey have been right all along. I cannot — and will not — marry the squire simply for the means he can provide us."

Edgemont seemed confused, and then he was clearly taken aback. "You were engaged last night, Alexandra," he warned.

"No, Father, you and Mr. Denney agreed to a betrothal, but no one has signed a contract, and I am not wearing a betrothal ring." She was firm.

He stood up; so did she. "We are signing contracts *tonight,*" he said ominously. "We are announcing the betrothal, as well."

She stiffened. "I will not marry him."

Edgemont's eyes widened. "You are the obedient one. You are the giving one. You are, in fact, exactly like your mother — the glue holding this family together. Of course you will marry Denney and save this family from ruin."

Guilt began. Clarewood seemed to give her a dark look, in her mind, as if he sensed she was about to back down and retreat. "I cannot marry him."

"You can and you will!" Edgemont shouted. "I am your father. I am head of this household. You will obey and respect me, Alexandra!"

She trembled. "Sign what you will. I am twenty-six years old, and legally, I am my own keeper — I cannot be forced into marriage against my will."

He trembled with rage, and Alexandra thought he might hit her, when he'd never laid a hand on her, not once in her life. "You will do as I say!" he commanded. "You will go to that altar!"

She shook her head, mouth pursed, hating having to refute him this way and reveal that he had no power, none. For, unless he physically dragged her into church, she was not going to marry Denney. They stared at one another, Edgemont trembling with rage, Alexandra grim with sorrow. Then she turned and left the room.

Her sisters were standing in the hall, Olivia holding a cup of coffee, both of them ashen. "What will you do now?" Olivia asked, her tone hushed.

Of course she could not tell them that she meant to accept Clarewood's indecent offer. She could not tell them that she meant to take him as a lover and accept payment in return. It was sordid. It was wrong. But her sisters would have a future, and it was better than a lifetime of pretense and compromise.

This time, the journey to Clarewood had been a swift and easy one — as far as the logistics of travel were concerned. Ebony had picked up a trot the moment she'd asked him to upon leaving the house, and he hadn't faltered even once since then. A glance at her pocket watch showed her that less than two hours had passed and they had just turned onto Clarewood's long shell drive, though the magnificent house was not yet in sight.

Her pulse raced. Her mouth was dry. She'd never been as nervous, not even the last time she had gone to Clarewood to return the roses and the diamond bracelet. He had won. Of course he had. Had the outcome of their contest ever been in dispute? she wondered.

And it would not be the end of the world. Some good would come of it. There would be no going back. Alexandra knew she was giving up all self-respect, but it seemed a small price to pay for her sisters' livelihoods.

And there was more. She might be losing self-respect, but when she thought of being in his strong arms, her heart leaped and raced, and her tension instantly changed in character. Her heart had been racing ever since leaving Edgemont Way. There was no denying that she felt anticipation as well as dismay. In a few more days she would be the Duke of Clarewood's mistress!

Alexandra inhaled. As Ebony trotted up the shell drive toward the fountain ahead, she reminded herself that she had to stay focused on the terms of their arrangement. She wished to have a complete and detailed understanding, one that would protect her interests — which included those of her sisters. She'd already decided to ask Clarewood to provide dowries for her sisters. The question was, how much more should she ask for?

Her stomach churned with revulsion. Corey had accused Edgemont of selling her off to Denney, but what she was doing now made her father's efforts to marry her off seem noble. She was selling her body to the duke. There was only one word to describe that. It would be so different if this was a love affair, or even one of purely physical passion.

She thought about turning back. It wasn't too late; they could continue on as they had for the past nine years. But Clarewood's image was so forceful now, compelling her, and her sisters' future was at stake.

"Ebony, whoa," she called, pulling on the reins.

And then she heard galloping hoofbeats coming up rapidly behind her. She twisted to look at the approaching horseman. And even before she could recognize the rider on the magnificent black stallion, she knew it was Clarewood.

He rode the way he did everything else — with power and authority, as if he were not just a prince but a king.

Her tension spiraled. He halted beside her carriage so precipitously that shells sprayed its wheels. As she stared, she realized he was even more dashing than usual in his riding clothes. And now that he was beside her, she once again had that odd sense of being safe.

Alexandra met his intense dark blue stare. It was filled with speculation. "Good afternoon," he said, his mouth softening. "Are you returning my horse?"

She trembled, her heart lurching. If she said yes, she would go home holding her head high. If she said no, she would begin a new journey, one that would change her life forever.

"Miss Bolton?" he murmured, still staring. "Can I entice you to come inside and take tea? Perhaps you can then work on forming the answer I wish to hear."

She wet her lips. "I am not returning the horse."

He started, and then, slowly, he smiled. "I see." He was obviously pleased. He gave her a direct look, one that caused her body to tighten impossibly, and he dismounted, leading his horse to the back of the carriage and tying him firmly there. Alexandra didn't move as he came around to the driver's side of her small vehicle. She wasn't sure she was even breathing. She was about to become his mistress, and she was acutely aware of the magnitude of that decision.

He smiled again. "May I?"

At first she didn't hear him, too busy staring at his handsome face, at his high cheekbones, that straight, patrician nose and those brilliantly blue eyes. She felt helpless and lost, a small rowboat churning in the sea of his charisma. Then, when he said her name, his tone more forceful now, she came to her senses, moving over so he could climb up and take the reins. "Of course."

But the moment he settled down on the seat beside her, it became even harder to think. Only centimeters separated them now. It was hard to breathe, even harder to pretend he did not affect her so completely. She was acutely aware of his big, male body, so close to her.

"I am thrilled to have your company," he remarked, driving the horse forward. "Can I assume the journey over was a pleasant one and that you are enjoying Ebony?"

She inhaled and realized he'd heard it. "It was very pleasant — in marked contrast to the other day."

He smiled, eying her closely now. "You seem overwrought, Miss Bolton."

She was not going to tell him how she felt, or why she felt as she did. "You are mistaken. I am . . . suffering from a mild migraine."

One brow arced upward, indicating mild disbelief. "We shall have to remedy that. My housekeeper has some miraculous potions. And how is your father?" he asked politely, as they rounded the fountain.

My father is furious with me. He continues to drink himself silly and to gamble our means away. She smiled. "Very well, thank you."

He gave her a sidelong look. "By the way, I happen to detest trivial speech and rarely find myself in the position of having to instigate it."

She turned to look at him, and their gazes locked. It was so hard to speak when he stared at her as he did, with slightly smoldering eyes. "If you must know, it has been years since I have been out in society. I'd forgotten how much casual banter there is. I am afraid I am now lacking in that particular social grace."

"Good," he said flatly, surprising her. "Can we agree that no conversation at all is better than the mundane and the inane?"

She inhaled sharply, surprised. "Yes, we can."

"So you will not mind long silences?"

She continued to stare, aware of how handsome he was, and now, how powerfully masculine. Did he know why she had come? Was he assuming there would be many more moments like this one? "I will not mind long silences."

He seemed amused. "Then you will be the first, Miss Bolton. And may I say that I find you refreshing and original in many respects?"

Her eyes widened. Surprise became an absurd pleasure. "Have you just flattered me, Your Grace?"

"I have." He halted the gelding in front of the house. "I have no patience for coquetry and am frankly bored with coquettes. I am glad you are not one of them."

She trembled, shocked. Was he implying that he was not only attracted to her but that he *liked* her?

He leaped down from the carriage with impossibly athletic grace, as if a man of twenty. Then, as a stable boy began running over to take the horse, he held up his hand to her. "May I?" He smiled.

She felt as if the earth were spinning wildly now. The regard he was sending her was so frank and so intimate that it was as if she were the only woman who existed.

If he truly cared, this would be so much

easier, she thought. Alexandra gave him her hand. And the moment she did, a jolt went through her, one very much like lightning. She let him help her down, hoping he hadn't noticed how affected she was by his praise, his warmth and his touch.

"You are trembling," he said softly.

She jerked and looked into his blue eyes.

"I am glad."

Realizing he still held her hand, she pulled it away. She'd meant to hide her anxiety, but his candor was tugging at her. "I am nervous."

His eyes widened. "Then I am sorry," he said. "Because, in spite of my reputation, I do not bite, and in spite of what is transpiring, I intend to be respectful." He gestured, and Alexandra preceded him into the house, even more surprised by his last words.

In the front hall, as she gave her coat to a servant, she said, "Your Grace, I was hoping to have a private word."

"I am hardly surprised. Shall I delay tea?" His gaze was searching now.

She nodded, wanting to get the impending negotiation over with. He touched her waist lightly — a gesture no stranger would ever dare — and Alexandra walked forward, thinking, *He knows.* He knew why she had come, otherwise he would not be looking at her as he was, or touching her so improperly, as if they were already intimate.

He guided her into his library, closing the ebony doors behind them. A fire burned in the green marble hearth, and Alexandra quickly went to stand there. There were no more doubts as her mind raced; instead, there was only the question of how to proceed and best protect her sisters' futures.

Suddenly his hard body bumped her from behind. She jumped, whirling to face him; he steadied her by clasping her elbows briefly. "You are very anxious. You need not be. Maybe I can make this easier for you." His gaze remained intent and searching. "You have come to accept my offer."

She nodded. "I have rejected the squire. There will be no marriage."

His eyes blazed. "Good. I never share."

She inhaled, taken aback.

"Alexandra," he said softly. "Come, let's be frank now. You will be my mistress. I expect absolute loyalty from you."

"God, it sounds so sordid!"

He took her arms. "There is nothing sordid about the desire we share. It is natural, my dear. It is hardly as if we are two young innocents."

She trembled as the conflagration instantly began, warming all parts of her body.

Because she *was* innocent, and moral, not that he would ever know.

"What is it? I can see doubt in your eyes."

She hesitated, tempted to tell him the truth: that she never had had a lover. Then she could ask him why he had assumed the worst of her. But she was afraid he might change his mind about their affair. It was so ironic. "How can you possibly respect me?"

His eyes widened. "You are a gentle-woman. It is my duty to respect you."

Lovely words, but they would not change her own lack of honor. "So you have respected your previous mistresses?"

He released her. "That is an interesting question." He stared. "No, actually, I have not."

She wondered at that. "But somehow I will be the exception?"

"Why are we dwelling upon respect?"

"It is important to me."

He was thoughtful for a long moment. "You are an interesting woman, Alexandra, and I find myself constantly intrigued. I am aware that, somehow, you are not like the others. You do not take our liaison lightly, obviously."

"No, I do not."

His gaze narrowed. "You truly wished to marry the squire and would have done so if

I hadn't interfered?"

"Probably. It was my intention."

"And was it my charm that has changed your mind?" He was wry.

She trembled. "I believe you know that you are very hard to resist. It is also obvious that you do not take no for an answer."

"I do not." He touched her cheek. "Especially not in your case, when so much desire rages between us," he added softly.

She was throbbing acutely in every fiber of her being now. "We must discuss our arrangement," she managed.

He became bemused and dropped his hand, but in such a way that his fingers slid across her jaw, sending a spiral of pleasure through her. "Very well, if you insist."

"I do." She stared, fearful.

"Although I will confess I have never had to do so before." He was reflective again. "You seem dismayed."

"What does that mean?"

"My previous lovers have eagerly pursued me and vice versa. I have never encountered resistance before. I have never had to assuage or reassure anyone, for any reason. I have never had to discuss the parameters of a liaison." He paused. "That is what you wish, is it not? To discuss the exact nature of our relationship?"

Alexandra was ashamed. "Yes. I cannot be like the others, Your Grace."

"This is undoubtedly about my promise to be generous. Do you doubt me?"

"No, of course not." She knew he would be a man of his word. "But I must know what you require of me — and vice versa."

His mouth curved, and he reached out and slowly pulled her close. "So you wish for details?" he murmured.

She wanted to soften in his arms, but she stiffened, instead, her heart pounding. "There is so much to discuss, even logistics to arrange. But mostly I wish for there to be a contract between us."

He released her abruptly. "A contract? Not an understanding?"

He was insulted, and that had not been her intention. "I do not mean that you must draw up a document, Your Grace, but I should prefer for us to verbally agree to some terms."

He stared. "Very well. And what are your terms, Alexandra?"

She hesitated, aware that her cheeks were on fire now. She wished he hadn't felt insulted, but there was simply no easy way to ask for what she had to.

He waited.

Finally she managed, "There must be

discretion. No one can know of our arrangement."

He folded his arms and said thoughtfully, "You live at home with your father and sisters — two hours from here. If we are being blunt, then I will tell you that I require your presence in this house on a nearly nightly basis."

She flamed. Images danced in her head, of her in his arms in a big, canopied state bed. "That is impossible."

His face hardened. "Really?"

"We will have to settle on the afternoons," she said thickly, hating this tangent. She added, "And that will be difficult enough for me."

He stared, his expression impossible to read now. "I will purchase a house close to Edgemont Way. We will be able to spend evenings there once I have done so. Until that time, we will have to manage with the occasional afternoon." His eyes darkened. "My time is valuable, Alexandra. Unlike most peers, I am preoccupied with great projects during my waking hours."

She shook her head. "I did not mean to anger you, Your Grace. And I do not wish to inconvenience you. But I must protect what is left of my name."

His stare remained direct. "I am a reasonable man, and frankly, I cannot fault you for that. You are the first in many regards, Alexandra. Your living at home, and being unwed, presents a difficulty I had not considered."

She trembled, this time in relief. *He had understood her reasoning. He was no longer angry.* "Thank you."

"What else do you wish to discuss?" When she hesitated, dreading raising the subject of remuneration, he said flatly, "Might I assume there is the matter of my generosity?"

She nodded and bit her lip. "I must do well enough to provide small dowries for my sisters."

He shoved his hands into the pockets of his tweed riding coat. "And what will that amount be?"

She so hated what she was doing. She'd intended to ask for more than dowries. The house needed repairs. They all needed clothes, and the pantry was bare. Instead, she decided to forgo those other things. "That is all. Olivia and Corey need dowries."

"You do not wish for a dowry for yourself?"

"No." She looked at the floor. Her cheeks were so hot she wondered if they were scarlet now.

"How much will your sisters need, Alexandra?"

She looked up, trembling. "One thousand pounds each, Your Grace, unless you think that is excessive."

His gaze narrowed. "I think the figure a low one." He shrugged. "Done."

She'd secured a thousand pounds for each of her sisters, but she felt no elation. He must surely disrespect her now. Humiliated, and wondering if she should undo what they'd just agreed to, she turned back to the fire. She felt close to tears.

He came up behind her again, clasping her by her shoulders, his breath warm on her neck and jaw. "No," he said firmly. "I am not letting you retreat."

She tensed, shocked by the feeling of his entire body, hard and warm, against hers. Her heart thundered. Her skin flushed. A terrible aching began.

He nuzzled her neck and murmured, "This is morally repugnant to you."

"Yes," she breathed.

He slowly turned her around. "Why? I know *I* am not repugnant to you."

"No, of course not." If ever there was a time to tell him the truth, it was now.

He rubbed her shoulders languidly. "I have assumed from the start that you are a woman of some experience," he said.

She tensed. If she confessed to her innocence, would he retreat from their arrangement? She looked into his smoldering eyes, her heart thudding with so much desire, and now, with some alarm.

He gave her an odd look. "I am correct, am I not?"

Her alarm grew. If she confessed, he was going to walk away from this pursuit. In that moment, she was certain. "There was someone once. I loved him."

His eyes widened and his caress stopped.

"I did not feel ashamed of my passion, because of that love. More importantly, we had planned on marriage." She searched his gaze, biting her lip. When he did not speak, she added, "Our arrangement is a calculated one, Your Grace. And that is the cause of my hesitation."

"Yes, it is. And who was this paragon?"

"Does it matter? He has since wed someone else. And I am here, concluding an illicit and immoral arrangement — for monetary compensation."

"It is to our mutual satisfaction," he said sharply. "We both benefit, Alexandra. As do your sisters."

When he stared, as he was doing now, it was impossible to look away. "Yes, they benefit," she whispered.

He released her. "I am sorry you are struggling with your conscience. Perhaps this will help. If I cannot satisfy you — enough to make you pleased with our relationship and content to remain freely in it — I will terminate our contract but compensate you in full."

It took Alexandra a moment to grasp what he was saying. She was stunned.

"I meant it when I said I am a generous man, Alexandra. Perhaps you should start taking me at my word."

CHAPTER NINE

The next day, Alexandra set about preparing the evening meal with her sisters, but she could not shake her encounter with Clarewood from her mind. As she peeled potatoes, she kept recalling their conversation in vivid detail, especially his seductiveness when he'd come up behind her. It was impossible not to feel his hands on her shoulders, his breath on her neck. She trembled and glanced at the kitchen clock.

It was only half past noon.

Clarewood had instructed her to return for luncheon on Friday. Tomorrow. She had almost been dismayed, for a part of her had expected him to begin his seduction then and there. But he had been expecting the dowager duchess within the hour, and obviously, there was no getting past that.

She reached for another potato and realized she had emptied the bowl.

I shall require your presence on a nearly

nightly basis.

She was already ridiculously tense, and her body had been in a state of fevered arousal since their negotiation. It was shameful. She did not know what was wrong with her. Being in his arms was wrong, yet it felt right.

She glanced at the kitchen clock again. Only five more minutes had passed.

"Why do you keep looking at the time?" Corey asked.

It was almost, Alexandra thought, as if she were looking forward to returning to him and beginning their affair, as if she were counting the minutes until she saw him again. "Am I looking at the clock?"

"Every five minutes," Corey said, her hands covered with flour.

The front door knocker sounded.

They never had callers; their neighbors were far better off than they were and hardly interested in the disgraceful Bolton family. Alexandra tensed. She had stopped by Squire Denney's yesterday on her way home to break things off with him. He had been stunned, and then he had been upset — understandably so. She had done her best to explain by telling him that she would never love anyone again, and it would be unfair for her to marry him considering that. He had argued with her, insisting she would become fond of him and that he would make her happy. It had been a highly awkward encounter.

When she left, he had insisted that she would soon come to her senses. "You are merely having bridal jitters, Miss Bolton," he had declared. "I am sure of it. But your sister is right. I have rushed you, so I will court you properly now."

"Please don't," Alexandra had tried. "I have truly changed my mind."

She knew he hadn't believed her because he hadn't *wanted* to believe her.

Her father had already been out when she had returned, so she hadn't seen him until a few hours ago, when he had been exceedingly cool to her. He no doubt still meant to try to force her to the altar, she thought grimly. But she wouldn't go, and in light of her understanding with Clarewood, his intent simply didn't matter.

Their caller knocked again. Alexandra took off her apron, as did Corey, afraid the squire was calling. All three sisters exchanged looks. "If it is Denney," Olivia said, "remain firm. That is the best you can do."

"I feel sorry for him."

"You would feel worse if you married him and had to pretend that you cared — for the rest of your lives," Olivia returned evenly.

"I'll get it," Corey said. "If it's the squire, I'll say you are not home."

But as she rushed off to answer the door, Alexandra followed. She did not intend to hide. To her surprise, the squire was not there; a petite, beautiful blond lady entered the house, instead. Instantly Alexandra recognized her from the Harrington ball. She recalled having noticed her with the duke.

"Hello, Miss Bolton, I presume?" the lady asked, smiling and taking off her gloves.

Instantly Alexandra tensed. The other woman's smile was cold, and the light in her eyes was somehow unpleasant. "Yes."

"I am Lady Witte, and I have heard your sewing extolled by Lady Lewis and Lady Henredon." She began removing her coat, and Alexandra helped her. "I do hope you will accept me as a new customer. I have a number of gowns that need cleaning and repairs."

"I am always taking on new customers." Alexandra smiled, relaxing now that the woman's supercilious attitude was explained and pleased to have a new client. For while that would mean additional work, there would also be added income.

"Oh, I am so relieved." Lady Witte smiled widely at her. "I have the gowns in my coach."

Alexandra turned. "Can you get them, Corey?" Then she faced Lady Witte. "It's rather chilly. Can I offer you some tea?"

"Yes, it is quite cold out, but I will pass on the refreshments. I simply wanted to meet you myself this first time. Next time I will send my gowns to you." She smiled again and said, "Did you enjoy Sara de Warenne's birthday fete?"

Alexandra steeled herself against any impending unpleasantness. "I did," she lied. "It has been a long time since I was out in society, obviously." She gestured at their run-down home.

"I can only imagine," Lady Witte said blandly. "You certainly made an entrance."

Alexandra tensed. "I wasn't feeling well," she said.

"It is fortunate Clarewood noticed you — and bothered to come to the rescue." Her smile seemed frozen in place.

And Alexandra knew now that this woman hadn't come simply for the fine repairs she could make to her gowns. It felt as if Lady Witte was prying into her relationship with Clarewood. But as they had barely begun, she thought she must be imagining it.

Though socialites did love to rumor-monger.

Edgemont came down the stairs just then, dressed for town. "I am taking the black," he said. "If you need to go out, you can use my mare."

Alexandra bristled inwardly, but outwardly, she smiled. "I have no plans to go out today. Father, this is Lady Witte, and this is my father, Baron Edgemont."

They exchanged pleasantries, and he went out to tack up Clarewood's horse. As he did, Corey and Olivia came inside with a dozen stunning dresses — Lady Witte's wardrobe had cost a small fortune. Alexandra saw some intimates in the piles of clothing: frilly, lace drawers and beribboned corsets, beautifully sewn and hand decorated, a few of the items black. No one had ever brought her their most intimate undergarments before. Corey's eyes were popping, and her cheeks were red. Alexandra knew her sister had examined each undergarment.

"You need not rush," Lady Witte said, as if oddly satisfied. "I prefer you to take your time and be as fastidious as you like."

"I am a perfectionist," Alexandra told her, as Lady Witte reached for her coat. "And I am proud of my handiwork."

Lady Witte looked at her with open pity. "Of course you are, Miss Bolton."

Alexandra helped her on with her coat and opened the door for her, now noticing the expensive lacquered coach in front of the house, a two-in-hand, the pair in the traces matching bay Hackney horses. As she walked the other woman out, Edgemont led Ebony from the stables, a few dozen paces from the house. "Thank you for coming," she said.

Lady Witte halted in her tracks and looked at Alexandra, unsmiling, her eyes growing even colder. Then she strode forward.

Confused, Alexandra followed. "Is something wrong?"

"Where did you get that gelding?" Lady Witte demanded.

Edgemont had heard and he halted. "What?"

"Lady Harrington was kind enough to loan us the horse when our mare went lame," Alexandra said carefully.

"Really?" Lady Witte sent her a scathing look. "That is one of Clarewood's finest, or I miss my guess."

Alexandra stiffened.

"You are mistaken," Edgemont said, looking back and forth between them. "The horse came from Harrington Hall. My

269

dearly beloved and deceased wife was a good friend of the lady Blanche. My daughter doesn't even know Clarewood."

Alexandra could not believe what was happening. Dismay mingled with the disbelief.

"Really? He rescued her at the ball, did he not? And then you were escorted home in his coach." In obvious disgust, she strode back to her coach. Her driver opened her door for her and she got in. He closed it after her, but she leaned out of the open window. "I have changed my mind," she said, her cheeks flushed. "I should like everything the day after tomorrow."

Alexandra rushed over to the coach. "That is impossible, Lady Witte."

"I am sure you will manage," the other woman said, slamming the window closed.

Alexandra stepped back as the driver got into his seat, releasing the vehicle's brake and lifting the reins.

"Alexandra?" Edgemont asked, as the carriage began to move off.

She forced a smile, exhaling before facing him. "Father, Lady Harrington gave us the horse. I can't imagine what is wrong with that woman."

He stared, impossibly sharp now — as if suspicious. Then he softened. "You would never lie. You don't know how. I'll be back for supper." He swung into the saddle.

When he trotted off, her sisters came to stand beside her. "What was that about?" Olivia asked in concern.

"How would Lady Witte recognize Ebony?" Corey asked in a low tone.

Alexandra felt oddly ill, and her heart was thundering. She tried to recall exactly how Clarewood had spoken to Lady Witte, and now she was certain the woman had been flirting with him, while he had been characteristically impassive and polite. In fact, if memory served, his gaze had strayed to *her*, as if he were not all that interested in Lady Witte.

Not that any of it meant much — except that Lady Witte knew enough about the duke to have recognized one of his horses instantly. Alexandra did not want to jump to conclusions, though it was hard not to. Lady Witte was a beautiful woman, and she was both impossibly elegant and probably not even twenty-five.

Did she really want her gowns cleaned and mended? Or had she come for more personal reasons?

"She hates Alexandra," Corey said, ashen. "But what I do not understand is why."

"I think she is a widow," Olivia said. "And

I think she is jealous of Clarewood's interest in Alexandra."

The following day Alexandra arrived at Clarewood fifteen minutes early. Guillermo showed her into the blue-and-gold salon where she'd become reacquainted with Elysse de Warenne and met Lady St. Xavier. "Luncheon is at one," he told her, unblinkingly. "His Grace is in a meeting, but he will be through shortly."

"Thank you," Alexandra managed, hoping he hadn't noticed that she was trembling. Her nerves were out of control.

It was almost impossible to believe that she was embarking on an affair with the Duke of Clarewood. Alexandra paced. She was breathless. Well, of course she was. In a few hours she might be upstairs — in his bed.

She wasn't ashamed now, or mortified. She wasn't anything except anxious. He would be a good lover, she was certain. She knew he could be kind; he'd been kind to her the moment they'd met — and more than once since.

She needed him to be kind now.

Even if he didn't truly care for her — and how could he? They barely knew one another — she needed him to pretend affec-

272

tion. He was very experienced; he'd been rumored to be attached to various beautiful women over the years. Alexandra was certain that he would put her at ease. In spite of his illicit affairs, he was obviously a gentleman.

Guillermo had left the doors open. She heard voices, one of which was his. Her heart jumped. She turned, and her eyes widened when she saw him pause before the threshold with Randolph. His gaze was direct, his smile suggestive. His eyes were unusually bright. Then he turned to the younger man. "Please make sure I have the answers I am expecting, preferably by tomorrow."

"Yes, Your Grace." Randolph turned and smiled at Alexandra. "Good afternoon, Miss Bolton. I hope you are enjoying Ebony."

She was too aghast to smile. "I am."

He nodded and sauntered off.

As Clarewood strolled into the room, carrying a stack of papers, she said, "We agreed on discretion."

He was amused. "Randolph is discreet."

"Having him see me here is not discretion!" Unthinkingly, she started for the door.

He barred her way and caught her shoulders. "You are beautiful today."

She froze, looking up into his smoldering

eyes. "I have been anticipating our rendezvous. I hope you have, too," he murmured.

She found herself staring at his mouth and slowly forced herself to look back into his eyes. "I suppose I have, though . . . I am somewhat nervous, Your Grace."

His smile deepened, revealing a dimple. "You have no reason to be nervous," he said. He slid his thumb along the high curve of her cheek. Alexandra shuddered. Sensation raced through her entire body, right into her loins.

"I pray you are right about Randolph," she whispered. "And what about Guillermo?"

He was amused. "If Guillermo wished to betray me, he could have done so a thousand times."

What did that mean? she wondered, thinking of Lady Witte.

He released her, sliding one hand down her arm in a casual caress as he did so. Her insides tightened anew. "He would never betray me."

"Do you know Lady Witte?" she heard herself ask.

"Frankly, I know her very well." He seemed mildly surprised by her question.

Alexandra stiffened. *They were lovers.* "She is a new customer."

He started, becoming annoyed. "You do not need customers, Alexandra. You need to heed me, and carefully. Now that we have agreed to this arrangement, I will take proper care of you."

She gaped. "What does that mean?"

"It means you need a wardrobe and some spending money, at the least." His stare intensified. "I said I was a generous benefactor."

She flushed, shaken. Was he kind and considerate? It seemed so. Maybe she had misjudged him on every score. On the other hand, there was his relationship with Lady Witte.

"I sense that there is more. Please, finish," he said softly.

She found her courage. "Is she your lover . . . even now?"

"She was my lover," he said, his expression impossible to read. "But it is over."

She was relieved. And now she understood why Lady Witte had pried — she must have sensed the attraction they shared at the Harrington ball. And as she knew Clarewood, she must have guessed he would make advances. Ebony's presence had confirmed it. No wonder she had been so imperious and so mean.

But it was over, he had said so. She tried

to hide a small smile. He knew — of course he did — because he added softly, "You are the woman I want sharing my bed, Alexandra. And if you do not yet believe that, you soon will."

She breathed in. His gaze was warm. She knew where they would end up the moment their luncheon was over.

"I do believe you," she whispered, aware that his face was inches from hers.

That was when she realized how silent the room was, and that she could hear his breathing and her own thundering heart. He straightened to his full height, holding out his hand; she slowly reached out to grasp his palm. His touch burned. There was that incredible jolt again, one defying all logic, all propriety. Her knees felt impossibly weak; he reached out and caught her by her elbows, steadying her.

"Why are you so nervous?" he murmured, slowly reeling her in. "You remind me of a schoolgirl being seduced by an older, worldly roué."

It was so hard to think now, when she was almost wrapped in his arms. And then he pulled her closer, crushing her breasts with his chest. As Alexandra slid her hands to his shoulders, the sensation of being held by him, of holding him, was dizzying. "Oh, dear," she said. So much fire was gathering beneath her skirts. Befuddled, she had to wonder if Owen had ever caused such an instantaneous explosion of desire.

"I wish to be a gentleman, the perfect lover, really," he murmured, bending over her, "but I am as impatient as a schoolboy, too." He rubbed his jaw against hers. "I have been thinking about you," he added in the same throaty tone, and now his mouth moved against her cheek.

She couldn't breathe adequately now. She clung, allowing her hands to roam down his hard, muscular back. "Your Grace," she whispered roughly, and to her horror, she heard herself sigh.

"Stephen," he whispered, and he rubbed his full lips against hers.

She went still, closing her eyes. The sensation was exquisite, but so teasing. And as he started to kiss her, remaining unrushed, she felt a massive hardness move against her hip. She flinched, but only in surprise. An acute throbbing began in response to that masculine urgency, while she opened instinctively for him.

His mouth hardened on hers, and then he kissed her.

She held on hard, letting him drag on her mouth, plunging deep, desperate for so much more. She cried out as he moved her backward, his tongue searching deep, and somehow she found herself lying on the sofa on her back. He came down fully on top of her.

She had one thought as she kissed him now, wildly and frantically — she had to love him. There was no other explanation for the urgency, the desperation, the passion or the oddly joyous bubble in her chest. Alexandra tore at his mouth. She shuddered in desire, longing to gasp in pleasure, too.

He suddenly caught her face in his hands and looked down at her. She blinked up at him, shuddering with an imminent wave of arousal. He said roughly, "I have never wanted anyone more. I wanted you from the first moment I held you in my arms."

She breathed, "I want you, too. Desperately."

His smile appeared — it was satisfied. "Shall we go upstairs?"

She was afraid to delay, afraid the magical passion might vanish. "No."

He chuckled, reaching for the buttons on the back of her dress. Alexandra sat up, turning her back to him, and was shocked when she felt his mouth and tongue on the bare skin of her nape. He nibbled her flesh, causing so much delicious sensation that she had to close her eyes, barely able to refrain from moaning, while he tugged open a button and moved his mouth lower. She shivered with pleasure, finally giving in, moaning. He reached her chemise — it was the only undergarment she wore, other than her drawers — and swiftly undid the rest of her dress and helped her out of it.

She faced him, standing, feeling more naked than not. His gaze was on her breasts as he discarded his jacket and waistcoat, tossing both indifferently onto a nearby chair. Her chemise was tired and old — and nothing like the beautiful garments Lady Witte had worn — but his eyes were blazing. He bent forward and nuzzled a taut nipple, clasping her waist and anchoring her in place.

Alexandra gasped in pleasure, seizing his head, wanting so much more.

He ripped off the chemise — she heard the cotton tearing — and sucked her nipple into his mouth. The pleasure was excruciating, and she did not think she could stand it — and then he slid his hands between her legs, against the shockingly wet flesh exposed by her slit drawers.

"Yes," he murmured, triumphant.

She clenched against him, holding on to him for her life. He rubbed her, and the explosion was instantaneous — she began weeping, the physical ecstasy too much to bear. The waves of rapture carried her away, but she was vaguely aware of his laying her down, of his heavy breathing, of his coming down on top of her. And then she felt his rock-hard phallus pulsing against her convulsing flesh.

But he didn't move, merely kissing her neck, as the climax lessened. Alexandra started to drift back to coherence, clinging to his shoulders. So this was what desire was all about, she thought, feeling as if she were floating. It was about love. And rapture . . .

He caught her face as she opened her eyes to see that his were ablaze. "Darling," he said, then kissed her hard.

Reality began to intrude. She'd just experienced rapture as never before, and he was as naked now as she was — and poised between her legs. Instantly, the sensitive flesh between her thighs began to swell as that terrible urgency began to build all over again.

She kissed him back, seeking his tongue, while exploring every inch of his muscular back and his hard hips. She writhed against his hardness, trying to pull him closer, totally mindless now.

He laughed roughly, breaking the kiss, moving lower, kissing her breasts. She gasped again, this time in protest, but he only continued to laugh, pausing only to lave each nipple in turn, reestablishing the acute restless need. She began to whimper, tossing, clenching his muscular shoulders, barely able to stand the lack of union. He murmured, "Patience, darling," and kissed his way down her belly. Suddenly realizing what he intended, she went still, shocked.

He was halfway between her navel and her pubis when he looked up, eyes agleam, his muscular arms bulging. "No one has ever tasted you this way?"

"No," she gasped, shuddering.

He smiled, then slid his tongue up against the heavy folds at the juncture of her thighs. Alexandra shuddered uncontrollably, falling back on the cushions, as his tongue moved slickly over her. She cried out. A moment later he had slid up her body and was pressing his length hard against her, his face set with strain.

Their gazes locked. "Hurry," she demanded, clawing him. "Hurry!"

He smiled tightly and drove into her wet, throbbing flesh.

Alexandra was shocked by the pressure and the pleasure of feeling him within her

— and then she felt him strike against her maidenhead. His gaze flew to hers, wide with shock. She was shocked, too — and beginning to whirl back into another wild explosion of rapture. *"Please."*

His face hard and tight, he drove past the barrier, and Alexandra held on to him, weeping in ecstasy now, as he pounded swiftly, rhythmically, deep.

When Alexandra awoke, she lay alone on the sofa, covered by a gold throw. She gasped, briefly confused, for she was stark naked and the salon was pitch-dark. In fact, the sky outside was dark and blue-black.

Reality came flooding back. *She had just spent the afternoon making love to the Duke of Clarewood.* She inhaled, clutching the throw. Obviously she had fallen asleep, still naked on his couch. As she began to blush, praying no one would walk into the salon, she realized she needed to get home immediately. But she did not move, other than to cover herself more thoroughly with the throw.

Her heart burst into a wild riot of emotions she could barely identify.

They'd made love twice, without pause. He was a magnificent lover. She hadn't realized that so much ardor could exist between two people. She hadn't realized she herself could be so passionate, so uninhibited. They were lovers now. She was the Duke of Clarewood's *mistress.*

She began to tremble, biting her lip, amazed. Happiness was growing inside her chest, like a balloon. *Being with him felt so perfect, so right.*

Her heart thundered, and she recalled the way he had looked at her, with so much warmth, as if he cared. But at other times he had looked into her eyes as if trying to look into her soul. She did not quite know what that searching gaze could mean, and she hugged herself. Did she dare think about him as anything other than her lover and benefactor? Did she dare think of him as a man?

She was helpless to restrain herself. He was such a paragon, handsome and wealthy and titled. He was generous. He was renowned for the charities he supported — had even founded. He was intelligent, dedicated. And he was a gentleman. . . .

She wasn't ashamed of what had just happened, not at all. She was *thrilled.*

They were lovers now.

She would not die a virgin, and she had avoided suffering Squire Denney's touch. But there was so much more, and she trembled at the thought. They hadn't dined. There had been so little conversation. Next time, perhaps they would share their thoughts and feelings over some wine. Next time . . . She smiled, dreaming about it.

In her mind's eye she saw herself at his table — which was beautifully set, of course — wearing a stunning and expensive gown, which he had purchased for her. He sat beside her, smiling, reaching for her hand, and there was candlelight. . . .

Smiling widely, she reached over to a small lamp sitting on the end table. She sought to turn the gas on and glanced around for her clothes.

Was she falling in love with him?

She trembled all over again, her pulse pounding. While in his arms earlier, while they were joined, it had certainly felt so much like love.

Could she have responded so passionately to him if it *hadn't* been love?

She blushed. She was a sensible woman. She did not believe in love at first sight, yet it seemed to her that she had fallen in love with the Duke of Clarewood the very moment she had first laid eyes upon him.

Did it matter? For they were on a new path now. . . .

She bit her lip, hoping to contain what

felt so oddly like happiness, and saw her clothing spread across the gleaming wood floors. Her chemise was ripped almost entirely in two. She blushed, hugging the throw to her breasts.

He had been impatient, even as he'd counseled patience. Simply recalling the intimacy they'd shared made her body tighten, heat, as a distinct and pleasurable aching began to grow.

Alexandra got up and slowly dressed, thinking about every moment they had shared. Her body tingled deliciously, while her heart kept dancing, no matter how she tried to warn it to behave, reminding herself to proceed with care. It was as if he was that force of nature she'd spoken of, one she could not resist. She smiled. Hadn't she said only a hurricane could stop her from marrying the squire? Well, she had found her hurricane, had she not? Now she anticipated walking from the room so she might speak with him for a moment before she had to go home.

Her heart raced harder, as if she could not wait to see him again.

She was fighting the buttons on the back of her dress when a light knock sounded on the door. She froze, alarmed, then called, "Do not come in!"

A woman said, "His Grace asked me to check on you, madam, to see if you need any help."

He'd sent her a maid. More pleasure unfurled. Alexandra called for the maid to enter, and a young woman in a dark uniform came inside, closing the door behind her. "Here, let me help you with that," she said.

Alexandra smiled gratefully at her, aware of what the other woman must be thinking. There was no possible excuse to make for being half-dressed in the duke's salon, with her hair completely down. "Thank you. What is your name?" she asked, as the maid swiftly buttoned her dress.

"It is Bettie," the girl said. "May I help you with your hair?"

"That would be wonderful, but we must try to find my hairpins." She flushed as she started looking about the floor and sofa for the missing pins. When she only found three, Bettie told her that she would go and find some more for her. When the maid had left and Alexandra sat down to wait, the duke returned forcefully to her mind. His handsome image curled her toes. She wondered what he was doing, and she got up and went to the door, which Bettie had left ajar. She opened it a bit wider and peeked out into the hall.

Directly across from her, the library doors were wide-open. Clarewood was standing inside the darkened room, staring at a blazing fire, his back to her.

But before she could move, he must have felt her presence, because he turned. The lights were not on in the library, just the fire, and she could not make out his expression. But clearly he was staring.

She hesitated — she knew her hair must be a mess, and she must look like a harlot — but then she slipped into the hall and quickly approached him, smiling hesitantly. When he did not speak, when he continued to stare, she became uncomfortable and confused — this was not the reception she had expected. She faltered on the library's threshold. "Your Grace? It is late, and I must go." She bit her lip, wishing she could say so much more, yet at the same time uncertain of what she might say if she could speak freely. She wanted to acknowledge what had just happened, what they had shared.

"Come in, Alexandra," he said tightly.

She flinched; his tone was so hard. She cautiously walked inside, and when she could make out his features, she saw that his eyes blazed and his face was a hard mask of controlled anger. "What is wrong?" she gasped, stunned.

"What is wrong?" he choked. Then he inhaled, and she realized he was so angry that he was trembling with his rage.

She took a step back, utterly confused. "What has happened? Have I done something?"

He crossed the few paces between them and towered over her, the effect distinctly frightening. Alexandra tensed, as if for a blow. "I do not like being deceived."

He was enraged, but he hadn't raised his voice. She wanted to back away, but she held her ground. "I do not know what you are talking about." But a terrible inkling began.

"You were a virgin, Miss Bolton," he ground out.

She recoiled, too deeply in shock to think clearly. He had retreated into formality just when she expected intimacy, and it hurt.

He walked past her and slammed both doors closed with so much strength that the floor shuddered. She had turned to keep him in her sight, still shocked by his anger, and very frightened now. He had assumed the worst of her, and, admittedly, she had deliberately misled him. But she had never expected such anger. "Is that why you are so angry? Because I did not have the experience you assumed I had?" she managed.

"I am well beyond anger," he said flatly. "You lied to me."

His words were worse than any physical blow. "I didn't think it important," she tried, suddenly aghast and near tears. But in truth, hadn't she sensed just how important it might be, why else had she let him believe the lie?

"You didn't think it important?" He was incredulous.

"I think there has been a terrible misunderstanding," she whispered, trembling.

He made a harsh sound, mirthless, and clapped his hands slowly together. "A laudable performance, Miss Bolton."

She jerked. "I do not know what you mean, Stephen!" But the moment she used his given name, as he'd instructed her to do during the height of passion, though she had been unable to do so at the time, she was sure it had been a mistake.

It was. "It is 'Your Grace,' " he said dangerously.

She backed up, still in shock, but now it was combined with absolute disbelief. "Why are you doing this?"

"Why?" He stalked her as she retreated, not allowing her to keep her distance. "I should have known that this was a game.

You are a very clever player, Miss Bolton."

She stared, too appalled by his assumption to say anything.

"After all, no woman has ever rejected my advances as you have, or played hard to get, but then, you sought to whet my desire, did you not? And giving back the bracelet . . . I must commend you for that ploy! I know of no woman in your circumstance who would refuse such jewels."

Alexandra was so disbelieving and so horrified that she sank into the nearest chair. But he had followed her, and he towered over her still. "There has been no ploy!" she insisted. "I could not accept such a gift."

"I beg to differ with you. There have been nothing *but* ploys, my clever one, and you have led me a merry chase." He paused, breathing hard. "This was a trap, Miss Bolton, admit it."

She cringed. "No," she whispered. "I do not understand what you are talking about."

"I am *not* marrying you."

She stared up at him, shocked all over again. Her befuddled mind finally managed to come to the conclusion he had jumped to earlier. "You think I meant to trap you into marriage?" she gasped.

"I *know* you meant to trap me into marriage."

She clasped the chairs arms, so sick that she felt faint and dizzy. But of course he would think that a ploy, too.

"But I must applaud your scheme. Many women have pursued me in the hope of becoming my duchess. You are the first to give me her virginity."

She choked, fighting down the bile, fighting the need to retch. Her heart was screaming at her now. He had pursued her ruthlessly, in spite of her sensibilities and morals, yet now he was accusing *her* of pursuing *him* — and of plotting to trap him into marriage. She felt so faint now. How could this be happening?

When at last she looked up, he was shoving a piece of paper at her. "Take it and get out."

It took her a moment to realize that he was holding a bank check. Without thinking, she looked down again and started to shake her head.

"Take it," he gritted, flinging it at her. "Use it for a dowry." Then, "My coachman will drive you home."

He'd flung the check at her bosom, and it had fallen onto her lap. Alexandra didn't move, she couldn't, not even to look up into his hate-filled eyes, but his fury was so intense that she felt it anyway.

She was afraid to move, or even breathe, because if she did, she would retch or faint or start weeping. And then she heard him striding rapidly from the room. She heard the doors hit the walls as he flung them open. She did not move a single muscle, not even her eyelashes, waiting until she could not hear his footsteps anymore. And then she glanced at the check on her lap.

He'd made it out for five thousand pounds.

She gagged, falling to her knees on the floor, her heart wrenching. She fought the rising sobs, fought the spinning floor. Somehow she found the check and, still on her knees, tore it into shreds.

CHAPTER TEN

The drive back to Edgemont Way was endless. Alexandra refused to cry, and fought the rising bile and the need to retch. She remained in shock. Every moment of the afternoon and evening kept replaying in her mind: she would recall Clarewood moving over her, smiling warmly at her, and then she would recall him flinging the check at her and telling her to use it for a dowry. It hurt so much.

But when the coachman twisted to look at her and said, "Miss? We will be at Edgemont Way in a few more moments," she somehow snapped out of her painful reverie, forced into a harsh new reality in which she had no doubt destroyed not only her own prospects — such as they had been — but her sisters' as well, and she stiffened.

No one must ever discover what had happened that day. She was in her own carriage, with Ebony in the traces, and the coachman had a mount tied to the back fender. She could not be seen being driven home; coming home alone at this hour was bad enough. But Edgemont would be out, as he always was, so at least she would only have to lie to her sisters. She closed her eyes, despairing. Of course lying would be a consequence of her terrible behavior.

What had she been thinking?

She had been thinking that he was a prince, her *prince. . . .*

A stabbing pain went through her chest.

A few minutes later the coachman was on his way back to Clarewood and she was driving her carriage up the small, rutted driveway of her home, then halting before it. The lights were on in the parlor, and she knew her sisters were seated there, worried and waiting for her. It must, she decided, be close to ten o'clock.

As she got down and prepared to lead Ebony to the stable, the front door opened and her sisters came running outside, wrapped in shawls.

"Where have you been?" Corey demanded, her eyes huge. "We have been worried sick about you!"

"You should have sent a note," Olivia admonished. Then, "Father is home, but he is in the library with two friends, and they are foxed."

Alexandra stiffened. They had to get Ebony put away immediately, and then maybe she could sneak inside and he would not know she had come home so late. "Can you help me unhitch and feed the horse?"

"Of course," Olivia said, staring. But it was dark outside, and Alexandra knew her sister had no idea of the distress she was in.

Corey led the gelding to the stables, Alexandra and Olivia following. Alexandra was grateful her sisters weren't pestering her with questions, but she knew their silence would be short-lived.

In the interior of the small, four-box barn, Corey lit a kerosene lantern. Alexandra had already walked to the horse's far side, so neither one of her sisters could see her face, and was unhitching the traces, ordering herself to find composure and, if possible, a disguise for her feelings.

As she led Ebony into his stall, Olivia said, "Well?"

Alexandra meant to smile, but she failed entirely.

And now, in the flickering light of the lantern, Olivia saw her and she cried out, "What did he do to you?"

Alexandra hugged herself, perilously close to tears, knowing that if she broke down, her sisters would comfort her. But they must never know what had happened. "You were right. His intentions were dishonorable, and I realized I could not lower myself to his immoral level." She closed her eyes, thinking about just how immoral she had in fact been.

Olivia rushed over and hugged her. "Something happened. I can tell."

There was no possible excuse to make. Alexandra pulled away. "I am exhausted. I am going to sleep." She started from the barn.

Olivia followed. "You cannot return looking as you do — utterly distraught and disheveled — and then simply walk away from us!"

Alexandra hurried across the yard, and the moment she grabbed the knob on the front door, she heard boisterous male laughter. She paused, bolstering her resolve, and then walked inside.

Her father was standing in the front hall, putting on his coat, with two elderly friends. He beamed when he saw her. "So you have come back!"

She still couldn't form a smile. "I don't know what you mean, Father. Hello." She nodded politely to the two gentlemen, whom she did not know.

"You missed supper. I saw the carriage come in a moment ago." He squinted, suddenly puzzled. "Where have you been until such an hour?"

"I took a very late tea with Lady Harrington." God, it was unbelievable how one act could lead to one lie, which then led to so many others. "I am sorry I missed supper, but Lady Blanche sets a wonderful plate at tea time. Excuse me." Aware of her sisters staring at her and not believing a single word that she had said, Alexandra rushed upstairs, into her bedroom.

She shut and locked the door, then slumped against it. And when she opened her eyes, she found herself staring at his red roses.

They were dying now. It was so unbelievably appropriate.

"I hate you," she said. "I do."

She hugged herself, because hating wasn't in her nature. But his image loomed, at once handsome and kind, his eyes warm, and then so hateful and mocking. He was not a prince, he wasn't even a gentleman, and he was nothing like Owen.

Owen *was* a prince and a gentleman. He had loved her, he had wanted to marry her, and he would never have condemned her as Clarewood had done.

Too late, she realized it was Owen she missed and loved, not the damned duke.

If possible, the following day was even worse. And she should have known, for the sky had clearly been an omen — black with an approaching storm. It was bitterly cold out, the wind gusting, making their outdoor chores terribly unpleasant. And her sisters were giving her the cold shoulder now, which was even worse than being pestered with questions she didn't dare answer. Clearly they were angry with her, just when she needed their love and support. And then the squire called.

It would be rude to send him away, and Edgemont was home anyway, inviting him to come in, while insisting that Alexandra join them. Denney was kind and charming, and clearly as good as his word — he intended to court her properly now. But nothing had changed for her, and the last thing she would ever do was go from the duke's bed to the altar with another man. She spent a miserable hour, trying to converse politely, while still failing to summon a single smile. Impossibly, her heart felt broken. And that was absurd, because she neither knew nor loved Clarewood. She had made the mistake of confusing Owen and

Clarewood, that was all.

Finally the squire stood up, indicating that he was ready to leave, though she noticed he had begun to look at her with concern. Edgemont pumped his hand. "Good of you to come by," he said. "Excuse me." And very obviously, he vanished into the library, leaving the two of them alone.

Instantly Alexandra was dismayed. To cover it, she took the squire's heavy mantle from the coatrack. "Thank you for calling," she said politely, careful not to inject any warmth into her words.

He did not take the mantle; he took her hands instead. Instantly she stiffened. "Sir," she objected.

He released them. "You seem upset, Miss Bolton. I pray I am not the cause."

She wet her lips. "Of course you are not the cause, and I am not upset, just fatigued. I have taken on extra sewing," she said quickly.

He was clearly dismayed. "I do not like your working yourself to the bone! What if you became seriously ill?"

He was such a caring man, she thought, but her feelings hadn't changed. "I am hardly that fragile."

"My dear, can I help you and your sisters somehow?" he asked gently.

She was ready to cry over his kindness, but it was Clarewood's image she saw in her mind. And, albeit too late, she knew there was nothing kind about him; he was cold, calculating and selfish, as ruthless and heartless as the gossips claimed. "We are fine. But thank you," she added, and this time, she meant it. "You are truly a good man," she said impulsively, still focused on Clarewood.

His eyes brightened. "Does this mean my suit has a chance?"

She tensed, dismayed. She did not know what to say. But he deserved honesty, not lies. "I meant what I told you the other day, sir. You deserve a woman who loves you."

"And I remain convinced that one day, you will return my feelings," he whispered.

They were at an impasse. Alexandra was about to lead him to the door when she heard a horse galloping up the drive. She ran to the door and saw Randolph leaping down from his chestnut gelding. She inhaled. What did this mean?

Had Clarewood had a change of heart?

Her mind leaped and raced — could Clarewood have sent her an apology? It was the least she deserved.

"That's young Randolph de Warenne. He was here last week, I recall. Does he call frequently?" Denney asked, scowling.

She trembled as Randolph strode up the walk, his cheeks red from the blistering cold. "No, he does not."

The squire made no move to leave, and suddenly Alexandra realized the implications of his remaining with her, and she tensed in some alarm. "He must be interested in one of my sisters," she said quickly.

"Perhaps. Or perhaps he is interested in the fairest, and most intriguing, of you all."

Before Alexandra could declare that Randolph was not courting her, he was standing on the stoop before them, nodding at the squire but looking directly at her. "Good afternoon, Miss Bolton."

She began to fidget. Denney had to leave before the truth crept out. But the squire seemed intent on staying, and he said, "It's a terribly long ride from Harrington Hall."

Randolph looked down rather imperiously at him. "I am clerking for His Grace, the Duke of Clarewood, and it is less than two hours from here." Then he turned to Alexandra, clearly dismissing the squire. "I would like a private word, Miss Bolton, if you do not mind."

"The squire was just about to leave." Alexandra found a smile for the first time since leaving Clarewood last night. Denney seemed ready to object, looking back and forth between them, clearly mistrustful of Randolph. But he finally bowed and walked away to his carriage, promising to return tomorrow.

She managed another smile and then ushered Randolph inside, not daring to hope. But her heart was racing perilously anyway.

He handed her a sealed envelope, which he took from inside his jacket.

"What is that?" she asked. Her heart hammered. If he was asking for forgiveness, she must not give it. But she would so dearly love an explanation for his having drawn such a terrible conclusion about her.

"I don't know everything that's inside. But I have been given a message — if you do not deposit the check, he will make the deposit for you."

She was so shocked that her knees buckled. Randolph steadied her as dismay began. She tore open the envelope — and saw his check inside, this time made out for the two thousand pounds on which they had agreed. There was no note.

She began to breathe heavily, harshly, with difficulty.

"Are you all right?"

She slowly looked up, trying to keep her

outrage from showing. "I am fine," she lied. She knew she would never be fine again.

He was ruthlessly determined to finalize his architectural drawings. Nothing would stop him — *no one* would stop him. In fact, he had stayed up the entire night, redrawing them three times.

"You look like a wastrel," Alexi de Warenne said.

Stephen looked up, startled, as Guillermo said, frowning, "Captain de Warenne has called, sir, and, as usual, refused to await your convenience."

Alexi sauntered into the study, smiling, but his blue gaze was sharp. "What is wrong with you?" he asked bluntly.

"Can you bring coffee, Guillermo?" Stephen asked, ignoring the question as he stood up. He realized he had yet to change his clothes from the day before, and he was so wrinkled, there was no point in unrolling his shirtsleeves.

He could not get that lying bitch out of his mind.

And what was even worse than recalling her tears — which had been pure theatrics — was that every time he looked up from his desk, he saw old Tom standing there, mocking him for his feelings of rage and betrayal.

As Guillermo vanished to do his bidding, Alexi walked past him and looked at the drawings on the desk. Then he turned. "Well? Have you been carousing?"

She had lied, she was exceptionally clever, but he had been played, and that made him the ultimate fool.

Tom said, as clear as day, "You are Clarewood. She is nothing. She *means* nothing. Your duty means everything."

His inner tension seemed unbearable now. And had the old man been alive, had he really spoken, he would have been right. Stephen would never marry her, not ever, because he never gave his enemies the satisfaction of defeating him. "I was working on those plans last night."

"How boring," Alexi drawled. "Why do you look like hell warmed over?"

Stephen folded his arms and stared. "I have been played, Alexi."

Alexi raised his eyebrows. An amused smile began. "Uh-oh. I can't wait to hear the gory details."

"It is not amusing."

"I'll be the judge of that."

And as her image filled his mind — not when she was in the throes of passion, but when she was about to cry, as if he'd devastated her — Stephen cursed and decided it was not too early for a stiff drink. He knew he hadn't hurt her. Players as consummate as Alexandra Bolton were heartless.

Mostly he was in disbelief. He had wanted her as he had never before wanted a woman; his passion had been out of control — passion he had never dreamed possible. And that made him even more furious.

He poured a brandy and took a sip. There was a slight tremor to his hand. "I began an affair with Alexandra Bolton," he said. "And she has turned out to be a scheming witch."

Alexi's brows lifted. "Really? And she is scheming for what, exactly?"

Alexi was amused, Stephen thought angrily as he turned. "She was a damned virgin, Alexi — and she did not say a word!"

Alexi choked, surprised.

Stephen remained in disbelief. He'd asked her — somewhat off-handedly, he admitted — and she had lied. She had gone on and on about the passion she had felt for a previous lover — except he hadn't been a lover! And that was when he felt Alexi clasp his shoulder. He turned.

Alexi's eyes were wide and utterly innocent. "I suppose that was your first time, too?" He was trying not to laugh.

Stephen shoved him off. "Laugh all you wish. I have never pursued an innocent, as you well know. I would have stayed far away from her, had I known."

"Really? And now what?" Alexi's stare remained far too wide and bland.

Before Stephen could answer, he heard the sound of several pairs of ladies' heels clicking in the corridor. The footsteps were rapid — he instantly suspected the identity of his visitors. He tensed. When Elysse and Ariella appeared on the library threshold, he knew he would never hear the end of his affair with Alexandra Bolton if Alexi let the metaphorical cat out of the bag. He gave his cousin a dark, warning look. "Your head will roll," he said softly.

Alexi laughed at him and strolled over to his wife, who instantly nestled against him. "If you have found the dowager duchess her match, why am I the last to know?" he asked her, then glanced at Stephen. "We have no secrets."

Stephen scowled at him. "I have a guillotine hidden in my closet," he snapped.

Alexi laughed again.

"We actually came to call for another reason," Elysse said, looking back and forth between the two men. "Why did Stephen just threaten to take off your head? What is wrong with him?"

"I have been working on housing plans all night, in lieu of sleeping," Stephen snapped.

Both women flinched. Ariella murmured, "Someone is in a very foul mood — as never before, I think." She shared a glance with Elysse. "Maybe he has heard the rumors."

Stephen went still. Had she leaked the fact of her de-flowering — at his hands? Did she think to pursue a marriage — to eventually force him into it — in spite of what he had said? "What rumors?"

"Charlotte Witte is a woman scorned, and she is doing her best to bring poor Alexandra Bolton down. You do recall Miss Bolton, don't you?" Elysse asked innocently.

"Oh, he recalls her — very well," Alexi murmured to her.

Instantly, Stephen couldn't help but recall the night he had met Alexandra and the humiliation she had endured — with her head held high. He refused to admire her for anything now, yet he had admired her then. He was disturbed, on many accounts. He had never trusted Charlotte to be a woman of grace or honor, but this . . . She had guessed that he had jettisoned her for Alexandra, and he hadn't considered that she would seek her petty revenge. "What lies is Lady Witte spreading?" Of course he did not care, he thought.

"She is claiming that you are having an affair with Miss Bolton, Stephen, and that she has been seen at this house on several occasions."

He breathed hard.

"Of course you would never pursue and ruin such an honorable woman, now would you?" Ariella said, staring rather coolly. "Because I have heard firsthand from my aunt, Lady Blanche, that a very well-off squire is about to ask for her hand. Miss Bolton has fallen on very hard times since I married Emilian. She deserves a better situation than an uncaring affair with you."

He took another draught of brandy. His problems would be solved if she married the squire. Except now he was oddly dismayed and even more disturbed. He could not understand why, but he didn't like the image of Alexandra in the burly squire's arms. Not that it mattered to him, of course. He heard himself say, "Denney has yet to ask for her. No contracts have been drawn. And I am hardly having an affair with Alexandra Bolton. Even if I should, it is not *your* affair, Ariella."

Both women gaped, but Alexi was even more amused now. "And how would you know that he hasn't asked for her?" He grinned.

Stephen could not believe he had let so much slip. And he hadn't had a chance to tell Randolph to call off his spies, although he'd meant to do so. He'd even been informed of the state of affairs that morning, which was why he knew that no proposal had been made. He thought his cheeks felt warm, as if he were flushing — but that was simply impossible. "The squire is welcome to Miss Bolton. He will have his hands full with her." He almost added, *and her games*. "I wish them well. I will be the first to send them my congratulations and a wedding gift."

Her face swam in his mind. Beautiful and proud, with the kind of dignity so few women naturally achieved. Except it was all a lie. *She* was a lie.

"Is he smitten?" he heard Elysse ask her husband.

"I am wondering that myself," Alexi said, chuckling.

Were they mad? Stephen thought. "Why would you even make such a preposterous statement?" he demanded. "Because I admired her briefly?"

"Yes, and because there is so much to admire," Alexi drawled. "You are always immaculate, but today you are red-eyed, unshaven and in general unkempt. You seem to know Miss Bolton's intimate affairs. And you are very out of sorts, Stephen. Surely you can admit that."

"I will admit nothing," he snapped, then turned to both women. "How is the hunt for a husband for the dowager duchess proceeding?"

Ariella hesitated. He knew she was debating the possibility that he might be keenly interested in a woman for the first time in his life. At last she smiled slowly. "I like Miss Bolton. I always have."

"Good for you." He was brusque.

"We are compiling a list, but we are not yet ready to show it to you," Ariella said, her gaze searching his as her smile widened. "She is so unlike all the women you have been involved with. She seems deeply intelligent, highly determined, and apparently she has done quite a bit to keep her family afloat in daunting circumstances." She looked at Elysse. "We should befriend her. It is time."

"I should love to do so," Elysse said quickly.

He was in disbelief. They would not dare to meddle now! Besides, there was nothing to meddle in. "That is hardly necessary." But now he thought about the fact that she had shredded his five-thousand-pound note. Of course she had — she had a much higher pot in mind. But he was uneasy. She had truly needed the funds, even he knew that, but he had been so angry that he had meant to insult her by handing her such a staggering check. He'd meant to indicate that she was a high-priced whore. He regretted that. So he had sent her the amount they'd agreed upon.

"Why don't you want us to call on her?" Ariella asked.

He'd had enough. "Do as you wish! After all, you both run wild. Your husbands allow you absolute freedom of thought and action, and if they cannot stop you, how can I?" Too late, he realized that his uncharacteristic explosion of his temper had given far too much away. As he strode for the doors, an utter silence had fallen over the room. He growled, "It is lack of sleep making me tense, nothing more."

No one dared to dispute him.

But he knew they were talking about him as he left.

Alexandra was in the kitchen, sewing one of Charlotte Witte's ivory silk chemises, when she heard her father coming down the stairs. It was late afternoon, and he had gone out earlier, but she hadn't heard him come in. He must have returned while she was in the cellars, she thought, looking for violet thread, while carefully stitching a torn piece of lace. She kept herself carefully composed as she worked the needle. She refused to think of who the chemise belonged to, or how it might have been used — or abused.

Edgemont walked into the kitchen.

Alexandra did not look up until she realized he had paused on the threshold and was staring at her in silence. Surprised, she looked up, smiling, but when she saw his severe, set face, she faltered. "What is wrong?"

"I heard rumors last night," he said harshly. "Very ugly rumors."

Alexandra laid down her sewing very deliberately. Her heart thundered, deafening her. Had he heard about her affair?

"I did not believe them. I refuse to believe you have been sneaking off to rendezvous with the Duke of Clarewood."

She inhaled. "Those are terrible accusations."

"I called on Lady Blanche today." His gaze was unwavering now, accusatory, but also bleak.

She could not breathe. Somehow, she stood up. *She was about to be discovered.*

"She never gave you the horse. You weren't there at any time this week for tea. Who gave you the horse, Alexandra?" He was shaking.

She trembled, too. "It is just a loan. Bonnie really is lame."

"Where did you get the horse?" he asked ominously. "It is Clarewood's, isn't it? As Lady Witte claimed? Clarewood gave you that horse!"

"It's a loan," she tried desperately. "Merely a loan."

He was panting as he dug into his pocket and produced a slip of paper. Alexandra went still as she recognized the bank check. "And is this a loan, as well?"

She blanched and bit her lip, shaking her head, stunned. "You searched my room?"

"What did you do to receive this?" he screamed at her.

"Nothing," she lied, cringing. "It's not . . ." She faltered. "Father, please, stop!"

Her sisters came rushing into the kitchen, their faces pale with shock. "What is going on?" Corey asked. "Why is Father shouting at you?"

"Go," Alexandra begged them, not taking her eyes from her father. "Please go away."

But they didn't move, and Edgemont waved the check at her. "What did you do to warrant his paying you off?" he roared at her.

Alexandra couldn't tell him, and while she knew she must lie to save herself, she couldn't do that, either. Helplessly she sat down, tears sliding down her cheeks.

"Did you spread your legs for that bastard?" Edgemont shouted, shocked. His cheeks were red now.

"Alexandra would never do such a thing." Olivia tried to defend her, but her gaze was wide and horrified.

Alexandra finally whispered, "I thought he was kind . . . a prince."

Edgemont gasped, clasping his head, backing away. He started to cry.

Olivia paled with shock, as did Corey. Neither sister moved.

"I thought he was our savior," Alexandra said, brokenly. "I was wrong."

"Oh, my God," Olivia breathed.

"You need to deposit it," Alexandra somehow added, now covering her face with her hands. She had never been as humiliated or ashamed, as mortified. Her sisters would never admire her again. And why should they? She was a harlot, after all.

Corey turned and ran from the room. The front door slammed as she left the house.

Alexandra dared to look up, sick with

shame. Olivia was still horrified. Her eyes simply said, *Why? How could you do such a thing?* "I am so sorry," Alexandra whispered.

Her father turned and said raggedly, "Are you seeing him still?"

She managed to shake her head.

"So he used you and then tossed you aside?" Edgemont asked harshly.

Oh, God, this was turning worse and worse. "No, it wasn't like that. . . . It was a mistake — for both of us," she said, aware of how ridiculous it was that she was defending him now.

Another silence fell. Olivia walked around the table and sat down beside her, taking her hand. Alexandra was grateful.

A long, painful moment passed. "You'll marry Denney now," Edgemont said. He stared at her firmly. "There could be a child. I'll tell him you have accepted his suit."

She trembled. She had tried not to think about the possibility of having conceived, but now she did not dare refute her father.

He started to walk out, then turned. "You'll be wed within the month."

The wisest course of action had been an instant retreat to her room. Alexandra shut the door, breathing hard, refusing to cry. The dying red roses stared at her.

She had lost everything now. Her good name, her dignity, her honor, her self-respect and the respect of her family. There was nothing more to lose — except for her freedom.

She hugged herself, thinking of the kind squire and the horrid duke. She took the roses and forced them into the small waste-basket by the bureau. Then she heard her door open and glanced up as Olivia slipped into her room.

"Are you all right?" her sister asked, closing the door.

"No, I am not." Alexandra pushed the roses down, crushing them. The thorns cut her hands.

Olivia put her arm around her. "I understand."

Alexandra pulled away. "Do you? Because I cannot understand myself."

"He is impossibly seductive — and, as always, you thought nothing of sacrificing yourself for us." Her gaze was searching.

"He *is* very seductive," Alexandra whispered, and her heart suddenly hurt so fiercely, it was as if it was broken. She felt another tear well. "I truly thought he was kind."

"He is despicable, to use you so callously," Olivia whispered. "I hate him."

Alexandra stumbled away, the tears beginning to fall. She had controlled herself thus far, but the task seemed impossible now. His rejection hurt so terribly. His accusations hurt even more. "I miss Owen, Olivia," she said.

Aghast, Olivia sat down with her and took her into her arms. "Of course you do. He was your true love." She sat back and stared. "But I know you, Alexandra. And I know you would not do what you did just for us. Do you love him?"

"I don't know . . . maybe. But how could I? He is cruel!" She finally started to cry.

Olivia held her again.

A long time passed while Alexandra wept over her broken heart and shattered dreams — dreams she didn't dare identify. But his image was with her — it always was — and it wasn't hateful or mean. It was warm, and it was kind. Too late, she was certain she had truly fallen in love with the duke.

When the tears were finally spent, when all that was left were her throbbing heart and battered soul, she pulled away. "I am sorry. I never cry."

"It's all right," Olivia said, her face strained. Very carefully, she asked, "Could there be a child?"

Alexandra closed her eyes. A part of her

would rejoice if that were the case, but he would think it a part of her trap, and she would have to make certain he never knew about their son or daughter — something marriage to the squire would no doubt take care of. Then she looked at her sister. "It is unlikely," she said, having made a calculation. She thought she was safe from an unwanted pregnancy.

"Please refuse Denney," Olivia said.

Alexandra blanched. "How can I? Father is devastated. You saw him. A marriage I abhor is surely my punishment now."

Olivia was now close to tears herself. "How have we come to this terrible moment?"

"It is entirely my fault," Alexandra said, "when all I ever wanted was to take care of you and Corey."

This time, it was Olivia who wept, in Alexandra's arms.

Alexandra knew she could not hide in her room indefinitely. She was in the kitchen now, having prepared supper as usual. Everything was being kept warm in the ovens as they waited for their father to return from Fox Run. Alexandra felt certain the squire would be with him, his mood celebratory. She had already set out an extra place.

Her stomach churned. But if this was her penance, so be it.

Corey was arranging a vase of dried flowers as a centerpiece. She hadn't said a word since she'd overheard Alexandra's horrible interview with their father earlier. She was ashen and grim, refusing to look at anyone, especially Alexandra. Alexandra knew her young, idealistic sister was in shock that she could have carried on as she had — and that she felt utterly betrayed. She did not blame her.

They all heard the front door open and close, but it was only one pair of booted steps that sounded in the hallway. Alexandra glanced at Olivia, saying, "Would you get supper from the oven?" Then she wiped her hands on her apron and took it off, going out to meet her father.

He'd gone directly into the library, and he was drinking a huge glass of straight gin. In the doorway, Alexandra froze, Olivia behind her. She did not know what to think, and she was too mentally exhausted to jump to any conclusions. "The squire wasn't at home?"

Edgemont gulped down half the drink and turned, his eyes blazing. "He was home.

And he has heard the rumors, too."

Alexandra tensed in absolute dread. She could not take very much more. "Can we discuss the squire tomorrow? Supper is ready."

"No, we cannot!"

Alexandra flinched, knowing the sky had fallen. Olivia took her hand.

Their father advanced. "He's heard every damned rumor about you and your damned duke! He wants nothing to do with you, and I do not blame him!"

She saw the blow coming, but she was incapable of trying to defend herself, although Olivia shrieked. Edgemont struck her hard across the face, sending her staggering backward into the side of the door, and then against the wall.

She'd never been hit in her life. Now, her vision blackened and stars exploded in her line of sight. Then the pain erupted in her right cheekbone.

"Father!" Olivia screamed.

Clutching her face as the pain overwhelmed her, Alexandra sank to the floor and waited for the room to come slowly back into focus.

Edgemont towered over her. "You are nothing like your mother!" he screamed. "You are a whore!"

Alexandra curled up, protecting her head to defend herself from another blow. From behind, Olivia and Corey, who had come running at the noise, leaped on Edgemont, pummeling him with their fists.

"Leave her alone!" Corey sobbed. "Leave my sister alone!"

Alexandra somehow got up, shocked at having been so brutally struck, and even more shocked by the sight of her sisters trying to physically maim their father. "Stop!" she cried.

Edgemont managed to free himself of the two women, then pointed at Alexandra, his hand shaking, tears streaming. "I want you out of this house!"

CHAPTER ELEVEN

Alexandra stared around in dismay. Corey and Olivia were with her. There had been no suitable lodgings close to home, and they'd taken a full hour to drive to London's southwestern outskirts. The neighborhood was filled with factories that belched dark smoke, as did the steamships coming into the harbor, while the brick and stucco buildings lining the thoroughfare were blackened from the constant soot. The air was foul and heavy, and the working men and women — and children — coming and going were thin with malnutrition, as well as pale-skinned and dirty. London had changed so much in the past decade that it was almost unrecognizable — mills and factories were everywhere, as was the belching railroad. The rooms they'd found that were closer to Edgemont Way had been incredibly expensive, from Alexandra's point of view, or impossibly dirty, or there had been unpleasant innuendos from the innkeepers as to what she must do to have the room. While this neighborhood was hardly hospitable, the room she'd let was cheap — and it was clean in comparison to the other rooms she'd thus far seen.

Except, of course, for the privy, which she would have to share with a dozen other tenants. As for bathing, she would do so in her room, with water pumped from the courtyard well.

"Father will change his mind," Corey said desperately, her eyes red and swollen from crying.

Thinking about Edgemont hurt too much. "I will take my bags and my sewing upstairs," Alexandra said, attempting a cheerful smile. "It's getting late, and you should go back."

"We can't let you stay here by yourself, Alexandra," Olivia said nervously, as two very drunken sailors sauntered by them, winking. "I don't think this place is at all safe."

"You heard Mr. Schumacher. The public doors are locked at ten o'clock." But she doubted the veracity of his words.

"I don't care what he says. Even if you bolt your door, I am afraid for you to stay here by yourself."

"I hate him!" Corey shouted, and Alexandra did not know if she was referring to their father or Clarewood.

"I am going to stay here with you," Olivia said firmly, picking up a satchel. "Corey, guard the carriage and the horse while I help Alexandra."

Corey's eyes widened. Clearly she had no wish to stand in the busy street by herself. At that time of day, it was congested with wagons and drays carrying every possible kind of cargo.

"Olivia, I can take everything up myself. And you are *not* staying here! You need to get Corey home. It will be dark soon. I am fine," she lied, for she was so sick in her heart that she could barely describe her own feelings, even to herself.

"Will you really be fine? How can you pretend that you will be fine?" Olivia's gaze became moist. "We can't leave you here. And *I* hate him, too."

"You cannot stay here with me. I brought this on myself. And this is a pleasant inn," Alexandra said firmly, as if she believed it. "I am going to turn my little room into a cozy, cheerful place. You can visit me as much as you like. But tomorrow you must get in touch with all the clients on the list I gave you, so they know where to find me now."

Olivia grimaced. "You should have the money so you no longer have to take in sewing. But Father took it, and he will gamble it away before the week is out!"

Alexandra had three bags, one containing the garments she was currently working on, and the basket of food. She also had twenty-five of the fifty pounds she'd saved for Olivia's dowry. Five pounds had paid for her room for a month. The repairs and pressed gowns that were ready to be picked up remained at Edgemont Way. "You need to start home. Please. I have enough to worry about, and I don't also want to worry about you getting waylaid on the highway."

Corey was crying now. Olivia hugged her, fighting tears, and Alexandra hugged her back. Then she kissed Corey. "I will be fine. When have I ever not risen to the occasion? Surely, Corey, some good will come of this. God always has a plan."

"No good will come of this, not unless the duke marries you — which is what he should do!" Corey insisted, her eyes flashing.

Alexandra tensed, her heart leaping unpleasantly. "I believe he is well out of my league, my dear." But the truth was, he seemed to despise her now.

"I saw the way he looked at you," Corey continued shrilly. "What is wrong with him? You are better than those stupid, silly debutantes!"

Alexandra hugged her, then managed to get her and Olivia back into their carriage. She gave the black gelding a pat, grateful they had, at least, a good and solid means of transportation. "Please get word to my clients tomorrow. And if you have time, come on Wednesday," she said.

They drove off, both girls in tears, but Alexandra kept a smile on her face and waved at them. When they were gone, however, tears instantly filled her eyes. She fought them. She was not going to feel sorry for herself. She had made the mess she was in, and she would never try to deny it.

As she reached for one of her bags, a man came to stand beside her. She tensed, only to realize it was her German landlord. "I'll carry yer bags up, Miss Bolton."

For the first time since negotiating the price of the room, she looked carefully at him. Mr. Schumacher was a big bear of a man, so big that he was intimidating, but his eyes were direct and not without a trace of kindness. She smiled. "I'd appreciate the help," she said.

When she was safely in the room, the door locked, Alexandra lit the single lamp, knowing she must buy another lamp or candles on the morrow. The room had wood-paneled walls and wood floors, a single window, a narrow bed, a small, rickety table with two chairs, a sink, an icebox and a small wood stove. Pegs on the wall would serve as a closet.

But it wasn't that bad — Alexandra had seen so much worse. The floors needed wax, but they had been recently mopped. The pale muslin curtains on the window were freshly laundered, and so were the thin cotton sheets on the bed — she'd noticed that right away. She'd brought her own blanket and pillow. She hadn't met Mrs. Schumacher, but had been told that the missus did the cleaning herself, along with their two daughters, as well as the cooking for the public taproom. Alexandra had no intention of dining there. She could not afford it.

She took off her coat and hung it on one precious peg, then opened up her bag of repairs, taking out five gowns, all of which she hung on the remaining pegs. She removed her needles, pincushions and threads, placing everything carefully on the table. Sobs seemed to be arising deep in her chest. She ignored them, taking out her iron and the heavy towel she would be pressing the gowns on.

Having arranged a work space, she then took out the few belongings she'd chosen to bring, refolding and then replacing them in a bag, which she put at the foot of her bed, as if it were a chest. She then went to unpack the basket of food. One of her sisters had put a bouquet of dried flowers inside. She started to cry.

Alexandra gave up. She threw her blanket on the bed, lay down and curled up. This was her fault. She'd made a terrible choice, trusting a man she did not know at all. She had no right to such misery and heartache. She had no right to be feeling sorry for herself. She had no right to be afraid.

But she was all of those things.

And worst of all, Clarewood's image remained in her mind, but not as she had last seen him. She kept seeing him at the Harrington ball, when he had rescued her and then her father — his eyes direct, intense and concerned. Then she saw him as he waited for her to alight from the carriage, his gaze blatantly sensual and seductive. And the way he'd looked at her while they made love was simply unforgettable. . . .

But damn it, she wanted to forget. She

had to forget! Her entire life was at stake now, and she had to focus on her sewing; otherwise, she would likely starve to death.

But he haunted her dreams that night, as he had done from the start, and she tossed and turned restlessly until dawn. She spent the next day cleaning every inch of her room. She scrubbed the floors, the walls, the sink, icebox and stove. Then she dusted. By the time her sisters returned, she'd taken some scraps of red and gold fabric and sewn cheerful if exotic slipcovers for the chairs, the design somewhat fantastic, and had tossed her own violet shawl over the foot of the bed as a pretty throw. She'd embroidered the window curtains. She'd bought a bright red Poinsettia plant and placed it in the window. She'd put out some family portraits and thought that, eventually, her small room might even start to feel like home, though frankly, it looked like a gypsy's abode.

Corey and Olivia returned at midday on Wednesday. They had done as she'd asked, leaving her new address with her clients. Lady Lewis had even picked up her dresses, leaving payment, which they eagerly gave her. They exclaimed over how pretty the room was becoming, and Alexandra decided they could afford to eat lunch downstairs.

True to Mr. Schumacher's word, his wife was a wonderful cook, and they ate the best potted chicken they'd ever tried, followed by lemon tarts. They'd giggled over lunch, due undoubtedly to the ale they'd been served, talking about all kinds of silly things — including the fact that their neighbor had fallen off his horse, landing in his neighbor's pig sty. It felt so good to laugh. Corey pointed out that it was too bad the victim of the sty wasn't the duke.

That sobered them all.

"I haven't heard a word about him," Olivia said hesitantly. "Or anything else."

Alexandra told her heart to stop racing at the mere thought of him. She wondered if Lady Witte had ceased her vicious gossip. "It doesn't matter," she said, but it felt as if it mattered very much.

It was a long trip back to Edgemont Way, and Alexandra realized that they were the only ones left in the taproom. She looked at her pocket watch. "It's three," she said softly, her heart lurching with dismay. "You really must be going."

"I don't want to go," Corey said, her smile vanishing.

Alexandra gave her a look as they got up, having already paid for their meal. Mr. Schumacher came running into the room.

"Do ye need anything else?" he smiled.

"That was wonderful," Alexandra said. "Thank you."

He looked at her and then at her sisters. "You should go home with your family."

Alexandra turned away, unable to tell him that returning to Edgemont Way was not an option. She walked her sisters outside, fighting the sorrow building in her chest. Having them leave hurt. Going back upstairs felt as if it might be the loneliest moment of her life.

Olivia hugged her. "We'll come back tomorrow."

Alexandra was aghast. "No, you won't! It's much too far to come every day. Wait until Sunday, Olivia, please. And don't abandon Father. You *are* taking care of him, aren't you?"

"Of course we are," Corey said, her mouth downturned. Then she hugged Alexandra — hard. "I miss you so much. I am sorry I said you shouldn't marry the squire. You were right — he is a good man."

"No, you were right, Corey — I would have been so unhappy, marrying without any affection." Alexandra wiped the tears from her sisters' cheeks.

Then Corey and Olivia climbed reluctantly into the carriage. Alexandra stood on the street, waving after them as they drove off. Even when they were no longer in sight, it was hard to turn around and go back upstairs to her room. She missed them so much, and it hurt.

Alexandra spent the next week immersed in her sewing. She had a number of clients who were expecting to pick up their things in the coming week, and though Lady Witte had made such a fuss over having her items finished the previous Friday, her sisters had said she hadn't bothered to return for anything, nor had she sent a servant. Which was lucky, Alexandra thought. She dreaded their next encounter, but she needed the woman's business, and had all of her gowns and underthings ready that Friday — a week later than she'd demanded. She hoped Lady Witte would send a servant when she realized Alexandra was no longer at Edgemont Way. She was the kind of woman to avoid the East End, so Alexandra certainly didn't expected her to show up in person.

But when Alexandra went to answer her door late in the afternoon on Saturday, it was Charlotte Witte who stood there.

She was smiling in a very unpleasant manner, as if she were gloating. Then Alexandra saw the diamond necklace the other woman was wearing. It had three tiers and was undoubtedly worth thousands of pounds. Oddly, the sight of it was hurtful, because Alexandra couldn't help but wonder if the duke had given it to her.

Charlotte's catty smile widened. She looked Alexandra up and down dismissively, then looked past her into the small, shabby room. "Hello, Miss Bolton. Are my things ready?"

Alexandra avoided eye contact. "Of course." All the items in question were hanging in a garment bag, and she turned to get it. She despised the other woman, and knew it had less to do with the woman's rudeness than it did her past relationship with Clarewood. She was embarrassed to realize she was the one being petty now.

Charlotte followed her inside, closing the door — as if she wished to stay and chat — her eyes sparkling with glee. "My, you *have* come down in the world. This is hardly Edgemont Way. In fact, the servants at Clarewood have better accommodations than this."

Alexandra tensed, the words a distinct blow, as she felt certain the duke's staff had exceptional housing. Alexandra held out the garment bag, fighting for composure. *She needed this woman's business.* "I can't imagine how you would know anything about the servants' quarters." The moment she spoke, she regretted it.

Charlotte's eyes narrowed. "How dare you speak disrespectfully to me? I know because the duke is so proud of his progressive ways, and he wanted to show me his exemplary arrangements. But you wouldn't know anything about the duke, now would you — except that he is very powerful and insatiable in bed." Her pale brows lifted.

Alexandra flushed. There was nothing to say. She had a terrible image of Clarewood in bed with Charlotte, making love to the petite blonde with the same frenzy he'd shown her.

Charlotte laughed with contempt. "You are nothing, Miss Bolton, and nobody, and if anyone has made that clear, it is Stephen, who has tossed you aside like the piece of used baggage that you are."

Alexandra gasped. "That is beyond rude!"

"But that is what he did, is it not?" Charlotte said. "Servants gossip, Miss Bolton, and I believe I could recite your last encounter with him word for word, if I should choose to bother. Did you *really* think to trap him into marriage?"

Alexandra was aghast. She was also hurt, shaken and sickened by the other woman's cruelty. "Why are you doing this?" she asked. "What could I possibly have done to you?"

"I am doing nothing," Charlotte snapped, taking the garment bag. "And now I hope we are clear. You belong below stairs, Miss Bolton, and make no mistake about that again!" She set the bag roughly down on the table, knocking over Alexandra's sewing materials and a recently finished gown. As she did, she knocked over a cup of cold tea. Alexandra cried out, diving for the cup, afraid the liquid would ruin the gown. The cup broke, but she was relieved to see the tea spill over the floor. She seized the gown, holding it like a newborn to her breast.

Meanwhile Charlotte opened the bag and began roughly yanking out the items.

"Everything is pressed," Alexandra gasped. "And everything is in there, I assure you, I am not a thief. I have a very good reputation."

"Really? Because everything looks horridly wrinkled to me." Charlotte threw a gown that had been perfectly pressed onto the floor. "Look at that!" She stared and then removed a chemise and said, "You have ruined this garment, as well."

Alexandra was stunned. "I haven't ruined anything. Why are you doing this?"

"It is torn," Charlotte said fiercely, "and useless to me now!" She ripped the seams open.

Alexandra was stunned into silence.

"Oh, and what is this? Have you burned my favorite dress?"

Alexandra began to shake. "You know I have done no such thing."

Charlotte eyed her hatefully. "You ripped my chemise and burned my best gown, you did not press anything properly, *and* you were late! You are worthless, Miss Bolton, truly worthless, and I shall tell everyone how inept you are."

Alexandra's knees buckled. "Why are you doing this? Why do you hate me so?"

"Because you have dared to try to rise to my station, dared to tempt the duke, my lover — you, a dirty servant, and that is simply not allowed!" Charlotte shoved the items into the bag and started for the door.

Alexandra realized what was happening and managed to say, "You haven't paid me."

Charlotte looked at her with contempt. "I would never pay you for such shoddy work."

Alexandra couldn't breathe. "You owe me twelve pounds, Lady Witte. I spent days on your garments!"

Charlotte smiled. "I owe you nothing," she said, and walked out with her clothes.

Alexandra's first instinct was to run after her. But what would she do then? Steal her purse? Force her to pay? The woman was already going to tell everyone that she had ruined her clothes. If she forcibly took the money owed, she would be accused of theft, as well. She stumbled to her bed and sat down.

Breathing hard, she told herself that she would get by. This wasn't the end of the world, even if it felt like it. Lady Henredon, for one, had always been kind. Still, she didn't think she had ever been treated so rudely.

The duke's image loomed. No, she *had* been treated this rudely before. Clarewood had treated her even more poorly than his horrid little mistress. God, they deserved one another. The tears fell. She wished her heart would stop hurting so.

"Are we intruding, my dear?"

Alexandra froze at the sound of Blanche Harrington's kind voice. She wiped her eyes, aghast to be caught in such an emotional state, and looked up. Lady Blanche stood in the doorway, beautiful and elegant and so incongruous to the setting, her husband, Sir Rex, behind her. She was smiling kindly, but her gaze, while compassionate, was concerned.

Alexandra shot to her feet. "I am fine," she managed, trying to smile. Lady Blanche hadn't been on her list of customers, even though, once in a while, she did send clothes for a significant repair. Most of the time she had her own staff clean and press her wardrobe.

"May we come in?" The other woman's kind expression never faltered.

She had been a good friend of Alexandra's mother, and she had been a kind neighbor after her passing and in all the years since. She had certainly been kind at the recent ball. "Of course." Alexandra began to flush. "I'm so sorry." She darted a glance at Lady Blanche's handsome, somewhat intimidating husband. Like most of the de Warenne men, he had an air of authority about him, and could not enter a room unnoticed or without commanding respect. "I have nothing to offer you, really," she said helplessly.

"I'll send for tea," Sir Rex said.

Blanche turned to him, smiling, and when he'd limped off, she came inside. "How are you, dear? I'm afraid the news of your taking up residence at an inn is quite the gossip now. I heard it from Lady Lewis last night."

Alexandra bit her lip. "Do you want to sit down, Lady Blanche?"

Blanche smiled and took one of the chairs. Alexandra took the other one. Blanche said, "Charlotte Witte is a disgrace. She is the least gracious person I know. I saw her leaving the inn as we drove up. Did she upset you?"

Alexandra inhaled. "We have made a bad start, unfortunately." There, that felt better. She breathed again. "She has decided to actively hate me, and to hurt me if she can."

"And how can she hurt you, my dear? Other than with malicious lies?"

Alexandra stared, and Blanche stared back. "She has threatened to ruin my sewing business. I do very good work, as you know. But she intends to tell everyone that I have ruined her clothes."

Blanche reached out and held her hand. "I will set the record straight."

"Thank you." Alexandra was afraid she was going to cry again.

"Alexandra," Blanche said softly, "when I heard you had left home, I felt I had to come and inquire after your welfare. Your mother would be so upset. Is there any chance of your going back home, where you belong?"

Alexandra looked at the table. How much did Blanche know? Then she looked up. It was time to stop lying. "My father will not allow me back. I cannot really blame him."

The other woman's eyes widened.

"I have made a terrible mistake," Alexandra admitted.

Blanche tightened her hold on Alexandra's hand. "So the blame is all yours?"

Alexandra flushed and decided she had better not answer.

A knock sounded at the door. Blanche got up before Alexandra could move and let one of Mr. Schumacher's daughters bring in a tray of tea. Alexandra could not hear what she said to Sir Rex, who was standing behind the girl, but he turned and left. Blanche smiled at the young girl, then returned to the table. When they were alone, she poured two cups of tea, handing one to Alexandra. "I am not going to pry. I have heard all kinds of stories, but I despise gossip. With good cause, by the way." She smiled and sipped. "A long time ago, society thought me a madwoman. I do think I lost my mind, actually. I knew everyone was whispering about me behind my back — until Sir Rex returned to town to save me." She smiled.

Alexandra was stupefied. "I am sure you are exaggerating."

"No, my dear, I was known as 'the madwoman,' and most of London was enthralled by my downfall." Then she smiled. "It was long ago — another lifetime ago, actually."

Her tea forgotten, Alexandra asked, "Why are you telling me this?"

"Because having suffered the cruelty of the ton, I refuse to heed the gossips. On the other hand, it was very noble of Clarewood to rescue you at Sara's birthday party. It was even nobler for him to help Edgemont home that night."

Alexandra hugged herself. "It was kind." Immediately she wanted to take back her words. Tears filled her eyes. He was not kind, he was cruel, but she would never point that out to Lady Blanche.

Blanche's soft gaze hardened. "I believe I am furious with him."

Alexandra was certain that the other woman knew of their affair.

"I'd like to help you, my dear." Blanche smiled now. "Would you come to Harrington Hall? I have been meaning to take on my own personal seamstress for some time. Especially with Marion about to be wed, between her and Sara and myself, and of course Randolph, there is so much to clean, restore, repair and mend. I would give you a fine bedroom on the upper floor. I'm sure you would be more comfortable there than here."

Alexandra was so surprised that she started, shaking the rickety table. It took her only a moment to realize that Blanche hardly needed a full-time seamstress, and that this was an act of charity. "I so appreciate your offer, Lady Blanche, but I couldn't possibly accept."

"Why not?"

"We both know you do not need me at Harrington Hall, mending and pressing your clothes. I am so moved by your consideration, but I can't accept such charity. I can — and will — take care of myself."

Blanche sighed. "I thought you would refuse me. You are every bit as strong, independent and proud as your mother."

Alexandra heard again her father's cruel words. *You are nothing like your mother.*

Blanche smiled and cupped her cheek. "She would be so proud of you now."

Dismayed, wishing it were true and knowing it was not, Alexandra bit her lip and shook her head.

"You can turn to me at any time," Blanche said firmly. "If you need anything, or if you change your mind, simply ask or say so."

Alexandra was moved. "You are so kind."

"I loved your mother, and I love you, too, Alexandra." Blanche stood up. "Does Clarewood know that you have left home — and that you have taken up residence in a common inn?"

Alexandra stood, so swiftly that her chair toppled over. "He won't care."

Blanche studied her closely for a long moment. "Actually, I think you are wrong."

Julia Mowbray balanced over her mare's withers, allowing the hunter to extend her stride. The rolling countryside became a blur as the mare's pace increased to a gallop, Julia's Great Danes running alongside them. Crouching almost like a jockey, Julia let the mare go forward a bit more. Horse and rider were one.

Several moments later, she sat her mount casually as they trotted back to the handsome two-story stone stables behind the house, the Danes now running ahead. She was out of breath, but no longer filled with the excitement of the furious ride. Instead, she was thoughtful.

Tyne Jefferson was firmly engraved on her mind. His image had become unshakable — a big, muscular, leonine man, bronzed from the sun, his brown hair shot with gray and gold. When his mouth curved, a dimple formed on the left side of his face. His chin was cleft, his cheekbones high. His nose was broad and crooked — she guessed it had been broken more than once — but that could not detract from his strong, masculine good looks. He did not look like any of her peers. He was so obviously an American, and not because his suits were ready-made or his hands heavily callused. It wasn't the scar running through one eyebrow. There was something strong and sure about him, like an ancient oak tree that had survived endless cycles of life and death. His shoulders were so broad that she thought he might be able to withstand just about anything life dealt him.

He was so obviously the antithesis of her late husband, the previous duke.

They'd met a week ago at a London dinner party. She'd noticed him in the salon the moment she arrived. He was standing with Cliff de Warenne, one of the land's wealthiest shipping magnates, and Sir Reginald Reed, the knighted lawyer widely renowned for his control of many of the country's railway lines. They were engrossed in conversation, and she'd had the oddest feeling that she'd met him somewhere, at some time, in the past. It was an intense but fleeting feeling of recognition, and her heart had leaped. Then, a moment later, she'd known she was mistaken. She did not know that man. And she was certain he was an American. He was too big, too bluff and too rough-edged to be anything else.

He'd glanced at her once or twice before they'd gone into the dining room to sit down, not rudely, just casually, the way one would glance across a roomful of people to remark who was there. He'd been seated across the dinner table from her, and that was where they'd been introduced. Julia had tried not to look at him, but several times their gazes had accidentally collided. His smile had made her heart race. She couldn't believe how foolishly she was behaving. She was rarely attracted to men these days, and never to strangers.

Since that night, she'd learned he was a California rancher, and while she didn't know what had brought him to Britain, he was apparently trying to convince Cliff de Warenne to extend a shipping line to the small city of Sacramento. He was enthusiastic about the railroad that would soon be able to ship his cattle from his hacienda to the town and beyond, to the Midwestern and Eastern markets.

After supper, as the gentlemen were moving off to smoke cigars and sip whiskey, he bumped into her, seemingly intentionally. Julia had smiled at him as she would any guest, determined not to reveal that she found him terribly intriguing.

"I am sorry, that was clumsy of me," he said, even though he'd only brushed against her arm. "I'm too big for your country."

The comment was unusual, and she started, looking deeply into his amber eyes. "Yes," she slowly said, "I have a feeling that you might be too big for this tiny land."

He blinked and looked closely back at her, then slowly smiled. "Did you just insult me?"

She realized she was smiling back. "That was a compliment." And suddenly they were staring at one another.

She coughed, about to make a trite remark, when his gaze slipped to her sapphire and diamond necklace. He quickly looked up and said, "You are my first duchess."

Suddenly she was warm. "I don't imagine you would meet many duchesses in America."

"None."

Julia was warm just recalling their first meeting. He was a man of few words, but she didn't mind. When he spoke, it was worth listening to what he had to say. That was so different from her peers.

She'd learned more about him at the ball. He had never married. He didn't have any children. He lived alone. Julia couldn't really understand that, but she would never pry.

She had reached the stables, and two grooms rushed out. As she dismounted, her thoughts remained on Jefferson. While she thought she'd made an excellent impression upon him last week, at first she had been flustered by his call. She'd been embarrassed that he would catch her so disheveled from her morning ride, but he hadn't seemed to mind. He had seemed admiring, instead.

Her heart skipped like a young girl's as she thanked the grooms and started back toward the house, the Danes keeping pace. She'd even given him an open invitation to call, and they had planned to ride together. But a week had gone by, and he hadn't called. Their paths had not crossed at any evening affair, either.

Her heart lurched with dismay. If he had any interest in her as a woman, surely he would have called by now. Wouldn't he?

Was she being foolish? She was fifty years old. She knew she remained a very attractive woman, and that she looked only forty, if that. She supposed her youthful appearance was due to her active lifestyle. She was a horsewoman and had been so her entire life — she spent two or three hours every day in the saddle, which kept her legs strong, and her abdomen tight and lean. And she was always busy. While she had had many responsibilities as the Duchess of Clarewood, as she did now, as its dowager duchess, she had also become involved in many of her son's charities. She didn't have time to sit around and sip chocolate.

And although she was well into her middle years, Jefferson had awakened something in her that she had thought long since buried. A yearning churned in her now, and it included the desire to be in his strong arms. She was a powerful woman, but he made her feel small, vulnerable and feminine. He made her feel desirable again.

She did not know how long he would remain in the country, but she clearly had a choice — to remain lonely and wistful, or be bold and take matters into her own hands.

Her stride lengthened. Matilda and Henry galloped ahead of her, tails wagging. Julia went into a small library, furnished mostly in shades of cream and gold, and sat down at the desk there. She hesitated, and decided to be direct. She penned Jefferson a very brief note, inviting him for the ride they had discussed. As she sealed the envelope, she was afraid he would refuse.

What if she had misread him? What if his responses to her had merely been polite? After all, everyone fawned over her.

Before she had a chance to change her mind, she rang a small silver bell. "Godfrey, please see that this is delivered by messenger to Mr. Jefferson at the St. Lucien Hotel."

When her butler was gone, she called the dogs over, petting them as she thought about Jefferson. He would receive the note that evening. Etiquette required an immediate reply. She should know where he stood by tomorrow at this time.

She thought about how Ariella and Elysse had shepherded him over to her. She knew both young women fairly well, as they were so close to Stephen — and Ariella was his natural cousin, as well. She had instantly assumed the call was not without subterfuge. The young ladies were so transparent. It amazed her that they might be matchmaking, but she hadn't minded. If Stephen ever learned what they were up to, he would be furious with them.

She sobered. Her thoughts were now fixed on her son and the ugly rumors raging about town. The gossips held that Stephen was having an affair with Edgemont's daughter, and they were thoroughly titillated. Julia did not know Alexandra Bolton, but she'd glimpsed her at the Harrington affair, and it had been obvious that she was an honorable gentlewoman, even if impoverished, and one of great dignity and character. She was not the type of woman her son would try to seduce. To be blunt, Miss Bolton was not mistress material. She was certain there was no affair, but she had seen how attentive he was to the girl. She couldn't help wondering if Stephen was finally and genuinely interested in a woman — even if he might not know it himself yet.

Julia decided that she should call on Miss Bolton. If Stephen had taken an interest in a proper woman, she would be thrilled, never mind the damned gossips. And if Miss Bolton had been mistaken in her choice of men so long ago, Julia would be the first to forgive her. It was so easy to make mistakes when one was young and naive and filled with silly dreams.

Godfrey returned. "Your Grace? Mr. Jefferson has called."

Her heart slammed and stopped. Then it thundered. It took her a moment to realize that Jefferson had come of his own volition. "Show him to the Turquoise Room, please, and tell him that I will be right down." All too aware of Godfrey's jaw dropping, she leaped from her chair, calling for her maids as she ran for the stairs.

Stephen sat with his steward in the study, writing checks. Clarewood might be thriving, but there were still monthly expenses, including personal ones. He stared at an account, brows raised, wondering at the item. "Who is George Lavoiser?"

The steward leaned forward to glance at the bill just as Randolph strode in, his tweed jacket, breeches and boots damp from the drizzle outside. "That is the florist you used last month, Your Grace."

Stephen's heart seemed to lurch. Ah yes, he'd yet to pay for the spectacular roses he'd sent Alexandra. His entire body stiffened. The tension remained, although he was doing his best to forget about her and her schemes, and it was damned unpleasant. The problem was, she remained oddly unforgettable. He could not seem to erase their last encounter from his mind — nor the hours of passion they had shared.

He remained angry and disbelieving. Yet he was never angry — he'd spent an entire lifetime learning to be calm and controlled. Just as she had shown him the kind of passion he thought impossible, she had somehow broken through his reservoir of composure, not that he would let anyone ever know that.

Stephen scrawled a check and handed it to the steward. "Would you excuse us," he said, and it was not a question.

Randolph stripped off his sodden jacket and moved closer to the fire in the hearth. Stephen stood, not bothering to roll down the sleeves of his dark blue sweater. It was a dastardly day, cold and rainy. He walked over, almost reluctant to find out what Randolph had learned from their litigators. But as rumors were flying all over town about the "affair," he was fairly certain what he would hear.

As Stephen poured his younger half brother a brandy, Randolph said, "It's broken off, Your Grace. Denney has ended the suit."

He was not surprised. Of course it was broken off. No man wanted a trollop for a wife. And she wanted a far better catch for a husband. He handed his brother a drink.

Randolph sipped gratefully and then said, his gaze direct, "Apparently he was furious. He's heard all the rumors." He hesitated, then said, "There's more."

Stephen shoved his hands in his pockets and stared at the flames dancing in the hearth, his back now to his brother. There was no reason to feel guilty. She'd plotted to trap him, even if he had been amused by having Squire Denney as a rival, one he knew he could squash with one single breath along the nape of her neck. And if she hadn't been such a conniving bitch, he would feel sorry for her. After all, she could have used the security of the match with Denney.

But if he did not know himself better, he would think that he actually felt sorry for her. Just a little. And that was absurd.

She would find someone else to trap into marriage, he thought.

Of course, there *was* one little fact that was bothering him. She was in her middle twenties. Why hadn't she used her virginity long ago to ensnare a wealthy husband if that had been her plan?

He did not like that nagging question. Stephen turned. "What more could there possibly be?"

Randolph winced. "Edgemont threw her out. Apparently he heard the rumors, too."

Stephen reeled. He wasn't sure he had ever been as surprised, as taken aback. "He tossed her out?" Oddly, his first instinct was to confront Edgemont. "Where did she go?"

"She's let a room in London. Apparently she continues to sew for various ladies and has set up shop there."

Stephen's heart did the strangest thing — it sank with dread. *She'd been thrown out of her home. She was sewing from a room in a London inn.*

He reminded himself that this was not his concern, and that he did not care. He immediately returned to his desk. "I'd like to go over some ledgers with you, Randolph," he said, refusing to think of Alexandra any longer.

Randolph approached. "The word is the neighborhood is a very impoverished one. I have an address, by the way."

Stephen stared grimly, meeting Randolph's gaze. He couldn't believe he'd actually heard disapproval in his brother's tone. "Are you blaming me for her fate?"

Randolph stared back. "I believe that I am."

Stephen was surprised. "So you will take her side?"

Randolph grimaced and said softly, "We are brothers. I admire you immensely — and I am terribly grateful for your being my mentor. But I do not think she deserves this set-down. I know you would never callously toss her aside as you did. I can't imagine what she did to raise your ire. Perhaps, whatever it was, you were mistaken, or you might forgive her." He added, "Your Grace."

As disturbed as he was, Stephen was briefly proud of Randolph. "Few men would speak to me as you have just done. But I am glad you are being candid with me."

Randolph smiled. "I do not mean to criticize. But I am concerned."

"Don't waste your time. Miss Bolton is a survivor. And I am sure the falling out with her father is a temporary one. After all, she holds that family together."

Randolph seemed incredulous. "You won't repair this?"

Stephen stood. "I never forgive betrayal, Randolph, and neither should you. She betrayed me — she *played* me — and she can find another benefactor to rescue her from her current straits."

Randolph shook his head. "And if no one does so? Then what?"

"Do not push me," Stephen warned.

"May I check on her?"

Stephen paused. It took him a moment to consider this course. "If you do so, you are on your own. I do not want a report — not a single word." And as Randolph looked at him with disapproval, he finished, "This is not my fault. This entire episode is of her own making."

"Of course . . . Your Grace."

CHAPTER TWELVE

Tyne Jefferson strolled as casually as possible into the salon as he was ushered inside by a servant. It wasn't an easy task — his pulse was racing, his tension was high, and there was nothing casual about his call. He'd meant to stay away, never mind her invitation last week. He'd decided that, given his growing interest in her, no good could come of any further interactions.

Now he looked at her and his heart roared. She was even tinier and prettier than he'd remembered.

Julia smiled at him. "Another pleasant surprise," she said softly.

He managed to smile back, though his heart was doing a few odd flips and he was taken aback by his surging pulse. But he didn't hesitate. "I hope you mean that."

She came forward, her eyes on his. They were warm; they sparkled. Her cheeks were still flushed from the outdoors. "I do. I am so glad you have called. I was just thinking about you."

The British were probably the most polite and formal people he'd ever encountered, but her comment just now wasn't polite, it was familiar. He was startled.

For one thing, he'd decided that her last invitation had been made out of that infamous British politeness, nothing more, while he wanted a bit more than a chitchat. But she was a great lady and a duchess; wanting more was wrong, so he'd decided to stay away. And then he'd tried not to think about her, which had proven impossible. Every day he'd wondered if they would bump into one another that night at a dinner party or the opera. And a part of him had hoped so. But he hadn't seen her at any of the evening affairs he'd attended. He hadn't seen her in the park, either, or shopping on Oxford Street. And he'd been disappointed.

Worst of all, he'd even dreamed about her. And that made him uncomfortable, because he couldn't control the nature of his dreams, which had been sexual and intense.

The Dowager Duchess of Clarewood was on his mind, there was no damned doubt about that. He wasn't very happy about it, either, because there was just nowhere for them to go. Even if she was a passionate woman, he knew he was not her type of man. She needed someone cultured and titled, someone who wore white gloves, actually liked the opera and had never chopped a block of firewood in his life, much less killed a man.

But he'd broken down. His time was running out; in a few weeks he would be returning to California, so he had decided to see her one more time. He'd been half hoping that when he did, he wouldn't have any reaction to her at all — that somehow, he'd made it all up in his head.

But he'd been wrong. He was having a reaction, all right. She took his breath away.

She turned to ask the butler for refreshments, giving him the chance to ogle every inch of her. She was so tiny that he thought he might be able to span his hands around her waist. And when the servant left and she faced him, he felt himself flush, because in his mind's eye, she'd been stark naked.

"It's going to rain," she said. "Otherwise I'd take you hacking."

He recovered somewhat. "In California rain is a blessing. We have long, dry summers."

"And shockingly cold winters — in the high country," she said.

358

He raised his eyebrows.

"I was curious, so I have been reading up on the history of America — and California." She smiled.

His heart jumped again. Why was she curious? He almost wished he could tell her about all that he had endured — most of his friends thought him heroic. But he wasn't sure she would admire him for wandering through a blizzard with frostbite, then finally digging a hole in the snow to wait it out until he could see where he was. "I don't claim to be a historian, but you can ask me anything."

Her gaze held his, her smile fading. "It's a difficult life, isn't it — on the frontier?"

It was very difficult, and he wanted her to know that none of her peers could survive all that he had — as if that would impress her. "Our summers are boiling hot. Sometimes there's no rain. Cattle — wildlife — die. Our winters are worse. The snow can pile up higher than the rooftops of our houses." He smiled and shrugged. "But we do what we have to."

Her eyes were wide. "I've started reading about the difficulties of crossing the country and settling the western lands. It sounds so dangerous, Mr. Jefferson."

It almost sounded as if she were worried

about him. "It *is* dangerous." He smiled at her then. "A man needs ambition, and if he has it, and he has the guts, he'll be fine."

Her gaze was wide and searching. "You know," she said, "you said you've never met a duchess before. I've never met a frontiersman before — if that is what you call yourself."

"I call myself a Californian."

She smiled back at him. "I like that," she said softly. "It says so much in so few words."

He stared, unsmiling, and her smile faded, too. He felt so much tension within his own body and wondered if she felt the same. What man wouldn't want to take her in his arms and taste that small, pretty mouth? he wondered. What would she say if she knew he'd built his ranch mostly by himself, with his own two hands? That he'd killed a handful of men, mostly outlaws and Indians? That he'd almost starved to death one winter, when lost in the wilds of Nevada? That he'd eaten raw meat, having killed a fox with his bare hands, in order to survive?

He suddenly turned away from her. He knew what she would say. She would be appalled. As she would probably also be appalled by the scars on his body. He had more than his share. He, on the other hand, could imagine the perfection of her body, and he wished he could put his hands all over it.

She was being polite, even now. And despite his earlier assumption, that was undoubtedly the only reason why she had told him he could call anytime, why she had offered to take him riding.

"I do have a question," she said. "You told me you had come to Britain for personal reasons. I don't mean to pry, but it does seem like a truly long journey if you were only soliciting Cliff de Warenne."

He crossed his arms, tensing, and suddenly, he wanted to tell her about his life — not just the good parts, but the bad. "My daughter is buried here."

She started. "I am so sorry!"

"It's okay. Donna died twenty-eight years ago. And I should have come to her grave a long time ago, but I never did."

She reached for his arm and slid her hand over it. He jerked, surprised. "I didn't know. I can't imagine what you went through. So you were married?"

"No. She left me, even though I'd planned on marrying her, to return to Brighton, where she was from. I didn't know she was carrying our child." There was still sadness in talking about it, but it was distant and faded now.

"Life can be so cruel, so unkind," she said feelingly.

Her intensity shocked him. But he'd heard the rumors — apparently her husband had been a real bastard. "Yeah, it can — bad things happen to good people all the time, and there is no justice."

For a moment she was silent, staring into his eyes. Then she said, "You deserve good things, Mr. Jefferson, I am certain of it."

She laid her small, soft hand on his arm as she spoke, and his heart lurched like a locomotive hitting broken tracks. For one moment, as his blood heated, it was hard to speak. "That's kind of you," he said gruffly, and he actually felt himself blush.

Alexandra walked slowly up the crowded street, zigzagging between the pedestrians while trying to avoid piles of refuse, sewage and potholes. She wished she could hold a handkerchief to her nose. The stench was so foul, she thought she might vomit, but she couldn't hold a kerchief, because she had two bags in her arms. One contained groceries, the other, sewing supplies.

She was beyond dismay. Twelve days had passed since she had moved into Mr. Schumacher's inn, which she had come to regard as a veritable paradise in this dank and fetid swamp of impoverished and hopeless humanity. Alexandra had been aware of the terrible conditions of Britain's working classes. She had always felt sorry for the working poor, especially the children. But reading about the conditions in factories and mills — and debating the various ways one might institute economic and social reforms — was so very different from living among Britain's poor. She hadn't realized how terribly most of England was suffering, and just how privileged even the destitute among the upper classes were.

Everyone here was ragged, tired and hungry. Even the children had gaunt expressions and dead eyes. It was heartbreaking.

And perhaps the worst part was that these men, women and children didn't realize she was just like them. They looked at her with respect, they doffed their caps to her, they called her "my lady," and even, sometimes, "Yer Grace." They understood that she was gentry and simply did not know that now she was one of them.

Alexandra wondered how she would live the rest of her life like this. The thought was dismal and depressing. She could bear the burden of her poverty, but she missed Olivia and Corey terribly, and she was always tired.

She tensed, an image of Clarewood coming to mind. She still thought of him all the time, with hurt and anger, with betrayal, even though almost three weeks had passed since their ill-fated affair had begun and so precipitously ended. But she would not blame him for what had happened. Too late, she knew she'd been weak; had she been stronger, had she resisted his advances, she would be comfortably at home right now.

And then Alexandra saw a beautiful closed carriage at the end of the street, with two handsome bay geldings in the traces. She halted, tensing. Only a very wealthy nobleman or merchant would own such a coach, but she did not recognize it. At least it did not belong to Clarewood, not that she ever expected to see him again, and it was not Lady Blanche's. She relaxed a little and decided that the carriage had nothing to do with her.

She pushed open the door to the inn with her shoulder, her arms filled with her groceries and supplies. Randolph had called on her a few days ago, inquiring after her welfare. It had taken all her resolve to remain calm and composed, and even indifferent, while in his presence. She'd met with him in the public room, claimed she was fine, and refused him when he had asked if she wished to stay as his guest at Harrington Hall. She hadn't told him about his mother's visit, but he was an admirable and compassionate young man.

Now, as she entered the front hall, the public room ahead, the stairs on her right, she saw a beautiful noblewoman seated at a table there, chatting with Mr. Schumacher. Instantly her landlord waved at her; as instantly, the blond woman turned and stood up.

Alexandra felt faint. Although they had never met, she recognized the dowager duchess of Clarewood instantly. She'd seen her at the Harrington ball.

Julia Mowbray glided toward her, smiling. "Hello, Miss Bolton. I believe I am being terribly bold, but I decided we must meet."

Alexandra clutched her bags, afraid she would drop them otherwise. What could Stephen's mother want? Her stomach churned with sickening force. "Your Grace," she somehow said.

"Can we go upstairs? Mr. Schumacher has promised to send us tea." The older woman smiled.

Alexandra met her gray gaze and realized that her eyes were warm, as if friendly. But that was impossible. Her stare was also searching. What could she possibly want?

She tried to find an excuse to send the dowager duchess away, but none came to mind. She managed to smile in return. "I'm afraid my accommodations will not suffice, Your Grace. I do not think you will be comfortable."

"Do you have two chairs in your room?" She did not wait for an answer. "I thought so. Come, let's go up. You can hardly refuse me, especially as it was an hour drive to find your lodgings."

Alexandra inhaled, now nauseous. She led the way upstairs, placed her bags on the floor and unlocked her door. As they went inside, she stole a glance at Julia Mowbray.

The other woman's face was grim as she looked around the small, tidy but dismal flat. However, when she caught Alexandra looking at her, she smiled. "You are very brave, my dear," she said. "And you cannot stay here."

Alexandra placed her bags on the counter, facing her breathlessly. "I am afraid I have nowhere else to go."

"Nonsense. You will come to Constance Hall."

Alexandra was alarmed. "You are inviting me to your home?"

"Is my son not responsible for your predicament?"

Alexandra turned away, inhaling. What did this woman want? What did her offer signify? Was she as kind as her son was cruel? She would never accuse Stephen of anything, especially not to his mother. "Clarewood is not responsible," she muttered uncomfortably.

"Really?" Julia approached and touched her arm. "My dear, I have heard all the rumors. I rarely heed gossip, but obviously something has happened to cause you to have fallen on very hard times. I also know my son very well, and I saw him at Blanche's, so I suspect that Stephen's interest in you has played a role in your downfall. Am I right?"

Alexandra turned. "No." She held herself proudly. She would never reveal what had happened — to do so was simply wrong. And she would never lay all the blame on Stephen, not when she should have refused his advances. As the dowager duchess looked startled, Alexandra said, "Choices are rarely simple. I have always felt that one should take responsibility for one's choices. Mine have led me to this moment, Your Grace."

Julia's eyes widened. "You are a remarkable woman. You will not blame Stephen, will you?"

"No — I blame myself."

"You still cannot live this way." Julia's stare had sharpened. "But your restraint, and lack of malice, is commendable. Do you hate Stephen?"

Alexandra gasped. "We had a misunderstanding," she said slowly. God, that was such an understatement — and so much pain remained. "But I could never hate him."

"Do you love him, then?"

She flushed and turned away, trembling. She was afraid to consider the question, much less answer it.

For a moment Julia was silent, but Alexandra knew she was staring at her back. Then she said, "Good. My son is an exceptional man, though also a difficult one." Alexandra slowly turned as Julia Mowbray went on. "He was raised to be a difficult man, Miss Bolton. His father was cruel, cold and critical. Stephen was never loved and never praised. When he failed in an endeavor, he was punished, often with a fist or a riding crop. He has learned to be hard and difficult. He has learned to be intolerant of those in his employ, in his household, in his life. But he is compassionate. I am certain of it. If wrong, he will eventually realize it. And you must know he is a champion of those who have been wronged, or who suffer hopelessly and needlessly."

Alexandra stared. She hadn't known anything about his childhood, and she cringed, thinking about any child being so harshly treated. And she wanted to believe that he was compassionate. Just then, she kept recalling the warmth in his eyes as he made love to her — his promises to be generous. And suddenly she recalled how safe she had felt in his presence — and in his arms. She shivered. "There is no right and no wrong here, Your Grace," she whispered. "And if you are suggesting that Stephen — I mean, His Grace — will champion me or my cause, there is nothing to champion. Sooner or later I will work things out with my father and return to Edgemont Way."

"Really? Are you refusing my invitation, then?"

Alexandra trembled. She could not imagine accepting, and not only because she was too proud to take charity. She was not about to live with Stephen's mother. Not under any circumstances, particularly these. "I cannot accept."

Julia Mowbray started. "You are too proud to accept my offer? You would rather remain here, as a working woman?"

"Yes."

"You are an unusual woman, Miss Bolton," Julia finally said. She picked up her gloves, which she'd laid on the table. "I am pleased to have met you, and now . . . I am not sorry you have turned me down." Alexandra had not a clue as to what that last remark meant. "And I must say, I am also pleased that you are the one who has come into Stephen's life."

Alexandra trembled. "I cannot understand."

"Oh, I don't expect you to, not yet. But you will." And she smiled, as if she knew something Alexandra did not.

"You do not have to announce me, Guillermo," Julia said, striding briskly past the butler.

His eyes widened. "His Grace has left strict instructions that he is not to be disturbed, Your Grace, and you did not send word."

Julia was wry. "Yes, he will be put out — I have not made an appointment, and I am interrupting some grand scheme for a new charity. Charity does begin at home, Guillermo." She did not pause as she crossed the hall, the butler hurrying after her.

"I beg your pardon?"

Though she could hardly explain, she had been referring to Stephen's former mistress, Alexandra Bolton, of course, a simply amazing young woman. "Is he in the study?"

"Yes, he is. Your Grace, please! Let me at least announce you."

Julia ignored him, pushing open the door to the study, where Stephen sat at his desk, flanked by two lawyers who also handled her own affairs on occasion.

He looked up, startled. "Mother? This is a surprise."

"I am sure it is. I'm afraid I have an urgent matter to discuss with you — and that I must interrupt." She paused, smiling.

Stephen stood warily, coming out from behind his desk. "Is someone at death's door?" he asked, as the two gentlemen nodded at her and vacated the room.

"I certainly hope not." She kissed his cheek. "I have just met Miss Bolton."

His face darkened. Ignoring her words, he said, "I have been thinking about you. In fact, I have decided to begin looking for a husband for you."

Julia knew he meant to startle her — and change the subject. And he succeeded. Instantly she thought of Tyne Jefferson. It had been almost two weeks since that afternoon when she had learned about the child he had lost. He had called another time, but the weather had been too poor for riding yet again, so they had chatted while touring her stables. And when she had shown him her horses, there had been so much tension between them that Julia knew she hadn't been mistaken about his interest. Nor had she mistaken his direct male glances.

Her heart thundered. She had been expecting him to call on her as a suitor after that. But he hadn't — and how could he? She was a duchess, he an American rancher. She was going to have to take matters into her own hands.

And now Stephen thought to come to her rescue — but this was not a rescue, it was a fate worse than death! "I will not marry," she told her son. "And I mean it, Stephen."

He stared. "Do not tell me you are still besotted with that American."

"He calls himself a Californio," she said, unthinkingly. Her heart raced again. "I do not think I will confide in you again."

"And that is a confession in itself." Stephen stared closely. "You seem upset. He does not return your interest?"

"I am not discussing Jefferson with you again," she said. "Are you aware that Miss

Bolton has been thrown out of her home, and that she now lives in a small, dank room, with no amenities, a room not even fit for a vagrant, much less a gentlewoman?"

He stared. "There is no stopping you, is there? I am aware she has taken a room at Schumacher's Inn." He folded his arms, scowling. "I cannot believe that you have thought to meddle."

"She is living in abject poverty, Stephen," Julia said. "And I believe you are the cause of her downfall."

He flushed. "That is unfair. If I were the cause, I would make amends. However, *she* tried to deceive *me*. She is a very clever woman, and I am sure she will manage her current circumstances well enough."

"I am disappointed," Julia said, meaning it. "And I think you had better call on her before deciding just how well she is managing her current circumstances."

"Randolph has already called on her! So have Lady Blanche and Sir Rex. Now you have called — I believe she has enough champions. My God, before I even know it, Elysse and Ariella will visit her and blame me for everything."

"So you will let her starve? Sew by candle-light? Share common bathing facilities?"

He suddenly slammed a fist onto his desk,

stunning her. "And what would you have me do? Marry her?"

Her son never lost his temper. She stared, then said, "Is marriage to Miss Bolton on your mind?"

"Of course it's not," he snapped. And he returned her regard, finally saying, "You are exaggerating her plight, are you not?"

She was grim. "No, Stephen, I am not. It is miserable — and unacceptable. I expect you to rectify this."

His only answer was to pace, his expression resigned and grim — and reflective.

Alexandra was beginning to wonder if she was ill. She was always tired, but then, she was not sleeping very well.

Several days had passed since the dowager duchess's surprising — and incomprehensible — visit. Alexandra remained shaken by the encounter, and she was trying to forget it — just as she continued to try to forget all that had happened with Stephen. But it was impossible.

She wished the dowager duchess had been mean, unkind and even cruel. Instead, she felt almost certain that if she ever came to the comprehension that she simply could not go on as she was doing, the dowager duchess would open her home to her. And that made no sense.

Alexandra slowly walked toward the inn. She had no funds left — she had just used her last few shillings to buy precious thread and enough groceries for a few days of meals. She was owed payment by several customers, and she was going to have to find a way of driving out to call on the ladies and beg for what was due her.

Two thin dogs ran past her, and Alexandra tripped. She did not want to let go of her sewing supplies, so she fell, letting go of the groceries instead. She landed hard on her knees and elbow, clutching the one precious bag. The other bag landed in a puddle of dirty water, and three potatoes, a cabbage and an onion rolled into the filthy street. Sitting back on her calves, Alexandra cried out as she watched two small children dive upon her groceries. One of the mongrels came up to her and licked her face, wagging its tail.

She looked at the happy black-and-white face, the dancing brown eyes, and she felt tears rise.

"Here," a child said.

Alexandra saw a small, dirty hand holding an equally dirty potato under her nose. She looked up and saw a solemn little girl, her dark hair in pigtails tied with small scraps of rags. She was razor thin. "You can have the potato," Alexandra said.

The girl's eyes widened. Then she quickly turned and ran off with her precious cargo.

Alexandra saw that the rest of the groceries were gone and felt like crying, but she refused to do so, even though she could not afford more, not until she was paid. Then she looked at the dog who was sitting beside her. "If you think there will be scraps at my table, you are wrong."

Alexandra was about to get up when she caught sight of a beautiful royal-blue silk skirt, just inches from where she sat. The fabric was expensive, and only a lady would wear such a gown. Instantly she prayed that one of her customers had come to offer her payment, but she immediately knew better — her clients paid their bills by sending a servant. She looked up.

Two extremely wealthy ladies stood there looking down at her. One was a matron, wearing far too many jewels, the other a breathtakingly lovely and young blond girl. The matron stared with contempt, the girl, with horror. Certain they knew her, and were, perhaps, new clients, Alexandra got up awkwardly. As she did, the girl reached out to steady her.

The matron said, "Do not touch her, Anne."

Anne dropped her hand.

Alexandra looked at the matron. "I tripped and fell."

"Obviously." The woman inhaled harshly. "You must be the infamous Miss Bolton."

So, she was infamous now. Alexandra held the bag of sewing supplies more tightly to her chest. "I am Alexandra Bolton. Are you looking for me?" She desperately hoped they were new customers.

"Yes, we were," the matron said with absolute condescension. "I had merely wondered if the rumors were true that he had tossed you onto the streets. I wanted to see for myself the trollop he chose and cast aside — when my daughter would make a perfect duchess. Let's go, Anne."

But the lovely blonde didn't move. "Mother," she whispered nervously.

Alexandra followed her gaze — and her knees buckled. Her heart pounded as shock ran through her. Turning the corner was a huge black coach pulled by six magnificent black horses — the Duke of Clarewood's red-and-gold crest emblazoned upon the doors. *What was he doing here?*

For one moment she could not think, could only stare, horrified. Then coherence began. She did not know what he wanted, but she knew she had to run. Yet still she could not move. Her heartbeat had become deafening.

"I cannot believe this," the matron said tersely.

From the corner of her eye, Alexandra saw that both women were as riveted to the coach's splendid approach as she was. And now a crowd had gathered, just as awed and entranced — and she began to think more clearly.

Clarewood hadn't come, of course he hadn't. It was a servant, or even Randolph. He would never pursue her, not in any way. He thought the very worst of her.

But then the door opened and Clarewood stepped out.

Alexandra gasped, shocked.

The crowd stepped back, but he just stood there, looking at her. Alexandra felt her cheeks begin to burn as their gazes locked. She did not want him to see her in such misery and poverty. Her humiliation from the last time she had seen him was nothing in comparison to how she felt now.

The two ladies curtsied.

She'd forgotten them. She tensed as he strode forward, the crowd parting for him. His mouth was tight with displeasure, and he never looked away from her.

Her heartbeat continued to deafen her. What did he want? Hadn't he done enough?

"Your Grace." The matron smiled obsequiously at him. "This is such a pleasant surprise."

"Your Grace," Anne whispered, blushing.

He did not even look at them — nor did Alexandra. As they stared at one another, the tension between them made her feel faint. He was angry, she saw that now.

Suddenly Stephen looked at the two women. "This is very much a surprise," he said coolly. "Is Miss Bolton taking on your repairs, Lady Sinclair?"

The matron's smile vanished. "I have heard that Miss Bolton is a highly skilled seamstress. I wished a word with her."

"Really?" he said, his tone filled with mockery. He glanced at Anne. "This street is not fit for ladies, and I am shocked that you would bring your daughter here."

Alexandra's stomach was churning in a way she was now all too familiar with. She prayed she would not be sick.

"We were just leaving, Your Grace. And of course, you are right — I should not have brought Anne. We will take your leave, then." She smiled.

He didn't speak, his hard expression never

changing, as the two women hurried off. Alexandra noticed their coach, drawn by two dapple grays, for the first time. Then her attention was claimed as, slowly, he turned toward her.

She trembled. Very queasy now, she turned away from Stephen's intense stare, wondering if she could vanish into the crowd. Why had he come? What did he want? She wanted him to leave her be! Because now all she could think about was the passion they had shared — and how he had accused her of scheming to trap him into marriage afterward. His accusations still hurt terribly. But the worst of it was that a part of her wanted to rush into his arms, where she would be safe — where she would feel loved.

He touched her arm, and she had to look at him. He stared grimly at her. "What happened?"

"I fell." Her heart stuttered. "Why are you here?" she managed.

"Show me where you are living."

She stared back, startled. "What?"

"You heard me. You have taken a room in that inn." He gestured to the building, which was a bit farther up the block.

"I am not showing you anything." She inhaled. "In fact, I have to go. Good day."

As she turned, he seized her arm, shocking her, and said, "Edgemont tossed you out because of our affair."

She inhaled harshly. "I do not want to discuss this."

His grasp tightened. "But I do."

She tried to tug free and failed. Desperately, she said, "He heard the rumors, obviously. I'm afraid I do not dissemble well — contrary to what you believe. As you did not start the gossip and have no real part in this affair —" her tone became bitter "— you can leave and go about your affairs without any guilt." She couldn't help adding, "I am sure Lady Witte will be thrilled."

His face tightened. "I want to see your room."

"Please release my arm," she whispered frantically. "Please go away."

As he looked at her as if he wanted to learn the truth, her heart ached. If only he would believe in her, she thought. And the moment she realized what she wished — that he would trust her and care for her — she was dismayed and tried to wrench away. As she did so, the bile rose up. She groaned, panicked, but it was too late. She let go of her bag, rushing to the street, where she vomited uncontrollably.

And when she was done, her humiliation was complete.

The cobbles below her feet slowed in their terrific spinning and she straightened, inhaling, ashamed and ready to cry. Surely he was gone now.

"Let me help you up to your flat," he said from behind her, and he touched her shoulder.

"Why are you still here?" Horror returned.

From behind, he passed her a handkerchief. She took it, and carefully wiped her mouth and bodice.

"It's been about a month since we were together," he said without inflection. "Are you with child?"

She stiffened. She had been afraid that might be the case, but determined never to reveal it, if it were true. "No. I am not." She attempted a breath and realized that she finally felt well, for the first time that day.

He was silent.

As she bent to retrieve her bag, grateful that the items had remained inside, he reached past her and took it from her, his arm and shoulder brushing her as he moved. Alexandra slowly looked at him.

He looked back. "How long have you been ill, Alexandra?"

Her mind raced. "I believe I must have eaten something spoiled last night."

His mouth twisted. "I see."

When silence fell, when he didn't speak and didn't move, she asked, "What do you want? Why are you here? Haven't you punished me enough? Why do you wish to see me so humiliated?"

"I do not." Then, "I'll take your bag up for you."

The Duke of Clarewood did not carry bags. "I can manage myself."

"Can you?"

She squared her shoulders. "May I have my bag, please . . . Your Grace?"

A cool smile began. "I have asked to see your flat, Alexandra. In fact, I believe I have asked to see it four times."

"There is nothing to discuss and nothing to see. I am not inviting you up."

"I believe there is a great deal to discuss. You cannot remain here." He was firm. And the look in his eyes told her that his mind was made up.

She backed away. "And where, pray tell, shall I go? I am not welcome at home. I have no funds left. Should I accept Lady Harrington's offer of charity? Randolph's? Your mother's? As if I were homeless?"

"You *are* homeless."

She trembled and reached for her bag. He let her take it, but his stare was so hard that she did not move even after the bag was securely in her arms. "I have a home. My rent is paid for an entire month."

He made a harsh sound. "You can accept *my* offer," he said. "In fact, I insist."

She did not know what that offer would be, but she would never forget what they had shared — and what he had done to her subsequently. "No. Whatever it is, I am not interested."

"You haven't even heard what I wish to propose."

"I don't have to hear your offer. I am not interested in charity, not of any kind, and especially not from you."

Exasperation showed in his brilliant blue eyes. "You are stubborn. And I am annoyed. The Mayfair Hotel is the best in town. I will get you a suite of rooms there."

"In return for what?" she asked, genuinely surprised. Surely he had no lingering interest in her now? "Why would you do such a thing? What do you want from me?"

"I ask for nothing in return."

She shook her head. "I refused charity from Lady Blanche, from Randolph and from the dowager duchess. I will never take charity from you. I can get on just fine with my sewing business. In fact, I have several new customers."

His face hardened. "Really? But you just

told me that you are penniless." He met her eyes squarely. "My check was cashed. Did Edgemont take it?"

She realized she was crying. "Yes, he did," she said. "Just go away, Your Grace. I will manage — I always do."

He glanced away. "I'm afraid I cannot." And suddenly he pulled her close, wrapping his powerful arm around her like a vise. And then he started for his coach, taking her with him.

"Stop! What are you doing?" She balked, shocked.

The footman opened the door, and Clarewood lifted her into his arms. "I actually think that if I deposited you at a hotel, you are so proud you would walk out — and return to this abominable place."

She was in his arms. She didn't want to be there, nor did she want to cling, but it was a matter of safety to hold on to his shoulders. She stared into his intense blue eyes, aware that their faces were far too close for comfort. In fact, her heart was thudding and shrieking incoherently at her now. She instantly recalled how his lips had tasted, and how their union had felt. Most of all, she kept thinking about how he had made her feel — joyous and loved.

But it had all been a sham.

His mouth had tightened. His stare had changed.

Her insides lurched and then tightened in a way she instantly recognized. Nothing had changed — the terrible, fatal attraction remained. No good could come of it. "Put me down," she whispered.

He stepped up into the coach, the footman closing the door behind them. He stared into her eyes, and she stared back, her heart lurching, and he deposited her onto the seat. She slid into the far corner, staring at him, breathing hard.

"You'll spend the night at Clarewood," he said. "And tomorrow we will discuss your plight."

Stephen walked into the library, closing both doors behind him. Then he simply gripped the brass knobs, staring at the gleaming polished wood and his own white knuckles. He was horrified.

How could she have lived like that?

He hadn't seen her room. He hadn't needed to. He knew what the room would be like — he'd seen slums before.

And it was his fault.

He wanted to deny it, wanted to think otherwise. He turned and strode to the sideboard bar and poured himself a scotch.

He trembled as he sipped. He was a highly moral man. There was right, and there was wrong. The difference between the two was almost always black versus white. Alexandra Bolton was a gentlewoman, no matter what she had intended. She did not deserve to live among the city's most downtrodden, as one of them. He was horrified, but most of all, he was filled with guilt.

This was his fault, he thought again.

He took a draught of the scotch, but he did not relax. The drive back to Clarewood had taken almost three hours. She hadn't spoken, and neither had he — he'd only stared out of the window, trying to hide his dismay and horror. He kept hoping she would fall asleep — he could tell she was exhausted — but every time his glance wandered to the far corner of the carriage, she was wide-awake and staring at him as if he might possess a hidden ax, one he intended to dispatch her with.

Now she was upstairs in a guest room, with a maid drawing a hot bath. He'd instructed Guillermo to have supper sent up, the maid to attend to her every need. As if that might make up for what she had suffered for almost an entire month.

He gripped the glass so tightly that a finer crystal would have shattered. He should have gone to London to investigate her plight sooner. But he had been too furious over her supposed plot to trap him into marriage.

Obviously he had misjudged her. Alexandra was very intelligent, and if she was a fortune hunter, she would have found another benefactor the moment Edgemont had thrown her out. And even if she had somehow failed to do that, as an opportunist, she would have gone to live with Lady Blanche and Sir Rex at Harrington Hall. Now he thought about how she had resisted his advances. He had assumed it was a game, one meant to whet his appetite. But he had been wrong.

She had resisted him because she was a virgin, and his intentions had been dishonorable.

He cursed and flung his glass across the room. The action gave him no satisfaction. She was twenty-six years old! Had she wished to marry a fortune, she would have done so years ago.

How had she survived for almost a month in that rat-infested, disease-ridden hellhole?

Admiration crept through the raging fury. He did not want to admire her courage, her pride or her strength. Somehow he knew such admiration was dangerous for him. Yet how the hell could he not admire her? He did not know of any woman, gently born or not, who would have taken up residence in such a slum, not after leading a far different life. But then, when they'd first met, he'd admired her for sewing to make ends meet for her family. She was not like the others, he thought, as he recalled their conversation.

I do not like being deceived.

I did not think it important.

You did not think it important?

Stephen cursed again. Every woman thought her virginity important. How could she be an exception? He realized that on his own, he would never understand why she hadn't told him the truth about her innocence. Maybe he could eventually convince her to explain to him.

He was rarely wrong about anything, or anyone. But he had been wrong about her.

And he had pursued her, seduced her and treated her abysmally.

He was staring grimly at the wall when the hairs on his nape tingled. Slowly, he turned and looked across the room.

Tom Mowbray stood there, scowling and furious. Stephen knew what his father would be thinking, if he were alive.

Don't even think of marrying that harlot.

Scheme or not, your duty is to Clarewood, and you will marry a woman of equal rank, a woman who will bring you lands, titles and a fortune. If she is with child, pay her off.

Instantly he felt sick.

Was she carrying his child?

She had said that she was not, but he was not about to give her the benefit of that doubt, either, though he hoped, very much, that she had indeed eaten spoiled food the night before.

He always took excessive precautions with his lovers to make sure no one conceived his bastard. He would never allow a bastard of his to be raised by anyone other than him — not because his childhood had been difficult, lonely and without affection, but because of principle. He doubted he would be a very good father, but he intended to try, and he would be better than old Tom — he would reward excellence, and he would never mock or ridicule a good effort. His children, all of them, bastard and legitimate, would be raised under his roof at Clarewood.

He hadn't taken any precautions with Alexandra. He couldn't imagine why he'd forgotten, except that he had been mindless with passion.

If she *was* carrying his child, he would

raise his son or daughter.

And if she was with child, she would stay at Clarewood, at least until that child was born. In fact, he now realized the benefit of having her stay with him. Within a few months, he would learn the truth of her condition. Additionally, at Clarewood she would also receive the best care.

His mind was made up.

Tom stared furiously at him. Stephen grimaced. "Don't worry," he said softly, "I know my duty. I swore to do it, and I never break my vows."

Stephen walked away from the glaring illusion. He had no intention of marrying Alexandra. His duty was to Clarewood — to seek to increase the Clarewood legacy through his marriage — and he could do better. But if Alexandra was the mother of his child, he would care for her for the rest of her life. She would lack for nothing.

A recognizable knock sounded on the library doors, and he called for Guillermo to come inside. "Has Miss Bolton settled in?"

His butler was suitably grave. "She has refused to allow the maids entry to help her, and she has sent away her supper, Your Grace. I believe she has locked the doors."

"She is undoubtedly tired. She may even

be so soundly asleep that she did not hear the maids." He would not blame her for that. In fact, he hoped she was asleep by now. "Leave a tray outside her door, Guillermo, just in case she awakens in the middle of the night."

But Stephen wondered if her actions were meant to be defiant, a protest. He thought so, and he was not amused. His first impulse was to go up to her room and order her to comply with his wishes — she needed sustenance, especially if there was any possibility she was with child. But he instantly changed his mind. She despised him — and he did not blame her.

CHAPTER THIRTEEN

She could not hide in her room forever.

Alexandra stared at her pale reflection in the mirror. The frame was gilded, matching the arms and legs of the two green brocade chairs on either side of it. She had expected to see a haggard shrew in the looking glass, but upon climbing into bed last night and pulling up the thick, warm covers, she had instantly fallen asleep. For the first time in a month — for the first time since their aborted liaison — she had slept deeply and dreamlessly.

She was a bit pale, but she looked better than she had upon arriving last night. She almost felt well, she thought carefully. But how could she feel well when Clarewood had forcibly removed her from her hotel room and then brought her to his home just as forcibly?

She trembled, her pulse racing. In the mirror, she could see the stunning room behind her. The walls were painted a pale mint-green, the moldings pink and gold. The four-poster bed she had so enjoyed last night was canopied, with moss-green-and-gold bedding. The fireplace was cream plaster, a floral sofa before it. A small dining table and two chairs sat beside one window, and beyond was a balcony with another table and chairs. At the other end of the room a small, centuries-old writing table held a vase of flowers, along with a sheaf of parchment, an inkwell and a quill.

Her heart lurched wildly. The room was the loveliest bedroom she had ever been in, and a gruesome contrast to the room she'd leased at Mr. Schumacher's, but she could not accept his hospitality. Yet how could she tell him that? He was a force of nature, and he would not back down. And she still did not understand why he had done what he had.

Did he feel guilty after all?

And then she was sick. Alexandra raced to the bathing room and retched drily, before sinking to her knees and closing her eyes in dismay. There was almost no doubt now that she was having morning sickness. *She was carrying Clarewood's child.* A child should be a wonderful and joyous event. She tried not to cry. Fear of his rage made her cringe. She would love her baby, of course she would, but now she would be tied to the duke forever.

She wiped her moist eyes and got up. He must never know. She didn't have to think about it to know that he would be furious and think it a part of her scheme to trap him into marriage. Worse, he would insist on keeping her and the child, and she didn't want his charity. She had no intention of being a kept woman.

But now the future was even more frightening than it had been before. She wished she were back at Edgemont Way.

Alexandra opened the door, surprised to see her bags sitting in the hallway, and went slowly downstairs. Tension had stiffened her spine. Because she didn't know her way around the house, she headed for the front doors, praying she might escape outside unnoticed. But as she approached the front hall, Clarewood stepped into the corridor, barring her way.

He was in a dark morning coat, a handsome emerald vest beneath and tan trousers. There were faint circles beneath his eyes. "Good morning. I hope you slept well."

He did not look as if *he* had slept well. And his big body and powerful presence took up most of the small hallway. She was dismayed to have encountered him so immediately — as if he had been awaiting her. "I slept very well." Her nervousness escalated. "You are staring, Your Grace."

"You are very pale. Are you ill?" he asked abruptly.

"No, I am fine," she said, trying not to think about the child she was probably carrying.

He seemed to reflect on that. "You declined supper last night," he finally said.

"I fell asleep."

His mouth seemed to soften. "I had assumed so. I am about to take breakfast. Please . . ." He cupped her elbow.

She leaped away. "What are you doing?" She was aware that she sounded frantic.

His gaze narrowed. "I was escorting you into the breakfast room, Miss Bolton."

She was famished, but she shook her head. "I think I will walk outside."

He caught her arm as she turned, and she had no choice but to face him. "You are my guest," he said softly. "I do not make a habit of excluding my guests from my dining rooms."

She trembled, her heart slamming, wishing he would let her go, wishing his tone wasn't soft and enticing, that he weren't half so handsome — and that his touch didn't make her yearn to fall entirely in his arms. But just then he felt safe, like a deep, enclosed harbor after a terrible storm at sea. But he *wasn't* safe. He was completely dangerous — especially now. "I am not exactly your guest."

His brows rose. "You are most definitely my guest."

She inhaled and managed, "Do you abduct all your guests, Your Grace? Because I recall being manhandled yesterday, and taken into your carriage against my will."

"If I manhandled you, I apologize. But I had no intention of allowing you to remain in that inn."

"That is no excuse."

His mouth curved. "Apparently not. In fact, you are right. I should have convinced you to willingly join me. But it doesn't matter now. You are, most definitely, my guest."

She trembled.

"I suppose that is better than being your hostage."

"You must be very hungry, and I am not making a request." He actually smiled. "I am trying to make amends, Miss Bolton. And dukes do not take hostages. Not in this era, anyway."

She somehow pulled free of his hand, trying not to soften and return his smile. "I suppose that I am a bit hungry."

"Good." He nodded, seeming pleased, and allowed her to walk ahead of him. Alexandra was acutely aware of him as they went into a cheerful, daffodil-yellow breakfast room. They had finally found a formal, polite ground on which to meet. That was certainly a relief.

And then she forgot about the duke. A vast breakfast buffet was laid out on a sideboard, where two servants stood at attention. The aroma of eggs, potatoes, sausages, ham and bacon coming from the buffet was so enticing that tears came to her eyes and her stomach gently growled. She didn't think she had ever been as hungry, but of course, she had been subsisting on potatoes and cabbage for the past week.

If he heard her stomach, he gave no sign. As the servants leaped forward, he shook his head, and they retreated to their places on either side of the buffet. As he casually pulled out a chair, Alexandra saw that two places were set at the table; he'd meant for her to dine with him. Not that she cared — not that it meant anything, really.

But his hands were large on the back of her chair, and she now had a flashing recollection of his hands on her body — everywhere. She flushed, almost forgetting about the food. Her stomach churned, but not with illness. She wished she could stop being so aware of him.

Once she was seated, he took the other chair, glancing briefly at the serving men. "In my father's day, we frequently had a full house. There would be four or five tables in this room, each place occupied. I almost never entertain that way now."

She didn't know why he was telling her this, or why he had decided to be genial. "It's a beautiful room."

"It used to be very dark and dull. My mother refurbished it the moment my father passed away."

The serving men put plates of eggs, sausage, ham and potatoes before them. Alexandra swallowed hard, but recalled the dowager duchess's revelations about his childhood. "You were very young, were you not, when the previous duke passed?" She looked up from the plate, trying to be casual about the meal, and saw him watching her carefully. She flushed. He obviously knew she was ravenous.

"I was sixteen when he died and I became the eighth duke. Please . . ." He lifted a fork, smiling congenially at her.

He was never congenial — he wanted something. But she did not care. Not now.

As she lifted her own fork, she saw that her hand was trembling. Worse, as she dug into the scrambled eggs, her stomach growled, this time very loudly.

She set her fork down. "I am so sorry!"

"Alexandra."

Her gaze flew to his. She was so hungry she felt faint.

"You have been in that hellhole for weeks. You gave your sisters and Edgemont the two thousand pounds. In exchange, you have been starving."

She brushed at an unexpected tear. "I am merely tired." Not to mention that she was too hungry to argue now. "They needed the funds more than I did."

"We will talk after our meal." His tone was one of finality, his face hard. "Eat."

It was a command — of course it was — but she no longer cared if he bullied her. Instead, she began to eat, trying to go slowly, when all she wanted was to inhale the eggs and ham. The eggs were the most delicious she had ever tasted, but the ham and sausage were even better — and the toast had butter! And then, when her plate was empty, another plate was set down in front of her, as full as the first. She didn't argue, and she didn't look up, aware that she must appear to be a farmer's wife. She didn't care about that, nor about the fact that he had finished eating long ago and was now watching her over the top of a newspaper.

When she was done — when her second plate was perfectly empty, not even a bread crumb remaining — that plate, too, was whisked away. Alexandra wiped her mouth gently with her gold linen napkin and glanced across the table, out the window and not at him. She was so full, and it was wonderful. She wished her sisters could enjoy such a bountiful meal.

"Would you like another plate?"

She tensed, wishing she did not have to look at him. But she did, and reluctantly she turned to face him. He was so handsome that she lost her breath. "I do not believe I could ingest another mouthful."

He smiled. "I happen to agree with you."

She froze. He so rarely smiled, and even more rarely did his eyes fill with warmth or humor. And then her heart leaped and raced. Why didn't he smile more often? "Thank you," she said slowly, "for such an agreeable meal."

"It is my pleasure," he said, just as carefully. But he kept eye contact. "I am glad you had a restful night in appropriate accommodations, and that you have enjoyed your breakfast."

There was no way to avoid a confrontation, she thought. But she did not know where to start. Very carefully, she said, "Thank you for such hospitality. However, it cannot continue. Your Grace, I will be returning to my room this morning."

His smile vanished. "I cannot allow that."

She stiffened. "You know as well as I do that I cannot remain here."

"You most certainly cannot return to that slum, while you most certainly *can* remain here as my guest."

She inhaled as his stare hardened. "Why are you doing this?"

He sat back in his chair. "I wish to make amends."

Alexandra hesitated. "Why?"

"I am very distressed to have caused you to suffer as you have."

Alexandra stared as she realized that he meant it. He had been furious with her for what he thought was a deliberate deception on her part, yet he had no wish to see her suffer in an impoverished London slum. "I don't understand you."

"Why not? I am a philanthropist. I have set up asylums for orphans and hospitals for unwed mothers. Yet because of me, a gentlewoman has lost her position in life and has been reduced to poverty. There is a terrible irony in this. I can't allow you to remain in such straits."

She stared, trying to understand him. She knew about his causes and charities — everyone did. So was she now simply one of his charitable cases? It seemed so. And it was ironic — she wondered if she might wind up in one of his hospitals. "You do not need to feel guilty. Perhaps we should both admit to having made mistakes, and then we can part company in an amicable manner."

His gaze narrowed. "I consider myself a man of honor. When I ended our affair, I never expected Edgemont to throw you out."

She tensed impossibly. "I do not want to speak about that."

"Why not? And which topic, exactly, do you wish to avoid? Your father — or our affair?"

She stood up. "I will need a driver to take me back to my room."

He had stood the moment she had — and now he seized her wrist. "I would like an answer, Alexandra."

If she spoke about Edgemont, she would quickly shatter — and possibly reveal how entirely broken her heart was. As for what had happened between them, that was territory she refused to explore, not now, and most definitely not with him, for the exact same reason. "It is senseless to dwell on the past."

"Usually — but not this time."

He hadn't released her. "I cannot stay here. What little reputation I have left, I must guard."

His gaze was penetrating, so much so that she felt as if he was trying to read her mind and uncover her most intimate thoughts, feelings and secrets. "I would like a private word with you, Alexandra."

Her alarm knew no bounds. She managed to twist free. "I have to go."

"You can't go — you have no means of leaving, not until I allow it."

"You said dukes do not take hostages!"

"You are my guest, Alexandra." He turned to the servants. "Leave us, and close the doors. We are not to be disturbed."

"Oh, my God," she breathed, realizing the two serving men had been witness to their heated argument. They'd been so still that she'd forgotten they were present. She wrung her hands as they left, shutting the doors behind them. "What do you want of me now?"

"I have said repeatedly that I want to

make amends. But you are right. There is more." He stared.

She backed up.

"No, you cannot escape." He followed her. "Explain why you misled me about your innocence."

"What?" she asked, bewildered.

"You insinuated that you shared a grand passion with your suitor of some years ago."

She'd hit the sideboard. "We did." She felt so helpless. This had all begun because of what she'd had with Owen, she thought, but Clarewood would never understand her dreams and yearnings. As they stared at one another, she realized that she was trembling as he awaited her reply. "I was going to marry Owen St. James. We were in love," she whispered, saddened. But oddly, she didn't know if the wave of sorrow was still about Owen or about the shambles her life had become — or about *him.*

His stare intensified, but otherwise he did not move and he did not speak.

She felt tears gather. "I loved him so. He loved me. We laughed and talked and gossiped — we held hands in the moonlight. And we dreamed of our future." She hugged herself. "I still miss him," she heard herself say.

Another moment passed before he asked,

"When was this?"

She met his dark gaze. "Nine years ago — a lifetime ago."

"And what happened?"

"My mother died." She shrugged helplessly. "How could I marry him? I loved him so — I still do and always will. But my family needed me. Father was drinking even then — although not as heavily as now. My sisters were so young — Olivia was nine, Corey only seven. I broke it off with him." She wiped at a stray tear. "I broke his heart. He said he'd wait — I begged him not to. There were a few letters. And then he gave up, as I wished for him to do. Three years later I learned he had married someone else — of course I was happy for him."

"Of course." He spoke without inflection.

Alexandra realized she'd been seeing Owen standing before her, and now she stared at Stephen.

"Do you still communicate?"

"No. I last heard from him when he wrote to tell me he was marrying Jane Godson." She shrugged but knew the gesture was hardly nonchalant.

"He must have been a true paragon of manhood, to have captured your heart so." His tone was bland.

"Owen was handsome, witty and charming. He was also kind. He came from a good family. His father was a baron, like Edgemont. But most of all, he was my dear friend." She somehow smiled.

His face was harder now. The angles and planes were more defined than ever. He offered her a handkerchief, his lashes lowered, so she could not see his expression.

"I am sorry. I miss him still. When you rescued me at the ball . . ." She stopped, realizing that she shouldn't explain how he'd made her feel that night, how joyous it had been to be in his arms, to have him look at her with interest and heat.

"Please continue."

Alexandra hesitated. "You are handsome and charming. I'd forgotten what it was like to be in a man's arms like that."

He looked up at her, his eyes blank. "So I remind you of your long-lost love. Or perhaps I was a replacement for him."

"You are nothing like Owen. You cannot replace him."

He made a sound and his lips curved, but there was no warmth, no mirth, in his smile.

Was he becoming angry? "I do not mean to be insulting."

"Of course not," he said flatly. "And if we held hands in the moonlight, if I whispered the requisite endearments in your ear, would I be like young Owen?"

Alexandra did not know what to say, and she did not like his expression or his tone now.

He added softly, "And did you yearn for his kisses, too? In the moonlight? Did you desire him?"

Alexandra knew she was blushing. "I *loved* Owen. Of course I felt desire."

He stared, and she stared back. Then, very softly, he said, "But you don't love me, so there is no possible explanation for the rapture you experienced in my arms."

His choice of words made her cheeks flame even more deeply. Why was he doing this? And while he sounded somewhat angry, he was most definitely mocking. "I do not want to discuss our liaison!"

"Why not? Because I failed to hold your hand?"

He was angry now, she thought, panicking. But why? "I refuse to discuss this any further."

He caught her arm before she could flee. "I can see that your desire bothers you."

"There is no rational explanation for the passion we shared," she insisted.

He leaned closer. "Desire is not rational, my dear. It is physical — it is carnal."

Her heart beat explosively now. Every

fiber of her being had tightened, warmed. "I don't know why we are discussing any of this."

"We are discussing it because I want to understand why you deliberately misled me."

She hugged herself. "I am shameless. . . . I tried to resist . . . but I wanted to be with you," she whispered.

He smiled without mirth. "And now?"

She went still. His eyes were dark and angry, but they were smoldering, too. "Please, don't. No good will come of this."

"Of what?" He slid his hand under her jaw. "Surely you want to forget your old flame? Surely you still want to be with me?"

He was leaning toward her. "Stop! Owen was long ago. He is forgotten."

He laughed. "You spoke of him earlier as if he were your lover just the other day. You haven't forgotten him, not at all."

"I have to go."

"But you have nowhere to go," he said, his gaze hardening. "And you know it as well as I do."

She envisioned her horrid room. She thought about the beautiful bedroom he'd given her. "I cannot stay here!"

"Why not?" He smiled savagely. "I still want you. You still want me. And most of all, you need a protector now."

Alexandra paled.

"Besides . . ." He smiled. "I believe I can make you forget your beloved Owen St. James."

Alexandra sat in the window seat of her beautiful bedroom, her legs curled beneath her, a piece of embroidery on her lap. But she wasn't sewing; she was watching Clarewood's huge black lacquer coach as it approached the house, moving along the pristine shell drive, pulled by that magnificent team of blacks. Her heart thundered.

It was late afternoon. She'd fled to her room after their breakfast, intent on escaping both him and the memories of their passion, which he'd so effortlessly aroused. But it was impossible. He *was* Clarewood, and everywhere she turned, she felt his presence and his power.

She remained in disbelief that he would approach her yet again. That disbelief was joined by dismay — and also panic. The sooner she escaped Clarewood, the better, she thought.

The coach was passing the white limestone fountain now.

She would never rekindle their affair. There was nothing to consider. He'd had his chance and she'd had hers, and they'd both made monumental mistakes. They were done. She did not need a protector. And even if she did, she would never accept Stephen in the role, not after all that had happened, not even if some lost, lonely part of her needed someone just then.

She tried to think about Owen, but that had become impossible now.

Instead, the shocking passion she and Stephen had shared kept returning to her mind, but it did not matter. She would never forget his cruelty after. She forced herself to recall every detail, every horrid word. She had been filled with joy and expectation after their lovemaking, and then he had hurt her terribly with his false accusations.

He was hateful!

But she *had* lied to him.

Alexandra hugged herself. She wished he hadn't rescued her from her London room. She wished he'd become a distant, blurred memory. She wished he hadn't fed her that delicious, desperately needed breakfast. But he had done all of those things.

She told herself that he was a tyrant, used to having both servants and noblemen jump to do his bidding, and that he had no idea as to what it was like to ever be refused. But she understood him a bit better now, and she could see how such a difficult child-hood, coupled with the power he now had, would have turned him into a hard, uncom-promising man.

She was so nervous she felt sick. And that was another reason to leave — the most compelling one of all: so he wouldn't find out about her condition. She never wanted to be accused of being a scheming fortune hunter again.

She could manage on her own. She *would* manage on her own. There was no other choice.

She was so close to tears, confused and uncertain. She thought about her father and, because it hurt too much, she instantly shoved the image of him screaming at her and throwing her out from her mind. De-spite his cruelty to her, she hoped that Olivia was looking out for him and Corey. She so wished she was at home with her sisters — and that she had never laid eyes on the Duke of Clarewood.

Images, heated and frenzied, flashed through her mind, images of her beneath him, in his powerful arms. His blue eyes were brilliant, blinding; his smile was warm. . . .

She sat up straighter, staring outside. She

must not recall the passion they had shared. The elm trees lining the long drive were now entirely red. The trees closer to the house were red and gold. The sky was a pale blue, but the sun was shining. She could no longer see his coach. In a moment or so, he would be entering the house.

Alexandra stood up. He was going to have to let her go. There was no other choice. It was time to go back to her tiny room. Her life was an impoverished one, and staying here for too long would simply make the return to reality worse.

Biting her lip, Alexandra put the embroidery aside and stood. She paused before the mirror. Her cheeks were flushed, her eyes bright. She'd pinned her hair up, refusing a maid's help, but the simple coil wasn't tight enough.

Dread churned in her belly, and she started downstairs. When she reached the ground floor, she heard male voices and knew he had company. She tensed. She would have to delay their battle — and she had no doubt it would indeed be a battle.

She had no intention of eavesdropping, but she could hear exasperation in Clarewood's tone. "You need to rein in your wife, Alexi, and your sister."

Good intentions forgotten, Alexandra

stepped closer to the library doors, which were completely open.

"Unlike you, I find a woman's independence admirable. And if Elysse has made up her mind to thwart you, I may even cheer her on. Someone needs to take you down, Stephen."

Alexandra could barely believe what she thought she was hearing — Alexi's wife was disputing Clarewood? And Alexi de Warenne was daring to speak to him as an equal? She crept still closer to the door and looked into the room.

Alexi was amused. He was a handsome man, standing there in riding clothes, grinning. Clarewood, however, was dangerously annoyed. "I don't know why I put up with all of you."

"You put up with us because we won't be jettisoned, though God only knows why we put up with you and your moods," Alexi said amicably. He went to the sideboard and began pouring drinks. "Have you ever thought about the fact that you were a dour boy — and now, you are a dour man — though thankfully not as dour as old Tom?"

"Have you come here to insult me? My complaints are justified. I specifically asked the ladies to find my mother a suitable match — not to shove her at the damned

American."

Alexi laughed. "As I said, independent minds." He handed Stephen a drink, and to Alexandra's surprise, they clicked glasses, Clarewood actually seemed to be softening. Alexi added, "I don't think your mother will obey you in this particular matter. Besides, they make a striking couple, don't you agree?"

Clarewood choked. "Do not provoke me."

"Why not? You are easy to provoke, and it is good for you when you are refuted, disputed and downright disobeyed."

Clarewood gave him a dark look. "I gave them an opportunity to aid me in finding the dowager duchess a proper suitor. Now I am dismissing them from this task."

Alexi saluted him. "If they are on a trail, they will be as eager as bloodhounds. They will not cease and desist, my friend."

"Lay down the law," Clarewood said.

Alexi gave him an incredulous look, then sobered. "By the way, Charlotte Witte was at Harmon House last night. I hope you are finished with her. She was beyond any pale."

Clarewood inhaled sharply. "What did she do?"

"She told Lizzie that Alexandra Bolton ruined her gowns, and then went on to elaborate that Miss Bolton has been thrown out by her father and is now living in a London slum. She was gleeful, by the by. And she seems bent on making certain that no one will ever give Miss Bolton their orders." He stared. "She had nothing pleasant to say on the subject of your latest paramour."

Alexandra suddenly felt so ill that she reeled and had to grab the door frame to right herself.

"Charlotte has gone too far." Clarewood slammed down his drink. "I made the mistake of allowing her back into my bed for a night or two. But I am tired of her rumor-mongering. Miss Bolton does not deserve it."

Alexi turned and spotted Alexandra. "She most certainly does not deserve any of this."

She froze with dread.

Clarewood whirled, and instantly he said, "Are you ill again?"

"No." She straightened. "I am sorry, I did not mean to eavesdrop, but I had thought to conclude our earlier conversation." She knew she flushed. *Did he intend to defend her from Charlotte Witte and her lies?*

Clarewood reached her, steadying her with a firm grasp upon her arm. She met his gaze and thought she saw concern there, then realized she had to be wrong.

He stared carefully at her, then asked, "Do you know my friend Alexi de Warenne? Alexi, come meet Miss Bolton, my houseguest."

Her heart thundered as she tore her gaze from Clarewood, expecting to see mockery, disdain or contempt on Alexi's handsome face. But he only smiled warmly at her. "Good afternoon, Miss Bolton. I believe you have recently met my wife. She spoke very highly of you."

Alexandra was so surprised, she felt her knees buckle. Clarewood grasped her again. "You need to sit down," he said firmly.

She turned to look at him, then said to Alexi, "I enjoyed meeting your wife and sister, sir. It is nice to meet you, as well."

He kept smiling as he looked back and forth between them, then said, "Well, I am off. I have been told I must be home by six, and as you know, my wife rules the roost."

Clarewood looked at him, shaking his head.

Alexi grinned, then bowed to Alexandra. "Do not mind this beast. Beasts can be tamed." He walked out.

Alexandra felt as if she'd been hit by a whirlwind. Clarewood was so different around Alexi de Warenne; clearly they were close, and just as clearly they cared deeply for one another. He was close to Elysse and Ariella, too, and — most amazingly of all — he was angry with Charlotte for her lies and attacks.

"You are staring," he said softly.

Did that make him human after all?

When she did not speak, he said, "Have you been ill again, Alexandra? I expect the truth this time."

He still held her arm, she realized, and pulled away. "I have not been ill. I have been embroidering this afternoon, and I saw your coach return." She breathed in. "Mr. de Warenne is as charming as his wife."

"Yes, he can be a charming rogue — when he wants to be." He left her side. Alexandra watched him pour a small sherry, then return and hand it to her. She shook her head, but he said, "I insist."

She took a small sip and realized she was staring into his dark blue eyes.

He said softly, "Have you reconsidered?"

Her heart slammed. He had meant to defend her. He wasn't entirely unkind. And he was beloved by some — the de Warennes seemed to care for him, at least, so perhaps he was not *such* a beast.

"I cannot," she said, but even as she spoke, her heart began to pound.

"Why not? You cannot deny that an attraction rages between us, and I wish to take care of you."

Breathlessly, she asked, "What will you do about Charlotte?"

"She will never utter another word, malicious or otherwise, about you." His gaze turned searching. "When I said I would be your protector, I meant it in every possible way."

And she believed him. Her heart lurched, racing all over again. She trembled, aware of the rapid warming of her body and the desire to step closer to him. If she did, he would take her into his arms — and she would be safe, as never before.

"I despise injustice," he murmured. "There has been injustice, has there not? I was terribly wrong to accuse you of scheming to trap me into marriage."

Tears arose. "I did not think my innocence important," she whispered. "I was afraid you would walk away."

He watched a tear fall. "Why are you crying?"

What could she say? That she had fallen in love with him at first sight? That he had hurt her terribly? That she missed her sisters, her home, and yes, even Edgemont? That she dreaded returning to her hovel of a room? That she hated being whispered about, being scorned?

His expression softened. He slid one large hand up her neck, then covered the side of her face. Holding her head still, he leaned forward. "You cannot deny me now. I want to make this right, Alexandra," he said, and he kissed her.

CHAPTER FOURTEEN

Alexandra found herself in Clarewood's powerful embrace. She tensed as his mouth hovered over hers, as his breath feathered her lips. She had never wanted anything as much as she did his kiss — and, frankly, his protection.

As if he knew, she felt him smile, and then he murmured her name. Helplessly she slipped her hands onto his shoulders. He looked at her. She looked back — and his blue eyes were blazing.

She felt his hunger. Desire fisted through her. But even so, she simply could not do this.

As he pulled her impossibly close, covering her mouth with his, claiming it fiercely, possessively, Alexandra hesitated, trying to resist him. But he kept kissing her, and at last she cried out, tightening her grasp on his shoulders, finally kissing him back.

He made a harsh sound.

Their mouths had fused. Now their tongues entwined. Desire made her dizzy, hollow, almost sick. She needed him desperately. His hands moved into her hair, and the thick waves fell down. He turned her and pressed her up against a wall. He pinned her there, every inch of his hard, restless body urgent and demanding against hers.

She had never wanted anyone this way, and in that moment she knew it. Just as she knew she loved him, foolishly, stupidly and, somehow, irrevocably. And that was why this could not go on.

"Stop," she managed, tearing her mouth from his.

He paused, his eyes widening in surprise.

"I cannot restart our affair," she gasped, pushing at him now. "Please, let me go."

He was so surprised, he was speechless. Then, reluctantly, he eased his grasp on her.

Alexandra ducked beneath his arm and moved a goodly distance from him. She was shaking, and her body felt as if it were in flames. But it was her heart that hurt the most now.

"I vow to take good care of you," he said harshly.

She turned and saw him watching her like a hawk. She truly did not want to resist him, but she had to. He was offering her an affair, and when it ended, her heart would be broken. She knew that now.

"I do not blame you for mistrusting me."

"I cannot accept your charity or your protection," she managed.

His gaze was solemn, searching. "I see that your mind is made up," he finally said. "You are a stubborn woman. But I am a stubborn man."

She trembled. What did that mean?

"I am also deliberate, determined and patient. Very well. I will respect your wishes — for now."

She gasped. "Do not think to wage another pursuit!" She already knew she was not strong enough to resist his advances, if he truly meant to continue them.

"You seem dismayed," he said softly, his eyes gleaming. "And I think we both know why that is the case."

She began shaking her head. "You must respect my wishes *entirely.*"

He folded his arms. "You are off the hook — for now. But I will make things right."

"What does that mean?" she asked warily.

"You will stay here — as my respected guest. I insist." And he smiled.

Her heart leaped. She knew she didn't want to leave Clarewood, especially not to return to Mr. Schumacher's room; no one in her right mind would. But still she said, "I cannot accept."

"You can — and you will." His smile became warm. "I have houseguests from time to time. It is hardly unusual."

"Everyone knows what happened between us! My name is already in tatters. They still whisper about me."

His smile faded. "Didn't I just tell you that I would protect you — in every possible way? There will be no more gossip. I promise you that. In fact, I will even set the record straight and see to it that the world believes nothing happened between us."

She was disbelieving. He would tell a few cronies that she was his guest and under his protection. She had no reason to be his guest — Edgemont Way was within two hours' drive. And though he would tell them that there had not been a seduction . . . She trembled. "No one will believe you."

"Probably not. But does it matter?" He was wry. "No one disobeys me, Alexandra — except, of course, for you. If I indicate my displeasure, this chapter ends."

She inhaled. God, she wanted nothing more than her good name back and the gossip to die! But though he could probably put an end to the worst of the gossip, she doubted that she would have her good name back — and there would still be scorn. Maybe not from everyone, but ladies like Charlotte Witte would always take out their knives when they saw her. Still, this would be a vast improvement. Society was used to all kinds of affairs. "Why are you being kind?"

"I am not an unkind man, Alexandra, nor as heartless as is claimed." He studied her for a moment. "I have an engagement tonight. Why don't you tell Guillermo what you wish to have for supper? Now, if you will excuse me — seeing as I have been momentarily rejected, I have some reading to do."

She simply stared.

He gestured at the door.

Alexandra realized he meant to read there in the library, and that he had just dismissed her. Still stupefied by every moment of their encounter, she rushed for the doors. When she paused to glance back at him, he was already at his desk, reading a stack of papers. He was absorbed, and he did not look up.

Her heart stalled. If only she could have accepted his offer . . . if only she'd had the courage to do so.

He glanced up.

Alexandra fled.

The next morning Alexandra learned that Stephen was an early riser.

She didn't know what time he had returned last night, because she'd gone to sleep at midnight, and he had yet to come in. She hadn't exactly been waiting up for him — she had been reading a novel in bed — but she had been acutely aware of the fact that he was absent. Reading had proven impossible, as he was front and center in her mind. She kept thinking about their conversation and that stunning kiss — and what he wanted from her now. She worried about how she would shore up her defenses against him, when she hardly wanted to — when she had such inappropriate feelings for him. It had been strange going to bed in that luxurious guest room, but it had been wonderful, too. She had almost felt cared for. She had to remind herself that he merely desired her, which was a far different thing.

How could she have fallen in love with him?
Because there was no other explanation for her wild, turbulent emotions, her inescapable memories and her intense, undying preoccupation with him. All told, they had shared a few hours together. In sum, she

hardly knew him. And for all the shared good times, there had been so much that was bad and hurtful. On the other hand, love was always inexplicable. One did not ever choose love — love chose its victims. And hadn't she heard that he'd left a trail of broken hearts across the country? Undoubtedly she was hardly the first foolish woman to take a single look at him and fall headlong in love.

She wished her errant feelings would vanish, but she was terribly aware of them now.

Alexandra started downstairs, trembling with uncertainty and anticipation. It was eight o'clock in the morning. She hadn't seen him since their last conversation, when he had said he would momentarily respect her wishes, and that she would remain at Clarewood as his guest. Guests would join their host for breakfast and politely chat about any number of mundane subjects. She hoped he expected her to join him. Foolishly, she looked forward to the encounter, even while cautioning herself that he must never know how she felt about him.

The breakfast room was empty, though, and only one place was set.

She tried to contain her disappointment as she sat down and was served another sumptuous breakfast. It crossed her mind that he might not have come home at all last night, and she thought of Charlotte Witte with a deep, wrenching dismay. She suddenly found she had no appetite, even though she'd had her morning sickness earlier, and she was always hungry afterward. She pretended to eat, reminding herself that whatever Clarewood did, none of it was her affair. That choice of words did not help. She told herself that she had plenty to do that day. She had two customers whose gowns were not yet finished, and they were planning to have them picked up tomorrow, in town. She would have to deliver them now. And she had letters to write to her sisters. There was so much to explain.

She didn't dare think about her father. If she did, it would hurt too much.

Alexandra left the breakfast room, intending to go upstairs, and set up an ironing board and a small sewing table, if she could find one, there. But then she heard voices and thought she recognized Randolph's, as well as Clarewood's. *He was home after all.*

After yesterday, she had told herself that she would never eavesdrop again, but she instantly changed direction and found herself on the threshold of a small workroom with two tables and many papers spread across them. Randolph was inside, as was the duke. Clarewood was in his shirtsleeves, which were rolled up. His shirt collar was undone, his tie hanging loose. Two clerks were with them, and all heads were bent over the papers on the longest table. Everyone was speaking at once — except for Clarewood. He stood a bit apart, carefully listening to the others.

Even in such a state of dishevelment, he looked every inch the powerful and wealthy peer he was. He dominated the room. He was handsome, masculine, sensual. Trembling at the sight of him, Alexandra realized that they were discussing windows and lighting. Just as she came to that conclusion, Clarewood straightened and turned. His gaze warmed as it found hers.

She knew she blushed. She felt like rushing forward to greet him. Instead, she did not move. "I beg your pardon, I hope I am not interrupting," she said quickly. Looking at him had sent a blow right through her chest — a fist not just of desire, but of her newfound love.

He smiled and came forward. "You could never interrupt."

Her heart was hammering madly now. He could be so charming when it suited him. "That is nonsense. You are very busy, I see."

"I am always occupied," he said genially, his gaze moving slowly over her features. "Did you sleep well?"

"Very."

"And did you enjoy your breakfast?"

"Yes, thank you." She did not know why she was so nervous. And no one in the room seemed to care that she was present. The two clerks were arguing back and forth over the placement and size of the windows, with Randolph listening carefully to them before he murmured something about costs.

Clarewood glanced at the trio and then returned his attention to her. She had the feeling that he hadn't missed a word. "I am designing progressive housing for the working classes."

She started.

"No one should have to live without adequate light, ventilation, plumbing and sewage."

She looked intently at him.

"There is a textile factory in Manchester in which I own some shares. I am building a model housing project there. If it succeeds, I hope to be able to convince other factory owners to attempt similar projects." He smiled at her. "Healthy workers will be more productive workers, which will benefit us all."

"That sounds wonderful," Alexandra said. It was one thing to have heard about his good works, another to see him in his shirtsleeves, with his architects, his eyes alight with enthusiasm for his good causes. "Why do you care about the working poor?" While it had become somewhat fashionable to espouse such causes in the upper classes, most peers didn't care about anything except their own purses.

"Because I have been given so much — without lifting a finger for it. It would be remiss of me not to use what I have been given to help those far less fortunate than myself."

Her heart warmed impossibly. *He truly cared.* "Was your father a philanthropist, as well?"

"No, he was not." His smile changed. The warmth left his eyes. "I owe a great deal to the previous duke, but he was interested only in the prosperity of Clarewood — and what it could do for him and his progeny. I do believe he might be tossing about in his grave if he knew the sums I've spent on those who live in abject misery."

She studied his handsome face. If Stephen spoke the truth, how did a son differ so vastly from his father? He was a good man, she thought, her heart aching. She hesitated.

"I have heard that your father was very demanding."

He raised his eyebrows. "You have heard correctly. He was impossible to please. He would not be pleased with me now."

She did not believe that. "I am sure he would be very proud of you."

"Really? I doubt it." He was wry.

Alexandra wondered at that. "I am sure your son will be as generous as you, and you will be proud of him."

His gaze sharpened.

She tensed, thinking of the child she carried, and wishing she hadn't said what she had.

"I hope so," he finally said, turning away from her. Then he glanced back at her, but his lashes were lowered. "And what will you do today?" He finally met her gaze, but his eyes were impossible to read. "I have a meeting in town this afternoon, and a supper party after."

He would be gone for most of the day and evening, she thought, reminding herself that she had no right to feel abandoned or be dismayed. "I have some sewing to do."

His gaze narrowed. "I find your ability to provide for yourself in these circumstances admirable, but while you are here, you will lack for nothing."

"I have two customers who are expecting repaired, freshened and pressed gowns tomorrow."

He folded his arms and studied her. "Pass the cleaning and pressing on to my maids."

"I would never do such a thing! In fact, I was hoping to find a table to put in my room, one at which I can sew and iron."

His mouth tightened. Then, "This is absurd, Alexandra. I have a staff of laundresses on hand."

"I have worked very diligently to acquire a loyal clientele," she said. "I cannot suspend operations now."

He was clearly disapproving. "I thought you might like to take a coach and go into town to do some shopping, or I have some amenable riding horses should you wish to hack. But clearly you intend to spend the day sewing."

"Clearly," she said tersely. And just as clearly, he'd forgotten she did not have the means to shop.

"And tomorrow? Will you be hard at your labors then, too?"

"I hope so."

He shook his head. "I cannot understand why you would not take advantage of being my guest. I have a suggestion to make. Send word to your clients that you are on holiday.

Enjoy your time here. You might even consider inviting some friends for lunch. Perhaps your sisters might join you? My chefs will prepare any meal that you wish."

Alexandra almost gasped aloud. She would love to have her sisters over for a luncheon. And she recalled how she'd imagined being Squire Denney's wife, envisioning luncheons with her sisters and him. But the fanciful image had entirely changed. She saw herself with her sisters at the duke's table now, and he was the one walking into the dining room to join them, his smile wide and warm — and reserved exclusively for her. Shaken, she backed up.

She must never imagine such a scenario again!

"What is wrong?" he asked mildly.

"I am writing to my sisters, as they do not know I am here. I'd like to get the letter out with today's post," she managed.

"I'll have someone deliver it for you," he said. "But if you invited them for lunch, instead of spending your time sewing, you could explain your visit in person."

It was so tempting. She said softly, "And when I must return to my humble abode in town? Then what, Your Grace? How will I feed and clothe myself — and pay for my room — if I have lost all of my customers?"

434

His eyes darkened. "Maybe, by then, you will have a benefactor as well as a protector."

She knew exactly what he meant, and she flushed, her heart lurching. Her simmering desire intensified.

He smiled, somewhat smugly. "I think we both know that you will only resist me for so long."

"I think," she managed, "that my determination might surpass yours in the end."

His gaze narrowed, and Alexandra felt tension knife between them then.

"We will see," he said, shrugging. But his eyes gleamed, and she had the feeling that he liked this challenge — when she hadn't meant to challenge him at all. Then, "I have a great deal to do today. I'm afraid I must excuse myself, even if I am enjoying our debate."

"I am sorry. I should have gone directly upstairs."

He reached out and grasped her arm, forestalling her. "Alexandra, you are my guest, and you do not have to hide in your rooms. My staff has been instructed to see to your every wish. I would be appalled if a guest of mine were not perfectly comfortable. If you need something, you merely have to ask Guillermo — or you may ask me."

She realized that he meant it. But his eyes had that smoldering warmth now, which she understood completely. "Thank you, Your Grace." She pulled away.

He let her go. After a pause, he said, "In case you aren't aware of it, I am rarely thwarted in my ambitions, Alexandra."

Her tension knew no bounds. "I must attend my sewing. Have a good day, Your Grace." And she hurried away, almost relieved to have escaped intact, though she felt his eyes on her back.

The next few days passed slowly and had a dreamlike quality to them. She was the Duke of Clarewood's guest, but it remained hard to believe. When she awoke in the morning in her huge, canopied bed, covered in down, surrounded by the finest furnishings, she was always surprised to find herself there. A tray of chocolate was always outside her door, piping hot, in the finest china. Breakfast was always awaiting her in the breakfast room upon the elaborate buffet.

She now knew she would not see him at breakfast, or even during the day — he was either closeted with his architects, associates or clerks in his study or library, or he was attending meetings in town. She had adopted the habit of reading while taking breakfast alone, perusing the newspapers he'd already read. She spent the rest of her day sewing, taking a simple sandwich in her room at noontime, or delivering the gowns she had repaired.

If he was out, her gaze kept straying to the lawns and the long shell drive — she knew she was watching for his return. If he was in, she strained to hear the sound of doors opening and closing downstairs, and his rich, warm baritone.

And she would bump into him when she was least expecting it — upon turning the corner in a hall, or on the stairwell as she went upstairs, or when returning to the house from the outdoors. The moment their paths crossed he would become motionless, his powerful presence and large body dominating the small space between them. He never failed to politely inquire after her, while his gaze always instantly warmed. He no longer asked what she intended to do that day — instead, she caught him looking at her hands. She usually wore a thimble, and the tips of her fingers had calluses on them. He kept his expression impassive, but she knew he still disapproved.

And every such encounter made her

breathless. Every such encounter, no matter how small and how brief, made her yearn for more. Whenever they were close, his body pulled at her, as a magnet might. The urge to leap into his arms grew daily. She was almost certain he felt the same tension.

But he had yet to launch another seduction.

Now she lifted her needle and thread. It was late in the afternoon, and he'd left for the day before she'd even gone down to breakfast. According to Guillermo, he had gone to Manchester and might spend the night there. She shouldn't be dismayed, but she was.

A moment later Guillermo informed her that she had a caller. She was surprised; who would call on her? She'd written to her sisters five days ago, but there hadn't been a reply. She stood up eagerly, hoping that Olivia and Corey had come. "Who is it?"

"Your father, the Baron Edgemont."

She tensed. She'd written to her sisters but not to her father, because she didn't know what to say to him. She desperately wanted forgiveness — as desperately as she wanted him to love her and be proud of her again — as if they could erase the past.

Alexandra began to tremble, and she took a quick glance at herself in the mirror as she left the room. She followed Guillermo downstairs, praying all would be well with her father now. He had been shown into her favorite salon, and he turned when she paused on the threshold.

She could not move. He wasn't smiling, but then, neither was she. She wished they'd never had their last conversation, that he'd never thrown her out of the house. "Hello, Father." She inhaled. "I'm so glad you have called."

He was grim. "Your sisters finally told me that you are the duke's guest."

She cringed. "I *am* his guest — and *only* his guest. I had nowhere else to go."

He looked at her hands. Then he said, "Why are you still sewing?"

She removed the thimble, and realized she was clutching a needle and thread. "I need the income."

Edgemont gaped. "Surely that is not the case, seeing that you are living here as Clarewood's *guest.*"

From the way he spat the last word, she knew he did not believe her. She hugged herself. "I am not having an affair, Father."

"Then what are you doing here?" he demanded.

"I told you," she shot back. "I have nowhere to go, and he has been kind."

"Kind?" he echoed, shaking his head, disgusted.

This wasn't how she'd prayed their meeting would be. "I miss you, Father. I miss Corey and Olivia." She wanted to beg him to let her go home. But she didn't. She started forward desperately. "I am so sorry to have disappointed you. I do not blame you for throwing me out. What I did was shameful — disgraceful. I so need your forgiveness."

Edgemont trembled. "You're my eldest, Alexandra. Of course I forgive you."

She stared at him warily. He did not look as if he meant it. His face was set in harsh, twisted lines. Even so, she wanted to rush into his arms, though she had the feeling it would be awkward, at best, and a disaster at worst.

"You're my eldest, the best of the lot. You're the sensible one — the saintly one," he continued. "And you're so much like your mother."

She thought he meant to be loving, but his words felt like a blow. *You're nothing like your mother.* The words echoed in her mind. "I made a mistake. Mother would never have done what I did." Elizabeth would have stayed strong; she would never have given in to temptation. "Do you truly forgive me?"

"Of course I do," he said grimly. "Or I wouldn't be here."

But he wasn't embracing her, and he didn't seem pleased. Alexandra sat down, shaken. Nothing felt the same. She'd opened up a rift between them, and she could feel it still. "How are you? How is Olivia? Corey?"

"Corey has cried herself to sleep almost every night. She misses you — they both do." He was blunt, and his words stabbed through her. He added, "Olivia has holes in her shoes — the cobbler has said he cannot make another repair. The boys in town are so rude to Corey that she won't go into the village anymore."

Alexandra stiffened. Had he already spent the two thousand pounds? Still, she had not a doubt that her downfall had made things worse for Corey. She could not bear that.

Edgemont looked at her almost balefully. "I believe Denney will court Olivia now. You broke his heart, but that was over a month ago, and he has come by twice in the last week."

She shot to her feet. "No."

"It's too late to decide you want the good squire back." And he gestured at the room. "You have all of this now, anyway."

"I am his guest. Olivia must marry for love

441

— someone her own age."

"And she needs a dowry," he said. "But you know that."

Alexandra stood very still. "The two thousand pounds — it was for my sisters!"

"But it is gone, and I am so worried about them," he said. "I am drinking myself into oblivion every night."

It was hard to breathe. She was so angry now, but she began to understand where they were going. "You must control yourself," she said.

"How can I? My creditors come to the house every day now."

She trembled, sick with dismay. "How much do you need, Father?"

He walked away from her, hands in his pockets. From across the room, he turned and looked at her. "Another thousand would pay the most insufferable of them off. An additional five hundred would buy shoes and clothes for the girls."

He'd gambled away the money, she thought angrily, and now he wanted more.

"You're not wearing jewels," he said.

She touched her bare throat. "You didn't come here to see how I am, or to forgive me — or to tell me that you still love me," she said. There was more pain now, rising in her chest.

"You're my daughter. Of course I came to see you, and I said I forgive you."

He'd come for funds. She wet her lips. "I am not his mistress. I am his houseguest."

"So he is already done with you?"

"That isn't fair."

"He wouldn't have you living here otherwise. Will you help your sisters?"

He could not mean this, she thought, trembling.

He stared at her when she did not answer. "You remain a handsome woman, Alexandra, and I am sure he will reward you well."

She did not want to become sick now, but it was so hard to breathe, and her stomach churned.

"Well? Will you help us? Or will you abandon your family now?"

It was so hard to speak. "I will try to help," she said harshly.

Edgemont stared. She stared back, her vision blurred. She wasn't sure when she had started crying.

"I don't know why you're crying. You are living like a queen."

She was crying because her heart was broken. Her father had asked her to prostitute herself. And she had agreed. "Yes . . . I am . . . I don't feel well, Father. I think I must lie down."

"You don't look well," he said, "and it is a long ride back home, so I should go."

Alexandra did not know how she managed to show him to the door, then stand there waving, a smile plastered on her face, until he was gone. She vaguely heard Guillermo ask her if she was ill, and if he could get her something. She did not know what she said. Somehow she made it up to her room and crawled into the bed. The anger was gone. There was only heartache. She cried.

"What is wrong?" Clarewood asked quietly.

She hadn't heard anyone come in. She wouldn't have let anyone come in, not when she was so undone, so grief-stricken, and especially not Clarewood. She sat bolt upright, wiping her eyes, keeping her back to the doorway where he stood.

"Alexandra? Guillermo said you were ill. I did knock, but you did not hear me, and the door was wide-open."

She fought to control her heart, to somehow pull the sheared pieces back together, to mend them swiftly, so he would never know what had happened. She used her sleeve to wipe more tears as she heard his footsteps. She somehow squared her shoulders and turned to face him.

He was expressionless, but his gaze was riveted to her tear-streaked face. "What is wrong? Why are you crying? Guillermo said Edgemont was here."

She choked hard. "I'm fine," she gasped. "I need a moment, that is all."

"You are not fine. And I am guessing that your father's call was not a pleasant one."

She realized that his gaze had gone very hard — frighteningly so.

"If you tell me what is wrong," he added, more softly, "perhaps I can fix it."

She heard hysterical laughter erupt — along with a sob.

He sat down beside her on the bed, clasping her shoulders, his gaze boring into hers.

"He wants me to whore myself out to you," she said. Tears blinded her. "He needs fifteen hundred pounds."

His expression tightened. "I see."

She tried to turn away from him — instead, his grasp tightened. She looked up at him and was surprised by the anger she saw simmering in his gaze.

"I am not angry with you," he said softly. "But I am disgusted with Edgemont — not for the first time."

"He is my father! I . . . Despite everything, I love him."

His face tightened even more. "Of course

445

you do. It's your duty to love him. Just as it was your duty to obey him and care for him. I will give you the money, Alexandra."

"No," she insisted. "I can't take it."

He caught her face in his hands. "Then I will give it to Edgemont myself," he said, his gaze searing. "Damn it!" And he kissed her.

She went still. As his mouth moved over hers, some of the terrible grief lessened. The need to be in his arms surged as never before. He was her safest haven. She knew that now. And then he pulled back and looked at her — and his eyes seemed filled with anguish, as if he was sorry for her, as if he understood.

Desire exploded in her, shocking in its intensity. "Stephen."

He was looking at her, and his eyes blazed, the desire she saw there mirroring her own. He still held her face, and now he kissed her slow and deep and thoroughly.

She closed her eyes and began to cry, even as pleasure washed through her.

"Don't cry," he whispered.

Her mouth opened for him, encouraging him now, her hands seeking his shoulders.

He grunted, deepening the kiss. Alexandra threw her arms around him, holding on to him tightly, hoping to never let go. *I love you,* she thought. *I love you so much.*

"I have missed you," he said hoarsely.

She thought she had misheard, but she didn't care. She touched his high cheekbone, his strong jaw. "Make love to me."

His eyes blazed, and he moved over her.

CHAPTER FIFTEEN

She had fallen asleep, and now, as she blinked, she was aware that it was night-time. She instantly recalled their making love several times, their passion shocking and frenzied. *She was Stephen's lover again.*

She sat up, clutching the down covers to her chin. He'd turned two lamps on, and now he stood on the other side of the room, tucking his shirt into his trousers. Her heart leaped wildly. She was so deeply in love, and he had been so kind about her father. She inhaled, not wanting to think about that catastrophic interview. He was facing the mirror, and instantly he turned to gaze at her.

Her heart hammered wildly. She prayed that he would be as kind now as he had been before. From this distance, in the dimly lit bedroom, it was impossible to see his expression. Too well, she recalled what had happened the last and only time they had been together.

He slipped on his silver brocade waistcoat and approached. Although anxious, watching him gave her so much pleasure, and joy burgeoned. She tried to control it.

He paused by her hip. His mouth was soft, his eyes were warm, and his gaze was searching. She let the joy blossom.

She didn't know what to say, and she was hardly used to being naked in a bed, much less after lovemaking, so she tried to smile. Instantly he smiled back. And to her surprise, he said softly, "Do you wish to remain abed? I don't mind if you want to sleep."

She hesitated. The joy was beginning to wash fully over her now. "What time is it?"

"It's almost nine." His gaze moved slowly over her features, causing her to warm and blush. "You are a very beautiful sight like this, Alexandra."

She thrilled. And now she thought perhaps he really had told her that he had missed her. "I am an old spinster, and you know it."

His mouth curved. "Really? You are younger than I am, and I do not consider myself old."

She smiled back at him, so oddly happy now.

His smile vanished. "Do you have re-grets?"

She tensed, her own smile fading. "Will there be hurtful and hateful accusations?"

"No."

She sat up higher, holding the covers as modestly as possible. "Then how can I have regrets, Your Grace?" She wanted to use his name but didn't quite dare, though she'd used it once or twice during moments of the most extreme passion. She blushed now.

"Not 'Your Grace.' Just Stephen," he said softly, sinking down to sit at her hip. "And I believe we have sealed our agreement, have we not?"

She tensed. If he offered her a check now, she would be dismayed — no, horrified — to be paid for what they had shared. Because this did not feel like an agreement or an ar-rangement — not at all. Yet her father desperately needed money and Olivia must not marry Denney. "I do not think I can go backward," she said softly.

"Good." His gaze roamed over her face. "And you feel better . . . I hope?"

She tensed, afraid he was referring to her father. "Of course I do."

His smile came, then went. "I don't want you to worry about anything." His gaze intensified. "I am going to take care of

Edgemont."

She felt relief — and alarm. "He is my problem, not yours," she said.

"Really?" His gaze kept moving over her face. "Because when I extend my protection, I do so without parameters or limits." He slid his hand onto her hip, leaning closer. "Surely you must know that," he murmured.

Desire reared up, sudden, intense and shocking. She could not take anything from him now. If she did, he would not understand that she had come to love him. But at the same time, she was worried about Olivia.

"You remain sad."

There was no escaping the topic, she thought. "No matter what he has said, or what he has done, he is my father."

He pressed his mouth against her neck. "I know."

She wanted to ask him what he meant to do. But he was rubbing his lips over the tense cords of her throat, making her start to forget that afternoon.

"I want you," he said softly.

Alexandra sighed.

The Clarewood coach turned onto a very rutted, ill-kempt drive. Bracing himself against a safety strap, jouncing hard, Stephen stared out the window at the small, two-story house where Alexandra had lived. The grounds were bare and neglected, the front lawns mostly mud, and the barn behind the house was tumbledown and possibly in danger of collapsing. He was certain that once he went inside, her home would be as poorly kept. He had seen much worse — single rooms with no lights or windows, housing extended families, at once so crowded one could not move and so dirty one could not breathe. But his tension escalated anyway.

Alexandra deserved palatial living arrangements, and he was pleased he could provide them for her.

His heart felt as if it had lurched, and it was so oddly warm inside the coach. He had a disturbing suspicion that his heart was trying to tell him something, something impossible and unlikely, and he refused to listen to it. Because it was impossible that he had come to genuinely care for her, wasn't it? He was a cold, heartless man. He was not capable of love. Not because society accused him of as much, but because he had been shaped in old Tom's image.

Yet his heart raced, and it felt genuinely buoyant. He couldn't quite recall ever feeling this way, at once so satisfied, and so pleased — so happy. He wondered if he was smitten — and if so, if he was becoming a besotted fool, like Alexi and his other de Warenne cousins.

A de Warenne loves once and it is forever. He tensed. He was very familiar with that old family adage, but he was certain he was the exception to that particular de Warenne rule.

He did not want to analyze his strange feelings. He was simply glad he had come to his senses about Alexandra and rescued her from that horrid urban slum. He would always feel guilty for triggering the events that had put her in such horrific circumstances, but at least he was making amends.

He softened in a way he once would have considered impossible as he thought about her, even as he stared at the ramshackle house and dilapidated grounds. She was such a proud and responsible woman, and he knew, without having to be told, that living like this, in poverty, with a drunken father and two dependent and unwed sisters, had been a terrible drain on her. Hadn't she mentioned that she'd turned down a love match in order to care for her sisters? The tension in him grew. That had been a long time ago, but even so, he hadn't cared to examine how much she had once loved another man.

He was certain that Alexandra had not given her heart lightly. She might even be the kind of woman to love once and forever, like his relations. On the other hand, he was certain she felt something for him.

His heart stirred. He wanted her fiercely attached to him, and fiercely loyal. Perhaps, after a few more nights of excessive passion, she would be thoroughly besotted with him. He intended to make it so.

He did not want her having fond, secret and loving memories of someone else.

His coach had almost reached the front of the house, and he grasped the safety strap more tightly. He wasn't certain when he had first begun to admire her. Perhaps it had been that first evening at Harrington Hall, when she had held her head high in spite of the vicious gossip. But his admiration for her was growing by leaps and bounds, more so each and every day. In fact, he wasn't certain he had ever met anyone as strong, adept and determined. They had more in common than anyone would ever suspect.

He rarely had regrets, but he had many of them now. He was sorry he had so badly misjudged her, and that she had suffered so much in direct consequence of that. But that chapter was over now. This was a new beginning for them. If he could institute justice for her, he would. Starting with taking care of Edgemont and her sisters. That was the least that he could do.

The coach had halted in front of the house. Now that she was his mistress, he would give her all that she deserved. He looked forward to showering her with amenities he never even thought about: lavish meals, fine wine, silk sheets and hot baths, a new wardrobe, shopping excursions, vacations in France and Italy. And he looked forward to showering her with jewels.

His footman opened the door, interrupting his thoughts, reminding him to watch out for mud puddles. Stephen thanked him and stepped down from the carriage.

The front door of the house opened.

He met the gazes of her two sisters, who were wide-eyed with shock. He instantly started forward as the younger one, Corey, cried, "Is something wrong? Is Alexandra all right?"

"She is fine," he called out, increasing his stride. He had treated her cruelly and unfairly, but he was making amends now. On the other hand, his treatment of her was nothing like Edgemont's. He *despised* the other man. Having reached the front steps, he bowed to the young ladies. "Good afternoon. Your sister is fine, but I have some business matters to discuss with your father."

Olivia was staring intensely at him now, her cheeks flushed. "Please, do come in. I am sorry, I do not know what has come over me." She stepped aside so he could enter the house, obviously flustered.

He smiled at her. "I could have sent word, but I'm afraid I decided the matter is a rather urgent one."

Olivia's green gaze was searching. He was a good judge of character, and he knew that she was a sensible, intelligent young woman, in some ways very much like her older sister. He sensed a deep strength of mind and character. The younger one, however, seemed far too innocent for someone so beautiful, and very impulsive. It crossed his mind that both sisters needed husbands.

He stepped into a clean and tidy but very shabby parlor. The upholstered furnishings were tired, torn and worn, as were the draperies. The rug in the center of the sitting area was threadbare. The wood floors were scratched, and a few planks were chipped. The walls needed both paint and plaster. One chair sat on a broken leg.

"Corey, get Father and make tea," Olivia said, staring uncertainly at him as the younger girl ran upstairs. "Why didn't Alexandra come with you?"

"I believe she has a great deal of sewing to do today." Olivia looked disbelieving, but he could hardly tell her that Alexandra remained asleep in his bed. "Why don't you and your sister call sometime soon? I am sure my chef would be delighted to serve you all a very pleasant luncheon, and I happen to know that your sister misses you both — she would be thrilled to see you."

Olivia hesitated, wetting her lips, the gesture so familiar. He realized then that she would love nothing more — and suspected that their father had refused to let the girls visit. His temper rose, as it did every time he thought of Edgemont. He reined it in with some difficulty.

Just then the subject of his thoughts came ambling downstairs behind his youngest daughter, clearly having hastily shoved on his jacket. He looked every bit the drunk that he was and as if he'd had a bad night — he was unshaven and unkempt.

Stephen looked at Olivia. "I do not wish to be interrupted."

She curtsied, took Corey's hand and hurried down the hall. Stephen closed the door behind them and looked at Edgemont with utter contempt. The baron bowed, however, smiling obsequiously. "Your Grace! I did not expect you. Had I done so, I would have been up and about, and preparations would have been made for your call."

"Don't bother trying to placate me," Stephen said, rigid with anger. "I will get right to the point. You are never to call on Alexandra again. You are never to speak to her in an unkind manner, you are never to suggest that she must perform any kind of service in order to provide for you — and you are never to ask her for funds. Do I make myself clear?"

Edgemont paled. "You are mistaken, Your Grace," he began.

He realized his fist was clenched and that he was a mere moment from striking the man. He, who never hit anyone — except, occasionally, Alexi. He trembled and fought for control.

"She is my daughter. I would never be unkind or —"

"Shut up," Stephen said harshly.

Edgemont shut his mouth instantly.

"She is under my protection, and no one mistreats anyone under my protection. Have I made myself clear?"

The older man nodded, ashen.

"How much do you owe?"

"What?"

"I believe you heard me, Edgemont." Stephen knew his stare was so hateful that if looks could kill, the baron would have keeled over.

Flushing, Edgemont mumbled, "About a thousand pounds, give or take a guinea or two."

"You will give me all your bills. I am going to pay them for you."

Edgemont gaped. "They are in the library, Your Grace."

"Do not move. There is more. I will be providing an income for you and your two daughters. The funds are to be used exclusively for food, clothing and daily expenses — not for poker games and roulette, for horse racing or for liquor. I am warning you, sir. If I find that you misuse the monthly allowance, I will have you removed from these premises and thrown in debtors' prison. Do you understand me?"

Edgemont said, "I do, Your Grace, I do, and I am delighted, truly delighted, but surely I will have some small sum with which to go out at night?"

Stephen's disgust was boundless. The man was sick. He would never be able to restrain himself, but Stephen had no intention of supporting his gaming or drinking. And while he knew he could never put Edgemont in jail, he could remove the sisters from his keeping. And if the man reverted to type, that would probably be for the best, he thought. Still, there was no harm in repeating a good threat. "If you abuse my good will, you will find yourself behind bars."

"I understand," Edgemont replied.

And because he knew the girls were at the door, undoubtedly pressing their ears to it and eavesdropping, Stephen said, "Ladies, please come in."

The door opened, and the two stunned young women walked forward, their eyes riveted on him.

He smiled and handed Olivia a very large check. "This is for new wardrobes and any other necessities that you and your sister might need."

She didn't even look at it. Instead, tears came to her eyes. "We cannot possibly accept this," she whispered, reminding him so much of her sister.

Corey jabbed her with her elbow and said quickly, "Thank you so much, Your Grace."

She was a kept woman now.

Alexandra smiled, unashamed, tingling right down to her toes. In fact, she was filled with joy and happiness. Stephen's handsome image was engraved on her mind. In it he was smiling, his eyes warm. They were lovers now — and she was deeply and irrevocably in love with him, as well.

It was midday, and she was working on one of Lady Henredon's older gowns, a very lovely Parisian couture creation of lace and chiffon. It was hard to concentrate. Several days had passed, days that felt like a dream come true, days in which she wandered about Clarewood very much like its mistress, while being thoroughly well loved at night. She did not feel like a mistress or, worse, a fallen woman. Oh, no. She felt like a bride.

She had to pinch herself, because she knew this was not a fairy tale, that she was not a bride, and that there would not be a happily-ever-after ending. But that knowledge could not change her feelings — feelings that seemed to be growing by leaps and bounds.

She'd fallen in love with him before taking up her place in his bed again, but her love seemed to intensify with every passing moment. And how could it not, when he treated her like a wife, and when even his entire staff was reverent and deferential to her? The chef had begun asking her to plan the day's menus. The housekeeper had begun to ask her which linens she preferred. Her own personal maid would ask her which of the new gowns he had insisted she buy she intended to wear for supper, and which for the next day. How could she not feel like a cherished bride? And most of all, it felt as if this interlude would last forever — as if he loved her, just a little, in return.

It was so hard to chide herself for thinking that. And her warmth increased as she thought of how he'd awoken her before dawn to make love again, this time slowly and tenderly, before he left for a midday meeting in Manchester. He'd even kissed her goodbye.

Alexandra paused in her sewing, smiling. *He was such an extraordinary man.*

She was living in a fairy tale with her own prince charming.

How had she ever thought him a cruel, unkind man? He had devoted his life to alleviating the misery of others. She had quickly come to realize that as much as he revered his duty to Clarewood, which was bound up with his sense of duty to his deceased father, the success of his philanthropies was even more important to him.

They had fallen into a routine, with each of them going about their affairs by day, and then sitting down together to a wonderfully intimate supper in the evening. He had stopped going out to attend other social engagements, though she knew those engagements existed — after all, he was a premier peer and had many social obligations. Yet ever since their relationship had changed, he had stayed in every single night to be with her.

She knew the time would soon come when he would begin going out again — more evenings than not, no doubt — and she told herself that she did not care. She refused to think about spending the evenings alone at Clarewood while he went out, or the fact that if she *were* a bride, she would be going out with him.

And he was as generous as he had said he would be. Alexandra looked down at her raspberry silk gown. It was the loveliest dress she had ever worn.

A week ago a very famous seamstress had appeared with two assistants, informing her that His Grace had insisted an entire wardrobe be made for her. She had tried to refuse. They had scattered the loveliest, costliest fabrics she had ever seen about the drawing room, making it so hard to breathe, so shocked had she been by the lavish display. She had itched to touch the gorgeous bolts of silk and chiffon, of satin and velvet. But she had refrained. Then they had piled up equally lavish samples of stunning and expensive trims. Alexandra had been in disbelief — why would he spend such a fortune on her? She had spent the day trying to refuse each and every suggestion, but in the end, if she so much as indicated that she liked something, the seamstress instantly decided to make a day dress or an evening gown from it. Five dresses and an evening gown had already been delivered. Clearly an entire team of seamstresses had been sewing ever since the day of the fitting.

But one terrible problem loomed. She hadn't told him about the child.

Alexandra instantly felt ill. He hadn't seemed to notice the ongoing nausea. Surely he would have said something if he had. Not a morning passed that she did not rush off to find a chamber pot, but he was already downstairs by then — or off the grounds and on his way to town. She cleaned the pots herself, though she thought her personal maid knew what was going on. He had accused her of deception once, but the deception she was now engaged in was far worse than misleading him about her innocence. A child's life and future were at stake.

She did not know what to do. She thought

every single day about the child she was carrying and his right to know about it. But
even though it seemed like a faraway
memory, she hadn't forgotten his rage when
he'd thought her a scheming fortune hunter.
She never wanted to be accused and hurt
that way again. She had been so certain he
would think the child a plot to trap him into
marriage if she revealed her condition to
him. Now, she was not so sure. Now she
wondered if he might understand that it had
been a fateful accident. Now she wondered
if he might continue their affair, even knowing she was pregnant.

She did not want to lose him — not yet.

He had every right to know that he would
be a father. And he would be a wonderful
father, she had no doubt. Her son or daughter had every right to the benefits of having
the Duke of Clarewood as a father. She
believed that with all her heart and all her
being. But when she told him, their relationship might end. If he thought she was trying to manipulate him yet again, it would
certainly be over.

Alexandra was so deeply in love that she
could hardly imagine their relationship ending. Yet she hadn't lost every shred of common sense that she possessed. He would
learn the truth in a few more months, when

her condition became obvious.

And since he was going to find out about the child sooner or later, it was becoming clear that she should tell him now. It would relieve her conscience. It was the right thing to do. Still, she remained afraid of how he might react. If he *could* accept the news, she would cling to their affair until he lost interest in her.

This might feel like love, and for her it might actually *be* love, but in truth it was only an arrangement, though Stephen made it so easy to forget.

Now Alexandra stood and stretched. She'd turned a small withdrawing room on the ground floor into her sewing room. She rubbed her aching back and walked over to the window. As she looked outside, she saw an oddly familiar carriage parked in front of the house. Tension instantly began to roil in her stomach.

Stephen was gone for the day, and she could not greet his callers. She stared, suddenly grim. She would have to hide until Guillermo sent the visitor away. So much for feeling like a beloved bride.

She was surprised when Guillermo knocked, the sound now familiar to her. She hurried to the door, thinking that there must be a problem. "What is it?"

"You have callers, Lady St. Xavier and Mrs. de Warenne."

She blanched. "No, that's impossible — they must be calling on the duke."

"The ladies have explicitly stated that they are calling on you."

Her alarm was instantaneous. "Send them away!"

"May I suggest you entertain them in the Gold Room, Miss Bolton?"

She was shocked. In the entire week and a half that she had been at Clarewood, Guillermo had never offered an opinion, much less advice. "No good will come of this."

"To the contrary, His Grace is very fond of both young ladies, and I believe he would insist you take their call." He left.

Alexandra was dumbfounded. She took a breath and decided that he would never have said such a thing if he did not believe it. And she was filled with dread — while she had liked both women, she couldn't imagine why they had called. She hadn't thought about it, but the entire town had to know that she was living at Clarewood, and the most vicious gossips like Lady Witte would surely be accusing her of being Stephen's mistress. He might have quelled some gossip, but their affair could not be a secret now.

Ariella and Elysse were in the Gold Room when she arrived, chatting about someone she did not know, a cousin named Margery. Instantly both women turned to her, smiling as if they were thrilled to see her.

She was relieved, but she was cautious, too, wondering if the daggers would soon appear. "Good afternoon," she said carefully. "It is so pleasant to see you both again. But I am afraid that His Grace is not in at the moment."

"We know," Elysse said, smiling. "But we are here to see you, and this call is long overdue. We wanted to make certain that Stephen is treating you well. You seem to be in one piece — one very lovely piece, actually."

Alexandra tensed. What did the other woman mean?

"Actually, we are going shopping," Ariella said, stepping forward. She gave Elysse a quelling look. "And we decided that you must join us."

"Do you want to go shopping? Stephen will hardly mind, and he is gone for the day, anyway. Although he can be so difficult," Elysse said. "By the way, we think you are very brave to be putting up with him. He is renowned as a terrible host."

Alexandra started.

"He rarely has guests here, and when he does, they do not stay for very long," Ariella explained. "It is not that he shows rudeness or ill will, but he is too preoccupied to entertain. Though he *is* intolerant of those who overstay their welcome."

They were trying to ascertain the extent of her relationship, Alexandra decided. "He has been an excellent host," she said carefully.

Both women seemed delighted by her response. When they simply smiled and did not speak, she added, "I'm sure you have heard that I had a falling out with my father. The duke was kind enough to suggest that I stay here until I could make other arrangements."

Elysse sobered. "That is awful, about your having to leave your home," she said. "We are both so sorry. However, we are pleased that you have not joined in the universal condemnation of Stephen as a host."

"I would never speak ill of him," Alexandra said tersely.

"Apparently he is capable of being a good host — when he wants to be," Elysse said with a smile.

Ariella said softly, "He must be smitten."

Alexandra tensed and bit her lip. She did not know what to say. Surely they knew she was his lover, not truly his guest. Yet these women were acting as if there was nothing wrong with her being Stephen's mistress. "He is a gentleman," she finally said. "He is kind . . . a pleasing and thoughtful host. If I have overstayed my welcome, I have not noticed it."

The two women exchanged another glance, both remaining delighted. Then Ariella laughed. "You are clearly welcome here. Very few know how kind he is, Miss Bolton. His reputation is that he is cold, demanding, difficult and heartless. And I will admit that with most people he *is* very autocratic and rude. Clearly he has changed."

"And you have not lost patience with him," Elysse added.

Alexandra's cheeks were on fire, and she was breathing with some difficulty. Did they expect a confession? "I doubt anyone would be foolish enough to lose patience with His Grace."

"I lose patience with him all the time. Stephen can be a boor. He can also be boring," Ariella stated.

Alexandra felt her eyes widen. "He is far too clever to ever be boring, and he is actually charming," she began, then stopped abruptly.

"Well, I am very glad —" Elysse grinned

"— to see you in such good spirits, and so utterly loyal. You must be terribly good for him."

Alexandra was speechless.

Ariella looped their arms together. "Miss Bolton, I have known Stephen since he was nine years old, and he and my brother are best friends. We are thrilled that he has finally found someone as genuine as you to light up his dark, dreary life."

Alexandra pulled away. "I don't know what you mean!"

"We knew he was uncommonly interested in you when he helped your father home at Sara's birthday party," Elysse said. "Because we know Stephen so well, and he would not have bothered otherwise."

She felt helpless — as if being pushed along by a huge gale into a confession she did not want to make. "I had nowhere to go, as I said. He was kind enough to offer me accommodations, that is all."

"Good," Ariella said. "As it was his fault you wound up booted in the first place — was it not? He is honorable. So he did what was right."

Alexandra sat down, only to realize she was being rude, as she hadn't allowed her guests to sit first. If she confessed her feelings to these two women, would they laugh at her? Mock her? Scorn her? She was beginning to think they were genuinely pleased that she was carrying on with Stephen.

Ariella sat down beside her on the sofa and took her hand. "Love is such a strange bedfellow. When I first laid eyes on Emilian, it was all over for me — though I thought him a Romany *vaida!* I was smitten, besotted, obsessed, never mind that he was partly Roma and my father disapproved. And it was a difficult journey, one that, at times, seemed impossible. But he is the love of my life," she said happily, and squeezed Alexandra's hand.

"I was eight when I first met Alexi," Elysse said cheerfully, sitting down on the other side of Alexandra. "I thought he was the most dashing boy I had ever seen — and the most annoying! We spent our childhood years trying to impress or outright ignore one another — until he rescued me from scandal and then abandoned me at the altar. But we found our way back to one another, and I could not live without him," she said, smiling.

Alexandra had to smile. Her heart was racing now. Those were beautiful love stories — so unlike her own. But they clearly knew she was Stephen's lover and even seemed to

472

know that she loved him — and to approve. "But this is wrong!" she burst out. "Why don't you condemn me?"

"Because we like you," Elysse said firmly. "I liked you the moment we met. And we love Stephen — enough to worry about him. And sometimes there is writing on the wall." She grinned.

Alexandra did not have a clue as to what she meant.

"Besides, love can be so impatient," Ariella said, somewhat wickedly. "Good, now that is settled." She stood. "Come on. We are going into town, I need gloves, and Elysse needs clothing for her baby. You can accompany us — I am sure there is something you might wish to buy. And don't worry, if we come across any jackals, we will fend them off for you."

"Better yet," Elysse said, "we will send them to Stephen, and he will dispatch them for us."

Alexandra bit her lip, hard. It seemed that she had somehow made two new and wonderful friends.

Alexandra hurried downstairs, hoping to catch Stephen before he became too involved in his daily affairs. The girls had kept her out past supper last night; she had gotten home at half past nine. He had been in the library, reading contracts, having delayed supper until she returned. He had seemed pleased that she had spent the afternoon with the two women, and had refused to let her apologize. And then they had forgotten about supper. He'd pulled her close, and they'd made love on the rug, in front of the fire.

Eventually they'd gone up to bed, and this morning she had overslept. It was half past ten. She ran down the hall just as Stephen stepped into the corridor. Not for the first time, they practically collided, but he caught her and steadied her.

She let him pull her close. "We didn't speak last night except for a moment, and I was afraid you'd be gone by the time I came downstairs."

He slid his hand up to the nape of her neck and into her loosely coiled hair. "I wasn't in the mood to converse last night — as you well know."

She blushed. He had been so terribly amorous. "I meant to send word that I would be late. I never meant for you to wait on me — and to miss supper. I am sorry, Stephen."

His smile was indolent. "I said I didn't mind, and I never say what I don't mean.

In fact, I am glad Elysse and Ariella got you out of the house. You never said — was it an enjoyable day?"

She nodded. "I did not buy anything, but I helped Elysse choose her baby things." She stopped.

He stared.

She was uneasy. When she made those kinds of slips, she had the distinct sensation that he knew she was with child. But if he knew, he would confront her, she was certain.

He broke the tension. "Were you treated well?"

She was relieved by the question. "The shopkeepers treated me like royalty, Stephen."

He smiled, pleased. "Then maybe you will start going out more often. And why didn't you make any purchases? Didn't you see anything you liked?"

She bit her lip. How could she tell him that she would never feel comfortable using his credit?

He pulled her close. "I thought so. It would please me, Alexandra, if you went shopping. In fact, it would please me very much if you spent an excessive amount on yourself."

She had to smile back at him. "I think you

mean it."

"I do," he murmured. Then, "Come into the library with me."

His eyes were so warm that for a moment, she thought he meant to make love to her there in the bright light of midmorning. But a moment later he was opening a locked desk drawer. He straightened to face her, and she could not see what he was holding. "It is my pleasure to give this to you, Alexandra."

He held out a velvet-covered jeweler's box. As he opened it, she glimpsed a diamond bracelet inside and, for one moment, thought it was the one he had tried to give her when they had first met, after the Harrington ball.

But then he lifted out the bracelet, and she saw it was far different — it was even more stunning and costly. She knew her eyes were huge.

"I want you to have this," he said roughly, approaching, and began placing it on her wrist.

She came out of her shock. She had never seen so many large diamonds. "Stephen . . . how can I accept this?"

"You can — and you will," he said firmly, fixing the clasp. His gaze met hers. "It is a token of my affection — my admiration —

my respect."

She inhaled — and tears flooded her eyes.

He tilted up her chin. "Remember, I never say what I do not mean."

She trembled, crying. This was not a payment for services rendered — it was a token of his affection. And he admired her. He respected her. "I love it," she whispered, thinking, *I love you.*

He slowly smiled, keeping her face tilted toward his, and slowly, his mouth feathered over hers. "I believe you are turning me into a shamelessly content man."

She was so moved, she was speechless.

And then he glanced past her, at the window. Alexandra followed his gaze — and saw her old, tired carriage outside, with Ebony in the traces. "My sisters have finally come to visit!"

He wrapped his arm around her and kissed her on the mouth. "Make sure they stay for lunch. I'll see you later."

"No, wait." She clasped his beautiful face in her hands and kissed him fiercely. "I do not deserve such jewels. But I love it!"

He smiled. "Go greet your sisters. And, Alexandra? Enjoy yourself."

Alexandra barely heard him now. She tore free, lifting her skirts so she could run. She raced through the house as swiftly as she dared, and when she reached the front hall, Olivia and Corey were just handing off their coats. They cried out as she skidded into the front hall, and everyone embraced wildly. Tears of joy filled Alexandra's eyes. "I have missed you so!"

"I have missed you, too," Corey said, hugging her hard one more time. "You are so elegant! Look at that dress." Then she saw the bracelet. "Oh, Alexandra!"

"He just gave it to me, as a token of his affection and respect," she managed.

Olivia held her hands, clinging, her eyes wide. "It is gorgeous — and you are so beautiful. You are radiant — as never before." Her gaze held Alexandra's, and it was searching now.

"I have hardly changed," Alexandra said, but she flushed as she spoke, her eyes still moist. She was an entirely different woman now — and they both knew it.

"He is good to you, isn't he? You are so happy — I can see it in your eyes," Olivia said softly.

Alexandra cupped her cheek, as Corey said, "He came to Edgemont Way. He set Father down and gave him a list of things he must never do again — including being rude to you!"

Alexandra gasped, stunned.

Olivia took her hand back. "He has given us a very generous monthly allowance. The pantry is full, as is the hay storage, and we have ordered three new gowns each."

She reeled. *Look at what Stephen had done for her family.*

"He is a good man, isn't he?" Corey asked, her gaze intent and searching. "He must love you very much, to take such good care of us, and to put Father down the way he did — and to give you that stunning bracelet."

Alexandra froze. What if Stephen loved her? Was it possible? *This is a token of my affection — my admiration — my respect.* She thrilled. "He is generous by nature," she managed. Then, swallowing, "I do believe he is fond of me."

"Fond?" Corey echoed. And she looked at Olivia, who returned her glance. Instantly, Alexandra knew that they had a secret.

Olivia said softly, "Are you in love with him now?"

Alexandra met her sister's searching gaze and knew that something was wrong. "What is it? What has happened? Something *has* happened, I am sure of it."

Her sisters shared another glance, but for once Corey held her tongue.

Olivia broke the silence. "Owen is in town,

479

Alexandra. He called yesterday — looking
for you."

CHAPTER SIXTEEN

Alexandra was so surprised that for one moment she thought she had misheard. But her sisters were staring expectantly at her. *Owen was in town?* Her heart skidded wildly.

She did not know what to think. He'd probably been to town many times in the past nine years — but he had never tried to call on her before. A month or so ago she might have been ecstatic, but now she was simply stunned.

Why had he appeared in her life again?

What could it mean?

Her heart lurched again as she fought for composure. Memories began flooding her, and in all of them Owen was as bright as the sun. He was smiling, and he was her best friend. But he was also her suitor, and she suddenly recalled being in his arms, in the heat of a passionate kiss. She tensed.

But even as she recalled his golden image, his smile, his dancing eyes turning dark with passion, Stephen's image loomed. Her tension spiraled impossibly, and she glanced at the dazzling bracelet on her wrist and thought of how he'd made love to her that morning. She loved Stephen now — Owen had married someone else a long time ago.

"Why did he call on me — after all these years?" she managed.

Olivia took her arm. "Maybe we should sit down, Alexandra."

She flinched, dread beginning to pool in her stomach. Olivia had further news — and it was not going to be good, she instantly decided. "Is he all right?"

Olivia smiled grimly, pulling her toward the closest open doors. "He is well enough, considering."

What did that mean? Alexandra followed her sister into the Gold Room.

"You are upset," Corey said, her tone odd, and she glanced again at Olivia.

Alexandra realized her breathing was shallow. "What aren't you telling me? This is clearly ominous. And of course I am upset." Owen had been the one true, great love of her life. She loved him still. Of course she did. She would always love him — and always consider him a dear friend — but that would not change her feelings for Stephen.

Olivia clasped her shoulder. "He is a widower now, Alexandra. He buried his wife six months ago."

Alexandra heard herself gasp. Her knees felt weak. Olivia caught her elbow, saying, "Will you swoon?"

Her shock knew no bounds. *His wife had died.*

And he had called on her. . . .

She went to a chair and sat down, breathless. Her temples felt about to explode, and because she knew Owen so well, she knew how filled with grief and mourning he must be, and her concern for him was boundless. But even as she thought that, Stephen's image was there in her mind, dark, powerful and somehow accusatory.

She inhaled.

She was with Stephen now. She was carrying his child. There was no reason to suddenly feel caught between two very polar and powerful forces threatening to pull her in opposite directions. She loved Stephen, even if she didn't dare admit it to him — even if she was only his mistress and would never be more. "Is he devastated? When did this happen?"

"I do not know if he is devastated, but he isn't happy. He is not as I recalled him," Olivia said somberly. "Was I wrong to remember him as being dashing and sunny, and always ready to smile or laugh? He was grim, Alexandra, and sad."

"He was *very* sad," Corey offered as soberly. "But he was eager to see you."

Alexandra's tension increased. "He is in mourning." She was so concerned for him, and that put her on firmer footing, somehow. "He must need a shoulder," she said. "He must certainly need a friend. No wonder he has sought me out." This wasn't about renewing their romance, she realized. Was she relieved? Dismayed? All she knew was that she had to see Owen and comfort him if she could. And Stephen would understand.

Olivia sat down beside her, staring. "He was very disappointed that you were not at home."

Alexandra looked at her, because of the innuendos in her tone. What was Olivia thinking? That they would renew their grand love affair? "He did not come to town with romantic intentions."

Olivia and Corey exchanged a new round of looks. "How do you know that?" Olivia asked carefully.

"Because it has been nine years, and he is mourning his wife's passing." She heard the sharp edge to her tone. And she wasn't certain, even as the memories of the years they had shared kept flooding her now, but hadn't he told her that he would never stop loving her — and that he would never forget her? She trembled, thinking of Stephen, distraught. She had the notion that he wouldn't like Owen very much. And Owen would certainly disapprove of her living arrangements. He might even expect Stephen to marry her. "What did you tell him? How did you explain that I no longer live at home?"

"I told him that you were currently Clarewood's guest. I don't think he understood." Olivia stared with significance.

Corey added, "He said he would call on you here. He will find out very shortly."

Alexandra inhaled. "I never had secrets from Owen, and I do not intend to keep them now. In any case, he will realize that I am Stephen's mistress soon enough." Her mind was made up. He certainly needed her as a friend, but he had *not* come to town with any romantic intentions. And even if he had, it didn't matter. "If he doesn't call tomorrow, I will call on him — I intend to renew our friendship. Where is he staying?"

"He is staying with Lord and Lady Bludgeon in Greenwich," Olivia said.

Alexandra did not know the couple. She

rubbed her throbbing temples. She realized she was now eager to see Owen, and comfort and console him, if need be.

Olivia took her hand. "Are you really all right? You are as white as a sheet."

"This is a shock," Alexandra admitted. "And I am worried about Owen."

"Of course you are," Olivia said, her gaze searching.

She met Olivia's kind, concerned eyes. And she did not like the question there. Olivia wanted to know if she had any romantic feelings for Owen.

"So what are you going to do?" Corey asked suddenly. "Once you see Owen again."

Alexandra tensed. "I will offer him comfort, Corey."

Corey and Olivia looked at one another again. "That isn't what she meant," Olivia said.

Alexandra leaped to her feet and began to pace. Her sisters did not know she was with child. Surely they would stop insinuating that something romantic might happen between her and Owen if they did. And they liked Stephen — they had made it clear how impressed they were with his generosity.

"You loved him so much once," Corey

said. "I remember your crying yourself to sleep."

Alexandra came to a stop. "That is the past!" Olivia was one of the most sensible women she knew — she had always been Alexandra's confidante, and Alexandra needed to speak with her privately now. "Corey, could you find Guillermo, who is the butler, and tell him that we are three for lunch today?"

Corey smiled. "Clarewood said we should come for lunch."

When their sister was gone, Alexandra looked carefully at Olivia, who said, "You seem remarkably composed, considering that you have just had the shock of learning that the love of your life has been looking for you and that he is now available."

"I am with Stephen now, and you know it as well as I do."

It was a moment before Olivia spoke. "Will Stephen offer marriage?"

Alexandra tensed, dismayed. "Olivia, come. You know as well as I do that he would never consider me eligible to be his duchess."

Olivia's mouth tightened. "There are dukes — and princes and kings — who marry commoners, for goodness sake. You would make a wonderful duchess."

Alexandra's heart missed a beat. "Please don't." She took Olivia's hand and exhaled. "Olivia, I sent Corey away because there is something I must discuss with you — desperately."

Olivia started. "What is wrong?"

"I am with child. You are the first to know — I haven't told anyone yet."

Olivia gasped. "Alexandra!" Then, her eyes huge, "You haven't told Clarewood?"

"No. I am afraid he will think my pregnancy a scheme to trap him into marriage." She stared at her sister now and said nervously, "The first time we were together, he thought I meant to trap him into marriage because of my innocence." Olivia had paled. "He was so very angry. I cannot bear such anger again."

Olivia inhaled, standing. "He should marry you, Alexandra. It is the honorable thing to do. No wonder you keep insisting that you are with Clarewood."

"That isn't fair — and you like him. You know you do."

"Yes, I do, but now that I know you are carrying his child, he *must* marry you. This changes everything! You are with child — this is actually joyous news! And surely he *will* marry you now. I cannot believe you have been afraid to tell him." She had begun to smile, no doubt thinking about the niece or nephew she would have.

Alexandra trembled. "I . . . I love him, but he is frightening when he is angry."

"Has he hurt you?" Olivia asked.

"No, of course not — not the way you mean. Olivia, I think he cares for me now, and that my news might even please him. But . . . I am so afraid I am wrong and that he will accuse me of scheming again — and then it will be over."

Olivia clasped her arm, grim and angry. "Alexandra, he should adore you. He should be head over heels in love with you."

"Stop!"

"The way Owen once was."

Alexandra pulled away. "That isn't fair. Owen has nothing to do with this."

"Really? I feel certain of one thing — Owen still loves you, and if Clarewood walks out, I am certain he would never let you bear a child by yourself."

"Stop! You can't possibly know any such thing." She hugged herself. "Please, you are being absurd. I care about Stephen, and this is hard enough as it is."

Olivia actually scowled, shaking her head. "You must tell him about the child — immediately. Then we will see what happens."

Alexandra could not believe Olivia expected Stephen to consider marriage to her — or that she actually considered Owen a knight in shining armor who would ride to her rescue if Stephen refused to marry her. But Owen *was* a knight in shining armor, she thought in despair. He had always been kind, caring and a man of honor. He would not care about the gossip — or her reputation.

Alexandra steeled herself not to feel the stabbing pain in her heart. "I have always known this affair was not meant to last forever."

"Why not? Because you are not good enough for him?" Olivia asked. "Clarewood has been very generous with all of us. But if he won't marry you, then you should rethink what you are doing."

Alexandra was silent — because a child's future was at stake, and maybe her sister was right.

Olivia barreled on. "I know you believe you love Clarewood, but do you really? Because I know how much you loved Owen. And I do not think a love like that ever dies."

Jefferson had not responded immediately to her written invitation, which a servant had delivered. When several days had passed without a reply, Julia had begun to think he meant to reject her invitation — which was an obvious rejection of her very cautious advances. But then his reply had come, with an apology — he had been in the south of Scotland. And when she realized he had accepted her invitation to join her for a ride about the countryside, her relief knew no bounds. She was thrilled.

She stole a glance at him now. Her mouth was oddly dry, and she was breathless. They were both mounted and walking their horses away from the stables; he hadn't said much since arriving, other than to greet her and offer some polite inquiries after her well-being. She'd tried to respond with her usual grace and a nonchalance she did not feel, but it had been almost impossible. He seemed larger and more masculine, and even more attractive, than before. He seemed to dominate the space between them. She was more aware of him than ever before. The tension she'd felt the last time he'd called had somehow become magnified, until it was almost unbearable.

She looked carefully at him and caught him staring, his regard male and bold. Her heart leaped. "Did you enjoy Scotland?"

"Yes, I did. My mother came from Glasgow."

She hadn't known. "I believe I have an

ancestor on my father's side who was born in the western isles."

"Then I suppose we have something in common." And for one moment their gazes locked, before he glanced away.

She wondered if something was wrong. He was so unusually quiet. "Have you enjoyed your time here?" she asked, hoping that nothing was wrong.

"Yes." He finally glanced at her, and his smile seemed forced. "I should have come to see my daughter's grave decades ago."

He had told her something terribly personal. She wished she could tell him more about her life — about Tom. She hesitated. "I'm glad you finally did. I hope it helped."

He was silent for a moment. "It did."

She heard herself say, "I decided years ago not to visit my husband's tomb."

He was staring intently now. "Why not, if you don't mind my asking?"

"It's been fifteen years, and I was tired of paying my respects." She shrugged. "Or pretending to do so."

"I heard it said he was a son of a gun."

She bit her lip. "He was a cold, difficult man . . . and frequently cruel."

"You deserved better. So why pay any respects, ever?"

She was surprised by the vehemence in

his tone. "It was my duty, Mr. Jefferson."

"Yeah, of course it was. Duty is everything over here." He glanced ahead.

She stiffened, dismayed. Something was wrong, she sensed it. "Surely you believe in duty?"

"I don't know, Duchess. Where I come from, a man needs pride, courage and ambition, not duty, in order to survive."

She felt as if she'd been slapped. She turned away, shaken.

"So we really don't have anything in common, now do we?" he asked softly.

She blinked back the sudden moisture in her eyes. Something *was* wrong — she was not imagining it. "Shall we gallop?" she somehow said, managing a bright, false smile.

"Can you control that mare? She looks hot-blooded," he said.

"Yes, I can control her," she said tersely, not looking at him. Without waiting for a reply, she urged the mare into a canter. She heard him following and sensed him just behind her, and the humiliation hit her, mingled with sorrow.

She was a fool. She had only imagined the attraction between them.

Then she saw the low stone wall ahead. "You can avoid the jump by veering right,

Mr. Jefferson," she called.

The wide, three-foot stone wall loomed. Julia didn't look back at him as she collected her mount for the jump. She was aware that he abruptly halted his gelding, but she continued to approach the wall and then soared easily over it. On the other side, she pulled up her horse, and for the first time in her life, she wasn't exhilarated. She was too distraught.

She gave her mare a quick pat on the neck as she turned back to face the way she had come. Jefferson remained on the other side of the wall, and she gestured to his right.

But he ignored her. And as he cantered toward the wall she stiffened, surprised — he intended to take the jump! She saw instantly that he knew nothing about taking a fence. His mount was out of the bridle, making a good jump difficult, at best. As if he sensed the problem, he urged the gelding to a faster speed — which could be a disaster in the making.

"Put him together!" Julia called. "Pick him up!"

It was too late. Horse and rider soared — badly — the gelding lurching awkwardly without the proper impulsion and then clipping the stone with his hind legs. Jefferson was already off balance, and she saw him lose a stirrup. As the gelding came down, he almost fell off, but he seized the gelding's mane and managed to right himself in the saddle.

As he dropped to a trot and then a walk, Julia bit her lip, relieved he'd made it to safety. Then she tried to feign indifference to the worst display of horsemanship she had ever seen. She kept her face expressionless as he paused before her, red faced. "Are you all right?"

"How do you do that?" he exclaimed.

"Oh, dear." She gave up and smiled. "You have never jumped a fence, have you?"

"We try to avoid jumping dead wood," he said, still red. "Our horses need to turn on a dime, stop on 'Whoa,' and push a cow up a fence."

She found herself genuinely interested, some of her dismay vanishing. "There is a technique," she said, then asked again, "Are you all right?"

"Other than humiliated?" He gave her a look and dismounted, then knelt to check his horse's back legs.

Julia slipped off her mare, kneeling beside him. "He's not even nicked — he'll be fine." She straightened.

He stood, too. "Thank God for that. I wouldn't want to hurt one of your horses."

And that was when she realized how close they were standing to one another. Instantly she went still, her heart slamming. Mere inches separated them, and it was hard to think about anything other than the man she was alone in the countryside with.

As if he felt it, too, he stared, and his gaze grew dark.

She knew she had to say something to break the moment, but she couldn't look away from his amber eyes, which were smoldering like coals now.

"You're full of surprises, Duchess," he said roughly.

She meant to speak. She truly did. But no words came out as she stared into his beautiful eyes — as he stared back at her.

"Hell," he muttered.

And then he leaned over her. She was stunned — but her blood roared. His hands settled on her shoulders — and she loved the feeling of his touch. "Julia," he said thickly.

She inhaled. "Tyne."

"I'm leaving soon," he whispered, pulling her closer.

She was in his arms, her thighs pressed against his legs, her bosom crushed by his chest. She looked at his mouth, desperately wanting him to kiss her.

His eyes blazed, and he pulled her impossibly close, wrapping his huge arms around her, as his mouth covered hers.

Julia cried out, stunned by the feeling of his lips claiming hers, and he deepened the kiss. Their mouths fused. His tongue went deep. And she felt every inch of his hard, aroused body. She clasped his shoulders, about to kiss him back. But he tore his mouth from hers and stepped away, breathing hard.

"I guess that was goodbye," he said.

Alexandra had just finished giving her sisters a tour of the house. And for that hour, as her troubles almost vanished, receding to the corners of her mind, it was so wonderful to be with them both. She knew she would be despondent when they left to return to Edgemont Way.

They were coming downstairs when Guillermo appeared at the bottom of the staircase. "Miss Bolton, you have another caller."

She was so surprised that she stumbled, instantly wondering if Ariella and Elysse had returned. But she did not think so — it was quite a trip from their homes to Clarewood, and she had just seen them. "Who is it?" And then, as she finished speaking, she suddenly knew, and not because she recognized the card on the silver tray Guillermo was holding.

She trembled, certain it was Owen. Guillermo confirmed her suspicions, saying, "Lord St. James has called, and he is in the Gold Room."

On the lower landing, she paused, her hand on the banister. "Please tell Cook that we may be four for lunch," she said carefully.

He nodded and hurried off. Alexandra crossed the hall, her sisters behind her. No one said a word.

He was standing beside a sofa, not far from the open doors, a tall, elegant figure. He turned.

Alexandra faltered. Nine years had passed. Once Owen had been a beautiful young man. He was thirty now, and he was even more handsome and more dashing — time had weathered him perfectly. She was trembling, but her heart warmed. She began to smile.

He wasn't smiling as he stared, taking her in from head to toe. "Alexandra," he finally said. "My God, it is so good to see you."

She started forward — so did he. They met halfway, instantly clasping hands. His were so familiar — large, warm, strong. And now she saw the dark light in his eyes. "It is so good to see you, too, Owen," she whispered. And she meant it.

"You haven't changed," he said roughly, his gaze slowly traveling across her features, "yet somehow you are more beautiful than ever."

She smiled again. "I am no raving beauty, and we both know it — and I am an old maid now, as well."

He smiled for the first time, and her heart leaped a little. His old smiles had been dazzling, and this was a poor shadow, but he had just lost his wife. "If you are an old maid, then I am an old man," he said. "And you are so beautiful — and it has been so long — that my heart is pounding madly."

She realized her heart had picked up a swifter beat, as well. She also realized that they still held hands. She gently dislodged hers and said, "I am so sorry about Lady St. James."

His smile vanished as his gaze met hers. "Thank you. She was a kind, gracious woman, and it happened so quickly that it took me a long time to recover from the shock."

She touched his elbow. "Will you sit? And will you join my sisters and me for lunch?" She turned. Olivia and Corey remained on the threshold behind her, uncertain. But they both smiled immediately at Owen.

He smiled back at them. "I should love to stay for lunch. Hello, Miss Olivia, hello, Miss Corey." He turned back to Alexandra. "I can't get over your sisters. When I last saw them, they were small girls. They are both so lovely — you have raised them well." But his eyes changed as he spoke, becoming searching as he glanced at her costly raspberry silk dress — and the bracelet she wore.

She flushed. She was dressed like nobility — and her sisters were in their ancient, well-mended and very tired gowns. "I did my best."

He said, "I take it the duke is out?"

"He is in Manchester today," she said, uneasy now.

He studied her. "We have a great deal to catch up on."

"Yes, we do." She smiled firmly. "Why don't we have lunch, as it is already half past one, and afterward we can stroll in the gardens and reminisce?"

"I would like that . . . very much."

They had finished dining, ending a superb luncheon of roasted guinea hens with lemon tarts and a fine sauterne. Owen had just pulled back her chair, and Alexandra smiled at him. Being with him again was as natural as being with her sisters. It was as if days had passed, not years. The initial awkwardness was gone. They were best friends — and they would always be best friends, she thought.

But more than that remained. Of course it did — there was the past.

They had talked about the parties and picnics and croquet games they had shared, and moments in Elizabeth's kitchen, waiting for her sugar cookies to finish baking. They had recalled too many small moments to count — moments Alexandra had forgotten until then. There was the time Corey had vanished during an afternoon of fishing and everyone had thought she'd fallen into the lake, only to find her asleep in the backseat of the carriage, buried beneath the blankets. There was the Christmas when Edgemont had just returned from Paris with thoughtful French gifts for everyone, and the time Owen had sprained his ankle so badly that Elizabeth had insisted he stay and recuperate with them. He had stayed in their guest bedroom, and Alexandra had been the one to entertain him with games of checkers, baccarat and cards. She had read to him, too, only to find out before long that his ankle had been fine, and he had feigned the injury so he could stay. She'd thrown his pillow at his head. He'd caught it and thrown it back at her, and they'd screeched with laughter, ruined all the pillows on the bed and wound up sharing a kiss. Elizabeth had walked in, frowning — but clearly she hadn't really minded. There had been so many good times. . . .

He had his hand on the back of her chair. Alexandra was very aware of him now. He remained as attractive as ever. She hadn't stopped caring, in spite of the passage of so much time, in spite of his marriage to another woman. But when he touched her hand, it was familiar, not stunning. It was comforting, not arousing. And throughout the luncheon, Stephen was there in her mind.

She almost felt guilty for being with Owen now.

"I suppose we should start home," Olivia said, rather despondently.

"I don't want to go home," Corey said flat out.

Alexandra shared a look with Owen, and when he smiled at her, she smiled back. She knew he was thinking what she was. "Why don't you stay the night? Obviously we have many guest rooms, and it has been so long — we have our own catching up to do."

Corey screeched in glee. "I would love to stay!"

Olivia looked from her to Owen and back again, then said, "Who will take care of Father?"

Alexandra sobered instantly, but Owen touched her elbow. "He can get on for a night or two without you, I have no doubt."

She looked gratefully at him. He was right. "We pamper him."

"Of course you do," he said, staring intently. And he slowly smiled. "You promised me a walk in the gardens."

She grinned. "I haven't forgotten." As they left the dining room, she gave instructions to the staff to get two guest rooms ready. Her sisters were shown upstairs, and she finally found herself alone with Owen. Suddenly nervous, she laid her hand on the smooth wood rail of the banister. Maybe reminiscing while alone was not the best idea.

He said, "I am glad your sisters are staying the night. Clearly you have missed one another."

She met his gaze and knew there was no avoiding a full confession now. "I miss them greatly. I miss Edgemont Way. . . . I even miss my father."

"Even?" He took her by the shoulders, so

503

they faced one another. "What is going on, Alexandra? We have never had secrets, and I must be blunt. Edgemont Way has fallen into such disrepair. What happened?"

She trembled, aware that he was edging carefully into the topic of her residency at Clarewood. "Father drinks obsessively — and gambles compulsively."

His eyes widened. "I heard something like that, but I had assumed it was vicious, untrue gossip. I am so sorry."

She inhaled for courage. "I have done the best that I could. It hasn't been easy. I sew for a living now."

He was shocked. "Are you serious?"

"Yes. I sew for those ladies who were once my mother's friends. Now they look down their noses at me, very openly, and gossip about me behind my back." She stopped, wishing she hadn't gone off in that tangent.

He flushed.

She looked at the ground, then up into his blue eyes. "We have no secrets, but you would never ask me directly, would you? Why I am living here?"

He was terse. "It seems quite obvious, but I am hoping that my suspicions are wrong."

She felt tears rise and touched his arm. "Owen, there was a suitor, after all these years, an older, kindly squire. But I simply could not bring myself to marry him. After what you and I shared, the fact that I felt nothing for him was glaring. And his suit brought back so many memories of our love."

He stared, and it was a long moment before he spoke, his mouth downturned. "You must feel something for Clarewood. I know you too well. You would never accept such an . . . arrangement, unless you were in love."

She trembled. "He began pursuing me the moment we first met. I resisted, of course I did. But he refused to take no for an answer." She hesitated. "Father found out and he — he has disowned me."

"I cannot believe your father!" he exclaimed, coloring rapidly now. "As for Clarewood . . . What kind of man stalks and seduces a good gentlewoman?"

"Don't! Owen — I do love Stephen, and he has been good to me."

"Really?" His tawny brows slashed upward. "He is wealthy, Alexandra, so do not be fooled. For him, that bracelet is worth a penny. It means nothing, because he is so rich."

She recoiled. "Please don't attack him."

"Why not? Unless he marries you — which he must do — he is the scum of this earth, and I don't care what his title is."

She'd forgotten how noble and honorable Owen was. She caressed his jaw. Instantly he pressed her hand more firmly there. Their gazes locked, and he said, "You do not deserve this life. You deserve more."

"We do not get to choose our fate."

"So you will accept this as yours?"

She did not know what to say. Owen would be furious when he learned of the child. "I am so glad," she finally said, slowly, "that we are still friends. I am sorry, though, that you have returned to town under such tragic circumstances." She caressed his cheek and then dropped her hand. Too much remained between them, she thought.

Owen said thickly, "I will always be there for you."

She brushed at a tear. "I know." And that was when she became aware of a new tension in the room, apart from the tension arcing between them. She glanced at the door.

"I see we have a guest," Stephen said, his tone mocking. He strode forward. "Do make the introductions, Alexandra."

CHAPTER SEVENTEEN

Alexandra felt her cheeks heat. She felt terribly guilty, though she had done nothing wrong. She was only entertaining an old, dear friend. And then she knew her own thoughts rang false. Owen was more than that — and she was guilty of having a deep affection for another man. Her gaze locked with Stephen's.

His expression had become impossible to read. His cool regard moved to Owen, who stood stiffly at attention. "I am Stephen Mowbray, the Duke of Clarewood. Welcome to my home."

Owen didn't smile, so to cover the awkwardness she said quickly, "Your Grace, this is Lord St. James, an old family friend."

Stephen didn't look at her now. His mouth curved, rather unpleasantly, as he said, "How wonderful for you. St. James? Are you any relation to the viscount Reginald St. James?" His tone was dangerously soft.

"He is my uncle," Owen said tersely. "How good it is to meet you, Your Grace." He still didn't smile, and his eyes were dark and angry. Clearly he did not mean a word he had said. But he kept his tone neutral and polite.

This was impossible, Alexandra thought, alarmed. "Owen was just leaving," she said quickly.

Stephen turned his searing blue gaze upon her.

She flushed. She had called Owen by his given name — in front of Stephen. She said thickly, "I have known Owen since I was a girl of fifteen."

Stephen stared, his odd smile fixed in place now.

Owen said, almost belligerently, "We were about to become engaged. My offer was accepted, but then the baroness died. Alexandra decided she must take care of her sisters and father, instead of starting a marriage with me. I was crushed," he stated flatly.

Stephen's tight expression never changed. "She has told me all about it, St. James."

Alexandra trembled, sick with dismay. She'd said almost nothing about it. "Lord St. James has just come to town. He is staying with Lord Bludgeon in Greenwich. I am delighted he has called. I invited him to stay for lunch, which he did." She realized she was speaking in a breathless rush. "And my sisters are here. They dined with us. It was delicious, was it not?" She smiled falsely at Owen now.

He stared closely at her, and she knew his unspoken thought: Why are you afraid of your lover?

She rushed on. "We had guinea hens stuffed with apricots. And I invited my sisters to stay the night — they are in their rooms, settling in. I did not think you would mind," she said. "We must plan a special supper tonight."

Owen continued to stare, and now Stephen was staring at her, too. He said softly, "You are so nervous, Alexandra."

She tensed, her alarm becoming panic. He had become an indolent but dangerous lion, and she was in his den.

Owen's already dark expression became darker. He said coldly, "Alexandra wished to make me and her sisters comfortable, Your Grace. She succeeded — she is an exceptional hostess, but then, she always was. However —" he smiled mirthlessly "— she promised me a stroll in your gardens."

Her alarm intensified as Stephen's fixed smile hardened. She instantly said, "It is far too chilly to walk outside now, and besides, you mentioned that you have a late tea in town. Don't you?" she lied, and heard the plea in her tone. He had to leave. Stephen seemed angry. She knew he couldn't be jealous, but she also recalled the terms of their arrangement — he expected her to be faithful to him. Once Owen left, she could explain, and then everything would be back to normal again.

Wouldn't it?

Owen looked ready to openly refuse. But with obvious reluctance he said, "I never meant to stay too long, and you are right, I have other obligations." Suddenly he took her hand and clasped it. "I am so glad we have had this chance to see one another again, after so much time. Thank you for the splendid lunch and the even more splendid company."

She tugged her hand free. "I am so glad, too." She glanced uneasily at Stephen. That odd smile remained, but his eyes were black thunderclouds. "I will walk you out."

Stephen folded his arms. "Bon voyage, St. James. Call anytime."

"Thank you for lunch, Your Grace," Owen returned as caustically. "And I may do just that."

They hated each other. Alexandra knew her

cheeks were crimson now, as she crossed the hall with Owen, acutely aware of him beside her, and just as acutely aware of Stephen standing on the far side of the room, staring at them. Owen lowered his voice at the front door and said, "Will you be all right?"

"I will be fine," she said breathlessly. "Really." Her smile felt horrifically fragile.

Owen glanced across the hall at Stephen. "He seems a heartless bastard. Send word if you need me." He bowed and strode out the open front doors, which the doorman closed after him.

She was trembling wildly now, her knees buckled, and she hugged herself. She felt sick, but not because of the child. *They hated one another!* she thought again, and briefly closed her eyes. What was she going to do — about everything? Only two things were clear: she must explain her relationship with Owen to Stephen, and now was not the time to mention her condition. Then she slowly — reluctantly — looked up.

Stephen's regard was scathing. Then he whirled and strode down the hall, vanishing from her sight.

She wet her lips nervously and realized she was afraid of him now. She'd seen his temper once and had hoped never to see it again. But there was no avoiding a confrontation now. She hurried after him.

As she entered the library behind him, he flung his coat onto the sofa. "So how is your long-lost love, Alexandra?"

She faltered. "Owen is my friend, Stephen. I am with you now."

He whirled to face her. "You loved him with all of your heart. You told me so. You planned to marry him. But instead, you sacrificed yourself for your sisters and father. Do correct me if I am wrong." He was dripping sarcasm.

"No," she whispered. "You are right. But that was long ago."

He made a harsh sound — like a mirthless laugh. "What does he want?" he demanded.

She shivered, unable to tell him what Owen had said.

"What does he want?" he repeated, his tone louder now, his eyes ablaze.

"I don't know," she said, trembling. "His wife died six months ago, and he decided to call on me so that we might reminisce."

His eyes widened. He was incredulous.

She turned away, her temples throbbing. Everything was so clear now. Owen still loved her — she knew that now. And she knew why he had come to town — and it wasn't to reminisce.

Olivia was right. Owen would be her knight in shining armor, if she needed one.

And she still cared so much for him.

From behind, Stephen seized her shoulders roughly, whirling her to face him. "I see," he said bitterly.

"No." She shook her head, frantic. "No, you do not see anything! I would never violate the terms of our agreement."

"And what terms are those?" he demanded, his gaze searing. "Do you love him, Alexandra? Or need I even bother to ask?"

"I would never be unfaithful to you!" she cried desperately.

"Really?" His grasp tightened. A terrible pause ensued. She could not look away — and now she could hardly breathe. "You didn't answer me. *Do you still love him, Alexandra?*"

She gasped. She meant to answer, she did. But no words formed. Instead her heart thundered, in fear, with panic.

"There are many ways a woman can betray a man," he said harshly. He flung her off, and she stumbled. "And you do not have to bother to answer me," he spat, stalking to the fire, "because I know the answer!"

She started to cry. "No, you do not know the answer."

He whirled. "You love him! You loved him nine years ago, and you still do! I am not blind. It is beyond obvious!" he was shouting. "Any fool can see that the two of you are in love!"

The tears flowed. "I love *you*," she whispered.

"You would lie to me now? Deny that you love St. James?"

She began shaking her head. "Of course I love him, but —"

He started toward her, livid. Alexandra tensed and flinched, thinking he meant to strike her. But he didn't raise his hand. "And would you have told me about this visit if I hadn't walked in on the two of you so tenderly in one another's arms?" He was shaking. "I saw the way you were touching him, Alexandra, so don't tell me that you haven't betrayed me."

She tried to tell him that she would have told him, but all she could do was whisper, "Yes," as the tears crept down her cheeks.

"How many times will you betray me?" he demanded. "How many times?"

She didn't know what he was talking about. "I haven't betrayed you!"

"Really?" He was breathing hard, as if he'd been in a footrace. "And what about the child? My child? For how long did you think to deceive me? Lie to me? Did you intend to leave me before the child showed — and pass it off one day as someone else's?"

She cringed, horrified. He knew. *Stephen knew about the child.* "How long have you known?" she managed.

"I have known since I picked you up out of the London gutter," he said vehemently.

She recoiled, and not just from the language he'd chosen — but from the hateful look in his eyes. "Please don't, Stephen. . . . I hated the deception!"

"Then why?" he shouted at her.

She shook her head helplessly. How could she tell him that his anger terrified her — that *he* now terrified her?

"I had every right to know that you are carrying my child — *my* child!" His arm swept out — a lamp went crashing to the floor, shattering. Alexandra leaped away, but he seized her arm and yanked her back, this time up against his hard, trembling body. "You have lied to me from the start. I am usually a good judge of character. But the lies will never stop, will they?"

"No!" She wept. "Stephen, I was going to tell you about the child!"

He released her, shaking his head, backing away. "Get out," he said.

And when she did not move, he roared, "Get out of here!"

Alexandra ran.

It was too late now. He stared out his carriage window, filled with what felt like hatred for a man he did not know, when he had never felt such vicious fury before. He had developed a deep affection for Alexandra. He knew that now — but it was too late, because he had lost her.

I loved him with all of my heart . . . my mother died, there was no choice. . . .

Of course I love him.

He cursed.

He had lost a woman he cared deeply for to another man.

And it bloody well hurt.

He began to laugh, without mirth, and he drank from his glass of scotch. He was the most eligible bachelor in the realm, the wealthiest, most powerful peer, and he had lost his mistress to another man. One day, he would think the terrible irony funny.

But he had never cared about a woman before. He had never spent hours talking to another woman, even while in bed, and he had never smiled as much as he had recently. Alexandra had brought so much light into his life, and he hadn't even realized how dark and dreary it had been before she had come into it.

He had been content, but not happy. Alexandra had shown him the difference.

Was he in love?

Did it matter?

She loved someone else. It had been so damned clear. And even though she'd never been with St. James, they looked at one another, silently exchanging their thoughts, as if they'd been lovers for years.

He wasn't just a suitor, he was my best friend.

He had never become her best friend. The thought hadn't occurred to him. He'd wanted to protect her, defend her, take care of her and make love to her. He'd always considered Alexi his best friend and now, damn it all, he wanted to know why he wasn't *her* best friend!

The jealousy seethed, as hot and angry as the anger. *St. James was her best friend.* He tossed the glass aside and drank directly from the bottle now.

He was jealous — another first. As for the pain in his chest, did that mean he had a broken heart? But that was impossible, wasn't it? He was cold and heartless, everyone said so. He was just like old Tom.

He closed his eyes in anguish, certain that

517

his father was somewhere close by, laughing at him now. *Dukes do not endure broken hearts. Get on with it.* He could hear him as clear as day.

Except that while Tom had done his best to form him in his mold, to make him into a cold, rational, decisive man bent only on duty, he wasn't Tom's natural son; he was a de Warenne.

A de Warenne loves once and forever.

He cursed when he wanted to weep. He had lost a woman he cared for, and if he dared to be honest, he loved Alexandra Bolton. There was no other explanation for his feelings now or for the light she'd brought into his life. He'd never met anyone like her. He'd known that immediately. She was so fiercely courageous, so determinedly strong, so adept and independent. And she was passionate. Amazingly, she had taught *him* passion. He'd never wanted to be with any other woman the way he wanted to be with her. He hadn't even realized he was a passionate man until he'd made love to her.

How many times had he looked at her while making love to her, wanting to tell her how he felt? And each and every time, old Tom had sat by his side, mocking him for such weakness.

He'd never told her that he cared. But that

was for the best, wasn't it?

He tensed, his gut contracting so tightly it hurt. No man in his right mind would declare love to a woman who did not return his feelings.

He couldn't help remembering himself as a young boy, wishing so terribly to hear those few words from the man claiming to be his father.

But he hadn't confessed anything to her. Still, he had thought she cared in return. She had touched him as if she loved him. Her eyes had shone as if she loved him. But she didn't love him — it had been a pretense, a game.

She loved St. James.

He flung the bottle at the other seat, hard, and it shattered. Then he covered his face with his hands. He was filled with anguish, and it felt unbearable! He'd never felt this way before. He had never been denied anything he dearly wanted!

And what about their child? Would she ever have told him about their child?

He wasn't sure, and he was so angry that he had no intention of giving her the benefit of the doubt. There had been so many moments when she could have told him — he'd intentionally given her openings. But she never had. Alexandra was so adept at lying to him. She had lied about her innocence, and she had lied about her pregnancy. His heart cracked widely apart now. He felt certain she'd intended to deceive him for as long as possible.

But what if she had been telling the truth when she said that she had intended to tell him about their child? His heart screamed at him.

His heart was not to be trusted, obviously. He was a rational man! And what she'd intended did not matter — because of St. James.

He would never let another man raise his child.

His heart lurched as he thought about that. He realized that the carriage had stopped. He turned to look grimly outside and saw Alexi's grand Oxford home, brilliantly lit up in the middle of a cloudy night. He'd bought it back when he and Elysse were estranged, and the magnificent country manor was set on ten acres, surrounded by gardens and a game park. Stephen got out, the footman carefully pretending he didn't know that the duke was drunk, and had smashed a bottle of old and costly scotch whiskey in the back of his once-clean coach.

Alexi did not keep doormen, and Stephen rang the bell and used the door knocker, rudely and loudly, simultaneously. Alexi greeted him a moment later barefoot, shirtless, clad only in a pair of trousers — and holding a pistol in his hand. His eyes widened. "Come in," he quickly said. "Has someone died?"

Stephen strode past him. "I could use a drink." He walked down the hall and into the library where he'd spent so much time with Alexi and his other cousins.

After closing the front door, Alexi followed him inside. Stephen was staring at the small fire burning in the hearth, wishing the pain in his chest would go away.

Alexi turned on several lights and said, "You have come a long way for a drink. But you certainly look as if you could use one — though you stink of liquor already. And you do not have a coat, though it is freezing out."

"I smashed a bottle of whiskey inside my coach." He turned to look at his friend.

Alexi's eyes widened again. "You never smash things — unless it is my nose." He walked over to the sideboard and began pouring drinks. "It is one in the morning, by the way."

Stephen looked at him. "I have something to tell you."

"I suspected as much." Alexi handed him a glass.

Stephen did not drink. "Alexandra is carrying my child."

Alexi's eyes widened, and he began to smile. Then he sobered. "Stephen, if you do not think this is good news, I will pummel some sense into you. She is a fine woman, and you do not have any children — and you certainly need sons."

Stephen made a dismissive sound. "I'm a bastard, and I swore I'd never inflict that stigma on a child."

Alexi smiled. "Then marry her, you dammed fool."

Stephen's grasp on the glass tightened. His jaw was so rigid, he wondered if he might crack his teeth. Of course he should marry her. She was carrying his child. And suddenly he could see a future with her as his wife — and it was a bright, cheerful future, filled with joy and light. Except he did not think she would choose him over her true love. He was certain she would turn him down.

"She loves someone else."

Alexi choked.

"Can you believe it?"

Alexi put his own drink down, in order to clasp Stephen's shoulder. "Are you sure?"

"Yes, I am sure — and not because I caught them together. She told me all about the one and only true love of her life — whom she meant to marry nine years ago." He stared at Alexi, wishing St. James were present, so he could throttle him and get him out of their lives. "He was courting her. She turned him away when her mother died, so she could sacrifice herself and her happiness for her family. But that," he inhaled, "is Alexandra."

"What do you mean, you caught them together?" Alexi asked carefully.

"I did not catch them in bed, if that is what you're thinking. I caught them with their heads together, in an affectionate embrace."

"And because of that, you think she still loves her old flame?"

Stephen nodded.

Alexi shrugged. "As I said, she is a fine woman. And you always get what you want, so if you want her, go get her. You are at your best when you have a rival. And by the way, we all approve — very much."

Stephen was disbelieving. "Didn't you hear what I said? She's in love with St. James!" And old Tom leered at him again. He would never beg for her love. No one should beg for love. It was either freely given

523

or it was worthless. "Oh, I forgot to tell you the rest of it — he's a widower now, so they can ride off together into the sunset, their wedding rings glinting." He choked on the last words.

How could losing her hurt so terribly?

Suddenly Elysse appeared in a nightgown and wrapper. "Stephen? Is everything all right?"

He felt like a child again, one living in the lonely splendor of Clarewood, doing his best to please the duke and always failing. He saw old Tom in a corner of the room, laughing cruelly at him. That old man had never once said he'd cared, was proud, or that he loved the boy he'd made into his son.

He turned his back on Elysse, trying to find composure. Alexi said, "We are fine, sweetheart. Go back to bed. I won't be up for a while — if at all."

Stephen heard her leave. He inhaled and said harshly, "I am sorry. I did not mean to be rude to Elysse."

"You have finally found love. Therefore you are forgiven."

Stephen faced Alexi. "You may be right, but do not start in on me with all that de Warenne myth and tradition. I am not a de Warenne, I am Clarewood — I am more old

Tom's son than I am Sir Rex's. And Alexandra is making plans to marry her beloved Owen even as we speak."

"Are you certain?" Alexi asked.

Stephen spoke with care, considering his own words. "Of course I am certain. I know Alexandra. She is the kind of woman to give her heart once in a lifetime." But oddly, just then, as his heart screamed at him, he felt some doubt. Still, he had seen them together. They had looked as intimate as lovers. He *hated* St. James!

Alexi began shaking his head.

"What does that mean?" Stephen demanded.

"It means a man blinded by love is exactly that — blind. You can't possibly see clearly — or think clearly — now. And Elysse happens to think Alexandra is perfect for you. She also thinks that Alexandra loves you. In fact, she told me that Alexandra is not the kind of woman to have an affair, not unless it is about love."

Stephen stared, breathing hard. He wanted to believe it, and for one moment, recalling the way she had caressed his cheek and looked at him with soft, shining eyes, he almost did. Hadn't he been her first? Hadn't she tried to refuse him on moral grounds? But then he recalled how he had found her and St. James in the front hall, and Alexandra had been caressing the other man's cheek just the way she'd caressed his. He could barely breathe. "You haven't seen them together."

"No, I haven't, but as I said, right now you are blind. Have you spoken to her? Really spoken to her?"

Stephen tensed and began to pace.

"I thought so. You had a terrific row and then you left. Why don't you go home and go to sleep, and when you wake up — and recover from tonight's overconsumption of whiskey — you can have a calm, rational discussion with her."

Stephen turned. "I do not think I will ever be rational again."

Alexi smiled.

"It is hardly amusing."

"Actually, Stephen, seeing you broken-hearted and taken down a peg or two by a good woman is very amusing — and well overdue."

A part of him did want to go home, awaken Alexandra and demand to know if she cared about him — if she loved him, even a little. And if he made love to her first, he could probably entice her into just such a declaration.

Do you love St. James?

I love you.
Do you love St. James?
Of course I love him. . . .

"Thank you for being so understanding," he muttered. But what if she did love him a little? After all, she was carrying *his* child, not Owen's.

Alexi came over and clapped him on the shoulder. "If you tell her how you feel, or even if you don't, and you simply offer marriage, I feel certain she will accept."

Stephen wasn't certain, not at all. And then he realized that didn't matter, either. What mattered was their child. They should marry for the sake of the child.

He stared, his heart hammering. "I am not going to tell her that I love her, given the probability that she does not love me back."

"Why not? What do you have to lose?"

"I have some pride left," he said brusquely. He somehow knew he could not withstand making that kind of confession, not if she did not say the words to him in return.

"And that might be all you have left, if you don't tell her how you feel," Alexi said. "So what will you do? Allow her to run off with St. James?" His stare was piercing.

Stephen felt his anger surge. "You bloody well know I would never let my child be

527

raised by someone else!"

"But you've told me a hundred times that you will be a terrible father — just like old Tom." Alexi's eyes were wide and innocent.

Stephen told himself that he was not going home to tell Alexandra that he had fallen in love with her, nor would he beg her to choose him over St. James. Dukes did not beg.

Dukes issued orders — and ultimatums.

Tom mocked him openly now.

"I never said Tom Mowbray was a terrible father. He was a harsh disciplinarian — but he has made me the man that I am."

"No, you are who you are because you are a de Warenne, Stephen, and you had Julia to offset Tom's cruelty."

"I have to go," Stephen said abruptly, turning.

Alexi followed him through the door. "What will you do?"

Stephen paused in the front hall. "We will marry for the sake of the child," he said.

Alexi's eyes widened. "I suggest you ask her *pleasantly.*"

Stephen smiled coldly. "I am not feeling very pleasant, Alexi."

Alexi groaned.

Alexandra sat in the window seat of her

bedroom at dawn, Olivia beside her, Corey curled up asleep in a nearby chair. A tray of refreshments sat on the small breakfast table to their left. Her sisters had apparently overheard them shouting at one another, and had come to Alexandra's room immediately. They hadn't left her even once during the course of the entire, endless night.

And endless it had been. Her eyes were red and swollen from crying. Her heart ached so much. She hadn't slept at all last night, and how could she? She had been shocked and hurt by Stephen's anger and accusations. It was a nightmare come true. To make matters even worse, he'd left Clarewood at midnight, returning three hours later. She didn't want to imagine where he'd gone, but there seemed to be only one possible explanation for a man leaving his home in the middle of the night like that. He'd sought comfort from another woman, she was sure.

Alexandra sat with her cheek on her raised knee. She was brokenhearted.

Olivia caressed her stiff shoulder. "What will you do?"

She lifted her head. "I will have to make myself presentable, go downstairs and continue the discussion."

Olivia's stare became searching. "That was not a discussion."

"No, it was not." Alexandra hugged both knees to her chest.

"How could he become so hateful to you when he was so kind and generous before?"

"I was afraid of this. I have never known anyone with such a temper. It is rare. But he apparently cannot withstand what he thinks is dishonesty." She felt like crying all over again. "I was going to tell him about the child last night. Can you believe it? And I would have told him Owen was in town, too!"

Olivia took her hand. "You were right and I was wrong — at least about Clarewood."

Corey surprised them when she said, "I think he loves Alexandra."

Alexandra jumped, surprised to realize her sister had awoken. "I wish you were right, but I am afraid you are wrong."

"No, I am right — two men love you, and he is angry because of Owen."

Alexandra did not think so. He was furious over the child, just as she had expected in her heart of hearts. She slid her feet to the wood floor, which was icy cold. "I should get up. He is an early riser." She trembled, already ill with fear.

But as she stood, a knock sounded on her

door, startling her. "Come in."

The door opened and Stephen stood there, so ravaged in appearance, his eyes so dark and determined, that she gasped in shock. Instantly she knew he'd not yet been to bed. She wondered if he'd been drinking, but it was impossible to tell. "I wish a word with you now," he said.

She was alarmed and looked at her sisters, but they were already standing, their expressions indicating the same worry and surprise that she felt. Olivia caught her eye, and Alexandra said, "I'll be fine," though she knew the words were a lie.

They hurried across the room and scooted past Stephen, who did not even look at them, much less greet them. When they were gone, his hands went to his hips, his posture aggressive.

Alexandra hugged herself. "I despise arguing with you."

"Then don't lie."

She debated defending herself yet again but was sure he wouldn't believe her. "I don't want to fight with you."

"Good. I have no intention of fighting with you, either — not now. Not when you are carrying my child." He paused, looking at her meaningfully.

She tensed. "Yes, I am," she said, unsure

as to his intent.

"We will marry, Alexandra, for the sake of the child."

She was shocked.

"You will not bear my bastard," he added. Then, "And if this was your plan, it has succeeded."

She began to shake. This had not been her plan, and while she loved Stephen, and marrying him was beyond her wildest dreams, he was angry with her, cold and distant, and he was suggesting marriage not because of any feelings for her or desire for a future with her, but for their child. How could she accept?

How could she refuse?

Instantly, she thought of Owen, who would offer for her because of the love in his heart.

"You are strangely silent," he said coolly.

She inhaled. "I am shocked."

"Really?" His tone was mocking. "I am the greatest catch in the realm, yet I haven't heard you accept my proposal."

What should she say? That she loved him too much to marry him this way? Or should she marry him anyway, *because* she loved him? "I am going to have to think about it."

His eyes widened briefly, and then he smiled dangerously. "I must admit, I did not expect that answer." His stare hardened and smile vanished. "I expected you to turn me down."

He was no longer furious, she thought, sickened with dismay, he was simply hateful. "I need to think about it, Stephen," she repeated.

"Really?" He laughed coldly at her. "Let me make myself clear, Alexandra. I have dreaded marriage for as long as I can recall — I have been searching for a suitable bride for a decade, at least. This will be another arrangement for us — for the sake of the child. I will not bring a bastard into the world."

She trembled. "Do you hate me?"

He started. Then, "No."

They had that, at least. She closed her eyes briefly. "I still have to think about it."

"Why? Because you want to wait and see if St. James will step up?"

Before she could deny that, he said, "Let me rephrase. This was not a proposal, it was a choice. You may choose to marry me, or you may run off with your beloved St. James." She cried out, but he barreled on. "However, if you decide to run off with your lover, the child stays here, with me, and we will be married first."

She gasped in disbelief.

His smile was cold. "The child is mine. You have a choice to make." He turned and started from the room.

She ran after him. "I cannot agree to either choice!"

He whirled, and they collided. He caught her savagely and said, "Oh, no, you will make a choice — it's me or St. James, and the child stays here."

Alexandra was too stunned to say a word.

He flung her off and strode out.

CHAPTER EIGHTEEN

As Julia entered the St. Lucien Hotel, heads turned. She hurried across the spacious lobby, ignoring the stares. Even those who did not recognize her could surmise that she was a lady of wealth and rank — her stature was obvious from her clothing, her jewelry and her comportment. But some clearly knew who she was, for murmurs of "Good morning, Your Grace," drifted in her wake. She did not look at anyone, nor did she respond. She simply couldn't think about anything or anyone other than Tyne.

He had kissed her briefly, but with so much passion — and she had kissed him back. Then he had told her he was leaving and pulled away. They had remounted, Julia in a daze, partly from desire and partly from shock. And when she had tried to make conversation as they'd returned to the house, he'd been quiet and withdrawn. He'd left before she could ask him if he wished to return and ride again.

He was returning to America tomorrow. She'd made inquiries.

She was ill with dismay and sick with dread. She hadn't slept in days, not since their outing — not since his kiss. She was smitten with an American stranger, and she was never going to see him again — unless she did something about it.

Julia had lived most of her life in isolation. While Tom was alive, she'd formed and maintained the appropriate relationships and acquaintances, but never any close friendships. To anyone who chose to consider the question, her life had been centered on her duties as a mother and a duchess. Secretly, her life had revolved around protecting Stephen from his father's criticisms, cruelty and rages.

After Tom had died, she'd maintained a portion of those relationships, while allowing others to wither and fade. She'd remained close to Stephen, as he was only sixteen, to help him with his new responsibilities. It had quickly become clear that he would manage Clarewood far more astutely and efficiently — and economically — than Tom had ever done. He hadn't needed her help, only her support.

Exulting in her freedom, she'd begun

building a new life for herself, one founded on her love for horses and dogs. New friendships were formed with other horsemen and women. But she was reserved by nature — and none of those relationships had become close.

Consequently, she had no one to confide in.

After Tyne had left, she had sat down by herself, with her Danes, to analyze her situation. She had realized her choices were few. She could do nothing and hope he returned to see her, or she could go to him and take matters into her own hands.

The truth was that she was lonely and wanted to be with Tyne. She wanted to walk with him, talk with him, ride with him — and she wanted to share his passion. She did not want him to disappear from her life. She even thought she might want to share her life with him.

And she knew he might not share her feelings — but there was one way to find out.

Now she paused at the hotel's front desk. Because it was so early, she was the only patron present. A clerk rushed to attend her.

She didn't even try to smile. "Is Mr. Jefferson in?"

"I have yet to see him come down, madam," the clerk said.

"What is his room number?"

He did not blink, merely turned to a ledger and gave her the information. Julia thanked him and headed for the wide wood staircase.

She knew she was being stared at as she went up. She didn't care, even if it was unheard of for a woman to call openly on a male guest in his room. The gossips would have a field day, she decided. Let them. It was so early that they couldn't believably accuse her of lechery. They would go mad, trying to decide who she had seen and why she had done so.

She almost smiled, but she was as nervous as a girl of sixteen. Would he be pleased to see her — or would he be dismayed?

If he was clearly dismayed, she wouldn't even attempt to flirt with him, she thought, her anxiety increasing. She hurried down the corridor, clutching her purse, already breathless. When she saw his room, she inhaled for courage and knocked on the door.

"One moment," he called.

Suddenly she flushed. What if he was with a woman? She would die of embarrassment.

And then the door opened. He stood there in his trousers and a shirt, the shirt half tucked in, as if he'd been undressed. His eyes widened when he saw her.

She knew her color remained high, and she could not look away from his amber eyes, but instead of reciting the lines she had rehearsed, she said thickly, "You are leaving tomorrow."

He slowly nodded, his gaze locked with hers. Julia was acutely aware of his powerful body, his heat, his scent. Tension seemed to fill the small space between them. He kept his hand on the door. Suddenly, his gaze never moving from hers, he stepped back, pulling the door fully open.

No invitation could have been clearer.

Breathing hard, trembling, Julia stepped past him, into his suite, and stopped. There was a desk and a sofa, but she saw only the bed. And now he stood just behind her, so close that her skirts touched his trousers.

He closed the door, saying, "I've been thinking about you."

She turned to him; it was impossible to think. She could only feel now, only want. "Tyne," she murmured.

Suddenly he gripped her shoulders, and his grasp was crushing. For one moment he looked at her, his eyes ablaze. And then he pulled her up against his body, wrapping his arms around her, so she was dwarfed by his huge embrace. She felt every hard inch of him as she breathed in his thick male scent, her cheek crushed against his chest.

His heart was pounding.

He tilted up her chin, and their gazes collided. Julia realized her heart was beating as hard as his, harder than it ever had before. He understood — and he covered her mouth with his.

His kiss was hard and demanding. She caught his shoulders, deliriously excited, as he forced her mouth wide, his tongue going deep. Julia began to whimper. To squirm. Nothing had ever felt as right as his kiss, his touch or his huge body engulfing hers.

They kissed wildly, frantically, moving across the room. The backs of her thighs hit the mattress. Julia caught his shirt as he broke the kiss, fumbling at the buttons. It never crossed her mind not to tear his clothes off. She couldn't breathe as his bare chest was revealed.

He caught her hands. "Are you sure?" he asked.

She slipped her hands over the shockingly hard planes and muscles of his chest. She inhaled sharply, and he groaned. "I have never been as sure. Make love to me, Tyne."

He tore off his shirt and flung it aside. Julia took one look at his huge, muscular and scarred torso, and almost fainted from the intense flood tide of desire. He lifted her into his arms and laid her on the bed, his mouth on the swell of her breasts, above the bodice of her grown. His mouth left small, hard kisses there while she stroked his hot skin, his nipples and his hard, rippling arms. She couldn't stand being apart or feeling so heavy and so hot. "Hurry," she whispered.

He lifted his head and looked at her, his eyes ablaze, but there was surprise there, too. Then he reached for the buttons at the back of her dress.

She sat up, panting, and suddenly she was the woman she'd once been, the woman she'd forgotten all about. As he unbuttoned the dress, she reached up and removed her hairpins and small hat, and as she slid her hands in her platinum hair, she looked at him. Her dress was unbuttoned, but he hadn't pulled it down, and he went still. Wanting him terribly, she suddenly lifted her hair, allowing it to spill free, while the bodice of her dress fell, revealing her to him. Her corset was Parisian, the chemise transparent silk. Her nipples had become so sensitive that even the soft silk hurt.

"You're so beautiful," he whispered roughly, reaching for her.

But she stood, breaking his hold, and slid the dress off, revealing her silk drawers and stockings.

Instantly, Tyne grabbed her by the hips. "You're so tiny." He sounded almost afraid.

She had never felt as desirable. As they kissed wildly, frantically, they fell to the bed. He fumbled with his belt and trousers, shedding them, and then his hands were all over her. Julia didn't know how she got out of her underthings, but his hands and mouth were everywhere, in places that hadn't been seen or touched in decades, and she wept in growing pleasure.

He caught her hips and said something, then settled his tongue low and deep. Julia exploded. Bursting into bright light, she wept in rapture, thanking him repeatedly.

He moved over her, breathing hard. She managed to open her eyes, look at him. *I love him,* she thought. And she wanted to please him, too. She knew what he meant to do, but she reared up, surprising him, to kiss him, wanting him to understand the magnitude of what he'd just given her, the depth of her gratitude. On his knees, his manhood fiercely stabbing at her, he went still, while she kissed him.

She bent low and tasted him.

He shuddered, groaned, and she knew he meant to protest, but she had no intention of stopping, and she moved her mouth over him, new desire making her dizzy and faint. He choked, breathing hard, and then pulled her up into his arms. For one moment they looked at one another with sudden recognition.

He smiled fiercely, and then they were joined. Julia wept as another release took her again, but they were tears of sheer joy. Finally he cried out, and she thought he wept, too.

When she floated back to reality, she was in his arms, their legs were entwined, and he was stroking her jaw with his thumb in the broad light of a weekday morning. She flushed with happiness. The urge to make love with him again returned. She wriggled her toes, smiling, and looked up at him, her small hand on his chest.

He smiled back, and his eyes were warm. "I never would have guessed," he said softly, kissing her forehead. Then he slid his hand into the waves of her long hair.

"It's been so long, and I've been so nervous about allowing you to see how I feel."

His smile faded. "How long, Julia?"

She said simply, "Fifteen years."

He stared for a long time. "You're so passionate. How could you manage like that?"

"There was no one I wanted," she said softly.

He went still. Then he tightened his embrace and moved over her, but now he stared into her eyes.

She remembered that he was leaving the next day. Dismay welled in her, accompanied by heartache. "I am going to miss you, Tyne."

His eyes widened, and she hoped she hadn't made a terrible mistake.

But he said only, "Do you have to go?"

She stared at him, confused.

"We can have a champagne breakfast in my bed."

If that was all he was willing to offer, she would accept. Julia clasped his strong jaw, her heart buoyant with her love, refusing to think about tomorrow. And then she lifted her face to his. He went still, and she kissed him slowly, until he pushed her down onto the bed.

He could not attend the drawings on his desk; the lines and notations swam in his vision, as if crooked and illegible, deluding him. Instead, Alexandra's image was in his mind, her eyes red and swollen — clearly she had been crying last night. Why?

Why was she upset? Her long-lost lover

had returned!

Then he recalled her shock when he'd told her that they would marry.

She had been so surprised; clearly she had not expected that response from him. But then, he had never thought the pregnancy was a scheme to trap him into marriage; it had obviously been an accidental conception.

After all these years, after searching for the perfect bride for over a decade, he was ready to marry the woman he'd pursued, seduced and then rescued, the woman he'd forcibly made his mistress. She had no good name, no means and no rank — she sewed for a living. God, it was an ironic twist of fate. They would marry because of the child, but he wanted to marry her because he was in love. He wanted to give her his good name and his protection, and all the finer things in life.

He cursed.

Several hours later, a steaming cup of tea was at his elbow, a glass of scotch, half-finished, beside that. He'd been trying to work since dawn — since he'd told Alexandra that they would marry, and that if she left him, she would also leave their child behind. His architects, Randolph and his steward had all vanished, clearly realizing he was in no humor to work with them.

Only Guillermo hovered. He'd brought sandwiches, which he'd refused, then eggs and ham, which he'd ignored. The butler's last attempt to entice him to eat had involved steak and kidneys. He'd sent the tray away.

He covered his face with his hands. He was so damned tired. He'd never expected Alexandra to ask him for time. But he should have guessed. She was intelligent, and clearly she meant to weigh her options. He did not know of a single woman who wouldn't have leaped at the chance to become his duchess, no matter the circumstances. But her response confirmed what he believed: she did not love him back. She loved St. James.

He looked up, across the large, dark library. Old Tom stood in the corner of the room, his expression one of scorn and condescension. Stephen blinked, and his father was gone.

A soft knock sounded on his door, which was ajar. It was Guillermo, and while his butler never changed his expression, Stephen took one look at him and stood, alarmed. "What is it?"

"I believe that Miss Bolton is leaving with her sisters."

It took him a moment to comprehend Guillermo's words. Then he strode past him, through the house and into the front hall.

Alexandra was there with her sisters, wearing one of her old, tired, unfashionable dresses, and they were all putting on their coats. He saw instantly that her sewing bag was on the floor, beside her — and that her wrist was bare. And he knew then that she was leaving him.

She turned, holding her head high, her eyes very swollen now. She walked slowly to him, pausing, her gaze on his. It was filled with what seemed to be sorrow or hurt or both. "I am going back to Edgemont Way."

Her words knifed through him, causing physical pain. "I see." He took a breath and spoke so calmly, he knew he surprised them both. "So you have made your choice."

She shook her head in denial. Tears slid down her face. "No. There was no choice to make."

He did not understand her words, but it was clear that she had chosen St. James over him and their child. He shoved away the pain and said, "I would prefer that you stayed here until the child is born — so you will have the proper care."

"I cannot stay here, Stephen," she said,

trembling. "Not now, not like this."

He inhaled, fighting to stay calm, fighting the pain. "What do you mean?"

"Staying here, after what has happened, would be unbearable."

He tensed. He wanted her at Clarewood, where she would have the best care — and where she would be nearby, where he could see her every day. He spoke carefully again. "Can't you wait a few more months before you run off with your lover?"

She trembled. "I am not running off with anyone. But I will not stay here. Surely you will not attempt to force me to do so?"

He stared closely, aching in every fiber of his being. "No, I will not force you to stay here." Somehow, he kept his voice to a monotone.

She seemed relieved.

She was clearly desperate to get away from him. He did not know how they had come to this impasse. "I will send servants to attend you at Edgemont Way, but you will return to birth my child at Clarewood. And we will marry first." It was a warning. His son or daughter would be legitimate, and would be born here. He would not have it any other way.

He was shocked when she shook her head again. "This is also my child, and I am afraid I cannot give it up, not even to you, the rightful father. Our child will stay with me, Stephen."

"I will never allow another man to raise my son," he informed her coldly, meaning it. Pain knifed deeply through him.

She backed away. "Maybe we can discuss the child more calmly when some time has passed — and we are both in better tempers."

"There is nothing to discuss," he said, breathing hard. "I will fight you as you have never been fought before, but the child will be raised here, by me."

More tears fell, and she flinched. "I am going home." She turned.

He seized her, the action reflexive.

She faced him, her eyes wide. A terrible moment ensued. She said softly, "I do not want to fight with you, not on any account."

"Then stay here and marry me now."

She shuddered. "I can't."

He released her. He could not breathe properly.

"I am sorry," she whispered. "So sorry." When he did not reply, she walked away, picked up her bag, then half turned and said, "The bracelet is on my dresser."

There were no more tears left. Alexandra

held on to the safety strap of the carriage as it bounced along the ruts of their drive, her small, ramshackle home just ahead. Nothing had changed, she thought dismally. The yard was muddy and unkempt, puddles had turned into ponds, one of the front steps was crooked, and the brick walk was missing pieces. Beyond, the barn looked in dire jeopardy, as if it might cave in on itself at any moment.

She trembled. She had thought herself cried out last night, but she had been wrong. She had spent the past three hours crying, and even her sisters hadn't been able to comfort her.

As their carriage halted in front of the house, Bonnie now in the traces, the front door opened. Edgemont stepped out onto the porch.

She tensed. She could not bear another difficult and hurtful confrontation now.

Olivia had been driving, and she set the brake and got down from the carriage. "Hello, Father. Alexandra has come home, and you will welcome her with open arms."

Alexandra looked at Olivia. Her sister had grown up, she thought. But she couldn't be joyful at that realization, for it was tragedy that had matured her.

Edgemont trembled. He was bleary-eyed,

but freshly dressed, and he didn't say a word.

Corey alighted, and Alexandra followed suit. As Corey led the red mare toward the stable, she followed Olivia onto the front porch, the steps creaking beneath their weight. Her heart lurched as she said, "Hello, Father." She prayed they would not have it out now.

His gaze was searching. She knew there was no disguising her distress, that he could see she had been crying. "Hello, Alexandra." His jowls quivered. "What has happened?"

She decided to make light of it as much as she could. "I seem to have made a habit of being tossed out on my rear," she said, trying to smile.

He did not smile back.

She picked up her sewing bag. "I must come home, and I am begging you to let me return," she said with all the dignity she had.

He choked. "I am so sorry I threw you out! I was simply distraught to realize what you'd done."

Alexandra had never been so relieved. "Father, I am ashamed. And I am sorry to have hurt you and disgraced everyone." Then she thought about her child and realized she couldn't have regrets. She would love her baby, no matter what happened next — and she feared that would include a terrible battle with Stephen. She would find a better time to tell Edgemont about the child in her womb.

His eyes became moist, and he blinked rapidly. "I am sorry, too. My God, Alexandra, you are the light of this family, and you are so like your mother. I was wrong, *wrong,* to say otherwise. Clarewood is a roué, and the world knows it. He seduced you, didn't he? The bastard! I've heard it said he has left a trail of broken hearts across the land. But I blamed you — when I should have blamed him. Well, I blame the bastard duke now!"

Even now, she wanted to defend him, but it was impossible. He meant to keep her child from her. He thought her a liar — a purposeful one. He'd leaped to the conclusion that she loved Owen, and meant to run off with him. He would force her into marriage! He did not trust her or understand her — or know her — at all. How was that possible? He thought the very worst of her!

She could not marry him if he disliked her, despised her, or, even worse, was indifferent to her. And she would not marry him, loving him as she did, when he so clearly did not love her in return. It remained unbelievable that he would marry her and then allow her to run off with Owen — and keep her child from her. "I fell in love with him, Father," she managed. "Otherwise I would have been able to fend off his advances."

She was amazed when he gently touched her cheek. "Of course you did. You would never have carried on otherwise, and I knew it even as I made such horrid accusations. I am so sorry, Alexandra. It was the gin — you know that, don't you?" he pleaded.

She took him into her arms as she might a grown but mentally impaired or physically defective child. As she held him, he started to cry, and she knew he was suffering from the effects of whatever he'd found to imbibe the night before as much as he was from anguish and sorrow. And it crossed her mind that her father was weak and had become useless long ago. The man her mother had married had died with her. But it didn't matter. He needed her to take care of him, and she would gladly do so. She would do so until the end of her days.

He sniffed and stepped out of her embrace. "Could you make me some eggs? No one makes an omelet as well as you do."

She smiled, feeling wan, tired and sad. Nothing had changed. She looked from her disheveled father to her sister, who was the epitome of impoverished grace, and then at the untidy, worn parlor just inside. No, nothing had changed — except that she was an experienced woman now, with a child on the way. She had come home to Edgemont Way to take care of her sisters, her father and now, her unborn child.

She had come full circle.

"Word has it that you have been locked in your library for most of this week. I have noticed that you have not returned my notes. I could not decide if things went well with Alexandra or if you remained mired in a lovers' quarrel."

Stephen had been engrossed in a proposal for financing a Northern European mining venture in which he was intending to invest. He looked up and found Alexi standing on the threshold of the library, Guillermo behind him. And because every shade was down, every curtain drawn, he was uncertain if it was day or night.

He was not in the mood for callers, and he had made that abundantly clear to his staff. Not even Alexi was to have the privilege of walking in on him unannounced now.

"Elysse insisted I call," Alexi added, staring very closely at him.

"I told Captain de Warenne that you were not receiving callers, Your Grace," his butler said. "But Captain de Warenne refused to heed me."

"I decided to let myself in, as I always do," Alexi said cheerfully. "I must say, I was rather surprised to find that Guillermo actually intended to bar me, your closest and perhaps only friend, from seeing you."

Stephen closed the file, annoyed. "I am much occupied, Alexi," he warned.

"Really? Elysse just heard a rumor — that Alexandra Bolton has returned home, and that she is being courted by a gentleman I do not know, one Owen St. James. I take it, then, that you were correct and I was wrong, and she turned you down?" He sauntered in. "Or did you lose courage and fail to ask her for her hand?"

Stephen stood, somehow managing to smile calmly. Five days had passed since Alexandra had left Clarewood. And the moment she had walked out of his front door, her intentions clear — she meant to keep his child from him and, no matter what she had said, run off with St. James — he had shut her out of his mind and his heart. He did not think about her. He did not feel anything now. And he would not think about the child until the spring, having estimated it was due in early August. In fact, he was feeling very much like his old self again — his life was the Clarewood legacy, as it should be. He rose early to attend his numerous affairs, both of the duchy and the Foundation, and he went to bed late, satisfied with the day's achievements. Nor did he go to bed alone. An expensive London madam had been providing him with a different courtesan every night. His only requirements were that they were foreign, healthy and did not speak a word of English.

But even though he smiled benignly now, his heart lurched unpleasantly in response to his cousin's comments. But he was not going to pay attention to Alexi's words, since he knew Alexi only meant to bait him. "Do come in, as you will not take no for an answer. How are you? How is Elysse?" He walked out from behind his desk, going to the sideboard. When Alexi did not answer, he asked, "Wine or scotch?"

"Actually, it's a bit early to drink, so I will decline," Alexi said.

Stephen poured himself a glass of scotch as Alexi came up behind him. "Guillermo, please open the drapes."

As sunlight began to fill the room, Alexi said, "What is wrong with you, and what has happened? Why did Alexandra leave Clarewood?"

"Nothing is wrong with me, Alexi. I have come to my senses, that is all." He smiled.

Alexi stared, his gaze filled with speculation. Then, "She refused to marry you — undoubtedly because you demanded a marriage, instead of tendering a romantic proposal."

Stephen tensed. He had indeed done just that, and he knew it. But he was not going to discuss Alexandra Bolton — nor would he think of her. He sensed Tom nearby — and knew he was pleased. "I am not a romantic, ergo I would never tender a romantic proposal. And the affair is over — I do not wish to discuss it." He got up and walked away from his cousin. Now, though, he had a slight ache in his chest.

Alexi followed, seizing his shoulder. "She is having your child! Or is it St. James's bastard?"

Stephen whirled, furious at the allegation, fist clenched, ready to smash Alexi in the nose for daring to insinuate that Alexandra had been unfaithful to him. His anger soared. It knew no bounds. And the moment he met Alexi's smug eyes, he knew he'd been successfully baited.

As if a dam had been breached, the pain

coursed through him in the wake of his anger, and he kept seeing Alexandra leaving his front hall with her sewing bag, her eyes red and swollen, her head held high. "Damn you!" he exclaimed. "The child is mine — and when he is born, he will be born at Clarewood. *I* will raise my son or daughter," he said harshly. "No matter what she intends. Damn her!"

"Stephen, what is wrong with you?" Alexi grabbed him by both shoulders. "Why won't you fight for her?"

Stephen wrenched away. "We have been through this before." Suddenly he could not breathe — he was panting harshly.

"My God, you are a man who has moved mountains to build hospitals and asylums and housing for the working poor, and now one man stands between you and the woman you want, and you are a complete coward!"

Stephen went still. Was he a coward? She didn't want him. She wanted St. James. Didn't she? "You don't know what you are talking about," he snapped, walking away.

Alexi followed. "But I do. Elysse and I hardly got off to a good start — years of pride and anger kept us apart. I think I know what the problem is. And it's not about pride — not for you. It's about love."

Stephen faced him scornfully. "Are you mad?"

"No. I think it is about the fact that you truly don't believe in love. And that is because of how you were raised — your parents hated one another, and frankly, I think old Tom hated you, never mind that he decided you'd be his heir."

Stephen choked in surprise. Hadn't he wondered, as a boy, if his "father" hated him? Too often it had seemed that way. And it had especially seemed that way when he was being punished.

"I think old Tom resented you because you reminded him, on a daily basis, that he couldn't sire a child. Every time he looked at you, he saw Julia and Sir Rex. But he would never let the world know that he was impotent, so you were turned into his perfect son, the future duke. He was so hateful, so cruel! I cannot blame you for your distrust of Alexandra — or your own feelings. But you aren't Tom, and she isn't Julia. Tom tried to make you in his image, but damn it, you are a de Warenne. And while we are proud and arrogant, we cannot get on without the love of a good woman. Look at me and Elysse. Think about your real father, Sir Rex, and Lady Blanche. I believe they secretly admired one another for years before they managed to find their way to one another. What about Ariella and Emilian? She defied society to be with St. Xavier. Or my father and Amanda? He rescued her at her father's hanging!" He took a breath and said, "You are a de Warenne, Stephen, and you are capable of a deep and undying love. Whether you know it or not, it is in your blood — and it is your right."

Stephen cursed as he sat down on the sofa, hard. His heart clamored at him, all the while breaking apart. He kept remembering his parents in heated and bitter arguments, while he turned and ran away, not wanting to see or hear them, as they fought one another as if to the death. He saw old Tom's livid expression as he raised his hand to strike him across the face, though he could not recall his transgression. Hatred had sparked in the man's eyes.

He covered his face with his hands. Was Alexi right? Because he had never believed in love until St. James had returned from the past, making him confront his feelings for Alexandra. Damn it. He did love her. But he remained impossibly hurt — no, devastated. *She had walked out on him. She had chosen someone else. Like old Tom, she didn't love him back.*

He felt raw and vulnerable, powerless —
like a boy of ten, not a grown man of thirty-
one who all but commanded an empire.

Alexi sat down beside him. "If you go after
her, you might live in a home filled with
warmth and laughter, not cold silence, and
damn it, I am not leaving until I have
convinced you to go climb this particular
mountain."

Stephen breathed hard, trying to hold
back the bone-deep pain of rejection. In his
mind, old Tom leered at him, pleased that
Stephen was undone. Of course he was —
he had despised love, and embraced hatred
and bitterness. He did not want Stephen to
be anything other than the cold, calculating
eighth duke of Clarewood. He wanted him
to wander its cold, silent halls alone.

Stephen slowly looked up. "I have a confession."

Alexi waited.

Stephen saw old Tom standing behind the
sofa, his face furious now. "My father
couldn't even express his affection for me
on his deathbed. I was desperate, even at
sixteen. Just once, I wanted him to say he
was proud of me, and that he cared."

Alexi laid his hand on Stephen's shoulder,
but only briefly. "I'm sure Tom couldn't say
those words, nor could he care about any-

thing or anyone — except the duchy. He was a cold, heartless bastard. But what about Sir Rex? He came into your life when we were nine. I heard Sir Rex praise you many times — he was always kind and attentive. You are every bit as much, if not more, Sir Rex's son as you are Tom's."

And suddenly Stephen recalled how Julia had been desperately determined to bury the past — how she never wanted to visit the mausoleum again. And he suddenly felt the same way.

He was sick and tired of having those talons in his back. He was sick and tired of looking up and seeing old Tom in the corner of the room, mocking him, ridiculing him.

He rubbed his neck. Blood was thicker than water, and he was a de Warenne — and he had fallen in love. There — he had admitted it. It hurt terribly. So now what should he do? Was Alexi right? Should he fight for her?

Why shouldn't he fight for Alexandra? He wanted her, *needed* her, and he did not want to fight her for their child — because he would win, and she would be destroyed.

He could never do that to her, he realized, sitting straighter.

"What is it?" Alexi asked.

Stephen inhaled, the pain vanishing. What

had happened to him? He always got what he wanted — he was Clarewood. He had pursued her once and won. Of course he would pursue her now. But this time, he would not make mistakes. Too much was at stake.

He turned to Alexi. "Is it true? St. James is now courting her?"

"I believe he calls on her daily." Alexi stared far too blandly now, trying to contain what Stephen knew was a satisfied smile.

Stephen wasn't sure Alexi was telling the truth, but it no longer mattered. He stood, deeply determined now. He was going to lose Alexandra if he didn't do something about it. "I have had it with St. James," he said softly. "Enough is enough."

Alexi stood, grinning. "And when this is all over, you will thank me properly, won't you? Because I believe you will be vastly in my debt."

Stephen ignored him, leaving the room.

"Advice is rarely free," Alexi called after him, laughing.

CHAPTER NINETEEN

"You seem to be in better spirits today," Owen said softly.

Alexandra smiled at him, but she was tense as she sat with him in the front seat of his gig. It was a sunny day, although cool, so she'd bundled up, and they'd taken a drive in the country. The leaves were red and gold, and soon the trees would be dark and bare. They'd brought a basket lunch with them and had eaten in a roadside meadow, not far from a herd of grazing sheep. It had been a lovely, lazy afternoon, though she should have been sewing. They would be home in a few more minutes.

Very carefully, she said, "You have lifted my spirits, but that has been your intention all along, hasn't it?"

He smiled. "Of course it has. I hated seeing you so glum."

She glanced away, keeping her smile in place. Owen had called every day. She anticipated his visits because his presence was warm and reassuring, and she enjoyed his company thoroughly. Chatting with him was so much better than hunching over her sewing, her thoughts dark with despair and her heart heavy with loss, her every moment filled with images of Stephen. Her heart was broken, and though she felt as if it would never heal, the truth was that she knew better. Once before, nine years ago, she'd suffered such heartbreak. Broken hearts did mend — eventually.

They had not discussed her return home or the cause for it. But he had told her that he was fiercely glad she had mended things with her father — and returned to Edgemont Way. Alexandra couldn't recall what response she had made. But she knew that Owen was aware that her affair with Stephen was over, and that he was pleased. Not a visit went by that he didn't offer up a remark that could lead to a very frank discussion of the affair and her feelings, but she had grown adept at steering clear of all such conversations. She could not, and would not, discuss her relationship with Stephen with him.

And it had become obvious that she was right — he was still deeply in love with her. His eyes shone when he looked at her, he often made jests to make her laugh, and his gestures were affectionate and flirtatious. But when he touched her, she flinched or even pulled away. She wasn't ready for a suitor — not yet, not now, and maybe not ever.

She cared deeply for him, but everything had changed — it was Stephen Mowbray whom she loved.

And Owen didn't know about the child, either.

Alexandra clasped her gloved hands together, deciding not to reply to his remark about her recent despondency.

In response to her silence he said, "We used to talk about everything."

She turned to face him, her eyes wide. "We can hardly talk about everything now."

"Why not? I am concerned about you."

"I know, and your loyalty has meant so much to me."

His gaze was searching. "When you are ready, Alexandra, I will listen. But you might feel better if you talk about Clarewood and what he has done to you."

Amazingly, she bristled, wanting to defend Stephen, even though his actions were inexcusable. "Owen, I accepted his proposition. We were both in the wrong."

His face hardened. "As much as I hate to

say it, he should marry you and make things right."

She inhaled, looking away.

He took her hand instantly. "I'm sorry. I know I've said as much before, and I swear I won't say it again. But I despise him, Alexandra. You deserve so much more."

She wanted to tug her hand free, but she didn't. And she wasn't going to argue about her lack of qualifications to be Stephen's wife and duchess, not when she no longer believed them. Olivia had been right. Noblemen married commoners for love — not often, but it did happen. He simply didn't love her. Love and lust were *not* the same thing.

"I hate seeing you so brokenhearted," Owen growled.

She did pull her hand away then. "I am fine — really."

"You are not fine, but you are incredibly brave and resilient." He then added, glancing ahead, "You have company, Alexandra."

She had already seen the coach in her drive — and recognized it. Elysse and Ariella had called, much to her dismay. Why had they come now? She wasn't with Stephen anymore, and they were his friends, not hers. Had they come to berate her for the falling out? Surely they had not come to comfort and console her.

"Who is it?" Owen asked softly, halting the gig beside the larger black lacquered coach.

"Elysse de Warenne and Ariella St. Xavier. They are recent . . . acquaintances."

He gave her a puzzled look.

Alexandra did not explain as they alighted and went inside, too overcome with new nerves. Olivia and Corey were entertaining them, a fire burning in the hearth, hot tea and scones on the table. Both callers leaped up as she came inside with Owen. They were smiling, as if pleased to see her once again, but they looked Owen up and down with great circumspection and speculation.

Alexandra took off her coat, coming forward. "This is a pleasant surprise," she said cautiously.

Elysse hurried over and hugged her warmly. "Do not stand on formality now — not after the wonderful outing we shared! We heard rumors, and we are so worried about you."

Alexandra looked into the other woman's kind, concerned eyes and was shocked. Elysse de Warenne did not have a mean bone in her body.

Ariella had also come close, and she patted her shoulder. "Are you all right?" she asked with concern, her gaze soft and warm.

Alexandra was undone by her concern, as well. They seemed to truly care. Her broken heart screamed for mercy. They were Stephen's friends from childhood, and maybe they could explain his behavior. Maybe, somehow, they could help. "I am fine," she lied.

"You do not look fine," Ariella said flatly. "Trust me, Stephen does have a very human heart beating beneath that cold exterior, but he can be impossible when he believes he has been crossed."

Alexandra trembled. "He is so angry with me," she whispered.

Ariella and Elysse exchanged looks. Elysse wrapped her arm around her again. "You have turned his very proper and perfectly ordered life upside down, Alexandra, simply by coming into his life and waking him up. Alexi tells me he is in dismal spirits."

Alexandra pulled away, glancing at Owen, who was looking grim and unhappy as he listened to them. "I haven't made the proper introductions," she said. As she made them, she was surprised to see how pleasant and polite both women were to Owen, when he was obviously a suitor and Stephen's rival, if such a word could be used. She paid little attention to their exchange, however. She kept thinking about what Elysse had just said — that Stephen was in dismal spirits. Why? Did he miss her? Was it possible? Or was he simply worried about the child?

Ariella and Owen were chatting, and Elysse took Alexandra's hand and dragged her into the front hall. "You cannot give up on him!" she exclaimed.

Alexandra bit her lip. "You do not understand. He thinks the worst of me. And he . . ." She stopped. She couldn't tell the other woman the truth. "He offered marriage, but for all the wrong reasons, and I refused him."

Elysse looked at her without surprise, and Alexandra realized she knew about the offer of marriage. Of course, her husband was Stephen's closest and oldest friend — and Alexandra immediately wondered what else she knew. As if reading her thoughts, Elysse took her hand and squeezed it. "Men can be such fools," she said softly. "How do you know that he offered marriage for the wrong reasons?"

Alexandra didn't know how to reply. "I love him," she finally said. "He doesn't love me back."

Elysse smiled. "Are you sure?" Then she said, in a whisper, "There is something you must know. Stephen is not an expressive man. He never shows his affection. He doesn't know how. He was raised by the previous duke, a cruel, difficult, harsh and hard man. An example was set, Alexandra."

"The dowager duchess said as much, but he can be tender," she whispered.

"And that is only because of the depth of his feelings for you," Elysse spoke with certainty now. "There is more. Stephen is very sensitive on the subject of fathers and sons — due in part to the horrid relationship he had with old Tom. But it is more than that. Are you aware that he has sworn never to allow himself to sire a child out of wedlock?"

Alexandra went still. "No, I did not know. Why? Many noblemen have bastards." She was certain now that Elysse knew about her pregnancy.

"I'm afraid he will have to tell you that himself. But this is a subject that can arouse him as no other." Elysse studied her.

Alexandra's mind was racing now. She knew she was being given important clues, and that solving them would somehow shed light on what had happened, but she couldn't fathom how to put them together.

"You should ask Stephen about his father — and why he has vowed never to allow another man to raise his child."

Alexandra began to tremble. If this was Stephen's Achilles' heel, it began to explain so much. "Are you certain?"

"I am very certain." Elysse smiled. "There is hope, dear. Unless, of course, you are in love with the oh-so-dashing St. James?"

"I love him, but I am in love with Stephen," Alexandra said. Was there truly hope? Because if there was, she would fight for her love, *their* love, and a future together with their child.

"I thought so." Elysse sounded triumphant.

They returned to the parlor, where Owen instantly caught her eye, his gaze concerned. She smiled at him to reassure him, but she was hardly all right. Her mind was racing. Stephen had an issue when it came to illegitimate offspring. She could not imagine why. Perhaps he had bastard siblings who had somehow suffered and it had affected him greatly. It was the only conclusion she could draw. But now she thought about his rage when she had refused to give him their child — and when he thought she would marry Owen, that she and Owen would raise that child.

She must explain things to him again, but more carefully, now that she knew he was so sensitive to the subject, she thought, feeling frantic.

A few minutes later Owen's expression changed. It became dark and grim, and he walked over to the parlor window, his hands in his jacket pockets. Alexandra turned to see what had caught his eye. As she did, Corey squealed in excitement. Olivia rushed past her, and Ariella said, her tone satisfied, "Well, I wonder what that is?"

As everyone rushed past her to look out of the window, Alexandra, too, stared outside. Randolph de Warenne was in the driver's seat of a farmer's wagon. The back was filled to overflowing with red hothouse roses. And Ebony was tied to the back fender, whinnying.

Alexandra's heart began to race madly.

Randolph leaped to the ground and started for the house. Corey looked at Alexandra, smiling, and then she ran from the parlor to open the front door.

The parlor had fallen frighteningly silent — the only sound Alexandra could hear was her heart thundering.

What had he done? What did this mean?

Randolph strode into the room, going directly to her and bowing. "Good day, Miss Bolton." And then he grinned.

She trembled — she could not breathe. "What is he doing now?"

"I believe he has sent you flowers, Ebony and a small token of his affections." Randolph smiled and produced a jeweler's box from his breast pocket. "I believe you know I am not allowed to return to Clarewood with the flowers, the horse or the jewelry."

She stared at the velvet box. *He had returned the bracelet.* "Why is he doing this?"

Randolph's brows lifted as he snapped open the box, holding it up for her to view the contents. "I believe His Grace is most insistent that you take this, Miss Bolton," he said, then added, "I believe he is finally smitten."

Alexandra could do nothing but stare at the huge diamond engagement ring.

Julia looked at herself in the mirror over the handsome mahogany bureau in Tyne's hotel room, morning light sneaking in past the curtains. He had stepped outside to allow her to dress. They'd spent the entire day and night since her arrival in his hotel room — making love, then talking about their lives, then making love again. They'd ordered room service for supper. And then they'd made love once more.

He was leaving today.

Julia trembled. She knew that she had never before looked so radiant, but she couldn't smile now, and her eyes were filled with despair. He was a strong, determined man, but a simple one in many ways. And his life was the homestead he had fashioned on the harsh California frontier over the course of two decades. Now she knew what that had entailed. She had seen the physical scars, and he'd shared the mental ones. He'd told her a dozen stories of miraculous escapes. It was amazing that he was even alive.

She trembled. Her life was a dutiful round of teas and balls, her horses and her dogs. Stephen hadn't needed her advice or guidance or even her support in years; he was a grown man, and a very successful, driven and accomplished one. And while she was sorry he wasn't settled yet, she felt certain that day was rapidly approaching. He was so obviously head over heels in love with Miss Bolton. Everyone seemed to know it except for him.

She knew that Tyne would love for her to visit, and she intended to do just that. But she couldn't bear the thought of his leaving now, when they'd just begun such an impassioned friendship, nor could she bear the probability that she might not see him for six months or even a year.

He knocked softly on the hotel-room door.

Julia managed a smile. "Come in."

He slipped inside, his smile brief, his eyes dark.

"I need help with the back of this dress," she said softly.

"Of course you do." He studied her as he approached. She gave him her back, and as he did up the last few buttons, she closed her eyes. Even his fingers skimming across her back felt so terribly right.

He clasped her shoulders and turned her around. "You don't seem happy today."

She met his unusually somber gaze. "Neither do you."

"What man in his right mind would want to leave now?" he asked simply.

She gasped. Then she seized his hands. "Then don't!" she said. "Stay a little longer — so we can further our friendship."

"And then what?" he asked. "I'll have to leave eventually, and your life is here."

She stared.

"What is it?" he asked sharply.

"I meant it when I said I want to visit you in California," she whispered.

His stare widened. "But you have a full life here, Julia. You are a dowager duchess."

"I *am*," she agreed, "and soon, if I do not miss my guess, there will be a new Duchess of Clarewood."

"What are you saying?" He gripped her hands tightly now.

"That my duties here can be escaped, but the Danes must come with us."

His eyes were wide and intent. "Julia, I have a confession to make."

She tensed.

"I am glad to stay on longer, to see you. But there is a problem. If you come with me to California, I may not be able to let you leave when you need to go."

"And what if I never want to leave? What if I want to stay?" She clasped his face. "I have fallen in love with you, Tyne, and there is nothing here for me now."

He pulled her close. "I can't believe it. . . . You'd leave everything you have here — for me? What if you don't like California? I have told you how hard life is there."

She slid her hands to his shoulders. "I am more than ready to start life over," she said softly, meaning it. "And I am tougher than I look."

He started to laugh before catching her by her waist and lifting her up, and then he hugged her fiercely. "For such a tiny woman you are very tough, but you no longer have to be, because I will be tough enough for us both. Julia. I love you."

Her heart exploded with joy. And she

knew then that everything else that had transpired in her life had been leading up to this moment — to Tyne.

She tilted her face up, and he kissed her, then murmured, "But I want to make an honest woman of you."

Holding the jeweler's box, Alexandra walked past Stephen's doormen into the front hall of the house. Guillermo beamed as he saw her, rushing forward to take her coat. "I will tell His Grace that you are here, Miss Bolton," he said. "He is in the study, of course, with his architects."

She trembled. Should she stand on formality now? "I know the way, Guillermo, but thank you," she said, her heart racing so swiftly that she thought she might faint. She had been up all night, staring at the engagement ring. A part of her was thrilled. She knew Stephen so well now, and she knew he would never be defeated in something he had decided he must accomplish. They had come full circle, hadn't they? He was pursuing her again. He would not take no for an answer. But this time, his seduction would make her his wife.

She loved him so much that she felt dizzy thinking about it. She loved him so much that she thrilled at the notion. But her pride remained, and so did innate caution. He was a proud, complicated and difficult man. He did not understand compromise. A marriage without mutual affection and understanding would be impossible. And he had to genuinely care for her in return. They could not marry simply out of convenience, or for their child. It would hurt too much.

Ariella and Elysse knew him as well or better than anyone, and they were certain that he loved her. But then why hadn't he simply said so?

She knew him well enough now to imagine that such a confession might be difficult for him. He wasn't demonstrative, except in bed. He might not even know how to express such feelings. And he certainly wouldn't think it necessary to explain himself, not even to the woman he wished to marry.

Alexandra paused on the study's threshold, praying that he truly cared for her, too. The door was wide-open. Sunlight was pouring into the room. Her heart slammed as she looked at Stephen, standing by the far desk, with two architects, his shirtsleeves rolled up to his elbows, his gaze trained on the drawings spread out before them. The sunlight illuminated his high cheekbones and the sharp bridge of his nose. Her heart slammed and filled with love, but the hurt remained. She needed him so.

He looked up, and their gazes locked.

Then his eyes fell to the velvet box she held. He straightened, his expression impossible to read. "Would you excuse us?" he asked the other men.

Alexandra didn't move as the two gentlemen smiled at her and filed out. She was absolutely breathless now. She prayed for a happily-ever-after fairy-tale ending.

He came forward, unsmiling, his eyes searching and somber. "I see that you're not wearing the ring. Have you come to return it?" He spoke quietly.

She bit her lip. "I have come to discuss it." That hadn't sounded right — it had sounded so detached. "I have come to discuss *us*, Stephen."

"Good," he said harshly. Then, "Is it true? Is St. James already courting you?"

She tensed. "Stephen, he has been calling, but as a friend. He knows I am heartbroken."

"And why would you be heartbroken, Alexandra, when your long-lost love has returned? I thought you would be delirious with joy."

"I am hardly delirious with joy." She inhaled. Was their inability to communicate so severe? "You never let me tell you why I couldn't agree to marry you," she said tersely.

"So you have come to reject me. Be warned. I have thought a lot about this. I am not going to back down, and I will not take no for an answer. Nor will I allow my wife to run off with another man."

"In a relationship, in our relationship, you must step down from tyranny, Stephen."

He winced. Then, "I am not giving up. I meant my every word."

Her heart thrilled, but she had to be sure. "Because of the child," she said. "Because you have a sore spot where bastards are concerned."

He stared. "Who told you that? Let me guess — Elysse? Ariella?"

"Yes, but they did not say why."

"Then I will tell you why, and if you ever use it against me, I will deny it. I am a bastard, Alexandra. My natural father is Sir Rex."

She cried out, shocked.

"With that background, how could I ever allow another man to raise my child?" he asked. "My child *must* have my name!"

She reached for his hand. "Why didn't you tell me?"

He didn't pull away. "It is a serious matter, never mind the rumors that abound, some of which are correct. One does not confess such a secret at the drop of a hat. Clarewood is at stake, should that truth ever be revealed and confirmed."

She was still reeling from his revelation. "If I had known, I would have understood why you were so insistent that we must marry — or that I must leave my child with you." It began to make so much sense now. She considered what Elysse and Julia had told her — that Stephen had been raised harshly and unkindly.

He studied her. "I had a difficult childhood. While St. James seems a reasonable man — and nothing like Tom Mowbray — I could not bear to leave my son or daughter in another man's custody. I simply cannot do it."

She touched his face, the comprehension surging. *He was afraid his child would suffer an unhappy childhood in another man's care.* "I am not marrying Owen. I am not with Owen. I am not in love with Owen, Stephen."

He seemed puzzled. "But you —"

"I love him, but you are the man I am in love with."

His gaze widened with disbelief. "What?"

"I think I fell in love with you at the Harrington ball, when you rescued me and then my father," she said, tearing up. "I've never believed in love at first sight, but not only were you an impossibly handsome prince, a true knight in shining armor, you were strong and kind."

He reached for her and pulled her close. "And that is what you desperately needed, Alexandra, and I felt it immediately. You needed someone else to bear the burdens you had been struggling with for so long."

She met his somber gaze. She had needed his strength and he had known it — he had offered it to her immediately. "I am strong, but I am tired, Stephen, tired of always having to be the strong one, of always having to do the right thing, of sewing until two or three in the morning."

He clasped her face. "You will never have to be tired again. You will never have to struggle again, and you will end that damned business immediately! Can't you understand? This isn't simply about the child. I want to take care of you. I always have — from that first moment we met. I *will* take care of you!" He wiped a tear away from her mouth. "And I need you, Alexandra. You have warmed these icy halls."

She wondered if this was his way of telling her that he loved her.

He added thickly, "I truly thought myself a heartless man, until you came into my life. You showed me love, and you taught me passion — now can you see why I can't allow you to leave me?"

She somehow nodded, crying. "I love you so much."

His eyes widened. He inhaled, trembling. "Do you really love me? You have seen me at my worst. I can't quite believe that you could truly love someone like me. You have seen my temper and my cruelty. How can you love me?" he asked harshly.

She took his face in her hands. She knew very little about his past, but he suddenly seemed to be a small, vulnerable boy, not a powerful grown man. He clearly needed reassurance, and she was glad to give it to him. "You have lost your temper, I agree, but very rarely, and you are not cruel. You are the kindest, most generous man I have ever known."

He glanced past her.

Alexandra turned. No one stood behind them. "What is it?"

As if he had just realized something, his expression became relieved, and he smiled at her. "Nothing. Alexandra? I have been miserable without you. I do not want to live alone at Clarewood, in these damned halls, without you."

She laid her hand on his cheek, surprised by the passionate admission. As he blushed, she said, "I have been miserable without you, too. I cannot live without *you,* either."

"Good," he said, pulling back. And suddenly he was the powerful, arrogant, confident Duke of Clarewood again. "Then that is settled. We will be wed immediately, without fanfare."

Alexandra nodded, crying all over again.

And he swept her up into his arms, smiling.

"What are you doing?" she asked, astonished.

"Carrying my soon-to-be bride over the threshold."

Julia paused on the threshold of the great dining room at Clarewood, and before Guillermo could announce her, she smiled. Stephen sat at the head of the table, with Alexandra on his right. Their heads were together, and he had his hand on top of hers. Both of them were smiling, but it was her son's warm, open smile that caused her heart to swell with joy.

She had been right about them, she thought, pleased. And she had been right to pray that Stephen would find love, not just a bride. He was so obviously happy, and she was thrilled.

"Your Grace? The dowager duchess has called," Guillermo intoned.

Stephen leaped to his feet. "Mother, you have impeccable timing. Guillermo, set another place."

The butler smiled and hurried off.

Julia entered the room, and he hurried over to kiss her cheek. She turned to Alexandra, who was standing, looking expectant. "How are you, dear?" she asked.

"I am fine, Your Grace. It is a pleasure to see you again," Alexandra said, her cheeks tinged with pink.

Julia glanced at her son and saw him staring at Alexandra with a besotted expression. She laughed, happy as never before.

He turned sharply. "Your timing is perfect because we have news to share, and I wanted you to be the first to hear it. But I must say, you are in very good spirits." His gaze had narrowed with suspicion.

"My spirits have never been better, and I also have news. But why don't you go first?" She was too deeply in love to be worried by her son's impending disapproval. Nothing would stop her from being with Tyne now.

Stephen turned toward Alexandra, who came around the table to stand beside him

— and he pulled her close. He faced Julia and said, "I have asked Alexandra to be my wife, and she has agreed."

Julia, overjoyed though not surprised, clapped her hands together. "I am so happy for you both!" She instantly reached for Alexandra and hugged her hard. "I am so thrilled, my dear. I thought and hoped this would be the outcome of your affair."

Alexandra beamed. "You are so kind. Thank you. I love your son, Your Grace, and I intend to spend the rest of my life making him happy — while teaching him a thing or two about compromise."

Julia laughed. Stephen was staring at Alexandra again, with the same smitten look. "Oh, dear," she said. "There is a wedding to plan. And I have a feeling Stephen has realized that sometimes a queen rules, not the king."

Alexandra laughed.

"We are eloping," Stephen said firmly. "Alexandra and I have already decided on it — and we did not even have to compromise." He glanced warmly at her again.

Julia wondered at that — every woman wanted a wonderful wedding. Alexandra had suffered many hardships, and she deserved a big event. "I refuse to be excluded," Julia returned instantly.

Alexandra took Stephen's hand. "That is what Alexi said . . . and Elysse and Ariella. And what about Sir Rex and Lady Blanche? They will surely wish to witness the nuptials — and so will Randolph — and my sisters, of course."

Julia grinned. Alexandra had no intention of eloping.

He sighed. "I had truly hoped to avoid a society affair."

"You cannot avoid such an affair, you are the Duke of Clarewood," Julia said firmly. And then she thought of her own plans with Tyne. He wanted to marry her. He loved her. It was a dream come true.

She smiled to herself. *Their* timing was clearly perfect, too. "But if you are truly in a rush, I could help — I am sure we could manage a small family affair within a month or so. I have an excellent caterer."

"Ah, that means just a hundred — or two hundred — guests." But Stephen smiled as he spoke.

Alexandra couldn't help it. She looked at him. "My sisters would love to be my attendants."

Julia said softly, "Sara and Marion would love to be bridesmaids, too."

Alexandra instantly thought of her two new and dear friends. "And Ariella and

Elysse, who gave me so much hope when I thought we were finished."

"I give up and I give in!" He put his arm around her. "I see I have been deluded all along. Very well. We will have a small affair, then. Under two hundred —" he scowled "— but as soon as possible."

Alexandra bit her lip in pleasure. She was becoming Stephen's wife, and they would have a beautiful wedding after all. "I hope I am not dreaming. Maybe I should pinch myself."

"You are not dreaming, and if I did not know better, I would think that the two of you conspired against me in advance." But he smiled.

"We are women — we think alike when it comes to weddings, darling," Julia said, smiling.

Alexandra could guess why Julia seemed so ecstatically happy, and she smiled to herself. Once in love, it was easy to recognize another person who was in the same state.

"Mother? I am now thoroughly worried. You keep beaming like a moonstruck girl."

Julia sighed. "I am moonstruck, Stephen — I am head over heels in love."

His horrified expression was comical. "Pray God you are not in love with that

American!"

"I am marrying that American, Stephen. In fact, we are eloping."

He stared at her, for once at a loss for words.

"I am happy as I have never been before, and we will be leaving for California after your nuptials."

He sat down.

Alexandra rushed to him. "Stephen, this is wonderful news! Your mother so deserves love and a good second marriage."

He looked up at her. "A good second marriage? In California? With an American?"

"Look at how happy she is," Alexandra said, taking his hand. "I know you want the dowager duchess to be happy, beloved and cared for."

Stephen looked at Julia, slowly standing up. "Are you really happy? I did have Jefferson investigated. Unfortunately, as he is an American, it will take months for my runners to learn if he has a shady past. But the one thing I know is that he does not have means, Mother, not as you do."

"And I don't care that his means are modest! He doesn't have a secret past. He is a good man, Stephen, and I would like you and Alexandra to join us for dinner tonight, so you can get to know him. After one evening you will realize how solid and dependable he is."

He stared grimly at her.

Alexandra looked back and forth between them. The dowager duchess was glowing. She had every right to this second chance at life and love and happiness. She hadn't met Jefferson, but she'd seen him that one time at the Harrington ball, and anyone could tell that he was a strong, sincere man. He had seemed as solid as an ancient oak tree.

And now that she knew a little about the kind of life Julia had led, about how she had sacrificed everything for her son, Alexandra understood her so much better.

She looked at Stephen. She knew how protective he was of those he cared about. But he was changing. He smiled often now. He laughed. He often took her hand and squeezed it. And he'd mentioned his childhood twice to her now, speaking first of Tom, and then of Sir Rex. She hadn't realized how cruel his "father" had been. He had suffered so much as a boy that she was amazed he'd become the good man that he was. And now, understanding him as she did, everything made so much sense. In return, she had shared the agony of her mother's passing and her decision to break up with Owen.

The past felt as if it was finally that, the past. It finally felt buried, as it should be.

And Stephen had stopped looking over his shoulder and into dark corners.

Now he wanted to start thinking about marriages for her sisters. He said it would be his first priority after they were wed.

But of course it would be. Stephen was that kind of man — a family man. His protection wouldn't extend just to her; it had automatically been extended to her sisters, and even to her father. He hadn't said so, but she was fairly certain he'd paid off all her father's debts.

There were no more secrets. There was no more pain. Clarewood's long, lonely halls were suddenly warm, suddenly bright, as if the walls had been painted the color of the sun. And there were so many daily callers now. Alexi was a frequent guest, as was his wife, Elysse. Ariella and Emilian, Jack O'Neill, Sir Rex and Lady Blanche came almost as often. The once infamous Captain Devlin O'Neill, Elysse's father, had even come for supper with his American wife, and it had been a fascinating evening. In fact, every de Warenne and O'Neill who lived within a county or two had begun calling on a regular basis. Nor did anyone come alone. Children — and grandchildren — of all ages were always in tow.

They hadn't made their wedding plans public, but Alexi, Elysse and Ariella knew — and Alexandra felt certain that therefore every de Warenne and O'Neill knew, as well, which was the reason for their sudden popularity. While congratulations weren't offered, there were plenty of winks and handshakes and kisses.

Clearly the fact of Stephen's paternity was common knowledge in this large, warm family.

Her sisters came weekly now, too, bubbling with smiles and eagerly discussing plans for her future. Obviously Olivia and Corey knew about the wedding, and they were overjoyed for her. They wanted to come more often, but they were busy with Edgemont Way's reconstruction now. After all these years, the house was being rehabilitated, inside and out. It was being refurbished, too. The stables were being razed and then rebuilt. And their new wardrobes had arrived. Her sisters were so fashionable and elegant now!

They were going to be thrilled that there would be a real wedding, not an elopement. Alexandra smiled — she couldn't wait to tell them.

But then she sobered, just a bit. She didn't know what it meant, but she had caught the notorious Jack O'Neill staring at Olivia while she wasn't aware of it. She hadn't known whether to be happy or dismayed by such intense scrutiny on his part. Although he was Captain O'Neill's son, he had only modest means and intended to return to America, where he was making his fortune. Additionally, he was a reputed rake. Alexandra had told herself that she was mistaken and he was not interested in her gentle sister, but in fact she was not entirely sure.

Alexandra smiled at Julia now and said, "We would love to dine with you and Mr. Jefferson tonight." She looped her arm through Stephen's. "I am sure we will become as fond of him as you are."

Stephen sighed. "Very well. As much as it pains me, I can see you have made up your mind. Not only will we dine together tonight, I will give him the benefit of the doubt."

Julia beamed, hugging him, and Alexandra smiled. She had not been in any serious doubt that Stephen would bend to Julia's wishes. He had changed too much. He would allow the dowager duchess to live her own life.

Just then Guillermo appeared on the

threshold once more. "Your Grace? Miss Bolton? The Earl of Adare has called. The countess is with him, as are several small children."

"Show them in, then see if Cook can accommodate everyone," Stephen said instantly. He gave Alexandra a look. "Do you mind? You have not met Tyrell yet, and his wife Lizzie is a wonderful woman."

"Of course I do not mind," she said. She hadn't met a relation yet who she hadn't liked.

A moment later six boys and girls ran into the dining room, followed by the darkly handsome Tyrell de Warenne and his plump wife, Lizzie. As introductions were made, Stephen pulled Alexandra close and let the cat out of the bag, announcing their wedding plans. The earl kissed her cheek and welcomed her into the family, while Lizzie hugged her, asking her if she needed anything. As she began chatting with the earl's wife, the children began playing with one another, their screeching and laughter filling the dining room. No one chastised them, because no one cared.

Across the room, she caught Stephen's eye. As one of his little cousins ran past him, bumping into him, he smiled at her, his eyes shining. She smiled back, her heart so swollen with love she felt as if she might drift to the ceiling. Alexandra realized that her prayers had been answered. There was going to be a happily-ever-after ending after all.

And as she looked around the room, she knew why Clarewood's rooms and halls were warmer and brighter now. It was because they now rang with laughter and were filled with love.

10/10 0